W9-AHZ-037

MYSTERY WRITERS OF AMERICA

Presents

THE PROSECUTION RESTS

MYSTERY WRITERS OF AMERICA
Presents

THE PROSECUTION RESTS

NEW STORIES ABOUT COURTROOMS, CRIMINALS, AND THE LAW

Edited by
LINDA FAIRSTEIN

LITTLE, BROWN AND COMPANY

NEW YORK • BOSTON • LONDON

Little, Brown and Company
Hachette Book Group
237 Park Avenue, New York, NY 10017
Visit our Web site at www.HachetteBookGroup.com

First Edition: April 2009

Little, Brown and Company is a division of Hachette Book Group, Inc. The Little,
Brown name and logo are trademarks of Hachette Book Group, Inc.

Library of Congress Cataloging-in-Publication Data
Mystery Writers of America presents the prosecution rests : new stories about
courtrooms, criminals, and the law / edited by Linda Fairstein. — 1st ed.
p. cm.
ISBN 978-0-316-01252-2 (hc) / 978-0-316-01267-6 (pb)
1. Legal stories, America. I. Fairstein, Linda A. II. Title: Prosecution rests.
PS648.L3M97 2009
813'.0108355—dc21   2008045351

HC: 10 9 8 7 6 5 4 3 2 1
PB: 10 9 8 7 6 5 4 3 2 1

RRD-IN

Printed in the United States of America

CONTENTS

CONTENTS

THE PROSECUTION RESTS:
AN INTRODUCTION

As a prosecutor in the great office of the New York County District Attorney for thirty years, I tried dozens of felony cases—murder, rape, robbery, burglary, and assaults of every variety. I worked shoulder to shoulder with the smartest cops in the city before ever taking the results of their investigations into the well of the courtroom and presenting the gathered evidence to a jury of the defendant's peers. My adversaries were among the most talented members of the defense bar, skilled in the art of advocacy and the ability to communicate with those good citizens chosen to judge the fate of their clients.

There were powerful moments of eliciting facts from witnesses that established the necessary elements of brutal crimes, a few terrifying occasions when the mendacity of my own complainants was exposed by the opposing counsel, the astounding triumphs afforded to my colleagues and me when a revolutionary scientific technique called DNA analysis was first introduced to the criminal courtroom in 1986, and every now and then a dazzling turn at cross-examination which nailed the hired gun, the expert witness of an opponent.

My favorite moment in the trial was always the point at which

I rested, at which I announced to the judge and jury that I had completed the People's case. It was the culmination of months of preparation and organization, mastering the facts and scrutinizing the details, interpreting the alleles and loci of genetic fingerprinting, and packaging everything I could gather to present to the jury in a logical, persuasive, and trustworthy fashion. Defense counsel had taken his best shot at my witnesses, and might or might not go on to offer his own version of events, but my burden on behalf of the state had been satisfied.

The old maxim claims that a trial is a search for the truth. But as all the participants know, that search should have been completed long before any of us walk through the courtroom doors to try to convince the jurors of our position. From the discovery of the commission of the crime, police officers are charged with the responsibility of evaluating the evidence they collect—eyewitness descriptions and circumstantial facts, and now the remarkable forensic tools that have so radically affected the criminal justice system.

Then district attorneys are called in on the cases. We take our witnesses as we find them—some of them "innocent" victims, but many of them flawed human beings—people who lie, cheat, steal, and have violated most of the other commandments before they ever raise their hands and swear to tell the whole truth and nothing but the truth. Defendants are arrested and indicted, hiring private counsel or assigned public defenders to represent them at trial. The search for truth goes on throughout the entirety of the pre-trial period—lawyers for both sides seek testimonial, documentary, and scientific evidence to corroborate their witnesses or exonerate those wrongly charged. Most of the time, I like to think, our system of justice has served us well.

The Mystery Writers of America invited authors—bestselling storytellers as well as new voices—to explore the complicated characters that inhabit the courtroom. In this wonderfully mixed collection of well-told tales, you'll meet rogue lawyers and victims who lie; people who want the system to work and those who use it for revenge or a more personal form of justice; the alibi witness who is eviscerated on the stand and the killer who gets away with murder. These are stories about the criminal justice system, and, may it please the court, I—for one—am grateful they are fiction.

I am delighted to offer the exhibits in this anthology to you as part of my case in chief. Again, it's like my favorite moment at trial. I've given you the best of my fellow MWA writers, and now I get to sit back at counsel table while you evaluate the evidence.

The prosecution rests, but I hope your enjoyment of these stories is just beginning.

—Linda Fairstein

MYSTERY WRITERS OF AMERICA

Presents

THE
PROSECUTION
RESTS

THE SECRET SESSION

BY EDWARD D. HOCH

J udge Bangor himself entered Harry Fine's chambers a few weeks following Harry's swearing in as the newest justice on the state's Court of Appeals. It was a snowy January morning with the windows tightly closed, and Harry's first thought was that the Chief would probably light up one of his cigars in violation of the building's no-smoking rule.

"Harry, do you have a few minutes?" he asked, closing the door behind him without waiting for a reply.

Judge Bangor was the ultimate father figure, a stern but fair man who'd headed the Court of Appeals since Harry was admitted to the bar a dozen years earlier. He was over six feet tall with snow-white hair and a commanding voice that had many attorneys quaking in their boots and rushing back to the law library after a session with him.

"Certainly, Chief," Harry said at once, rising from his chair. "What can I do for you?"

"Sit down, sit down!" He took the maroon leather armchair opposite Harry's desk. "What I'm about to tell you is in confidence. I'd hoped I wouldn't have to tell you at all, but something's come up which may require our action."

3

"You certainly have my curiosity aroused," Harry said with a smile.

"Did you ever wonder what prompted Colin Penny's resignation, opening up the seat for you?"

"He said he wanted to spend more time with his family and maybe return to private law practice."

Judge Bangor snorted. "I doubt if you'll see him in a courtroom again, at least not in this state. Any sitting justices, especially on the Court of Appeals, are open to bribery attempts. It goes with the territory in this state. Certain accusations were made against Judge Penny, accusations that could damage a person's career even if they went unproven. Rather than allow these to be made public, we convened a secret session of the court—"

"A what?"

"Perhaps that is the wrong term to use. In any event, all five justices—including Judge Penny—gathered in private to examine the charges and rumors circulating about his conduct. Much of the evidence concerned a large political donation, beyond the legal limits, made by a lumber company that won the bidding to cull a portion of state forestland. Another bidder had sued, claiming the winner had prior knowledge of the bidding. His claim was rejected by a lower court, but it was working its way up to us. That was when Penny accepted a large political donation from the lumber company."

"Why are you telling me this?" Harry Fine asked. There was something unsettling about the conversation and he wanted it to end.

"Because it has become necessary, Harry. In our secret session we heard the case against Colin Penny and listened to his meager defense. Then he left the room while the four of us discussed his fate. I must tell you, the vote to force his resignation was not unanimous. Susan Quinn was on his side and spoke vigorously in his defense, but the vote was three to one, or three to two if we count Judge Penny's own vote. He was told he would have to resign."

"He went along with that?"

"He had no choice. The reporter who had the story agreed to kill it if Penny offered his resignation. Otherwise it would have been all over the papers."

Fine shook his head. "Highly irregular," he muttered.

"This is my court, Harry. I will do everything in my power to douse any flicker of scandal before it ignites."

"You still haven't told me why I need to know this."

Judge Bangor paused and reached for a cigar in his breast pocket, then thought better of it. "The reporter who threatened to break the story about Penny's illegal contributions now says there is a second member of the court involved. I see us going through this whole nightmare again. That's why I've come to you."

"Who's the reporter?"

"Maeve McGuire. You've probably seen her bylines."

Harry Fine nodded. "She's a pretty good writer. Ran a short interview on me after my appointment last month."

"I read it. That's why you're the perfect one to contact her."

"Contact her about what? I can't ask her to kill a story."

"Of course not. But you can have a friendly conversation with her, find out what's going on. All I have is a tip, and I can't pursue it personally for various reasons."

"Couldn't one of the other justices—?"

"Hardly! If the information she has is accurate, any one of them might be involved."

"Surely not Susan Quinn!" The feisty brunette judge, only a few years older than Fine, had introduced him to his new position by tutoring him in the arcane rituals of the Court of Appeals.

Judge Bangor shrugged. "It might be Quinn or Frank Rockwell or Zach Wanamaker. Find out what you can."

"I doubt if she'll reveal any big secrets, not to me at least."

―――

FINE PHONED MAEVE McGuire and invited her to lunch the following day. Not wanting it to appear clandestine in any way, he suggested they meet at the Temple Bar, a restaurant across from the appellate court that was frequented by lawyers and judges. As the hostess showed them to a table near the window, he saw Judge Rockwell at a nearby table, raising his eyebrows.

Maeve saw it too and commented, "Does he think he's spotted a blooming romance?"

"I hope not. My divorce isn't final yet."

She was an intense, attractive young woman who rarely smiled even when joking. Harry Fine read her columns intermittently and had seen her around the courts on occasion. He had consented to last month's interview after winning the appointment to fill Colin Penny's term.

"I hope you phoned to give me the inside scoop on the appellate court," she chided him now. "The word is that Bangor rules with an iron fist."

"You probably know more about it than I do," he told her. "What's the latest scandal?"

She shrugged. "One a year is quite enough. I assume you know about your predecessor."

"Judge Penny? I've heard talk. I've even heard he might not have been the only one accepting illegal campaign contributions."

"Tell me more!" she urged, flashing one of her rare smiles.

"I was hoping you could tell me."

The smile faded as quickly as it had appeared. "Did Judge Bangor send you?"

"Let's enjoy our lunch and not worry about who sent me."

She shook her head. "Look, Judge Fine, I interviewed you for my paper, but that doesn't make us lifelong friends. I have nothing to tell you. As you probably know, I agreed to kill a story about Judge Penny because he resigned from the court. That was a one-shot, and it won't happen again. Anything more that I discover about illegal contributions or bribes will end up on our front page."

"Of course! I'm not trying to influence you in any way."

But the luncheon went downhill after that. She dashed off as quickly as possible, pleading another appointment, and he finished his coffee alone. He was just paying the check when Frank Rockwell stopped by his table on the way out.

"Courting the press these days, are you?" he asked.

"Not really. She interviewed me last month and I felt I owed her a lunch in return."

"Never get too friendly with the press," the gray-haired justice advised. "They'll screw you every time."

Fine smiled. "Thanks for the advice, Judge."

Whatever Bangor had hoped would come of the lunch with Maeve McGuire, it hadn't happened. Fine hated to admit failure to the Chief and decided to try another possibility on his own. With no pending sessions that afternoon, he drove out to Willow Road, where his predecessor Colin Penny resided. It was an upper-middle-class neighborhood of older colonial homes, and Penny's house was only a few doors away from Judge Wanamaker's, where Fine had attended a New Year's Day open house a few weeks earlier.

Zach Wanamaker was at the courthouse, of course, and there was no sign of his wife as Fine drove past the house. He was in luck with Penny, though. The former judge was sweeping a light coating of snow from his driveway in an obvious make-work effort to keep busy at something. Fine pulled up and parked.

"I was driving by and saw you out here," he said, getting out of the car.

"Hello, Judge."

"I think you can call me Harry," Fine told him, already regretting that he'd stopped. "How are you doing?"

"Okay. I think I'll be going back into private practice soon. Taking good care of my old office?"

"Sure," he answered with a smile. Penny was a decade older than him, a hard age to be starting over. Already his face was lined, and he seemed to have aged since Fine had last seen him. The word was that his wife had moved out after his forced resignation and was staying with their son's family in Arizona. "Stop in and see us sometime."

Penny tried to smile but couldn't quite make it.

"I don't think that would be wise. I'm the black sheep these days."

"I'm sure you weren't the only one who took a contribution now and then."

"No," he agreed, "but I was the only one Maeve McGuire found out about."

"Well—" Fine glanced up at the sky, searching for a way out of the conversation. "Think we'll get any more snow?"

"Any minute, now that I've finished sweeping." He turned away and headed back to the house. "Good seeing you, Judge."

Fine returned to his car and drove back to the office.

―――

HE REPORTED TO Judge Bangor later that afternoon. Judge Susan Quinn was present too and was especially interested in Fine's brief conversation with Penny.

"How did he seem?" she wanted to know.

"Maybe a little bitter," Fine said. "But it's hard for me to tell. I never knew him that well."

Judge Bangor wasn't interested in Penny's feelings.

"Did he say anything about someone else on the court being involved?"

Susan, at age forty-six, still wore her hair at shoulder length despite some traces of gray. She was married to a successful surgeon, and the two were popular partygoers in local society. She interrupted to defend Penny. "Isn't it bad enough you forced his resignation?" she asked.

He turned to her and said, "My dear, this appellate court is the most important thing in my life. I intend to keep it pure and uncorrupted no matter who suffers. Now then, Harry, what, if anything, did Colin Penny say to you?"

"Nothing, really. I remarked that there were probably others who'd accepted donations, and he replied that he was the only one the reporter found out about."

"Was he speaking specifically of the appellate court?"

"I don't know. It was just a general comment."

Susan shook her head. "Chief, you're carrying this to extremes. Harry has told you everything he knows."

"Very well," Judge Bangor agreed. "We'll adjourn this session for now."

THE REST OF the week passed quietly. January was often a slow month on the court calendar, and the Chief called only one joint session on Friday concerning a statute of limitations case. Zach Wanamaker cast the deciding vote to uphold the lower court's ruling, and everyone scattered for the weekend.

Fine went down to the parking garage with Wanamaker when it was over. "Going skiing this weekend?" he asked, knowing that the older man spent time on the slopes whenever he could. He was in good physical shape, with a ruddy outdoor complexion.

"You bet!" Judge Wanamaker replied. "I'm driving up to the mountains tonight, meeting some friends there."

Fine didn't particularly care whether his friends were male or female. They were just making elevator conversation. "We'll see you on Monday, then."

Wanamaker nodded. "I'll be driving back early Monday morning. Have a good weekend."

Fine spent Saturday and Sunday reading up on earlier appellate court decisions. He had a good working knowledge of the law, but Judge Bangor could leave him in the dust with citations of obscure cases. Fine's law clerk had assembled enough reading matter to keep him occupied for the weekend, and he almost felt guilty slipping away on Sunday night for dinner with a lady friend.

He was preparing to leave for the courthouse that sunny Monday morning when Judge Bangor phoned. "I just wanted to alert you, Harry. That reporter, Maeve McGuire, was killed by a hit-and-run driver about an hour ago, on her way to work."

———

By ELEVEN O'CLOCK the five justices were assembled in the Chief's spacious office. Judge Bangor rapped his knuckles on the desk to signal for quiet, though no one had said a word since entering the office. He took out one of his cigars, but it remained unlit, perhaps in deference to Susan Quinn, the most outspoken justice on the subject of smoking.

"You all know why we're here," Bangor said.

"Miss McGuire made charges against Colin Penny that forced his resignation. And recently I've heard rumors that she was about to make accusations against another of our number. Her death this morning is tragic, of course, but it has nothing to do with us. I would suggest that if any of us are contacted by the press we merely have no comment other than to express our sympathy to her family."

"The press will be all over this," Frank Rockwell said. "She's one of theirs."

He brushed back his gray hair with a familiar gesture and added, "Harry had lunch with her last week."

Wanamaker turned toward him, a bit surprised by this news, but the Chief hurried to his defense. "I asked Harry to contact her because she'd recently interviewed him. I thought he might learn if the rumors were true that another justice was involved."

Fine nodded in agreement. "Unfortunately, I learned nothing from her."

Susan Quinn spoke next. "Where did you hear these rumors, Chief?"

"I'd rather not say."

"Come on!" Judge Wanamaker insisted. "We have a right to know."

Bangor squirmed uneasily. "All I can tell you is that it was someone at the newspaper who knew what she was working on. It was the same person who tipped me off about the situation with Judge Penny."

"What time was she killed?" Susan wanted to know.

"The police tell me it was about seven forty a.m. She started work at eight. They have alternate side of the street parking and she was crossing the street to her car. A neighbor heard the thump when the car hit her, but no one has come forward yet who actually saw it happen."

"Are the police checking garages and repair shops?" Harry Fine asked.

"Of course. That's the first thing they think of."

There was little more to be said. None of them wanted to suggest, even obliquely, that Maeve McGuire had been killed to keep her from revealing anything further about bribery or illegal campaign contributions. Even Judge Bangor finished the session by remarking that it was a terrible accident.

And yet, the driver hadn't stopped.

———

FINE WENT BACK to his office and tried to work, but the memory of Maeve McGuire was too strong to shake off. He ate lunch alone at a little coffee shop down the street and returned to find a pale Susan Quinn waiting in his office.

"What is it?" he asked, immediately on guard.

"I received a message meant for Judge Wanamaker," she said in a hushed voice. "I'm not sure what I should do."

"What was it?"

"It was on my voice mail, but it was for Zach. His garage called with an estimate on repairing his car. He's to phone them."

"You haven't told him?"

"He's not back from lunch."

Fine stared out the window for a moment. She was asking him what she should do, and he didn't know what to tell her.

"Can't you just give him the message when he returns?"

"Harry, what if the car was damaged when he hit—"

"Don't even say it," he cautioned. He wasn't willing to accept the notion that Zach Wanamaker, or any of the other justices, could be a murderer.

"Should I tell the Chief?" she asked.

"Not yet. Look, it may be nothing. It may be a ding in his door or a damaged tire."

"You don't usually get estimates on jobs like that."

She was probably right, but they needed more information before taking it to the Chief. "Look, could you phone the repair shop and say you're Judge Wanamaker's secretary calling for the estimate? Find out what repairs it's for."

"I—I don't know if I should do that."

"I'd do it myself and say that I'm Zach, but they might know his voice."

"You really think we should?"

"We have to know, Susan, before anyone else does. If the police are starting to check repair shops—"

"All right," she decided. "I'll call." She put on her reading glasses to make out the number on her note and punched it into Harry's phone.

"Make it sound good," he told her, shutting the office door.

"Hello?" she said. "This is Judge Wanamaker's secretary. You phoned him about repairing the damage to his car? He's wondering how much that would be." She listened and jotted down a figure.

"Nine hundred eighty-five dollars," she repeated, raising her eyebrows toward Fine. "And what would that cover? The right front fender and the right headlight. And you've already notified the insurance company? Very good. When will it be ready? Not till Friday? All right, I'll tell him. Thank you." She hung up.

"You should have been an actress instead of a judge," Fine told her.

"Sure, or maybe just a secretary."

"He hit something with his car, or someone."

"I can't believe it, Harry. We'll have to tell the Chief."

"All right," he agreed. "We'll go in together."

Judge Bangor looked up as they entered his office and closed the door. "What's up?" he asked, looking from one to the other.

Susan told him what they'd done, about the mistaken message and her call to the repair shop. "It's probably nothing," she told him. "But in view of what happened this morning—"

Bangor shook his head. "I've known Zach for twenty years. He couldn't do anything like this."

"You'd better ask him," Fine suggested. "I think he's back from lunch now."

A few moments later Zach Wanamaker joined them in the Chief's office, puzzled by their grim expressions.

"What's up?" he asked.

Judge Bangor asked, "Did you have an accident with your car, Zach?"

"Accident?"

"A call from your repair shop was on my voice mail by mistake," Susan told him. "Nearly a thousand dollars' damage."

"Oh, that!" He shrugged it off. "Driving back from the mountains this morning I hit a deer. Killed it dead."

"Did you report it to the police?" Bangor asked.

"Of course! You think I'd break the law? I got home a little after seven, showered, and took the car into the shop. Luckily I could still drive it."

"We'll have to confirm your story."

"Confirm all you want," Wanamaker said, his ruddy complexion turning a deeper red than usual. "I damn well didn't kill your girlfriend, if that's what you're thinking!"

Everyone seemed to freeze at his words, and Fine had the bizarre impression of time standing still. He feared what might happen next, but there was an opportune knock on the door and Judge Rockwell entered. "Am I interrupting something?" he asked.

The Chief recovered his composure, as if Wanamaker's words had never been spoken. "Not at all, Frank. Come in. We're just discussing the McGuire situation."

"Terrible! A terrible accident."

Judge Bangor spoke as if announcing a verdict, without looking at Zach Wanamaker. "It was no accident. I'm calling a secret session of this court for Wednesday morning at eleven, to consider the murder of Maeve McGuire and any possible involvement by a member of this court."

BANGOR REMAINED IN his office with the door closed, admitting not even his law clerks, until late in the day.

Then he summoned Fine. Lighting one of his cigars, he said, "Harry, I want you to check out Judge Wanamaker's alibi about hitting the deer. See if there's any truth to it."

"I don't know that you should refer to it as an alibi, Chief. He hasn't been accused of anything yet."

"Just see if the state police have a report of his car hitting a deer this morning."

"All right." He hesitated, knowing he was on slippery ground. "What he said about you and Miss McGuire—"

"—is no one's business. We were friends for a time and she tipped me off about Penny."

"What about the latest rumor?"

"She didn't give me a name. By that time we'd broken up. That's why I sent you to see what you could learn."

Fine tended to believe the last part, and it was none of his business if they'd been more than friends.

"All right," he said. "I'll check on the accident first thing in the morning."

But a call in the morning brought only a request for the time and place of the accident, and he had to go to Judge Wanamaker's office for that information. The judge was not in a mood to cooperate. "He's really going through with this secret-session business tomorrow?"

"Apparently," Fine told him. "But if I can dig up some evidence, I can act as something of a defense attorney for you."

"I'm well able to defend myself, thanks. The accident occurred about six forty-five a.m. I know because I was listening to a morning show on the radio. I used my cell phone to report it, but it was ten minutes before a trooper arrived and filled out an accident report. Luckily I could still drive the car, and I got back to my house before seven thirty to shower and change."

"Where did it happen?"

"Route nine, just south of the city line."

Fine phoned the state police again and gave them the information, requesting they fax him a copy of the accident report. Ten minutes later it was on his desk. It seemed straightforward enough: "At 6:57 a.m. I responded to a 911 call and found a silver SUV at the side of Route 9 near the 13-mile marker. A young buck deer, dead at the scene, had run onto the highway in the dark from the woods on the eastern side, hitting the right front fender of the northbound vehicle. A large piece of the plastic fender was broken off, and there was blood and deer fur at the point of impact, but no other damage. Driver and sole occupant of the SUV was Judge Zachery Wanamaker of the Court of Appeals. He was uninjured and was able to drive the car home after filing the report. I phoned the highway department to remove the deer carcass and remained on the scene until it was picked up at 8:05."

That seemed to be proof enough for Fine. He poked his head in Wanamaker's office and said, "I have a fax of the police report."

"Good! One more thing I forgot to mention. I have a witness who saw me arrive home with the damaged car."

"Who would that be?"

"Oddly enough, it was Colin Penny. He's a neighbor of mine."

———

AT ELEVEN O'CLOCK Wednesday morning, when Judge Bangor gaveled the secret session to order in his office, all five justices were in attendance. Fine shared the leather sofa with Susan Quinn while Judge Wanamaker sat alone in the far corner and Rockwell pulled up another armchair to be closer to the desk.

"All right, the session will come to order," Bangor announced. "I hadn't expected the need for another of these so soon after the last one, but the untimely death of Maeve McGuire has made it a necessity. As I stated before, this session is in no way a trial.

It is more of an informal inquest to determine the truth or fal-sity of the rumors going around. I've asked our newest member, Judge Fine, to handle the investigation as it concerns Judge Wa-namaker, and he will report to us now."

Fine rose to his feet, feeling a bit out of his element. He stepped away from the sofa into the neutral area at the center of the room. "Your Honors, Maeve McGuire's violent death came shortly after she hinted to the Chief that another member of the appellate court had accepted bribes and illegal campaign contributions. It was the same charge that forced Colin Penny's resignation and my own appointment to this august body. Miss McGuire was killed by a hit-and-run driver in an early-morning accident near her apartment. When we learned of dam-age that morning to Judge Wanamaker's vehicle, a natural suspi-cion arose. The judge's story was that he hit a deer while driving back from a skiing weekend. This is the story I was asked to investigate."

"It's not a story," Wanamaker interrupted. "It's the truth."

"I'm inclined to agree," Fine told the court.

"In fact, I have here the state police report on the incident." He read them the report and then continued, "I also have a wit-ness that I'd like to bring before this session."

Judge Bangor immediately objected. "This entire session is informal and extralegal. We could not admit a stranger to these proceedings."

"This is no stranger. In fact, he played a major part in your most recent secret session. I'm referring to Colin Penny."

It was Judge Rockwell who spoke up then. "There's no need to revisit that affair. Penny has resigned from this court and we're the better for it."

But Susan Quinn protested. "Colin's not here to get his job back! Apparently he can verify Zach's movements on Monday morning, and we should hear him out. By inviting him in here, we're not telling him anything he doesn't already know from firsthand experience."

Judge Bangor sighed. "All right. When can he be here?"

"I asked him to come at eleven fifteen," Fine replied. "He should be waiting outside now."

"Pretty sure of yourself, aren't you?" Bangor asked.

"I am, yes."

"Very well. Bring him in."

Fine went out to the reception room and found Penny seated nervously in one of the chairs. "They're ready for you, Colin."

"I still feel it's a mistake to come here like this."

"It's not a mistake to help clear an innocent man."

He followed Fine into Judge Bangor's office, nodding to the others. Only Susan Quinn made an effort to put him at ease. "We've missed you, Colin. How are you doing?"

"Well enough. I'm going back into private practice next month."

"That's great," she told him. "You'll probably be arguing cases before us."

"Let's get on with this," the Chief ordered.

"What evidence do you have to supply, Penny?"

The former judge cleared his throat. "I was wheeling my trash Dumpster out to the curb on Monday morning—"

Fine interrupted to ask, "What time?"

"Before seven thirty, but close to it. I was back in the house in time for the seven thirty news. I had just reached the curb when Judge Wanamaker's car turned into the street. I saw its headlights, though it was getting light by then, and I noticed a large piece out of the right front fender. He slowed down, lowered the window, and told me he'd just hit a deer. He was going to change his clothes and take the car in for repairs."

"What did you do then?"

"I wished him good luck and went back in the house."

"Tell me something, Penny. Did you ever have a hint that another member of this court besides you was receiving illegal payments?"

"A hint," he admitted. "I never knew if it was true."

Bangor asked a few more questions and seemed satisfied there was no more to tell. "Thank you for coming in," he said as Penny left. "I know it couldn't have been easy for you."

When he'd gone, Zach Wanamaker spoke from his corner chair. "Satisfied now, or do we get the deer in to testify?"

"We owe you an apology for even considering the possibility that you killed that woman. But the fact remains, someone killed her, either accidentally or deliberately." Bangor shuffled the papers on his desk. "This court cannot afford a scandal, and I will do everything in my power to prevent one."

Susan Quinn spoke up. "Are you still thinking one of us accepted a bribe for our vote? With Zach cleared, that only leaves Frank and myself."

"And me," Bangor reminded them. "I'm not above suspicion."

"Wait a minute," Fine said. "We're assuming she was killed to prevent her naming a second member of this court accepting bribes. But suppose the motive wasn't in the future but in the past. Suppose she was killed in an act of vengeance over something she already did?"

"What would that be?" Judge Rockwell wondered.

"She was going to publish the information about Colin Penny. When he saw the damage to Judge Wanamaker's car, it gave him an opportunity for revenge. He could have driven over to her street, less than ten minutes away, saw her crossing to her car, and run her down, knowing that Wanamaker would become at least a temporary suspect."

"I can't believe that!" Susan responded with a touch of anger in her voice.

But Judge Bangor nodded. "It's certainly a possibility."

She turned and lit into him. "Haven't you done enough to the poor man already? You drove him from the bench, ruined his career!"

"Not without cause," Bangor reminded her.

Fine tried to calm them down. "I only mentioned it as a possibility to be considered. There's no proof that he killed her."

"There'd be proof on his car," Bangor said.

"I'll have the police take a look at it."

Zach Wanamaker cleared his throat. "If you're done with this little charade, I'll be getting back to work." He picked up a folder and departed.

Fine glanced down at the state police fax on the table in front of him. He was sorry now he'd ever gotten involved in this. Was he as bad as Bangor in besmirching an innocent man?

"Wait a minute!" he said, staring at the fax as if seeing it for the first time. "There's something wrong here."

"What's that?" Susan asked.

Fine didn't answer her. Instead, he grabbed the fax and followed Judge Wanamaker out of the office, ignoring a question from the Chief. He strode quickly across the reception area to Wanamaker's door and went in without knocking.

The judge looked up from his desk. "What is it now?"

"You killed her after all, Zach," he managed to blurt out. "You really killed her, didn't you?"

Judge Wanamaker stood up, his face aghast with shock or anger. "What are you talking about, Fine? You just proved my innocence."

"That was my mistake, wasn't it?" He tossed the fax down on Wanamaker's desk. "Read it and weep, Zach."

"What? This is the state police report. I admit I killed the deer. This has nothing to do with McGuire's death."

"Doesn't it? He says you had a broken right front fender, with blood and bits of fur on the car, but no other damage. Yet your garage is installing a new fender and a new right headlight."

The judge tried to shrug it off. "So the trooper missed the headlight."

"Hard to do when it was still dark out. He might not have let you drive home with just one headlight."

"It might have been damaged and failed on the way home."

Fine shook his head. "No, because Colin Penny mentioned seeing your headlights when you turned into the street."

"That was almost seven thirty. How could I have showered and changed and still killed the woman?"

"You didn't shower and change till later, if at all. You were only ten minutes from the spot where Maeve McGuire was run down and killed." As he spoke, he was aware of the door opening behind him, and out of the corner of his eye he saw Judge Bangor enter the office.

"That's crazy," Wanamaker tried to argue. "It was morning by that time. Even on her little street there might have been traffic and pedestrians to see what happened, to take down a license number."

"But there weren't, were there? If you'd seen another car or person, you'd just have driven on and done nothing. It was a crime of convenience, though not too convenient for Maeve. You had to silence her before she revealed the bribery charges against you, and that was a perfect opportunity."

"Do you think you can prove any of this?"

"I do," Fine told him. "If the headlight was broken when you hit her, there'd have been pieces of glass at the scene. I'm sure the forensics lab will be able to match them to your headlight."

Wanamaker turned to the Chief. "Do you believe any of this?"

"I do," Bangor said. "You're finished, Zach."

"At least give me the deal you gave Penny. Accept my resignation. The whole thing can be hushed up for the good of the court."

But the Chief only shook his head. "You killed Maeve, Zach. You killed her, and there's no way I'm hushing that up. If it means a black eye for my court, at least her death won't go unpunished."

"Judge—"

Bangor shook his head and pronounced his verdict.

"You're guilty as charged."

DESIGNER JUSTICE

BY PHYLLIS COHEN

Never long on patience, Harold Vekt was beginning to think about giving up. His feet hurt and his beer-laden bladder was trying to get his attention.

His luck, he decided, stank. Forty minutes had passed since he'd positioned himself behind the hedges leading to the elaborate teak-and-glass entryway of the Waterside Club, on the edge of the river that divided the city. Every departing couple had been ushered into a taxi hailed by one of the plushly uniformed doormen, or into a limo that glided up to the entrance at just the right moment.

Half the women wore furs, although the night was mild. Many of the men, and some of the women, carried leather briefcases. All were well dressed and well groomed. Jewelry with possibilities showed on all the women and many of the men.

Didn't any of them live within walking distance?

He was about to take a chance on assuaging his bladder in the hedges when the door opened once again and a baritone voice declared, "No thank you, Antonio. It's a fine evening. We'll walk home." Vekt gritted his teeth and zipped up.

The couple appeared to be in their late forties, a few years younger than Harold's mother. Though with their easy-street life, he thought, they could look like that and be much older. The woman's hair was honey gold and sleekly coiffed. She wore a beige fur jacket over an amber silk dress, oval earrings of gold rimmed with tiny diamonds, a thick gold bracelet, and a ring that was simple in style but held a diamond of several carats. The man, in a three-piece gray suit, wore a gold pocket watch and carried a tan leather briefcase of the old-fashioned envelope style, with a flap and two buckled straps.

The man and woman walked up First Avenue, busy and well lit, and turned east on 56th Street. Vekt stayed three-quarters of a block behind them. They crossed Sutton Place; here no one else was about, and the bare but thickly branched trees dimmed the street lighting. Vekt grasped the weapon in the pocket of his gray hooded jacket and increased his pace until he was about twenty feet from them. "Excuse me, sir."

The couple halted and turned. "Yes?"

He moved closer. In his upturned left hand was a slip of paper. "I'm looking for Ninety-two Sutton Terrace."

The man pointed toward the river. "Sutton Terrace is around that corner, but as far as I know, there's no ninety-two."

Vekt had closed the gap between them. He brandished the scrap of paper, and then his right hand was out with a slim-barreled black handgun and his left arm was tight around the woman's waist.

"Okay—the rules are: one, be quiet; two, open the briefcase and put your wallet in it. And if you happen to have a gun, remember that I can shoot her before you could even aim at me."

Staring, rigid, the man complied. Gargling noises came from the woman's throat. Vekt jabbed the gun into the back of her armpit and whispered fiercely. "Shut—up!"

He turned back to the man. "Now, your watch, with all its attachments." Into the briefcase went the Patek Philippe with its heavy gold chain and fob and Phi Beta Kappa key. "The wedding band too." It was of textured gold and about half an inch wide.

Vekt turned to the woman, keeping the gun in place. "Now your stuff—into the briefcase. First the purse."

"There's no—"

"Quiet. The purse." Her husband held out the briefcase; she dropped in the small cream leather bag with its mother-of-pearl clasp. "Your jewelry. All of it."

She started with the bracelet, using her teeth to undo the difficult catch. The earrings were next, then the solitaire, followed by a diamond wedding band that Vekt hadn't noticed.

He took the briefcase with his left hand. "Now, if you make any noise before I'm out of sight, I'll be back here before anyone else has time to show up. In which case you won't live to tell them anything." Shifting his gaze back and forth between them, he walked backward, aiming the gun.

He was ready to turn and run when a glint flashed in his left eye. It came from the base of the woman's throat.

Vekt dashed forward, grabbing at her neck for the thin gold chain with its small disk pendant.

"You stupid bitch—I said all of it!"

"NO!" she shrieked, flailing at him. "Not this! My baby! You can't take it! You can't have her!" She scratched his eyelids with one hand and pulled his greasy blond hair with the other.

He shoved the gun between her breasts and pulled the trigger. The husband was clawing at him; he shot without aiming and flew off down the street just as the first window opened in an adjacent building. He had not taken the chain.

———

VEKT FLUSHED THE toilet, huffing with relief, and jumped into the shower, making the water as hot as he could stand it. He soaped himself until he was coated with white, and then rinsed for ten minutes, gradually changing the mix until it ran ice cold.

Wrapped in a huge, thick, white towel, he strode with damp footsteps into the kitchen and pulled a bottle of Heineken from the refrigerator. But he put it back without opening it; his gut feeling told him that this was more than a beer occasion. He poured three ounces of Glenlivet over two chunky ice cubes in a thick tumbler and carried it into the living room, ready to assess the evening's proceeds.

Vekt began with high hopes and ended with exultation. Cash: $1,145 in the wallet, $312 in the purse. Credit cards: five, including two platinums. Jewelry: the best, and plain design, easy to dump. Except the watch: an intricate antique; he'd have to hold it for a while. Maybe even wear it; he could afford a three-piece suit. Except the earrings too, damn it. The name of a well-known brand of costume jewelry was stamped on the back. The bitch!

———

VEKT'S FRIENDLY NEIGHBORHOOD fence was in a good mood. "These two"—the diamond rings—"let's say five thousand."

"Seven."

"Fifty-five hundred."

"They're at least twenty-five retail."

"Six."

"Done. How about the gold stuff?"

"The bracelet—mmmm—four hundred. This ring's a problem—it has initials inside."

"So remove them."

"I will, but it ain't easy. And it leaves scars—reduces the resale value. Seventy-five."

"Come on, Lou, it's a five-hundred-dollar ring."

"One hundred's the best I can do. Better than you'll get elsewhere."

Vekt conceded. He coaxed Lou out of fifty for each of the credit cards and for the leather briefcase. He was now clean of almost all the evidence. The purse and its trivial contents had been thrown down a sewer; the gun and the blond wig went with it. Only the antique watch remained, in the movable heel of a brown leather boot, lined up in a closet with all his other footwear.

———

VEKT WAS STARTLED by a hand touching his left forearm. His eyes and mind had been wandering around the courtroom, from the gold chains around the neck of a pudgy middle-aged juryman to the reporter who had all her parts in the right place under clothes that showed them off.

He turned toward his attorney after a second nudge. "You must, I repeat, must, pay attention," the man growled. "If a witness says anything that you can challenge, write it down—push the paper to where I can see it from the corner of my eye."

It was still a mystery to Vekt how he had lucked out with this lawyer. Wilson Herrera was nationally known for his high acquittal rate and his six-figure fees. "Every attorney gets to do court appointments once in a while" was all he'd said in explanation.

The prosecutor's six-foot-two-inch frame, with its hint of a paunch, moved agilely in its charcoal-gray vested suit as he faced the witness over rimless granny glasses. Vekt took a perverse comfort from Luther Johnson's dark brown skin. Only two of the jurors were black. Maybe the other ten wouldn't buy it from one of them.

———

"Detective Swayze. Tell us why you decided to arrest Harold Vekt for the murder of Annabelle Jagoda."

"Her husband, Morris Jagoda, identified him in a lineup."

"And why did you include Mr. Vekt in the lineup to begin with?"

"Mr. Jagoda had identified his picture."

Vekt watched Herrera write, with a silver-plated Parker pen, *pic→l'up.*

"Is this the picture?"

The detective studied the stiff 4 x 6 paper. "Yes."

"What was the source of the picture?"

"Police files." Herrera underlined his cryptic notation.

"Describe the person as you see him in the picture."

"Long, narrow face, short, light brown hair, narrow eyes close together, sharp, straight nose, down-curved lips, small ears close to the head."

"Do you see the person in this courtroom?"

"Yes. The defendant." He pointed to Vekt with a jabbing motion. Johnson glared at Harold, then with deliberation shifted his gaze to the jury.

"Pass the witness."

Herrera rose. "Detective Swayze, did Mr. Jagoda provide a description of the person who had robbed him and shot his wife?"

"Yes."

The lawyer held out a page. "Does this statement include that description?"

Swayze scanned the printed sheet. "Yes."

"Please read the outlined phrase."

Swayze cleared his throat. " 'Shoulder-length blond hair.' "

It was Herrera's turn to look pointedly from the defendant to the jury. "Detective, you say Mr. Jagoda selected Mr. Vekt's picture and then identified him in a lineup. Was anyone else whose picture he was shown included in the lineup?"

"Uhh—no—the others were cops or civilian employees of the precinct."

"When Mr. Jagoda was viewing the lineup, what did you say to him?"

"I asked him to ID the perpetrator."

"To be more specific, did you say, 'Is the person who shot your wife among them?' or did you ask, 'Which of these people did it?'"

Swayze looked perplexed, then shrugged and shook his head. "I really don't remember." Herrera opened his mouth, then waggled his fingers in a dismissive gesture.

"Now, Detective, after Mr. Vekt was arrested, was a search of his apartment conducted?"

"Yes."

"Who conducted it?"

"I and my partner—Louis Walters—and two uniforms. Uniformed police officers."

"Describe the search—how thorough was it?"

"We looked in every closet, every drawer, every pocket, every cushion, every shoe, every food container. The toilet tank, the freezer."

"In other words, every possible place of concealment?"

"That's right."

"And what, if anything, did you find related to the robbery?"

"More than eight thousand dollars in cash."

"Just cash? No jewelry? No papers from Mr. Jagoda's briefcase, or the briefcase itself?"

"No. But Vekt could have easily—"

"Buts are not allowed, Detective. Was there anything at all that identified any part of the cash as having belonged to the Jagodas?"

"Why would a guy like Vekt have so much cash around unless—?"

"Please answer the question. Could you single out any of the cash as being proceeds of the robbery?"

"No."

"No further questions."

Johnson jumped up. "Redirect, Your Honor." The judge nodded.

"Considering the hair discrepancy, why did you accept Mr. Jagoda's identification of this picture and of Mr. Vekt in the lineup?"

"We had cautioned Mr. Jagoda to pay more attention to the permanent than to the changeable characteristics. He looked at this picture for a long time, turned the page, and then, suddenly, turned it back, saying—"

"Objection. Mr. Jagoda is the best source of what he himself said."

"Sustained. Mr. Johnson, you may pursue this when Mr. Jagoda is on the stand."

———

VEKT LOOKED AT the ceiling as Morris Jagoda entered the courtroom and walked stiffly toward the stand. Herrera jabbed his thigh. "The jury is watching you!" he hissed through clenched teeth.

Luther Johnson's body language managed to suggest deference and compassion as he began to question Jagoda. "I know, sir, that this is extremely painful for you. But it's necessary if justice is to be done. Please tell us what occurred on the night of March twenty-first last year."

Jagoda licked his lips. He rested his right hand on the ledge that held the microphone; his left arm hung at his side, bent slightly at an unchanging angle.

"We were on our way home from dinner, walking along Fifty-sixth Street. Someone called out to us, asked for directions.

Then he pulled a gun and grabbed hold of Annabelle and demanded our valuables. We gave them to him—he instructed us to put everything in my briefcase—and he ran off. But he must have caught sight of the chain Annabelle was wearing with our daughter's pendant on it. He became enraged and ran back and grabbed for it. Annabelle became hysterical and tried to fight him off. He shot her, directly into the heart."

"Objection. Mr. Jagoda is not qualified to describe the course of the bullet."

Judge Patrick Quinn raised his bushy eyebrows. "Well—it hardly matters. The medical examiner has already testified to that fact." Herrera shrugged. The judge signaled Johnson to continue.

"Why did your wife, after surrendering all her other jewelry, resist his taking this item?"

Jagoda's eyes lost their focus. He seemed to have left the courtroom emotionally. The judge said, "Mr. Jagoda?"

"Yes—sorry.

"Felicity was our only child. We were nearly forty when she was born—our last chance. She was bright, lively, loving. Not the prettiest little girl in the world, but the most interesting, delightful, creative personality. For her third birthday we gave her a little round gold pendant, engraved with her initials intertwined with ours, as though we were all holding hands.

"A few months later she became ill. She died of leukemia two months before her sixth birthday, after a great deal of suffering. She was brave too—did I say that? Annabelle put on the pendant and never took it off. She slept with it, she bathed with it. In the end, she defended it with her life, as though it were Felicity herself."

So that's what set the bitch off, Vekt thought. He scanned the jury out of the corner of his eye and squirmed.

Johnson waited a few seconds in the silent courtroom, then

placed himself between the defense and prosecution tables. "Mr. Jagoda, did you get a good look at the person who shot your wife?"

"Yes. He is that man"—pointing—"in the light blue shirt and dark blue jacket."

"Please note that the witness has pointed out the defendant, Harold Vekt." Harold began to open his mouth but was glared down by Herrera.

"Would you tell us, Mr. Jagoda, if the defendant's appearance differs in any significant way from what it was at the time of the crime."

"His hair is different. It was blond, and much longer."

"Then how can you be certain it was he?"

"When I first saw his picture at the police station, there was something about it, but I passed it up because of the hair. But then I remembered that I'd been told to pay more attention to the permanent features than the changeable ones. And I suddenly recalled that as my wife pulled the robber's hair it had appeared to shift slightly, backward from the hairline.

"The eyes and mouth, the shape of the chin were exactly as I remembered them."

"One more question, sir. For how long a time would you estimate you had an opportunity to observe the defendant's face and become familiar with it?"

"I can't tell you in minutes or seconds. For as long as it took him to ask for an address, and for me to answer him; and for him to threaten us with his gun and demand our valuables, and for each of us to remove our valuables and put them in the briefcase, and for him to back away several feet and run forward again."

"I appreciate that you can't know the exact time lapse. But between two minutes and half an hour, which is closer?"

"Two minutes."

"How about between two minutes and fifteen minutes?"

"Fifteen. Definitely."

"Thank you, Mr. Jagoda. Pass the witness."

Herrera, four inches shorter and considerably bulkier than the prosecutor, rose from his chair but stayed behind the table. "Mr. Jagoda, may I offer my sincere condolences for your losses." Jagoda's expression did not change. "But you must appreciate that describing the tragic nature of a crime does not provide evidence that any specific person committed it."

"Objection."

"Sustained. Save it for the summation, Mr. Herrera."

"Sorry. Mr. Jagoda, you estimated the time you and the robber were in each other's presence as between two and fifteen minutes, closer to fifteen. During how much of that time were you actually looking at his face?"

"I don't understand."

"Let's start with the time before he pulled the gun. When he asked directions and you answered him. Were you looking at his face throughout that time?"

"Well—I suppose so. What else would I have looked at?"

Vekt scribbled something. Herrera threw it a stony glance and took an audible breath before continuing.

"Was he, for example, holding anything in his hand?"

Jagoda hesitated. "Ye-es. A bit of paper. I assumed the address he wanted was on it."

"You assumed—so you didn't actually see it?"

"I tried to, but it was out of reach."

"You tried to. So then, for part of that time, were you not looking at the paper rather than at the man's face?"

Jagoda was silent.

"Please answer."

"I would have to say yes."

"Now—let's get to the rest of the time, after the gun was displayed. How did you react when you first saw the gun?"

"I was horrified—paralyzed."

"Where were your eyes? What were you looking at?"

Jagoda sighed and closed his eyes. "The gun, mostly."

"And when you were putting your valuables into the briefcase, what were you looking at?"

"The items I was handling, and the gun, and his face."

"When he turned his attention to your wife, what were you looking at?"

"Primarily the gun. It was jabbed into her side. I was terrified that it would go off."

"So, would it not be accurate to say that for most of the duration of this event you were looking at the gun, not at the perpetrator's face?"

Jagoda's gaze left the attorney's face and swept out a semicircle across the floor, coming to rest on a far wall. Barely audible, he said, "Perhaps. I can't be sure."

Herrera nodded gently, as though he and the witness had arrived at an understanding. Then he moved a few steps closer to him. "Now, sir, is it correct to say that you identified the defendant first from pictures shown you by the police and then from a lineup of six people?"

"Yes."

"What did Detective Swayze say to you as you prepared to view the lineup?"

"Objection. Your Honor, you've already ruled that the speaker is the best source—"

"In this instance," Herrera interrupted with a touch of indignation, "the speaker has already said he doesn't remember."

Judge Quinn looked from Herrera to Johnson to Jagoda, then pursed his lips and said, "Overruled. The witness may answer."

Jagoda nodded. "He instructed me to view each of the men carefully and select the assailant."

" 'Select the assailant.' Were those his exact words?"

"I don't believe so, but—"

"Let me put it another way. Did he say, in effect, 'Is it one of them?' or did he say, 'Which of them is it?'"

"The latter is closer."

"Let's clarify that. He asked not *if* one of them did it, he asked *which* of them did it. Is that correct?"

"Yes."

"Now, Mr. Jagoda, you said that shortly after your first sight of Mr. Vekt's picture you suddenly remembered that the robber's hair had seemed to shift as your wife pulled it. Why did you not say this in your first statement to the police, when you described the person as having shoulder-length blond hair?"

"I didn't remember it at the time. You must realize, I was in a state of shock."

"Yes," Herrera said softly, "tell us about that." Vekt looked up at him, puzzled.

Jagoda, focused inward, continued. "The police had found me sitting on the ground, in a complete daze, with Annabelle in my arms. I didn't realize that I had also been shot. They took me to the emergency room, where my arm was treated, then to the intensive-care unit to see her.

"As we entered I heard a doctor say to the detectives, 'She's still alive, barely. Frankly, with that wound, we don't know why.'

"I looked through a glass partition at a mass of technology: tubes, machines, all attached to this papier-mâché creature: yellowish-gray skin, concave cheeks—surely not my Annabelle."

Vekt stared at Herrera. Why was he permitting, even encouraging, this ploy for sympathy?

He drew a huge question mark on the yellow pad, but Herrera either failed or chose not to see it.

"The doctor was explaining to me," Jagoda was saying, "that all her functions were being mechanically supported, but his words floated by me, carrying their meaning away. The electronic beeps speeded up, and there was a great deal of to-ing and fro-ing, but then the sound changed to an unmodulated signal, and everyone suddenly stopped moving. The doctor looked at his watch and"—Jagoda inhaled deeply—"pronounced Annabelle dead, at two forty-six a.m.

"Very soon afterward, the police took my statement. So you can see why I might have left something out."

Herrera sighed, as though moved. "So what you mean to tell us, Mr. Jagoda, is that because of trauma you had forgotten about seeing the hairline shift, but that on a later occasion you suddenly recalled it?"

"Yes."

———

Two correction officers escorted Vekt to the defense table at 10:15 a.m.; everyone else, except the judge, was in place.

Herrera looked at him. Vekt straightened his tie. "How are you?" the lawyer asked.

"Slept lousy. That tear-jerking stuff—the jury ate it up. How come you let him go on like that?"

"Because it makes a very bad impression if you negate the victim's suffering." Vekt raised his eyebrows. "And," Herrera continued coldly, "we shall probably make use of it later in the trial."

Vekt opened his mouth, but just then Judge Quinn entered. "Remain seated, please. Mr. Johnson, have you any more witnesses?"

"One bit of redirect for Mr. Jagoda, Your Honor."

Morris Jagoda seemed to have lost weight since just the day before. Johnson asked him one question: "What was there about Mr. Vekt's picture that drew your attention to it despite the fact that the hair looked different?"

"The eyes and the shape of the mouth are rather unusual."

Vekt reflexively touched the betraying features. Herrera also had one more question for Jagoda: "What time was it when this person first approached you?"

"I can't say exactly. But we'd left the restaurant at about ten oh-five and walked slowly, because Annabelle was wearing high heels. Probably ten twenty or so."

"Ten twenty. Thank you, Mr. Jagoda."

Vekt followed Jagoda's stiff descent from the witness chair and saw him take a seat at the end of the first row, next to a couple in their fifties who'd been there every day of the trial.

"What's he doing there?" he hissed. "I thought he wasn't allowed in."

"That was before he testified. Now it doesn't matter."

"It matters to me!"

Herrera's cheek muscles twitched. "His *wife* was murdered."

"Yeah."

THE FIRST WITNESS for the defense was Harold's mother. "Mrs. Vekt, where, to your knowledge, was your son on the evening of March twenty-first?"

"He came to my place for dinner."

"Where do you live?"

"In Yonkers."

"Do you remember what time he left?"

"About ten minutes to ten."

"How do you know that?"

"We watched *Celebrity Poker* for a while, and he helped me unload the dishwasher. Then he had to rush off to make sure of catching the ten o'clock bus."

"And that bus arrives in the city about what time?"

"Maybe ten to eleven, if the traffic's light."

"Thank you, Mrs. Vekt. Pass the witness."

Johnson positioned himself about six feet from the witness stand. "Mrs. Vekt, how often does your son visit you?"

"Two or three times a month."

"How is it, then, that you remember this one instance so clearly?"

"It was the last time before he was arrested." Johnson blinked and turned his back to her momentarily.

"Mrs. Vekt, do you love your son?"

"You bet I do. He's a great kid." Harold smiled, hoping she wouldn't mention the gifts he'd given her.

"Wouldn't you, then, lie in order to keep your son out of prison?"

"I don't know."

"Please respond with yes or no."

"Objection," called Herrera, but Theresa Vekt spoke over him.

"I can't say yes or no. A person can't answer that sort of question unless they really need to decide about doing it. But I don't need to because I'm telling the truth."

"Right on, Mom," Harold mumbled, eliciting another squelching glance from Herrera.

"Sustained," the judge said, finally. He looked at Johnson. Anything further?"

"No," the prosecutor grunted.

"Call your next witness, Mr. Herrera."

"Please call . . . ," Herrera said before he noticed that Harold was beckoning him. "Just a moment, please." He sat down, and Vekt leaned over to speak into his right ear.

"Put me on the stand. I'll knock 'em dead, the way Mom just did."

Herrera winced. He glanced around at the nearest spectators, then placed his mouth next to Harold's left ear and shielded it with his cupped right hand. "I thought we'd settled this. You have a legal right to testify, and if you are adamant I can't stop you. But in my *experienced* professional opinion, it would be extremely unwise—in fact, disastrous. So much so that I am unwilling to stake my reputation on it, and if you insist, I will apply to the judge to withdraw as your counsel. He might not consent, but the fact that I've asked will not do you any good."

The lawyer rose without waiting for a reply. Vekt stared at his back, no longer uncertain if Herrera knew he was guilty.

———

"PLEASE CALL DR. Madeline Smithers."

"Objection! We see no legitimate purpose—"

"You certainly understand the significance of—"

"Let's not have cross-talk between the attorneys. Come."

Johnson and Herrera leaned across the bench. Vekt strained to hear the whispers.

Herrera: ". . . acknowledged expert . . ."

Johnson: ". . . no relevance . . ."

Herrera: ". . . solely on . . . severely stressed witness."

Judge Quinn: "Gentlemen, lower your voices." The discussion continued inaudibly for about ninety seconds, and then the judge waved the attorneys away.

"The witness may be called. But, Mr. Herrera—and you too, Mr. Johnson—she may be questioned only regarding her own expert knowledge, and not about the specifics of this case. Is that understood?"

The attorneys, each looking dissatisfied, mumbled, "Yes."

———

MADELINE SMITHERS DIFFERED from most witnesses in not swiveling her gaze furtively from defendant to prosecutor to jury as she entered the courtroom with brisk, sure steps. She took the oath firmly and swept the back of her taupe wool skirt free of wrinkles as she seated herself in an erect posture. She was slender, with smoothly groomed graying dark hair and a long, oval face. Vekt's assessing eyes found only a plain gold wedding band and a hint of gold watch under the left sleeve of her suit jacket.

Herrera was standing between the defense table and the jury box. "Please state for the record your full name, title if any, city of residence, and place of employment."

"I am Madeline Curry Smithers, PhD. I reside in Chicago and am a full professor in the psychology department at West Chicago University."

"Please describe the area of psychology in which you specialize."

"For the past seventeen years my associates and I have been engaged in experimental investigation of perception and memory, in particular, the accuracy of eyewitness description and identification."

"In general terms, what have been your findings?"

"Unfortunately, inaccuracies and erroneous identifications have proven to be very common."

"Objection. What does 'very common' mean?"

"There will be more specific testimony."

"Overruled, provisionally."

Herrera turned back to the witness. "In your expert opinion, Dr. Smithers, what are the causes of eyewitness inaccuracies?"

"There are many influences on what we believe we remember. The wording of the questioning, for instance, can be crucial."

"Please give us an example."

"When a witness is asked to identify someone from among a group—either by photograph or in person—the police sometimes ask, 'Which of them is it?' rather than 'Is the person you saw among them?' Witnesses then tend to assume that one of the choices must be correct and select the one closest to their recollection, however remote the resemblance.

"A witness may also sense, through subtle—usually unintentional—tonal and behavioral cues, which choice the questioner would prefer and respond accordingly."

"Doctor, can a traumatized person be suddenly 'jogged' into remembering what he previously did not?"

"Sometimes; however, trauma obstructs observation, and what is not initially perceived cannot be recalled. Our findings contradict the common assumption that everything we are in a position to observe is stored in our minds and available for retrieval. Perception tends to be very piecemeal; we construct whole memories by using these pieces as raw material and filling in the logical gaps. Such sudden 'remembering,' therefore, is often resolution of uncertainty rather than accurate recall."

"Regarding this transition from uncertainty to spurious certainty—"

"Objection to the word 'spurious.' Implies that such remembering is always inaccurate."

Quinn looked skeptically from Johnson to Herrera, then said, less than forcefully, "Sustained."

"In that case," Herrera intoned, "I ask you if indeed such memory recovery is always spurious."

"Not one hundred percent, but often enough so that one should be wary about relying on it."

"Objection! It's up to the jury to decide what testimony to rely on."

"Sustained. Strike everything after the word 'percent.'"

Herrera blinked and turned back to the witness. "Please tell us in what way, if any, accuracy of observation is affected if there's a gun involved in the traumatic incident."

"The tendency is for one's eyes to remain riveted on the gun, largely screening out everything else."

"Including faces?"

"Yes, I'm afraid so."

Herrera returned to the table and scanned a printed sheet. He rattled the page briefly, and Vekt's half-closed eyes snapped open.

"Dr. Smithers, have any of your studies involved the procedure known as a police lineup?"

"Yes. I've run two such studies, one with college students as subjects, the other using the general population. Identical studies, with closely matching results, have been carried out at several other universities.

"In each trial an incident was staged, and witnesses were later asked to identify the 'perpetrator' by choosing among six people in a lineup. In sixty-seven percent of the trials the wrong person was selected, whether or not the right one was among the six.

"Witnesses tend to select someone they've seen before in any context if that is the only familiar face. In one study, a man who had come into the room to empty wastebaskets just before a staged assault was lined up with five men who had not been present at all. Fifty-eight percent of the witnesses identified him as the one who had punched the 'victim' in the jaw."

Herrera allowed a silence of several seconds before asking, "Is this type of erroneous identification—that is, of persons who have been seen in other contexts—always of someone who has been seen in person?"

"Not at all. It may also result from a television or newspaper sighting, or from having been shown a photograph by the police."

"From having been shown a photograph by the police," Herrera echoed.

"Yes. Especially if no one else whose picture the witness was shown is included in the lineup." Herrera nodded.

"Please keep in mind," Smithers continued, "that such witnesses are not deliberately lying. They firmly believe that they are recalling what they actually saw."

Herrera impaled a juror in the back row with his eyes. "They firmly believe what is not in fact true. That is just what makes this especially dangerous and frightening."

"Objection!"

"Sustained. Please don't editorialize, Mr. Herrera."

"Sorry."

Vekt smirked.

———

"HAS THE JURY reached a verdict?"

The foreman's long, narrow body, in jeans and a green sweater, seemed to uncoil rather than just stand up. "Yes, Your Honor, we have."

Vekt's left leg began to tremble. The judge instructed him to rise; Herrera rose with him.

"Read your verdict, please."

The foreman, not smiling, said, "On every count, we find the defendant not guilty."

"WHEEE-OOOO!" Harold took great gulps of breath and seized his lawyer by the upper arms. "Great job, Herrera. Great job!" The attorney remained expressionless.

"The defendant is free to go," Judge Quinn announced. Harold snorted with pleasure as he saw the prosecutor and his assistant looking at each other disgustedly. Morris Jagoda sat with his head in his hands.

Vekt reached out to shake Herrera's hand, but the attorney was bending down to retrieve his briefcase from under the table. He removed a small manila envelope.

"I was instructed to give you this in the event you were acquitted. I have no idea what's in it, or from whom it originated. I don't want to know." Herrera swept his papers off the table into the briefcase, clicked shut its combination lock, and stalked out of the courtroom. Harold stared after him briefly, then shrugged and turned his attention to the envelope.

It was 6 x 8; nothing was printed or written on the outside. Its metal tab closing was reinforced with two strips of transparent tape.

"What's that?" Theresa Vekt had come up behind her son.

"I don't know—something from the lawyer."

"Not a bill?"

"Nah—the court's paying him. I'll look at it later." His implication that it was none of her business was accepted matter-of-factly. "How about celebrating at Dinky Jones's?"

The dimly lit wood-paneled tavern had survived through all the years of change in Harold's childhood neighborhood. They sat on stools at the far end of the bar and had a couple of beers each, talking little except for toasts to each other and Herrera and Smithers and the jury. Then Harold took his mother to the Yonkers bus, promising to come for dinner in a couple of days.

———

BACK IN HIS flat, he put the thick envelope on the coffee table and studied it, pressing it between his palms. Fetching a steak knife from the kitchen, he cautiously slit the seal and peered in, then eased out the contents: two tape-bound stacks of currency and a folded sheet of white paper. He flipped his thumb through the bills; they appeared to be all twenties. Then he unfolded the paper.

Mr. Vekt—

I have need of a person with your skills and stamina to do a job of work for me. Of several people considered, you appear to be the best qualified.

The job is a one-time errand, whose nature you will learn at the appropriate time. It is essential, and in your best interests, that you say nothing to *anyone* about this, starting right now.

If you wish to accept, please come to 774 West 32nd Street at 9:30 on Friday night. The building has several entrances; use the door at the far end, closest to the river. It will be unlocked from 9:25 to 9:35. You will be met and given further instructions. Please do not bring your own weapon.

Enclosed is an advance payment of one-tenth of your fee. The rest, if you earn it, will also come in small bills. Should you decide against taking the job, you may keep this money. The only thing that will be expected in return is silence.

The message was unsigned, but the stiff formality of its wording had a certain familiarity. Vekt wondered if Herrera himself had written it.

One hundred and twenty-five twenty-dollar bills. Times two. Five thousand dollars. One-tenth. He didn't care who. His career as a mugger, supplemented by occasional legitimate odd jobs when he was up against it, would scarcely produce that much in two years. It was creepy, but he could take care of himself. He knew it, and the guy, whoever he was, that wanted to hire him knew it too.

————

LIGHT RAIN FILMED Vekt's face as he walked west. Unexpectedly, the wait for the downtown bus had been only three or four minutes, and he reached his destination at 9:15. On the designated door the numbers 774 were formed out of bright blue plastic tape.

Vekt tugged on the unyielding vertical door handle, then knocked, futilely. The appointed time, apparently, was firm.

Shivering from the dampness, he hugged himself and stamped his feet, glancing at his watch with increasing frequency.

Just as 9:25 popped in, Vekt heard a metallic scrape. He tried the handle again; this time only the door's great weight held it back. Slowly, he was able to pull it open.

Inside, there was total darkness. "Hey! You there?" Though he'd spoken softly, his voice reverberated. Suddenly there was blinding light, as multiple fluorescent bars fluttered on. He squeezed his eyes shut, then blinked several times before adjusting to the brightness.

He was facing a long, narrow corridor with whitewashed concrete walls. Blue tape arrows pointed down the center of the white floor. Vekt could not see where they ended.

"Anyone here?" He was louder this time, and so was the responding silence. Harold felt his scalp clench. His palm itched for a gun, but his only choices now were to accept the circumstances or forgo any possibility of earning a quick $45,000.

He proceeded warily about sixty feet along the blue trail, which made a left turn and an almost immediate right. A strip of blue disappeared under a battleship-gray door, which pushed open easily into a small bare rectangular room. The arrows continued at a diagonal. The head of the last one was angled toward a doorway in the corner.

"Son-of-a-bitch! What kind of stupid game is this?" Vekt aimed a punching shove at the narrow door, but it gave so easily that he lost his balance and stumbled through it into an unlit area. The lights in the room he'd just left cut off. With a loud clang, the door closed behind him.

"What the fuck is this?" He groped at the door, could not budge it, could find no knob or handle. "Turn the goddamn lights on!" He pounded on the door with both fists.

Suddenly the darkness was a bit less than total. He turned to see a small pool of light coming from a naked 25-watt bulb hanging by its wire about six feet above the floor. Directly beneath it was a small square table, and on the table was a sheet of paper. He crossed the murky space and gingerly picked up the page, printed in the same typeface as the letter that had directed him here.

Dear Mr. Vekt,

Welcome to the rest of your life.

I own this property. It has been disused for several years. No one ever comes here. The walls, inside and out, are eighteen inches thick.

Behind this table is a door leading to another room, the only other place you will ever be.

In that room are a refrigerator, a sink (cold water only), and a toilet; also a rolled-up mattress with a blanket and two spare lightbulbs.

In the refrigerator is a small supply of food. Use it sparingly; it will be replenished, but who knows when?

The door to the room is on an automatic time lock set to open twice a day, at 8:00 a.m. and 8:00 p.m., and stay open for twenty minutes each time. (This will help you to know the approximate time of day after your watch battery runs out. That is, if you manage to keep track of day and night—there are no windows in your new environment.) During those intervals, do whatever you need to do and get out. The room has no outside air supply. If you need urgently to urinate at any other time, use the storm drain in the center of this room.

You have no hope of deliverance, even if you've broken the rules and told someone where you were going. All the blue tape will soon be gone, including the numerals on the door. (There is no 774; the highest number on this street is in the five hundreds.)

You will live, at most, as long as I do—or perhaps a few days longer if there's food left when I die. My own life expectancy is problematic—my heart was torn out by my wife's death, and when I've finished with you, I'll have nothing left to do.

Now, of course, you know who I am. Have you figured out yet that it was I who paid for your defense? Attorneys such as Wilson Herrera do not ordinarily serve in "routine" cases, even by court appointment. Dr. Smithers doesn't come cheap either. Neither knows the origin of their fees.

Why have I done this? I prefer—for myself, at any rate—personal vendetta to "criminal justice." I want to control the exact specifications of your punishment, so that I may savor it.

When you've digested the contents of this letter, put it in the other room. It is the price of your next supply of food.

There was no signature.

Harold Vekt commenced his accommodation to his fate by vomiting into the storm drain.

FOLLOW UP

BY JO DERESKE

Jeff squinted through the snow and saw her—almost too late—standing beside the butt end of her car waving both arms. The nose was so deep in the ditch the rear wheels kissed air. Hopeless.

He hadn't passed another car in an hour. She'd freeze to death before any snowplows came by.

He eased the Cavalier to the side of the road, pumping the brakes. It fishtailed anyway. He turned into the skid and saw her running after him, arms frantic now.

She pounded on his window while he was cranking it down. Snow blew in and stung his cheeks, sucking at the warm air in his car. Her head was uncovered, hands bare, hair whipping with snow and ice. Her cheeks had passed from red to white.

"I need . . . ," she said. "I need . . ." He thought she was going to pass out.

"Get in the back." He reached behind him and pulled up the lock.

"My purse."

"Get in," he told her.

"Have to get it." And he'd be damned if she didn't turn around and start stumbling back toward her car.

"Get in," he shouted again, this time leaning back and feeling for the rear door handle. "I'll get it."

She fell into his car. "On . . . front seat." She spoke through clumsy lips. Shaking and unsteady. It was impossible to tell how old she was, what she actually looked like, even though, after all these years, he was good at that.

Jeff threw his jacket over the milk crate of files on the front seat and took the car keys with him. "I will be right back," he told her, saying it loud and slow like she was stupid. She didn't answer, but in the dim snowy light, he saw her nod.

It was hellish outside. He came prepared when he held hearings in the Upper Peninsula: extra clothes, boots, flares, water, blankets. He ran to her car first, his head bent against the wind. The snow was filling in the path she'd made around the driver's door. He jerked it open and grabbed a black plastic purse off the seat. It was an old car, and he'd bet the tires were bald as snot.

Last, he checked the backseat in case she'd forgotten a kid or a dog. He'd seen it happen.

Nothing. Back to his car. He opened his trunk, pulling out the red plaid blanket he kept in a plastic zip bag. His eyelashes were heavy with snow, his sweater layered with white. He brushed off as much as he could before he got back in the driver's seat and started the engine, switching the heater and blower to high.

In the backseat she rocked herself, and he pulled out the blanket, unfolding it before he passed it back. She grunted and jerked it from his hands.

"We'll sit here a minute until the windows clear," he told her. He wiped the inside fog from the windshield with a bar rag he kept beneath his seat, next to a sawed-off baseball bat.

Be prepared.

The snow had started at two that morning. Jeff knew because

he'd been sitting at the pitted desk in his motel room, paging through the Danny Hartman file.

He'd felt it, even inside, with the wall heater going like sixty. That weird softening and slowing down, like falling slow motion into a pile of cushions. He'd risen and parted the dusty venetian blinds, big old-fashioned blades like those his mother had wiped down every week with vinegar water. Flakes as big as bird wings drifted through the yellow lights in the parking lot, dusting the cars. As innocent as a glass-bubble Christmas scene.

But that was then. This was six hours later.

"You doing okay?" he asked over his shoulder.

"Better" came her muffled voice. And then, "Thanks."

She didn't say any more, and when the defrosters had done their work, he pulled back onto what he hoped was the highway, hunched over the steering wheel, trying to see through a windshield that kept slabbing up with the damn stuff, weighing down the wipers until he had to pull over, get out, and shake them loose.

"Where are we?" she finally asked. The car was warm enough, so he slipped off his gloves. He smelled alcohol.

Jeff glanced at the odometer. "Seven miles along the Seney stretch of Highway Twenty-eight."

The Seney was a twenty-five-mile straight ribbon of nothing. Pines lined both sides, leading off into swamps and more pines. No towns, no houses. Deer or bear might wander onto the pavement, but that was it. Garner, before Jeff, had fallen asleep on this road and been so busted up he had to leave the board.

"When's the next town?"

"Shingleton, in about twenty miles. You can probably get a wrecker there. A phone, too, if you need to call somebody."

She didn't answer at first, then she asked, "Where are you going?"

He said it casual, like it was the truth. "Just past Shingleton. But I'll make sure you get there okay."

"I'm going to Marquette," she said, as if he'd asked. "How far are we from Marquette?"

He glanced again at the odometer, knowing he was exactly 71.7 miles from Marquette. "Seventy miles or so," he told her.

In his rearview mirror he saw her rocking again. Back and forth like his brother, who'd been a real mental case. She was between forty and fifty, a big woman with hair plastered to her head. She wasn't wearing any makeup.

"Shit," he said aloud, pulling the wheel to the left to avoid a pine branch the size of a Christmas tree. The Cavalier slid a little, and he easily corrected. He'd driven in this stuff all his life, not in the UP, but in lower Michigan, where they were more likely to plow when it snowed.

He heard her whimper from the backseat, and he said without thinking, "Everything's okay, just a little slippery," reassuring her as he would a passenger he'd invited into his car: a friend, one of the other board members, his sister.

"I know, I'm sorry. I'm just nervous," she said, matching his unintended warmth. "I have to get there by ten."

He was supposed to be there by ten, too, but his eighteen cases weren't going anywhere. They'd been waiting for years. His arrival carried all the expectations of the Coming. A few extra hours meant zilch.

"Do you think I can get a ride from that town . . . Shingleton, to Marquette?" she continued. "If I don't get there by ten . . ."

He didn't want to know where she had to get, or why, what tragedies her story held. He wanted a deadly dull drive, not this. During the long, boring rides he did his final run-through of the cases, thumbing out files from the old plastic milk crate on the passenger seat, one hand on the wheel, glancing between pavement and reports. Easy decisions dropped in the front of the crate, tough ones slid to the rear for later, in a coffee shop or a motel room. Like the Danny Hartman case the night before.

Danny Hartman's parole hearing was today, just like the other seventeen men waiting for Jeff. Chuck and Paula, the two other board members on Jeff's panel, had apologetically but firmly deferred the decision to him. Cop-outs. "You've dealt with him. Whatever you decide, we'll back you up." It had happened before, and those were the cases he hated the most. Danny's was the only one that was all his on this trip. In six years Jeff himself had never begged off making a decision. That's why Chuck and Paula thought they could. The price you pay for dependability.

He represented the great State of Michigan, the man with the power. Yay or Nay. Yup or Nope. The Roman with the thumb: up and you got a chance in the real world, at least until your next fuckup; down and you're back inside until your number rolls around again.

"My son's parole hearing is today," she said.

"Shit," he said again.

"Yeah, I know," she misinterpreted. "That's where I'm going."

"Can family members attend parole hearings?" he asked. He knew the answer, natch. They couldn't.

"No. But I have letters." She held up her purse so he could see it, patted it. "An envelope full of them. I was sick, so I didn't mail it to the parole board in time. I'm taking it. In person. That's why I have to get there by ten. Before the hearings start. They said they'd take it."

He wondered who'd told her that.

"I had my gallbladder taken out," she went on, her voice relentless from behind him. "The doctor said it was one of the worst cases he'd ever seen. And then I thought his hearing was coming up *next* month, not this month. It got away from me, you know." She sighed.

"But these letters." He heard the soft pat of her hand on her purse again. "His old boss at the mill says he'll take him back. He can live with me until he saves enough to get his own place. He wants to learn welding; he told me he did."

That was part of the parolee's criteria: a job, a place to live, a plan for the future. A life of purpose outside, no drifting. A con without a plan meant landing back inside, and 40 percent of them did anyway. He didn't answer her, but she didn't stop. And he wasn't surprised by what she said next, not really. The day had that kind of feel to it.

"I promised Danny I'd get the letters in on time. Even Reverend Stokes wrote one, telling Danny's good points, how Danny helped at the church. The reverend believes in him."

Still, when he heard the name "Danny," he reflexively stuck out his hand as if she could see the files in his milk crate. Danny. Danny Hartman?

"What's your son charged with?" he asked, making it casual.

"He kept bad company," she said, sounding like she was going to begin one of those long stories, and then stopped, simply saying, "He robbed a Seven-Eleven."

Yup. Danny Hartman. Jeff thought of Humphrey Bogart in *Casablanca*. *Of all the cars in all the towns in all the world, she gets into this one.*

"It was a bad mistake. Don't think I'm making excuses for him, because I'm not."

He only nodded, hoping she'd quit, maybe fall asleep. The shadow of a car came out of the snow, and he let up on the gas, steering as close to the edge of the road as he dared. For thirty seconds after the two cars met, he drove in a whiteout, holding the wheel steady.

"Prison's been hard on him," she said, and he heard her sigh again. Every time she spoke, the alcohol smell got stronger. "He's never been cooped up before. He's had trouble."

That was the truth.

"But I know once he comes home, he'll do good. When he gets outside again. He was a good boy."

"Mmm," Jeff murmured.

"His boy misses him too," she said.

There hadn't been anything in the file about a son. Jeff glanced in the rearview mirror again. She was looking out the window, not that anything was visible out there. Snow billowed up behind the car like dust.

Her eyes were far away. Her nose bent to one side like that of a boxer who was lousy at protecting himself. "I've been raising his son since the boy's mother died the way she did."

The way she did. He loosened his grip and flexed his fingers, one hand at a time, then hit the radio's Scan button. The numbers ran up the dial in a static blur, AM 540 to 1700. Nothing. He flicked it off, and she took it up again.

"He's a sweet little boy. I'm trying to be a better mother to him than . . ." She trailed off.

He wanted to tell her to shut it, he'd heard hundreds of stories just like hers over *his* six years. He was the man who drove from Lansing in a crappy state car two times every month of every year, bad weather or good, an eight-hour drive up the middle of the state and across the big Mackinac Bridge strung between the peninsulas like a glittery web. Up to the prisons tucked as far away as the state could legally push them. Going so often that finally the other six took it for granted. "Jeff, will you take this to the new warden at Kinross next time you're up there?" "Bring back beef pasties this time, can you, Jeff? From Sally's." Until finally, the UP became his, as regular as a mailman's route.

Twenty to thirty prisoners might pass before him in a day, and he hit one or two prisons a trip. Kinross, Marquette, Baraga, even Shingleton. Last year, in 1986, there were over 20,000 prisoners in Michigan, and a growing portion of them were housed in the UP. The new prisons were about the only thing that kept this stretch of nothing alive.

What happened next wasn't because of the prisoners waiting to con him in Marquette or the mothers and babies anxious to hear whether Jeff would set Daddy free; not the victims who somehow got lost in it all. Not because of the mothers like her. Or maybe it was. There was no reason; nothing changed. The snow, the warm car, her voice from the backseat.

But the Cavalier drifted as if the steering had gone out, sliding like a graceful skater into the oncoming lane, then spinning backward across the highway into their own lane. Big lazy circles.

She screamed. He steadied his milk crate and rode it out. It ended when the passenger side slammed into a snowdrift and the engine killed. Just like that. Snow pressed against the windows and the light inside the silent car shifted to eerie white.

"Are you okay?" he asked her. She was rubbing her head, leaning against the snowy side of the car. She hadn't been wearing her seat belt.

"Can we move?" she cried out. "I promised him."

"I'll see how bad it is," he told her as he put his shoulder against the door. The car tilted toward the drift, raising the driver's side.

He checked the rear first, hunching his head close to his shoulder to protect his face. He'd bet the temperature wasn't above zero. The right tire was buried in the snow. But it didn't look so bad. Then he walked around to the front. The sliding car had rammed so hard into the snowbank that it had hung up. Cavaliers were front-wheel drive and no way could the front tires grab hold in this.

Jeff knelt in the snow, leaning down and squinting at where the front axle should be. The snow was packed tight. When he shoved at it with a bare hand, it thunked like concrete.

A muffled sound came from above him: a car door slamming. He started to rise; his foot shot from under him and he landed flat on his butt. By the time he hauled himself up on the front bumper, he saw her in the road waving at oncoming lights. A dark pickup swerved past, then stopped, and like a film that had been rewound, she ran after it, just as she'd run after Jeff, arms waving.

She opened the pickup's passenger door and climbed in. He wondered what she said to the driver that gave him permission to drive away from Jeff and his stranded car without offering to help or call a wrecker for him.

But there it was, she was gone. Wasn't that what he'd wanted? In seconds, the truck's taillights disappeared into the snow and he couldn't hear a sound except wind in the pines.

In his car, he first checked his files. His jacket still rested on the crate. Nothing had been touched. The backseat was damp with melted snow. She'd taken her purse and left an empty beer bottle on the seat. It must have been in her jacket pocket. He picked it up and dropped it in the plastic trash bag hooked over the glove compartment latch. *Keep Michigan Clean*, it said.

Jeff wrestled in the front seat, putting on a wool jacket and hat, lined leather gloves, lined boots, and a scarf he tied over his mouth and nose. Then he pulled out the shovel stowed in his trunk next to a fifty-pound bag of sand and got to work.

An hour later, the Cavalier was free. Jeff huddled in the driver's seat, heater whistling, his eyes closed and hands tucked between his legs, waiting to come back to life. That took almost as long as digging out the car.

He drove the Seney stretch slow and easy, never once glancing at the files he hadn't read yet, not Danny Hartman's either. He didn't take his eyes off the snow-laden vista, watching for a dark pickup in a snowbank, a woman waving a black purse at traffic.

He reached Shingleton, mostly shut tight, and stopped for gas.

"You see a woman in a dark pickup in the last hour or two?" he asked the attendant, who wore a hat with earflaps even inside the station.

"What you want to know for?" he asked.

Jeff shrugged. "Her car went into a snowbank and I wondered if she made it okay."

"Haven't seen a pickup or anybody like that," the attendant said, and popped the top on a Coke can.

———

HE REACHED MARQUETTE at noon. Seen through the snow, the ancient stone prison looked like a tortured dream. White-capped turrets, barred windows, and glass so thick it looked greasy. Cell-block wings—four tiers high—jutted off each side of the administration offices in the rotunda.

He drove the length of the parking lot, but the only dark pickup was layered with a foot of snow. It had been there for hours. He pulled in next to it anyway and carried his milk crate up the long steps to the offices. Two men in heavy brown work suits shoveled the stone steps and sidewalks: trustees from Magnum Farm, the minimum-security camp a couple of miles southeast. Neither one of them looked his way.

He balanced the crate against his leg while he opened the big oak door and stepped inside, letting it bump against his back. He had to wait outside the first set of iron gates for the guard to get off the phone.

"Hey, Jeff. Fun drive today?"

"You bet, Sam. What's new?"

"That a joke?"

"Anybody been here looking for me?"

"Nobody." The big guard locked the gates behind him while he signed in, and another guard casually checked his crate for contraband. That done, the second gates opened into the rotunda.

Prison offices circled the rotunda on two floors. It was Victorian-impressive, reminding a prisoner just what a wretched bastard he was. As Jeff stood there, two guards escorted a prisoner through the iron gates from one of the blocks. The guy gazed up into the rotunda like God was waiting up there to smite his ass.

He turned to the left, toward the hearing room, nodding to a couple of guards he recognized.

It took him five minutes to get ready. He pulled the files from the crate and set it in a corner, made sure he had extra pens, a pad of paper. A pitcher of water sat on the table; the ice had melted. He cleaned his glasses and cracked his knuckles, then sat at the conference table and waited.

A new guard escorted Roger Batenzcheski into the room. Roger sat in the chair across the table, the only other chair in the room. It was bolted to the floor. The guard stood to the side, watching.

"Roger," Jeff said, opening his file while he watched the man. He hid his hope pretty well. He looked fresh groomed.

"Mr. Willett, sir."

"Tell me what got you in here, Roger."

He didn't flinch. "I stole a car out from under a guy."

"Ever try that before?"

"A motorcycle once."

"Out from under a guy?"

"From a parking lot." He was a cool one.

Roger had done everything right since: been a good prison boy, taken a few prison classes, kept his nose clean. He had a job waiting for him, a girlfriend with an apartment.

"Did you know her before you ended up here?" he asked. It was the women who trolled for prisoner pen pals, thinking they were going to play savior, who were bad news.

"Yes, sir. We been going together for two years before."

It was an easy one. "I'm recommending parole," Jeff told him. Paula had screened Roger's case at the office and she'd agreed. "You'll receive official notification within thirty days. I don't want to do this again with you, got it?"

"Yes, sir." He finally gave himself away. "Thank you, sir."

"I mean it," Jeff said.

Five more. Three he paroled, two he passed on for another twelve months. One of those lunged forward to upend the table on top of Jeff, maybe hurt him. Jeff didn't flinch; the table was bolted to the floor too, just like the chair.

He took a break and grabbed a cup of coffee in the staff lounge. The room smelled like stale popcorn.

"Had a call about you this morning, Jeff," the warden said, leaning into the room. He was slowing down, getting ready to retire.

"Yeah? What about?"

"Hard to make out. I think she was hoping you were ass-deep in a snowdrift somewhere and hadn't showed up yet."

"That's about what happened." He dumped powdered cream into his cup. It floated.

"Well, she's hot to bring you some papers. I don't know what. She wouldn't tell me her name, but she knew yours. Mr. Willett, she called you. Know anything about her?"

"News to me."

He walked around the old rotunda, listening to voices echo and thinking that if the prison were built today there would be an uproar against wasted space. For five minutes, he stood in front of a window that faced the road. There weren't any vehicles moving out there, but at least the snow was letting up.

When he returned to the conference room, the guard asked, "You want Danny Hartman next?"

"Hold off," Jeff told him. "I want to look at his file again."

"Okay. Salzer, then."

He granted paroles to Salzer and eleven others, rejected four, and was taking one case back to Lansing for discussion. Then only Danny Hartman remained. He took off his glasses and pinched his nose. "Give me ten minutes," he told the guard.

He opened the file as if it might give him a new clue. Danny wasn't anything special. The 7-Eleven was his first major offense. The problems began after he landed in Marquette. Disobeying orders, fighting, being out of place, contraband alcohol—the typical laundry list of a malcontent. The guard ushered Danny Hartman into the room. He was twenty-eight years old, slight. Sullen and hunched. He sat with knees pressed together and looked over Jeff's left shoulder. Nobody's home, Jeff thought.

"Danny."

He gave a single curt nod.

"Tell me what got you in here," Jeff said.

Danny shrugged. "The Seven-Eleven, I guess."

"You've had some trouble here."

"Some."

"Do you have plans when you get out? A job? School?"

The kid shook his head, still looking over Jeff's shoulder.

"Anybody out there have a job for you?"

"Not that I've heard."

"You have family waiting for you?"

"Nobody."

Jeff moved papers as if he were reading Danny's file. "What about your mother?"

Danny stared back, hard. "My mother doesn't have anything to do with this."

"But she'll help you?"

He shrugged. "It's not her problem."

"I'm beginning to think you like this place," Jeff said, leaning back.

"It sucks."

"Then it's up to you to have a plan for resuming your life after prison," Jeff said, and waited. He closed the file. Sometimes that scared them and got them talking.

Finally, Danny mumbled, "It was supposed to be set up."

"Who by? What was it?"

"It didn't work, that's all."

Jeff waited again, but Danny's lips pinched tight. The kid was done. That's all she wrote.

"Anything else you'd like to say?" Jeff asked.

"Nothing."

"Then the board is extending your term for another twelve months," Jeff said as he wrote out the terms. "You'll have another hearing then. This gives you a year to clean up your act. Obey the rules, straighten up. Put together a job, a place to live, school, whatever. A solid plan." Jeff thumped his finger on the table. "Help me out here. Are you hearing me?"

Danny nodded, and there was nothing else Jeff could do but let him go. He nodded to the guard, who motioned for Danny to stand and then escorted him out. Danny didn't look back.

"Late day," Sam commented when Jeff signaled for him to open the iron gate.

"Yeah. I got a late start. Things look pretty quiet around here." He shifted his milk crate to get past Sam.

"Like the tomb. I saw a plow go by an hour ago, but I'd stay in town tonight if I were you. See you in a few weeks."

It was dark outside, but the snow had finally quit. By the prison lights he couldn't see if the sky had cleared up or if more snow was on the way. Six inches of snow was piled on his car. He brushed the worst of it off with the scraper from his glove compartment and got in. The Cavalier's engine cranked twice before it started, rough at first. Then he drove to a motel on the edge of town, drank two glasses of bourbon, ate a bag of Cheetos from the machine in the lobby, and slept until nine the next morning.

He found the sheriff's phone number at the front of the motel's phone book. "I gave a middle-aged woman a ride partway up the Seney stretch yesterday," he told the woman who answered. "She struck off on her own, and I was concerned about her."

"What's her name?"

"She didn't tell me."

"I haven't heard about any lost women, so she's probably okay. You can call back later if you want, once all the plows have been out."

"Thanks."

He drove slow between Marquette and Shingleton. The plows had pushed the snow into banks and the traffic had picked up from yesterday. He wore sunglasses against the bright white and squinted into every pickup he met. He passed two sedans and a semi off the road before he reached Shingleton.

The lights were on in Steve's Tavern, and he pulled in. The parking area was the best-plowed spot in town. It looked sculpted.

"Old Milwaukee," he told the bartender, who obviously lived behind the small bar. "Are you Steve?"

"Bill. Steve's my dad. He died ten years ago." He was using a rag like the one under Jeff's car seat to wash beer glasses.

"Were you working yesterday?"

"Ain't nobody else *but* me."

"I gave a woman a ride. Her car went off the road on the Seney stretch. She was heading to Marquette."

The man rolled his eyes. "Big? Nose like this?" He pushed his nose to the side with a forefinger.

"That's her."

"Fenn Schultz brought her in. I can tell you, she didn't get to Marquette yesterday. She spent the whole day in here with Fenn, tossing 'em back and shooting pool. They left together about six." He shook his head. "And that's all I know."

"Thanks."

Jeff drank his beer and glanced now and then at a soap opera on the television above the bar. He used the men's john, which was cleaner than he expected, and when he came out, the bartender was waiting for him. He held a thick white envelope.

"This might sound crazy," he said, "but the woman you mentioned? She dropped an envelope on the floor. It's addressed. You're the only one who's asked about her. You wouldn't be Jeff Willett, would you?"

Jeff waved at him and headed for the door. "Sorry."

In the parking lot he transferred his milk crate to the trunk and drove straight through to Lansing.

BY HOOK OR BY CROOK

BY CHARLIE DREES

I set the compact tape recorder on the scarred table and watch Dexter Bass pace back and forth in the cramped room. He's six-three—give or take an inch—with a sinewy build and long, sun-bleached blond hair. The police file indicates he's been a guest of the state on two prior occasions, but his muscles appear to come from hard manual labor rather than from pumping iron on a prison bench. Watching Bass, I feel more like an audience than his court-appointed attorney. He catches me glancing at my watch and slides into the chair on the other side of the table.

"Am I boring you?"

"Mr. Bass, I've been appointed—"

"I've had lawyers like you before," he says, fixing me with his charcoal-colored eyes. "Just going through the motions—and I did the time."

I settle back in my chair. Due to a shortage of public defenders in our jurisdiction, judges pick from a rotating pool of defense attorneys and assign them to defendants who can't afford legal counsel. And they frown on attorneys who do a less than stellar job with the assignment. As luck would have it, I'm at the top of the list this week. I can't afford to annoy the judge, so I swallow my pride. I haven't had much practice, and the words stick in my throat.

"Mr. Bass, I apologize. I'm not bored. I'm just eager to get started."

Bass studies my face, checking for any sign of deceit. It's hard to fool an ex-con, but he's overmatched and he looks away after a few seconds. Hey, I'm a lawyer. I've had plenty of practice looking sincere.

Bass brushes his blond hair off his forehead. "What do you want to know?"

I click on the tape recorder and grab his file. "Let me go over what's in the police report, then you can tell me your version, okay?"

"Sure." He glances at my briefcase. "You got any cigarettes?"

"Sorry. It's a no-smoking facility."

Bass snorts. "Figures. They want me healthy so they can stick a needle in my arm."

Like most cons, Bass knows the law. I open the case folder. "You were arrested early this morning at the Shamrock Bar following a fight with Cletus Rupp. Rupp died from injuries he sustained during this fight. Witnesses claim you two had been arguing." I peer at Bass over the top of the file. He's busy scrutinizing something trapped underneath his fingernails.

"After your arrest, the police discovered a gym bag in your car containing ten thousand, three hundred dollars in cash. They also found a hammer covered with blood and strands of hair, a man's Rolex watch, and a wallet containing sixty-three dollars. The driver's license and credit cards were issued to Steven Toscar."

Everyone knows who Steven Toscar is. Was. Toscar made tons of money in real estate. Two years ago, he shut me out of one of his projects, costing me a chance for a big score. It upset me at the time, but I got over it. It appears not everyone is as forgiving as I am.

"Toscar's wife called nine-one-one at eleven thirty-eight p.m." I rustle the pages until Bass looks at me. "The police are checking to see if your fingerprints match the ones found on the hammer. So what's your story?"

"Rupp was self-defense. He attacked me. But I swear I didn't kill Toscar."

"The evidence suggests you did."

"Cops plant evidence all the time."

"Are you saying that's what happened here?"

"All I'm saying is I didn't kill Toscar. Somebody must've planted that evidence."

A con's typical defense. I lean back in my chair. "Why don't you tell me what happened."

Bass rests his hands on the tabletop. They're large hands, tanned and callused as though they're used to hard manual labor. Like swinging a hammer.

"Two months ago," he begins, "I'm sitting in a bar, having a few drinks, minding my own business, when this guy grabs the stool next to me and orders a beer. I don't pay any attention until he pays for it. That's when I see the hook."

"A hook?"

"Yeah, a hook."

I arch an eyebrow. "Like a pirate's hook?"

"Not exactly," Bass says. "It had these pincers that were curved on the end. He didn't have any problem digging the money outta his wallet." Bass pinces his fingers together. "He was really . . ."

"Adroit?"

Bass frowns. "Huh?"

I dumb it down a notch. "Skillful?"

"Yeah, skillful. I never met anyone with a hook. We had a few beers, got to talking. He said his name was Cletus Rupp and he owned a swimming pool business. He asked if I wanted a job."

"Rupp offered you a job?"

Bass nods. "I told him I was an ex-con. He didn't care. There aren't that many jobs for ex-cons, so I said sure. The first contract he gave me was the Toscars' pool. That's how I met Eve."

I recall a picture from the society pages of a young, attractive woman thirty years younger than Toscar. "You got involved with Toscar's wife?"

Bass's dark eyes look haunted. "Mr. Cleary, I didn't stand a chance."

I watch the tape spin for a few moments. "What happened?"

"I worked on the pool twice a week," Bass says. "At first, Eve acted like I wasn't there. Then one day she asked if I wanted a drink. I told her I wasn't supposed to drink on the job. She said it was just lemonade—and she wouldn't tell anyone."

"Were you nervous?"

"Hell yes," Bass says. "I'm not stupid. I figured she had something on her mind."

"And did she?"

"Yeah. She wanted to know if I'd kill her husband."

The tape runs out. I fumble the little plastic cassette out of the tape recorder, flip it over, and shove it back in. Before I start the tape, Bass asks for something to drink. I step outside, talk to the guard, and he brings us two Pepsis. After he leaves, I push the Record button.

"Mrs. Toscar asked you to kill her husband?"

Bass unscrews the top on his drink. "Not in so many words. First, she told me she knew I was an ex-con. I asked if that mattered. She said no. And that's when she told me to call her Eve." Bass faces me. "Mr. Cleary, I've been in some nasty prison fights, but when she said that, she scared the hell outta me."

"What happened?"

Bass sips some Pepsi before replying. "She told me how her husband didn't pay any attention to her. How a woman like her had needs." He takes a deep breath. "One thing led to another, and we ended up in bed."

My heart ratchets up a notch. "Go on."

"Afterward," Bass says, "she kept telling me how much she hated her husband." He rakes his fingers through his hair. "This went on for a month. Eve would say she wished we didn't have to sneak around. I'd laugh and tell her she'd never settle for an ex-con. She'd pout until I'd say I was sorry. It was weird, but it felt kinda good too. It made me feel . . . special."

"So when did she ask you to kill her husband?"

"Last week," Bass says. "I showed up for work, and Eve was crying, said her husband accused her of having an affair. She denied it, but it didn't matter. He wanted a divorce."

I lean forward. "So what's the problem? In this state, she'd get half in a settlement."

Bass nods. "That's what I told her. But Eve said there was a prenup and she wouldn't get a dime. She said she deserved something for all she put up with over the years. She wanted him dead and asked if I'd do it. She told me he kept money in a safe in their bedroom. She said I could make it look like a robbery gone bad."

"What'd you tell her?"

"That I had to think about it. That's when she mentioned the life insurance policy."

This just gets better and better. "How much?"

"Five million dollars."

I tent my fingers. "So once Toscar's out of the picture, Eve's a rich lady. And she wants you to come along for the ride. Sounds like a sweet deal."

Bass scans the cramped room. "You think?"

I shrug. "A fortune and a fine-looking woman to share it with. What's not to like?"

"Murder, for one thing," Bass says. "Look, I've made my share of mistakes, but I never killed anyone."

"What about the evidence?"

"I told you. It was planted."

"You don't seriously believe the cops planted it, do you?"

"Doesn't have to be the cops."

That gets my attention. "What do you mean?"

"I think Eve got tired of waiting for me to make up my mind and found someone else. Cletus Rupp."

"Are you serious?"

Bass nods. "When I saw Eve yesterday afternoon, she was hysterical. Her cheek was bruised. She said her husband hit her. She said if I loved her, I'd kill him, so we could get his money and be together." Bass picks at a callus on his palm, avoiding my eyes. "I told her okay."

I sit up. "Wait a minute. I thought you said—"

"I was just gonna scare him," he explains. "Get him to reconsider. Eve said she was going to stay with a friend, so Toscar would be home alone. She gave me the combination to his safe and said she'd unlock the patio doors. I got to their place around ten thirty. There was a light on in the study. That's where I found him. He was already dead. I got the hell outta there."

"Why didn't you call the police?"

"With my record?"

I nod. "I understand. Then what happened?"

Bass drains the rest of his Pepsi. "I drove home. Around midnight, Rupp called and told me to meet him at the Shamrock. He said it was important, life or death. I got there about a quarter to one, but Rupp didn't show up until one fifteen. The minute he got there, he said he'd followed me to Toscar's place and he'd seen the body. He wanted ten grand to keep his mouth shut."

"The amount the cops found in the bag."

"Yeah," Bass says. "I told him I didn't know what he was talking about. He went ballistic. Said to pay up or he'd go to the cops. He wouldn't shut up, so I left."

"But he followed you outside," I say, imagining the events in my mind.

Bass nods. "He pushed me. I told him to leave me alone, but he just wouldn't back off. He swung at my head with his hook. I ducked and shoved him hard as I could. He slammed up against a pickup and dropped to the ground. He started jerking. I rolled him over and saw the hook stuck in his throat.

"The cops showed up, and I told them it was self-defense," Bass adds. "They arrested me anyway. They didn't charge me with Toscar's murder until later." He leans back in his chair. "And here we are."

"What if they find your fingerprints on the hammer?"

Bass shrugs. "It means I used that hammer for some reason, and Cletus took it. With his hook, he wouldn't leave any prints." Bass must notice the doubt on my face. "If I was gonna kill Toscar, don't you think I'd be smart enough to wear gloves?"

I sip some of my Pepsi. "Then explain how the gym bag got in your car."

Bass's leg starts bouncing. "Cletus must've planted it there while I was waiting for him. That's why he wanted me at the Shamrock by one. He would've had enough time to kill Toscar, clean up, and dump the bag in my car."

"But if he already had the money, why argue with you about it?"

"I don't know. I haven't figured that out yet."

"So you think Mrs. Toscar and Rupp set you up?"

Bass stares into my eyes. "Mr. Cleary, I know they did, but I can't prove it. With Cletus dead, it's my word against hers. Who do you think a jury'll believe?"

My silence tells him all he needs to know.

Bass slumps back in his chair. "That's why you gotta help me. Look, I'm a two-time loser. If I'm convicted, I'm looking at a death sentence. I need you to fight for my life."

I stare into his dark eyes. "Mr. Bass, I'll do all I can."

The guard pokes his head inside the room and tells me my time's up. I shake hands with Bass and promise him I'll be in touch. I exit the building into the early-afternoon heat and smile when I see the vanity license plate on my silver BMW: SHARK. Who says lawyers don't have a sense of humor? I toss my suit coat in the back and sink into the soft leather seats. After loosening my tie, I crank up the air-conditioning. The interior is cool by the time I leave the parking lot.

I turn on the radio. My fingers tap a rhythm on the steering wheel while I ponder Bass's story. All in all, he has a good grasp of how he's been set up. Just not of *who* set him up. But that's the beauty of this plan. After all, why would he suspect his court-appointed lawyer?

I take the exit for Channel Drive. A few cars pass me, but I'm not in any hurry. I know where I'm going and I know who'll be there when I arrive.

———

EVE TOSCAR STANDS in the front doorway clipping on a pearl earring. It matches the necklace around her neck. They contrast vividly with the sleeveless black dress she wears. The dress is demure enough for grieving, but it clings here and there, hinting at the lush body beneath it. Eve looks good. It's something she takes for granted. Like breathing.

I step inside and close the door. "Where's Inez?"

"I sent her home. She's a wreck. She worked for Steven for a long time." Eve brushes past me and heads toward the kitchen, leaving a hint of her perfume in the air. "What did Bass say?"

"About what we figured." I watch the way her hips twitch beneath the dress. Her jet-black hair is piled on top of her head, and a few loose wisps graze her neck. Her cheek is bruised from where I hit her, but her makeup hides most of it. "He knows he was set up—and that no jury will believe him."

"He's right." Eve fills a glass with ice from the dispenser on the refrigerator door. She adds a splash of vodka from the open bottle sitting on the granite-topped counter and takes a sip. She peers at me over the rim of her glass, her dark blue eyes locked onto mine. "Want one?"

I drop my briefcase on the floor, pry the glass from her fingers, and set it on the counter. "I had something else in mind."

Eve turns her head, and my kiss lands awkwardly on her cheek. A tiny ember of worry sparks deep in my gut. "What's wrong?"

She smooths the front of her dress. "We don't have time. The funeral director is coming by to talk about the memorial service." She avoids my gaze. "Besides, I've been thinking maybe we should cool things for a while, at least until after the funeral."

The ember flares into a full-fledged blaze. When Eve showed up in my office six months ago, I confirmed the details of her husband's will: she would never see a dime of his money if they divorced. She profited only if he died. When I didn't hear from her, I thought that was the end of it. But two weeks later she called. During our follow-up appointment, I found myself plotting Steven Toscar's death. In my defense, it should be noted that my trousers were bunched around my ankles at the time. Since then, I'd come to think of Eve as my personal 401(k).

So I don't like the idea of my retirement plans going up in smoke. I put on my sincere face—the one I used on Bass. "Don't worry, everything's under control."

She sips some of her drink. "That's easy for you to say. You didn't have to talk to the police."

"What'd you tell them?"

Eve fidgets with the strand of pearls. "What we talked about. I was with my friend Anne. I came home and found Steven dead."

"Anne will back you up?"

She nods. "Of course."

"Good. Stick with your story and the cops can't touch you."

"They want to talk again. You said once they arrested Bass we'd be in the clear."

I brush a stray hair off her cheek. "And we are. Look, with Rupp dead, there's no way the cops can link him to us. As for Bass, it's his word against yours. And with his history, you'll win every time. Just stick to our plan and you'll be spending Steven's money in no time."

She smiles. "I'm going to be rich. And I have you to thank for it."

The burning in my gut fades. "Glad I could help."

Eve inches closer. "You were so smart to use Rupp to find a loser like Bass."

I shrug. "He owed me a favor."

"Don't be so modest," she coos, molding herself against me.

Eve's good looks distract a lot of people—you'd have to be blind to be immune—but her matchless gift is how special she makes you feel. Bass nailed that right on the head. Pretty soon, you do whatever you can to hoard her for yourself. By then it's too late. You're hooked, and you'll promise her anything. Addiction is an ugly thing.

I smile. "It *was* clever."

Eve nips my earlobe. "Very clever. And making sure you were assigned as Dexter's lawyer was pure genius."

My heart hammers against my ribs. We both know I'm going to give in, but my ego wants her to work for it. I untangle myself and step back. "You know, you may be right. Maybe we should cool it for a while. I don't want to jinx anything."

She unbuckles my belt. "In that case, we should make this memorable."

I grip the countertop. "I thought you said we didn't have time."

"Shhh," she says, placing a finger over my lips. "This won't take long."

———

FROM THE MOMENT we hatched our scheme, I planned to help Eve spend her fortune. That's the main reason I sweated the details plotting Toscar's murder. Sure, love entered into it—the love of money. So I'm not a romantic. Sue me. Now with Rupp dead and Bass in jail, all the pieces have fallen into place.

So I'm stunned when a herd of cops shows up at my house three days after my meeting with Dexter Bass. The one in front is wearing an off-the-rack navy blazer and wrinkled khaki slacks, spotted with the remnants of his lunch. His thick-soled black shoes tell me he spends a lot of time on his feet, and the bags under his bloodshot brown eyes tell me he isn't getting much sleep. He shows me his gold badge.

"Jack Cleary?"

"Yeah?"

"I'm Detective Frank Hall. We have a warrant for your arrest."

"Wait a second," I say, backpedaling as several cops crowd past me. "What's this about?"

He hands me the warrant. "It's all in there, but I'll make it easy for you. You're under arrest for the murder of Steven Toscar."

———

BEFORE HALL BEGINS the interrogation, I look at the one-way mirror built into the wall. "I want to talk to whoever's back there."

Hall shakes his head. "You aren't in any position to make demands."

"Then we're finished here."

Hall gives me his best tough-cop stare. When I yawn, he glances at the mirror. After a moment, the door opens. Assistant DA Lois Stone strolls in and deposits her briefcase on the table.

"I'll take it from here, Detective," she says. After Hall vacates his chair, she sits down. "Hello, Jack. Fancy meeting you here."

Lois Stone is the best prosecutor in the DA's office. Defense attorneys call her "Stone Cold" because she shows no mercy in court. But she's no ice queen. Cinnamon-colored, shoulder-length hair frames a face that is more striking than beautiful, and the bookish, tortoiseshell frames she wears complement a pair of jade-green eyes a Mayan would covet. We met years ago when I worked in the DA's office and she had just passed the bar. I took her under my wing and taught her everything she knows about prosecuting the bad guys. Now I'll find out if I did a good job.

Stone adjusts the glasses on her nose. "Did they read you your rights?"

"Yes."

"And you're consenting to this interview without a lawyer present?"

"I'm a lawyer, remember?" I always respected Lois Stone, but the look on her face suggests the feeling isn't mutual. It'll be a pleasure to wipe that smirk off her face.

"How could I forget?" She points to the built-in video camera on the wall. "Okay if we tape this?"

"Sure. I've got nothing to hide."

"Okay, then let's get started."

"I didn't kill Steven Toscar. I'm innocent. I'm being framed."

Stone tilts her head. "Really?" She opens her briefcase and pulls out a folder but doesn't open it—a ploy I taught her to make a suspect sweat. "You sound a lot like Dexter Bass," she says. "Except I'm starting to believe him."

"That would be a mistake." I stare at the folder. My heart speeds up. It's a whole other world on this side of the table.

"Didn't you defend Cletus Rupp?" Stone asks. "Something about him stalking his ex-wife?"

I meet her gaze. "The woman was imagining things. She needed therapy."

Stone shrugs as if conceding the point. "Had you seen Rupp recently?"

"I hadn't spoken to him since his trial." Rupp and I met face-to-face. There won't be a telltale message on his answering machine for the cops to find.

"No chance encounter?"

"None."

Stone locks her green eyes on me. They're still as hypnotic as I remember. "Where were you last Monday evening between nine p.m. and one?"

Thank God for TiVo. "I was home watching TV."

She looks skeptical. "Anybody there with you?"

"No."

Stone lifts a corner of the file. "Did you make any calls, or did anyone call you?"

"No." I try to peek inside the folder, but she closes it. It's another tactic I taught her, but my chest tightens anyway.

"Did you go anywhere? Have a pizza delivered?"

"No, I stayed home all night. Look, I'm sorry no one can vouch for me, but I didn't think I'd need an alibi."

Stone ignores my tone. "So what you're saying is that you didn't kill Steven Toscar and frame Dexter Bass."

I lean close enough to smell her perfume—a hint of lilac. "Yes, that's exactly what I'm saying."

Stone twists the ends of her hair around her fingertips. "Well, Jack, I guess that makes you a liar *and* a murderer."

I jerk forward in my chair. "Now just—"

"Save it," Stone snaps. She stares at me and flips open the folder. It's full of pictures—8 x 10 blowups—and she hands me the top one.

"This is a photo of you and Cletus Rupp. That is your Beemer, right? The one with SHARK on the plates?" She doesn't wait for my reply. "You notice the date in the bottom right-hand corner? It was taken two months ago."

"You can program a camera to any date."

"Is that your defense, Jack? That someone faked the date?"

I stare at the photo. "I'm just saying it's possible. So, where did you get this?"

"We found it in Rupp's office. You want to tell me about this, Jack?"

My brain kicks into overdrive, trying to come up with an explanation Stone will buy. I snap my fingers. "I remember now. Rupp wanted to borrow some money. I told him no, and that was that. It must've slipped my mind."

Stone leans back in her chair. "I wonder why Rupp felt the need to photograph your meet."

"You'd have to ask him."

"Too bad we can't." Stone pauses. "I'd be worried if I were you, Jack. You're too young to have Alzheimer's."

Beads of sweat snake down my ribs. "We met one time. That's the truth."

Stone nods. "The truth is good. Who knows? Maybe it'll set you free."

My mouth goes dry. I glance at Hall, and he smirks. I drop my gaze and stare at the scarred tabletop. Stone rattled me with the picture. The pupil has learned some things on her own.

"So you met just once with Rupp?"

I look up. Maybe she's tossing me a lifeline. "Yeah, just the one time."

She takes a deep breath and shakes her head, a look of disappointment on her face. She pulls more photos from the file and lines them up in front of me. The dates and locations differ, but each of them shows the same thing: Rupp and me sitting in my car.

"You know what I think? I think you hired Rupp to murder Steven Toscar and frame Bass. Why? I'm not sure."

"That's crazy."

She shrugs. "Maybe, but right now I feel sorry for Dexter Bass."

I hold up my hand. "Wait a minute. Maybe Rupp did this on his own. Maybe after I turned him down, he asked Toscar for money. Rupp had the service contract for Toscar's pool, and Bass did the work on it."

"Bass worked for Rupp?"

I nod. "For the past two or three months."

Stone grabs the file and heads toward the door. "I'll be right back."

After she leaves, Hall counts ceiling tiles while I try to figure a way out of the jam I'm in. Neither of us speaks. Stone returns in a few minutes and hands me a Pepsi.

"I didn't know Bass worked for Rupp. Thanks for the tip."

I take a sip to ease the dryness in my throat. "Anything to help clear me."

Stone places the folder on the table and hooks one arm over the back of her chair. "So how do you think the evidence got in Bass's car?"

I lean forward. "Rupp must've found out Toscar kept a lot of money in his safe. He knew Bass had done time for burglary. Maybe he offered Bass a cut to pull off the job. Maybe Toscar surprised Bass during the robbery and things got out of hand.

My guess is, Bass threw the hammer in his car and planned to ditch it later. But he and Rupp got into a fight at the Shamrock and he never had the chance. That's why it was in his car."

I sit back in my chair and feel some of the tightness leave my chest. I've always done my best thinking under pressure. It's why I've done well in court. I've given Stone a scenario that fits the facts—and she's got to know my version offers a jury enough room for reasonable doubt.

But she won't let it go. "You're saying you didn't have anything to do with the gym bag found in Bass's car?"

"How could I? I was home all night."

Stone reaches into the folder once again, pulls out more photos, and spreads them in front of me. Seconds later, I realize I'm facing the death penalty.

"Last year," she says, "after being robbed three times in two months, the pawnshop across the street from the Shamrock installed state-of-the-art surveillance cameras." She pauses and picks up one of the photos, then places it back in front of me. "As you can see, they offer a pretty good view of the Shamrock's parking lot."

Stone taps the photo farthest on my left. "In this one, you've just arrived in the parking lot. I can even make out the writing on the baseball cap you're wearing." She squints at the photo. "What do you know? We listen to the same radio station."

I stare at the photos, unable to avert my eyes.

"See how clear your face is in the one where you're putting the gym bag in Bass's car?" She leans closer to me. "And guess what? We found your prints on the hammer used to kill Steven Toscar."

My head snaps up. I know I didn't leave any fingerprints. I wrapped the handle in plastic and wore gloves. The latex made my hands sweat. I rack my brain, searching for an explanation.

All at once, I know who set me up, and the realization leaves me light-headed. I bend over and suck air into my lungs.

"What's wrong?" she asks, her green eyes sparkling. "Cat got your tongue?"

I look into her eyes. "Why'd you keep looking when you already had Bass in custody?"

Stone scoops up the photographs and slips them into the folder. "The fingerprints on the hammer didn't match his. We expanded our search and got a hit on yours. You remember getting printed when you worked in the DA's office? After we got the photos of you and Rupp—plus the ones from the pawnshop—all the pieces fell into place."

The walls seem to close in on me. "I'll tell you who set this up, but I want a deal."

She considers this for a moment. "I'll have to talk to my boss."

I slowly nod. "I'm not going anywhere."

Stone pauses in the doorway. "There's one more thing."

"What's that?"

"You're slipping, Jack. I'd call another lawyer if I were you."

———

I FOLLOW STONE'S advice and call Curt Beyer. Beyer is the best defense attorney I know. He's expensive, but from what I've seen in court, he's worth every penny. I make the call, and forty-five minutes later he shows up. After two hours of hurried meetings with me and the DA, he hammers out a deal: I testify for the state and the DA won't seek the death penalty. There's even the slim possibility of parole in the distant future. When Stone returns, I agree to the deal.

She leans back in her chair and peers at me through her lenses. "So, what've you got?"

With my lawyer's blessing, I spill my guts, from my initial

meeting with Eve Toscar to the night of the murder. Stone listens quietly. She doesn't look impressed.

"This is your big exposé? That Toscar's wife wanted him dead?"

I didn't expect high-fives or pats on the back, but I thought she'd be more excited. "That's right. Eve wanted his money, but due to the prenup, she couldn't get it any other way."

"Jack, do I look stupid?" Stone's voice drips with scorn. "Don't you think we'd check her out?"

"Of course, but—"

"We put her under a microscope," she says. "She came off smelling like a rose. Everyone we talked to—including Toscar's friends—said the marriage was rock-solid. Hell, Jack, Toscar recently changed his will to dissolve their prenup."

The news hits me like a sledgehammer. "What?"

Stone smirks. "Didn't know that, huh? Here's something else I bet you didn't know. When we asked if her husband had any enemies, she gave us your name. She swore Toscar told her you threatened him when he cut you out of a business deal."

"That's a lie!"

"So you say. She also denied knowing Dexter Bass, and he confirms that."

"No way. I've got him on tape telling how Eve asked him to kill her husband."

Beyer grabs my arm. "Shut up, Jack. You can't divulge anything Bass told you in confidence."

I jerk my arm free and look at Stone. "You want to hear it?"

Lois Stone sits back in her chair and taps her lush lips with her index finger. "Curt's right. Whatever Bass told you is covered by attorney-client privilege. It's not admissible."

"Screw privilege," I say. "The tape's in my briefcase at home."

Hall clears his throat. He's been so quiet, I forgot he's in the room. "His briefcase is in the evidence lab."

Stone's eyes narrow. "You're kidding, right?"

Hall can't meet her gaze. "We, uh, brought it just in case."

Stone looks at me and shrugs. "I guess I can't stop you from playing the tape."

Ten minutes later, over Beyer's repeated objections, I pop open the locks on my briefcase and pull out my tape recorder. After I met with Bass, I never listened to the tape. Why bother? But now, with my life on the line, I'm glad I taped it. My hand shakes as I press the Play button. The tape spins. Nothing.

"Are you sure it's the right tape?" Stone asks.

I paw through my briefcase, searching for other tapes, but the rest are still in their cellophane wrappers. I fast-forward the tape, hoping to hear Bass's voice, but all I get is faint static. Then it hits me.

"I had the tape when I went to Eve's house after meeting with Bass," I explain. "She would've had plenty of time to grab the tape while I was in the shower."

"You have anything else to back up your story?" Stone asks.

I scour my memory but come up empty. My meetings with Eve took place after office hours, after everyone had gone home. She wanted to keep our meetings hush-hush, so I never logged them in my appointment book. And I never billed her, since she paid me in her own special way.

"No," I mutter. "Nothing else."

The door opens and a uniformed officer hands Stone several sheets of paper. She studies them, then looks at me.

"While we've been talking, the police checked Rupp's employee records. There's no record that Bass worked for him. No job application, no W-2, nothing. We even checked the service records for Toscar's pool. All the forms were signed by Dan Dorsey." She hands me the sheets of paper. "See for yourself."

I glance through the pages. "Maybe Bass used that name as an alias."

Stone shakes her head. "Rupp's secretary said Dorsey has worked there for years. We talked to Dorsey, and he confirmed that he did all the work on Toscar's pool."

The pages slip from my hands and flutter to the floor. Stone stands up and walks to the door. "Jack," she says, then waits until I look at her. "You've got zilch. No deal." She looks at Hall. "See that Mr. Cleary gets back to his cell."

———

AT MY ARRAIGNMENT, Beyer works his magic and gets me out on bail. It's a miracle, but that's why I'm paying him the big bucks. I have to wear a tracking bracelet on my ankle, but it beats sitting in jail. Stone objects, but the judge cuts her off and calls for the next case. After I'm released, I go home, make a couple of phone calls, and wait.

Three hours later, I stroll into the Shamrock Bar. At this time of day, even the hard-core drinkers have other places to be, so it's easy to spot Dexter Bass waiting in the booth in the far corner. With my arrest, his claim of self-defense rang true. His new attorney didn't have any problem getting the charges dropped. Bass raises his glass when he notices me.

"I didn't think you'd come," I tell him.

"I'm a curious guy," he says, a sly grin creasing his face. It quickly fades. "So, what'd you wanna talk about?"

"How did you do it?"

Bass sits up straighter. "Hold on there, Counselor. How'd I do what?"

"Cut the crap," I hiss. "I'm looking at life, maybe even the needle. The least you can do is tell me how you and Eve set me up."

"I don't know what you're talking about." Bass finishes his drink and starts to leave. I grab his wrist, stalling his exit. I need to hear the truth, and to get it I'm gambling that his ego is bigger than mine.

"C'mon, you can tell me. I'm pretty bright, but I know when I've been outsmarted. It was your idea, wasn't it?"

Bass jerks his hand free. "You wearing a wire?" I tell him no, but he isn't convinced. "Follow me."

We head to the bathroom and Bass motions me inside. The smell stings my nose, and I watch where I step. Must be the maid's day off. Bass locks the door.

"Unbutton your shirt."

I undo the buttons and show him my bare chest. He spins me around and shoves me against the wall. He frisks me, leaving no place unchecked. I've had less thorough exams at my doctor's office. Bass seems satisfied.

"It was Eve's idea," he says.

My stomach churns as Bass guides me through the double-cross. He and Eve worked a few scams in Vegas until he went to prison and she reinvented herself. When he got out, they hooked up again and looked for a patsy. I fit the bill. After I contacted Rupp, Eve had Bass take the photos of my meetings with him. Then Bass "bumped" into Rupp in the bar. Once everything was in place, he and Eve waited for me to murder her husband. And while I was busy killing Toscar, Eve snuck into Rupp's office and planted the photographs.

"How did my fingerprints get on the hammer? I wore gloves that night."

He gives me a smug grin. "It's your hammer."

"I don't understand."

"Eve took the hammer from your garage," Bass explains. "She gave you your own hammer and said it was one I'd used. But I never touched it."

My cheeks burn. "What about Dan Dorsey?"

Bass smirks. "What about him? I never met the guy. I visited Eve on the days Dorsey wasn't scheduled to be there."

I step toward him. "Was it worth it?"

Bass jabs his fingers in my chest. "Don't go righteous on me, Counselor. You tried to frame me too."

"Aren't you worried she'll set you up?"

"No. Lucky for me, Eve likes outlaws better than lawyers."

There isn't much to say after that. Bass looks at his watch and tells me he has a plane to catch. He unlocks the bathroom door and walks out.

The bartender is clearing the table where Bass was sitting. As I walk by, he puts his hand on my chest. I recognize him as one of the cops who searched my house.

"Stone's waiting for you across the street," he says.

I push through the back exit and cross the street to the pawn-shop's parking lot. I knock on the side door of the gray cargo van parked in the shadows. Lois Stone opens the sliding door and steps out into the afternoon heat. She's wearing a dark green pantsuit that complements her auburn hair. There's something on her lips—lipstick or gloss—that leaves them shiny. I'd like to think she did it for me, but that's wishful thinking.

"Did you get it?"

"Loud and clear. There's enough for arrest warrants. Eve Toscar and Dexter Bass won't be spending her money anytime soon."

"How'd you know he wouldn't find the bug?"

Stone grabs the van's door handle. "Jack, guys like you and Bass always think you're smarter than the rest of us. That's your downfall. Once he frisked you and didn't find anything, I knew he'd stop looking. There was no way he'd suspect we bugged the john."

I know she's right. "So is our deal back on?"

"Yeah, it's back on. You've got until Monday to get your affairs in order."

I shake my head. "I'm gonna die an old man in prison."

Stone's face softens for a moment. "Cheer up, Jack. With good behavior, you could get paroled in fifteen, twenty years. You'll still have plenty of life left."

"Not quite what I had in mind."

She shrugs. "A word of advice?"

"Sure, what've I got to lose?"

Her eyes sparkle. "When you're in the shower, don't drop the soap."

THE LETTER

BY EILEEN DUNBAUGH

The rag-and-bones man was the terror of my childhood. "Useless girls, like useless things, go to old Rags," my mother would say if I slacked on the chores she'd assigned. We knew him only as "Rags," the small, swarthy collector of junk, until the day my father got saddled with him as a client. Despite my mother's constant warnings, Daddy always seemed to be in the courthouse at the wrong time, when some judge or other was assigning lawyers to represent the latest crop of indigents who'd come before the bar. There were no public defenders back then, and the fool lawyer who ended up at the end of a judge's pointing finger took the case pro bono. It was possible to decline, but woe to the attorney who did if he found himself before that particular judge again.

I don't know why Daddy was always at the courthouse, unless it was because he was lonely. Each evening before he came home my mother would comb her hair and change her dress—and then spoil it all by talking at him, endlessly, and mostly in the same groove, telling him that a smart lawyer would keep away from the courthouse except when it was necessary to be there on a paying case, and that the way to feed your family was with last wills and testaments. I used to imagine that she was a record and that her voice would distort and finally stop if only I could figure out how to make the machine wind down.

She and Daddy had moved to Chicago from Missouri, mostly because of Mama's "aspirations." That was the word she used, proudly and without irony; she "aspired" to a better life. So instead of taking his share of the family farm, my father went to law school, moved to Chicago, and set up a one-man office on the fifth floor of a building on State Street. For a while, my mother was satisfied. The business boom of the twenties was big enough to bring well-paying work even to unambitious lawyers. And it wasn't that Daddy was lazy; his "problem," as Mama put it, was that he "pondered" too much. In the evenings he'd read, and when he could get away from the office, you'd find him puffing contemplatively on his cigar as he threw his fishing line into the stream not far from our house. We lived on the North Side then, in a tiny one-story, two-bedroom wood house that had seen better days. The neighborhood grew all around us in the twenties, but we still had country at our backs.

If Mama reminded me of a record, like all records of that time she played only two songs. She didn't like the grammar I picked up from the children of the slaughterhouse-working Poles and tried to arrange for me to play with the daughters of Dr. Adams, from our street, instead. She nagged my father until he built a playhouse in the backyard, thinking the Adams girls wouldn't be able to resist it. When they didn't come, her song for me—her "wayward Sadie"—became a lament.

I preferred it to the song reserved for my father—a relentlessly upbeat march, as if he only needed the example of others put before him to catch the rhythm and fall in line. He *must* have been lonely, for how can you confide your secret fears and doubts to someone who responds by pointing out that others don't have any? I think he had one friend, a man called Tom Fenton, who dealt in stocks and had an office in my father's building. It was a name, at any rate, that sometimes came up at the dinner table. He never brought Tom Fenton home, though, and in my partiality to my father I assumed it was because he didn't want to subject his friend to my mother's endless talk.

I would run a dozen blocks to meet my father on his way from the streetcar each evening. It may sound irresponsible to let a child wander alone through city streets, but it wasn't unusual—before the murder anyway. Children weren't supervised much as long as they chipped in around the house and were respectful in sight of a parent. Outdoors—and out of adult sight—we mostly did as we pleased, playing on construction sites amid broken glass, asbestos, and oil; sneaking in and out of hobo camps; climbing trees in the snatches of woods that remained. It was anything but a childproof world, but then accidents, even inside homes (where the absence of insulation in walls and on appliances made tinder boxes of the houses), were accepted as part of life.

What was not accepted was the default of trusted institutions such as the banks with the stock-market crash of 1929. I was nine. Old enough to sense even before Daddy came home ashen-faced on "Black Thursday" that something was wrong. My mother sat him down in a chair and knelt on the floor to take his hand. It was the tenderest moment I ever witnessed between them. I wasn't told until years later that my father'd heard a gunshot that afternoon and rushed to the next-door office of the broker named Tom Fenton to find he'd shot himself through the mouth.

We all knew our life was about to change. Now my father hung around the courthouse hoping to hear of paying work—any paying work. People didn't need a lawyer to draft a will when all they had was two sticks to rub together.

My mother started her own small millinery business from our house, and it was then that her threats about the rag-and-bones man began in earnest. She needed my help, and I was getting old enough to provide it. Gone were the Polish washerwomen who'd sloshed and wrung and hung and ironed our laundry. I watched Mama do it herself, surprised at the strength of her hands, which I'd never seen put to such hard work before. We didn't have the powerful detergents then that came out after the war; you got things clean with water heated in a tank without a temperature or pressure control, and with a washer that didn't rinse or spin. Before long my mother's hands turned lobster red from the scalding water, just like the hands of those sturdy Polish women. We both looked out at my playhouse as if it were a relic from an irreclaimably happy past, and for the first time I understood her "aspirations."

All three of us now lived in fear that we'd end up even worse off than where she and Daddy began. We never lost our tiny house, but we knew we could, and unlike many others who had family they could move in with, my parents had too thoroughly severed their ties back home to expect help in a crisis.

My mother passed her anxiety on to me through her threats about old Rags. I was young enough to take her seriously, and what made it worse was that Rags used to park his cart, which was pulled by a bony horse with an overlarge head, half a block down our street while he stopped to get a soda from a nearby shop. You couldn't see the shop from where he parked the cart; he chose the spot, I suppose, because there was a big tree there that shaded the horse on hot days.

For me, his parking place was a constant worry. It meant he didn't just pass our house shouting "Rags and old iron!" at a pace that allowed people to run out with their recyclable trash—the old clothes, bottles, tin cans, and iron he'd pay a penny or two for. My mother would have an hour each Tuesday to catch him and sell me to him.

If my mother was an unsympathetic adversary to me during

those years, she surprised me by showing a strong streak of compassion and generosity toward others. She had something mildly
disparaging to say about just about everyone whose background
wasn't exactly like ours. But she never let her prejudices stop her
from giving assistance to anyone who needed it. She even used
our few saved dollars to buy extra food for the endless stream
of homeless men who knocked on our back screen looking for
work.

Old Rags, as we called him until the day he became Daddy's
client, had a name that was unspellable, let alone pronounceable.
Something with a jumble of z's and other consonants. Naturally
that made his background a subject for discussion at our dinner
table. A Russian, my mother was certain, but Daddy said no, he
was Hungarian. A Gypsy, then, my mother insisted.

But Rags's roots were not discussed with my mother's usual
nonchalance. Her voice was hushed, because of the horror of
the thing he was said to have done. It was my father's first murder case, and not one he'd elected to take. Why he'd taken it at
all, even at the behest of the judge with the pointing finger, my
mother could not understand.

A little girl had been found dead in Rags's cart, under some
pieces of iron and a lot of loose clothing. I was ten, and they
felt no need to shield me from their conversation as one would
protect a child's tender ears today. As I listened, I was filled with
new loathing for my mother. I thought her a hypocrite, without
knowing the word. So this was what happened to girls who were
sold to old Rags. And my mother had threatened me with it a
hundred times. I wondered if my father knew how close I'd come
to being the girl on that cart.

No one could change Daddy's mind about representing the
ragman. We were already feeling the impact of the Depression,
and my father's health, by this time, had also started to give out.
My mother was right that he shouldn't be subjecting himself to

the strain of such a notorious case, but he'd heard other lawyers murmuring that they'd give Rags short shrift if he was assigned to them, and he wasn't going to turn his client over to someone who'd get him summarily convicted.

We never knew exactly what was wrong with my father, just that it was some kind of wasting illness that made him more gaunt with each passing month. He'd consulted a doctor, who could find no cause, and that was not an era when people got "second opinions."

If anything could have made my father's situation worse, it was that the body was identified, three days after its discovery, as that of Margaret Hilgendorf, a girl whose older sister was once a classmate of mine. When my mother heard the news, she *tsk*ed over the length of time it had taken the family—who were German immigrants—to report the girl missing. Their reluctance to trouble the police only reinforced her opinion that there was something sheeplike and unquestioning in the German character.

My impression of the family didn't fit my mother's stereotype at all. Mrs. Hilgendorf was a broom-wielding Brunhilde of a woman who made me think of bears, not sheep, and she stood no nonsense at all from any of her three daughters. I'd stopped at their house after school two or three times back when Gretchen was in my class, and Gretchen had immediately ushered me out of her mother's presence to a recess under the basement stairs that she'd turned into an Aladdin's cave. We were playing there one day when Mrs. Hilgendorf came clattering down the steps above us in pursuit of four-year-old Margaret, who ran into the narrow space behind the water heater to evade her. Mrs. Hilgendorf had given up that day, content to shout a threat at the little girl and retreat back upstairs with her broom. But the incident had frightened me, mostly because of the sheer size of the woman.

When Margaret's body was identified, the pressure on my father intensified. The family lived right in our neighborhood, and that seemed to provide a nail for Rags's coffin, since our street was near the end of his Tuesday round and the place where he parked his cart to take his late lunch at the soda shop. The Hilgendorf house was a block down the street that intersected with ours to the west, but this was still the outskirts of the city, and there was a large open field that ran from where the horse and cart were parked along the backyards of the houses on the Hilgendorfs' street. Most of the backyards had been privatized by fences or bushes, but the Hilgendorfs' had been left wide open and could be seen from where the horse was tied. The district attorney's theory was that Rags had spotted the pretty child playing in her yard and used the cover of the bushes and fences that backed the other yards to travel the few hundred feet to kidnap her.

What Rags's motive was, no one could say. There was speculation that it was something "indecent," and perhaps something involving torture, for Margaret's body was covered with third-degree burns all along one side. When the coroner's report came back saying she had not been sexually assaulted, Daddy breathed a big sigh of relief. But there were still the burns, and the talk continued that Rags was a "pervert" who tortured children. A pervert my daddy was defending.

My father's case was weak, and the dimmer the junkman's prospects looked, the more my father insisted on our referring to him with respect. We weren't allowed to say "Rags" anymore. Now it was Mr. Keresztnévz.

Mr. Keresztnévz's defense, as Daddy presented it, was that he hadn't the nerve to kidnap or kill a girl and then coolly partake of his lunch at the nearby shop. Several witnesses put him at the soda shop for at least a half hour, and others testified to seeing him leave the shop, collect his cart, and proceed up our street in the opposite direction from the Hilgendorfs'. The only time Mr.

Keresztnévz's movements were unaccounted for was the time *before* he sat calmly sipping his soda and eating his sandwich.

Another point in Mr. Keresztnévz's favor was that the autopsy showed no evidence of Margaret having been bound or gagged; and it established that she'd been burned while still alive, which suggested to my father that she'd been killed *before* ever being put in Mr. Keresztnévz's cart, in some private place where a gag was unnecessary. He told us over dinner one night what he thought had happened: that Margaret had wandered away from home, stumbled into a vagrant's camp, and burned herself accidentally on a barrel fire. A hobo would be frightened by a burned little girl's screams and might have panicked and killed her while attempting to shut her up.

Two boys rummaging in the rag cart for metal pipe with which to make smoke bombs had found Margaret's body at dusk, about two hours after Mr. Keresztnévz parked for the day, in a shed not a half mile from our house. That was plenty of time for someone other than Mr. Keresztnévz to have put the body in the cart and disappeared without leaving a trace. So went Daddy's argument. But he knew very well that under pressure of cross-examination, some of those witnesses who accounted for the ragman's whereabouts during the crucial afternoon would break down and say maybe they weren't so sure what time it had been after all. And besides, Mr. Keresztnévz was always going to be Rags to the people on that jury—a hunched little man with unfathomable, deeply hooded eyes who wore a dirty coat. What my father needed was someone who could testify unequivocally that no body had been in Rags's cart when he left it in its parking place that night.

It was wishing for the impossible.

But then the impossible happened. . . .

It was September, a week before the trial was to begin. I'd run out to meet my father as usual, but he stepped down from the streetcar deep in conversation with a pretty woman in a red feathered hat. I got a welcoming pat on the back, but they were too busy talking about some book they'd both read to bother with introductions. We were late getting home because my father insisted on walking by a much longer route that was on the woman's way. We'd only just come in and sat down together with the comics when a heavy hand thumped on the door.

That time of the evening, it could only be one person. The oldest Hilgendorf girl, Adelaide, delivered coffee cakes and strudels for her mother's at-home bakery business. We had a standing order for Tuesdays, but now that Daddy was representing Mr. Keresztnévz my mother was embarrassed to answer Adelaide's knock.

"Will you get it, please, Sadie?" she called out. For once I understood how my mother felt. I tried to avoid Gretchen at school for exactly the same reason. If only the Hilgendorfs would just refuse to deliver to us anymore. But they remained as faithful as the rising sun. The only time Adelaide had ever missed a delivery was the Tuesday Margaret disappeared.

The knock sounded again as I slid off the couch, grabbed some change from a dish near the front door, and swung the door open with my hand out ready to pay Adelaide.

But it wasn't Adelaide. It was a rough-looking man with a couple of days' growth of beard, wearing a tattered vest over a dirty work shirt.

The murder fresh on my mind, I shouted "Daddy!" with such alarm that both my parents hurried to the door.

Mama didn't know what to make of the unexpected visitor, but my father seemed to recognize him and invited him to come sit on the back porch, a glassed-in space that had the advantage of being away from my mother's ears and mine.

I think my mother and I both assumed the man's business had something to do with Rags, because none of my father's normal acquaintances dressed so shabbily or had such an air of furtiveness. When the man was gone, though, Daddy stubbornly refused to say what it had been about.

He didn't open up until the next night, when he came home with resolution and worry and hopefulness all mixed on his face and told us he had a witness who would prove that the dead girl was put on the cart after Mr. Keresztnévz finished his rounds. The man worked for Mr. Keresztnévz occasionally, helping him sort the things he collected and deliver them to whoever was willing to pay. The afternoon of the murder he and Mr. Keresztnévz had been sifting through the cart looking for cotton clothing, having been offered ten cents a laundry-basketful by a local printer who would use them in press cleaning. They'd poked through the whole bed of the cart, pulling out shabby garments that could be torn up to make that ten cents, and it was impossible, the witness claimed, that a body could have remained unobserved.

A problem with this testimony was that Rags had not said anything about sorting through the cart with his sometime employee when he was interviewed by the police. If he had, it would certainly have been known to my father. The only possible explanation, if this witness was telling the truth, was that Rags failed fully to understand the nature of his situation. And truly he *hadn't* seemed quite right in the head since his arrest; clearly terrified, he'd mostly rocked back and forth and moaned, instead of helping Daddy figure out how to save his life.

The last-minute emergence of a witness for the defense was a big break, even if there were holes in the story just waiting for the prosecution to rip open. For the first time, a ray of doubt about Rags's guilt started to shimmer in my mother's eyes. She was so absorbed in this new turn of events that we were on dessert before she imparted *her* big news. Someone had stolen her grocery money, which was kept in a coffee can on a high shelf near the door to the back porch. Our doors were usually left unlocked, and my mother was convinced that a hobo had come inside while she was out and found the money.

"I've told you before to lock the doors, Alice. . . . Let's all try to be more careful," my father said, putting a reassuring hand on hers.

———

THE DAY BEFORE the *State of Illinois v. Keresztnévz* went to the jury, a letter addressed to my father arrived with our morning mail. On light blue stationery, marked *Personal and confidential,* it sat on the kitchen table, where my mother and I hovered over it like bees every time we passed.

Daddy came home that night well past dinnertime, as he had throughout the trial, but early enough that I was still up doing homework. Mama and I exchanged a look when we saw that he was as surprised as we'd been by the letter. He took it out to the porch to open it, though, causing suspicion to cloud my mother's face. Then he came back into the house, put the blue envelope in his breast pocket, grabbed his coat, and said he had to go back to his office.

He must have come home sometime in the early morning to wash up and change his clothes, but neither of us heard him. It was his day to sum up for Mr. Keresztnévz, and then the junk collector's fate would be in others' hands.

Mama woke me up that morning slamming doors. I assumed she was upset over the unexplained letter on what was clearly a woman's stationery. But whatever jealous thoughts might have been eating at her, she was determined to be at the courthouse for the summation. I begged her to let me take off school and come with her.

It was the first and only time I ever saw my father in a court-room. Rags had someone there too. In the row behind the table where the accused sat, there huddled a tiny woman with a babushka on her head and a toddler clutched to her breast. "Mr. Keresztnévz's wife," Mama whispered as the court was being called to order.

I shrank inside my thin dress as the prosecution lawyer got up and had his say. I'd never been able to stand up to vindictiveness, and I didn't expect that my father would be able to either. But I learned something that day. When it was his turn to speak, some fire rose up in the man I'd known only as a gentle father. He commanded the room in a way the prosecuting attorney had not, for all the harsh accusations he'd flung about. And it wasn't my father's words that moved his listeners either; it was the faith in Mr. Keresztnévz that resonated in his voice. When he'd finished, Mama and I looked at each other and the thought passed silently between us: *That jury's got to let Rags go.*

There was nothing for it now but to wait for the verdict. My father gave Mr. Keresztnévz an encouraging pat on the back and made his way to the back of the courtroom, radiating gratitude at the sight of us. My mother affected a stern look at first, punishment, I suppose, for his mysterious behavior over the letter. But by the time we reached the streetcar, they'd linked arms and offered me a hand. My mother was proud of her husband, and of me. I think jealousy made her see that.

We'd just reached the house, and I was about to suggest we all go out to dinner, when my mother took a good look at my father's haggard face and stopped in her tracks.

"Dear God, Matthew," she said, putting a hand on his forehead, "we need to get you to bed."

She bundled him up with a hot-water bottle and extra blankets and sat with him through the night. By morning I could hear the rasp of his breathing all the way down the hall. A doctor was called, with the effect of frightening rather than comforting me, because money for a house call wouldn't be spent except in the worst case.

About the time the doctor pulled up in his Essex, a messenger came to the house to say that the jury was back. My father managed to raise himself up and get out of bed. Compassion outweighing his disapproval, the doctor drove us to the courthouse and waited with us while the verdict was read.

After the calling to order of the court, the judge's questions to the jury, and the unbearable moments of silence while the judge read what was written on the paper handed from the jury foreman to the clerk to him, the words—"not guilty"—rushed through me like a tonic. The pressure was off. Daddy would recover now, and our life would go back to normal.

But it wasn't to be. When my father turned from the defendant's table, he was a spent man. And this time when he was laid down on his sickbed, he wouldn't ever get up again. We sat with him for two days while he tossed uncomfortably—murmuring, in his waking hours, that he had to get to his office, that there was something he had to do.

At first Mama thought he was raving. "It's all right, Matthew," she kept repeating, "Mr. Keresztnévz's been acquitted." But finally she ushered me out, shut the door, and sat talking to him for a long while alone.

When she opened the door again, it was to tell me my father had died.

The agony of that moment comes back to me in the small hours of lonely nights to this day. But there was no time for it to sink in then, because my mother would not let us rest. She arranged for the funeral to be the next day. There were few mourners besides the Keresztnévzs, who laid a huge wreath on the fresh-covered earth, and no sooner had the tiny reception concluded than Mama told me she would be keeping me home from school to help clear my father's office.

Clearing the office was a pretext for finding that mysterious letter, I suspected, but my mother would not discuss it. When she found the blue envelope she opened it right away, scanned the single sheet inside, and tore it all to bits. Then she made me help her tear up several folders full of other papers, and we tumbled all the pieces together in the garbage can.

I never dared ask her what was in the letter.

Our lives resumed, though with a different dynamic. With my father's death, my mother was transformed. She never threatened me again. Evident as her own grief was in the premature gray that quickly frosted her hair, she set her mind immediately to protecting me, using the small savings we had left to pay for a typing course. Before long, she'd landed a job as a secretary.

There was another surprising turnabout too: My father wasn't two weeks gone when she started urging me to resume my friendship with Gretchen Hilgendorf. "They've been through a lot, those children," she said. "You should ask her to come home with you one afternoon, Sadie. It's the charitable thing to do." And instead of avoiding Adelaide when she made her Tuesday delivery, my mother now insisted on bringing the girl inside for a cup of tea and a chat, often over Adelaide's strong objections that she still had other deliveries to make.

Clearly Mama was trying to make friends with the Hilgendorf girls, but whether her purpose was to atone for my father's defense of Mr. Keresztnévz I couldn't be certain.

My own picture of my father was slowly, inexorably changing. While I wouldn't have tolerated anyone else saying it, I wondered if the term "philanderer" had applied to him—because I couldn't get that letter on a woman's stationery out of my mind. I remembered the smile on his face as we'd walked with the pretty woman in the red feathered hat and wondered if she had written it.

In time, my transition to adulthood pushed such questions about my father into the background. What would I do when I finished high school? It was Mama's wish that I go on to college, where, I suppose, she believed I would meet an appropriate sort of man.

She scraped together enough money for me to enroll at the city campus of the state university, where I met a plucky young Irishman called Pete O'Rourke, whom my mother came to adore, her prejudices about the Irish notwithstanding.

By the time I graduated, the war was on. Unwilling to marry a man who was shipping off overseas, I did something that shocked my mother speechless: I enrolled in law school.

It was three years later, on the day I learned I'd passed the bar exam, that she sat me down and turned my whole world inside out.

"Do you remember that letter that came for your father during the trial of Mr. Keresztnévz?" she said.

In an instant I was covered in pins and needles—as if after nearly fifteen years I was coming painfully awake. I wanted to shut her up, tell her not to speak—protest that there was a time when I had wanted to know, but not anymore.

Before I could object she continued, "You must have wondered who wrote it."

"No—what's the point? He's gone."

My mother laughed. "You think there was another woman, don't you? Your father and I were in love, Sadie, whether you knew it or not. There was never another woman."

Women of my mother's generation looked nothing like the fifty-somethings of today's boomer generation. They looked old: hair gone to white, middles stout and barrel-shaped. I found it hard to connect what I saw before me with being in love.

"What, then?" I said, fear starting to crawl up my spine.

"It was about the murder. I'm telling you now because you are about to enter your father's profession. Because you have just been admitted to the bar, and if he'd lived, your father might well have been *dis*barred. You aren't going to be accepted easily, a woman in a profession like that. You'll need to be careful.

"Maybe I'm also telling you because I've spent all these years wondering what I would have done in your father's shoes."

It was a punch to the solar plexus. Several moments passed before I could draw a normal breath.

"You remember that terrible man who came to the house, the witness who saved Rags?" she continued.

"Of course."

"Your father paid him." Bald as that, it came from her mouth. "He took the grocery money from the jar where I kept it and he paid him."

"Paid him to give his testimony, you mean?!"

"Worse. He told him what to say."

I flushed so hard it felt as if my skin would burst.

"Don't judge him too harshly," my mother said, studying my face. "That's why I never told you when you were younger. You idolized your father so. I always saw his faults, and I loved him anyway—"

"We're not talking about *faults* here!" I interrupted. I stood up and leaned toward her, staring her down as if she were before me in a witness box. Anything to make her recant her terrible testimony. "We're talking about lying. Breaking the law!"

"He was so certain Mr. Keresztnévz was innocent," she said calmly. "And there was little doubt he'd be executed if your father lost the case."

"What has the letter got to do with it?"

"The letter was from someone who had information about the real killer. The trouble was, it came too late. Your father's witness had already testified, and if what the letter said was true, Margaret Hilgendorf's body must have been in Rags's cart—without Rags realizing it—before he parked it for the night."

"And if Daddy had taken the letter to the police," I said, seeing where this was going, "it might have come out that he bribed his witness to concoct a false story."

"That's right. And there was no guarantee the prosecution would believe what was in the letter and drop the charges against Mr. Keresztnévz anyway."

"What did the letter say, Mama?"

I still stood over her, but less menacingly now.

She hesitated for a long while. Finally she said, "It was an anonymous letter, from one of the Hilgendorfs' neighbors. It said that on the afternoon Margaret Hilgendorf went missing, the letter writer was in an upper-story room of her house, which gave a vantage point above her backyard fence. She saw Mrs. Hilgendorf, or someone who looked like her, running along the backs of the houses with a bundle in her arms. She deposited that bundle in Rags's cart."

"Why didn't she sound the alarm right away then?"

"Because there was nothing unusual in someone forgetting they had something for Rags and catching up and putting it on his cart. There was no reason to think there was something wrong until Margaret was discovered dead. By then, Rags had already been arrested. And the letter writer wasn't confident she'd be believed if she said something against the grieving mother when the whole city already had its scapegoat. When her conscience finally got the better of her, she laid the decision at your father's door instead of going to the police. I'm sure she was surprised that nothing ever came of her writing that letter. She couldn't know that your father's hands were tied by then."

"But it can't be true. You're saying that Mrs. Hilgendorf killed her own child!"

"No, Sadie. I'm not saying that. But just in case there was something to the letter writer's story, I tried to keep an eye on those Hilgendorf girls over the years. I let them know there was another adult they could come to."

I looked at the white hair and worn face of the woman I'd been about to visit my wrath upon and my heart expanded. *Yes, you did,* I thought. *And I never knew why.*

I sat down and recalled my own childish fears of Mrs. Hilgendorf and her broom. I'd seen her more often in recent years, since Adelaide and Gretchen had married. She still baked for old clients like my mother, but she had to deliver the cakes herself with her girls gone. She was anything but scary in the twilight of her life. Bovine and passive was more like it, with big, sad eyes.

Surely she could not have killed her own child. And yet . . . I remembered those strange burns that had run down one side of Margaret's body. And suddenly I knew what had caused them.

"She did it, Mama!" I said.

She stared at me.

"No one ever explained the burns, did they? I mean, I know Daddy thought they were from a hobo's fire, but why straight along one side like that?"

She said nothing, just continued to stare.

"It was the water heater. Mrs. Hilgendorf used to chase Margaret and Margaret would hide behind the water heater. I saw it with my own eyes. But the day Margaret died, when Mrs. Hilgendorf found her daughter out of her reach, she must have been unwilling to give up. If she could just catch hold of one of Margaret's arms she could yank her out and punish her. I think she banged Margaret's head accidentally—but fatally—and scalded the side of her body against the heater as she tried to pull her out."

My mother put her hands to her face as if she was sorry she'd ever started down this road.

"Not Mrs. Hilgendorf," she said at last, folding her hands sadly in front of her. "Mrs. Hilgendorf was training Adelaide to join her in the business. They were saving to open a real bakeshop when Adelaide finished high school."

She sighed and looked regretfully into space. "The day Margaret was killed, Mrs. Hilgendorf had to go downtown with her husband. It was a proud moment for Adelaide, who was entrusted with baking the coffee cakes—the stollen—for the first time. Only Adelaide and Margaret were home. Adelaide thinks Margaret must have envied the attention her mother paid her. Whatever got into her, she waited until the stollen were all braided and left out to rise and Adelaide had left the room, then she picked them up and threw them onto the floor of the kitchen fireplace. I remember those rages a four-year-old can get into from when you were little, Sadie. . . . Anyway, when Adelaide came back and saw what her sister had done, she was determined to thrash her, but Margaret slipped past her and ran for her hiding place in the basement, taunting Adelaide all the way. Adelaide was more persistent than her mother. She caught hold of her sister and pulled. And then it was just how you say. She banged the little girl's head."

"She told you this?" My whole body went cold. "It was *Adelaide?*"

My mother nodded. "I'd given her a cup of tea one evening. You weren't home. . . . I asked after her mother and her face collapsed. Then it just . . . came out—along with her sobs.

"I believed her, because it made sense of something I'd been unable to reconcile: how a mother could put her own child out with the rubbish. It wasn't Mrs. Hilgendorf who put Margaret there, of course. It was Adelaide—tall, big-boned Adelaide. Wearing her mother's apron, she'd have looked a lot like her. Big as she was, though, she was only fifteen, still a child. She did what a child instinctively does—tried to hide the evidence of her crime.

"I'm sure she expected me to tell her mother. Maybe that's why she confessed it all to me. Because she didn't know how to tell her herself."

"But you didn't," I said, bitterness creeping into my voice.

"I let her grow up and decide for herself, Sadie, to wait on her own conscience.

"And I wasn't going to be the one to destroy your father's good name. That's what will happen if the case is ever reopened. You won't do it either."

———

SHE WAS RIGHT. I never did. I settled quietly into my job at the Cook County Public Defender's Office, which was formed soon after "Rags" Keresztnévz's trial. And I stayed there until the scandal of 2000, when the convictions of several men we'd inadequately represented were overturned, causing the governor to put a moratorium on the death penalty. They did a clean sweep of ancient warhorses like me then, even though lack of funding was to blame—or so I told myself.

Much as I loved him, I was never quite able to forgive my father for risking my future, my mother's happiness, and even justice for Rags Keresztnévz. It's only now that I'm old and have my own doubts and regrets to contend with that I think I might have done the same thing. Because in those days, when almost everyone lived on the edge of poverty, we could all see a little of ourselves in a frightened, indigent defendant like Rags.

SPECTRAL EVIDENCE

BY KATE GALLISON

Waitstill Winthrop smoothed his cravat and adjusted his wig, preparing to enter the courtroom, which doubled as Salem Village's meetinghouse, and take his place with the other judges who were to preside over Governor Phipps's first court of Oyer and Terminer in the case of the accused witches. Some of the nine judges were the same Salem magistrates who had first brought the witchcraft cases forward, Judge John Hathorne for one. But the other jurists had been chosen by Governor Phipps from among the most illustrious men of the Massachusetts Bay Colony: Nathaniel Saltonstall, Lieutenant Governor William Stoughton, and of course Winthrop himself. Men of Boston, Harvard men, men who had been educated as Christian gentlemen, men well prepared to deal with an assault on the Bay Colony by no less an adversary than the Devil himself. Nathaniel Saltonstall slid over and made room for Winthrop on the bench.

A great throng of spectators had come to Salem Village the morning of Goodwife Rebecca Nurse's trial. They were afoot and on horseback, so many that the proceedings had been moved to the meetinghouse from a room in Nathaniel Ingersoll's inn. As far away as Topsfield the farmers left their ploughs and the goodwives their spindles to ride into town and watch the witch's trial. Boston merchants came to the village in carriages, bringing their ladies, dressed in their best. Many found seats in the meeting-house, where they sat murmuring until Judge Stoughton brought them to order. The jurors, farmers and merchants for the most part, waited in respectful silence.

Ten seats in the front had been kept open for the afflicted girls. Winthrop was eager to see them. He had heard all about them, of course—who in Massachusetts had not?—young victims of satanic persecution who fell into fits, sometimes to be tortured by witches, sometimes to have their spirits dragged away to the infamous Witches' Sabbath, where they were forced to observe their neighbors committing sacrilege and murder.

Winthrop was well prepared for the trying of this case. Legal precedents abounded. All the judges had studied these with care and attention, in particular Reverend Richard Bernard's *Guide to Grand-Jury Men* and the writings of Cotton Mather, for how else were they to know the procedure for trying a case of witchcraft? The Bay Colony was nothing if not subject to the rational rule of law.

But before the girls came into the courtroom, the bailiffs had to bring in the prisoner. Judge Stoughton commanded, and it was done.

Winthrop could not but marvel that such a broken heap of bones as this person could threaten the welfare of the entire Massachusetts Bay Colony. Goody Rebecca Nurse had lain in gaol for months. She smelled like an old woman in need of a bath. In a pitiful last-minute attempt to appear respectable, she had combed her few wisps of white hair and tucked them under a fresh white cap. Her clothing at least appeared to be clean, probably brought to her by one of her many daughters, sitting together with the rest of her family in the first few rows of seats. Still, the dark blue dress failed to give the old woman the dignity she sought, since it no longer fit her but hung on her as though draped over a bare tree branch.

"Goody Rebecca Nurse, you are charged with the crime of witchcraft," Judge Stoughton intoned. "How do you plead?" As was customary in witchcraft trials, Goody Nurse was not invited to take an oath before her testimony. No witch was suffered to place her hand on the Holy Book, nor would any oath of truthfulness necessarily bind her, as the Devil, her master, was well known to be the father of lies.

The old woman raised her head and looked at Judge Stoughton, blinking her eyes, which were the same dark blue as her gown, but red rimmed like the eyes of a pheasant. Winthrop feared for a moment that she would refuse to plead, forcing upon the court the truly unpleasant necessity of applying *peine forte et dure,* where stones must be piled upon the defendant until he agreed to plead one way or the other to the charge, or until he died. But then she cupped her hand around her ear, indicating a problem hearing the judge's question. Apparently the Devil, her master, had not included the restoration of Goody Nurse's failing power of hearing among the rewards he gave her for his service. Judge Stoughton repeated the question loudly.

"I am not guilty, Your Honors," she said.

"Bring in Goody Nurse's accusers," Judge Stoughton said.

The crowd threw open the meetinghouse door and parted to make an aisle for the girls. A gust of spring air preceded them, soft with the smell of new grass. What pretty creatures! Some were young women, some were children trembling on the threshold of womanhood, the rosy kiss of spring upon their cheeks. Judge Saltonstall, as new to the case as Winthrop himself was, murmured to Judge Hathorne, "Do you not find it marvelous that the girls appear so well, given that Goody Nurse and the others are accused of causing their bodies to pine and waste?"

"Pining and wasting need not have any permanent effect in

order to meet the conditions of the law," Judge Hathorne explained. "The girls pine and waste for as long as they are in their fits, and that is torture enough for the poor things. We need not insist that they pine and waste at other times. See the last one in line? That's the unhappy Betty Hubbard. The child falls into trances, where she remains for hours, insensible to her surroundings. To see her would melt a heart of stone." As though to confirm his words, when the girls caught sight of Goody Nurse, they began to scream and writhe most affectingly, all but the Hubbard child, who sank into her seat with glazed eyes and her little mouth agape. Winthrop's very bowels were wrung with pity.

"Who's the big one with the red hands?" Judge Stoughton asked.

"That's Mercy Lewis," Judge Hathorne said. "A maidservant at the Putnams' house. Her parents were killed in the Indian raids at Falmouth some years ago, when she herself was captured." The way the girl was howling, Winthrop would have thought she was still in the hands of the savages.

Judge Stoughton directed the bailiffs to restrain the defendant. He shouted to be heard over the din of the girls. The bailiffs bent over the old woman and held her hands, which she must have been using to work some evil magic upon the helpless creatures. At once they fell silent, got up off the floor, and took their seats.

"Goody Nurse," Judge Stoughton said, "why do you hurt these girls?"

"I do not," she said.

"Why do you afflict them?"

"I do not afflict them." She shook her head, and the afflicted girls shook their heads in imitation of her, but in such an exaggerated manner that they must surely have hurt their necks. They all cried out in pain.

"What!" Judge Stoughton said. "You practice witchcraft here in the court, before our faces!"

"I know not what afflicts the girls. It is not I."

"Goody Nurse," the littlest moaned. The rest of them took it up. "Goody Nurse . . . Goody Nurse . . ."

When order was again established, Sergeant Thomas Putnam of the Salem militia, upright farmer and churchgoer, read to the court the notes he took at divers times when his wife and daughter were in their fits at his home. All one day and night his wife, Ann, had struggled with the specter of Goody Nurse. The witch had nearly wrenched Goody Putnam's arms and legs from her body in the effort to get her to sign the Devil's book.

"My wife was as stiff as a board," he said. "I tried to take her on my lap to comfort her, but her body could not be bent. Her screams were pitiful to hear." He went on to tell how Goody Nurse had assaulted his daughter, also called Ann, in many similar incidents, all duly documented. The smallest girl, she of the red cheek and sparkling eye, Winthrop understood to be Putnam's daughter. The person sitting between the little girl and Mercy Lewis had to be Putnam's afflicted wife. An uncommonly handsome woman, almost as fetching as Winthrop's own wife, whose arms he had left so reluctantly that morning.

Sergeant Putnam's deposition was followed by that of the Reverend Mr. Samuel Parris of the Salem Village Church, who stood up and confirmed everything Putnam had said, reading from notes of his own. He named the neighbors who had come into Sergeant Putnam's house and seen these events, in case the honorable judges wished to call them as witnesses. Goody Nurse stared at him reproachfully the whole time he was reading, but the minister never returned her gaze.

Then a man in the group of Nurse relatives approached the judges. "That's Goody Nurse's son-in-law," Judge Hathorne muttered. "Be advised."

"Your Honors, I wish to place in evidence a petition from

Goody Rebecca Nurse's supporters," the man said, showing a sheaf of paper several pages thick to Judge Stoughton.

"Your name, sir?"

"Thomas Preston."

"You are the husband of Goody Nurse's daughter?"

"One of her six daughters, yes. This godly woman—"

"Read your petition," Judge Stoughton said.

Goodman Preston read it out. The petition droned on and on about Goody Nurse's qualities, how long she had been a member of the church, how blameless among her fellows, in what a Christian manner she had raised her family. Her proud daughters raised their chins. The afflicted girls began to murmur.

"They say that witchcraft is passed from mother to daughter," Judge Hathorne said. "Was not Goody Nurse born a Towne? I've heard it said that her mother was a witch also." Judge Saltonstall frowned at him.

Betty Hubbard came out of her trance, blinking. "Goody Nurse's mother was a witch! Her sisters, Goody Easty and Goody Cloyse, too. Foul witches, all of them," she muttered, and drifted away again. A bead of drool formed on her chin.

Goodman Preston looked at the afflicted child, sideways and slightingly, and returned his eyes to the petition. He went on to read a list of the names of those of Goody Nurse's supporters who had appended their signatures to it. They were legion and included not only the Nurse kinsfolk but also many others, respectable churchgoing people, as he averred, one of them a Boston minister. When Preston was finished, Judge Saltonstall looked doubtful again.

"We'll soon clear this up," Judge Stoughton said. "Call the confessors."

The bailiffs brought them from the gaol, Tituba, the black Indian woman who was the Reverend Mr. Parris's slave, and the bold wench Abigail Hobbs. Judge Hathorne explained that the girls had identified these women at previous examinations, at which time the two had confessed to being witches and described the famous Sabbath held in Mr. Parris's pasture. "If any further proof were needed," Judge Hathorne said, "they cried out on a number of other people whom they saw there at the Witches' Sabbath. We are holding those men and women now in Salem gaol, of course."

"Of course," Judge Stoughton said.

Goody Nurse stared at the confessors. "These used to be among us. Are they come now to speak against me?"

Judge Stoughton gave her a curious look. "Among you at the Witches' Sabbath?"

"Among us in the gaol," she said.

"Tituba Indian. Give your testimony," Judge Stoughton said. "Tell us how you saw Goody Nurse at the Witches' Sabbath."

Trembling, the young slave approached the judges' bench. For a long time she stood staring at her feet. When she spoke, it was in the soft accents of the West Indian islands.

"I know nothing about any Witches' Sabbath. Mr. Parris, he beat me and make me say I am a witch."

"What?" Judge Saltonstall said. A sound like an intake of breath came from the afflicted girls. Betty Hubbard, deep in her trance, stirred a little.

Judge Stoughton flew into a rage. "Give your testimony, I say. Or can it be that you are back in the Devil's snare? We have a rope for unrepentant witches."

Tituba looked from one to the other of the nine judges' faces, sighed deeply, scuffed her toe, and hung her head. "Yes, sir. The witches meet in Mr. Parris's pasture. The king of the witches, he blow a trumpet, and all the witches they come from . . ." She glanced at Mr. Parris. He nodded slightly. ". . . from Salem Town, and Topsfield, also Andover and Boston and such places."

"Goody Nurse?"

"Goody Nurse with them. She ride on a pole."

"And?"

"Oh, the others . . . the king of the witches, he wear a high-crowned hat—"

"The Devil, you mean?" Judge Stoughton asked.

"No, Your Honor, a minister." She glanced again at the stony faces of Sergeant Putnam and the Reverend Mr. Parris as if for confirmation, but they gave no sign of approval or disapproval.

"And what was done there, at the Sabbath in Mr. Parris's pasture?" Judge Richards asked.

"They eat red bread, drink red wine. The Devil promise us things and make us sign the book."

"The book," Judge Saltonstall said.

"Little red book."

"And so Goody Nurse was there, and she . . . ," Judge Stoughton prompted.

"Goody Nurse was there," Tituba said. "And she say, Make your mark in the book or else I hurt you. Choke you, or stick you with pins. So I—"

"Tell us about the man in the hat," Judge Hathorne said. "The minister you spoke of. What was his name?"

"Don't know his name. He have black hair."

"Was he tall or short?"

Tituba glanced at the six-foot Reverend Mr. Parris and said, "Short."

This was a strange thing, and terrible if true, that a minister of the Gospel should be in league with the Devil. The men of the jury stared at the wench as if they expected her to sprout horns and a tail. "No wonder our poor colony is in such straits," Winthrop murmured. "A minister."

"This is not to the present case," Judge Saltonstall pointed out.

"True," Judge Stoughton said. "We will pursue it later. Abigail

Hobbs, your testimony, please. Tell us about Goody Nurse and the red book."

Young Abigail came swaggering up to the bench with her fists on her hips and an insolent sneer on her face, hardly the deportment one would have expected from a well-behaved Puritan maid. Of course, it was the influence of the Devil, plain as daylight. Winthrop could almost smell the brimstone on her. "*She* made me sign it," she said, pointing at Goody Nurse. The old woman sat with her hands in her lap.

"Goody Nurse made you sign the red book?" Judge Stoughton said.

"Yes. She said, Here, sign this, the Old Boy gave it to me to sign, and you must sign it as well or else I will hurt you, choke you, stick you with pins, tear off your arms and legs. Would Your Honors like to see my witch mark?"

"The Old Boy," Judge Stoughton said. "You mean the black man?"

"I mean the Devil."

"So on the Devil's behalf she gave you the book?"

"It was a little red book. She caused me to prick my finger and make my mark in it in blood."

"You signed your name?"

"I cannot write, Your Honor. But I saw many names in the book."

"Indeed." A murmur went around the courtroom. Was she going to reel off the names? Whom would she name? "Whose name did you see?"

"Goody Nurse's name, sir. And Tituba, and Mr. Burroughs, and Goodman Proctor . . ."

Judge Saltonstall said, "Can you read, Abigail?"

"No, Your Honor."

"But then how—"

If ever a scream could have actually curdled blood, the scream uttered by Mercy Lewis at that moment would have done it. Under his wig, Waitstill Winthrop felt his back hairs rise. The girl was on her feet, pointing at the ceiling.

"See!" she shouted. "See where she sits on the beam!" Every eye flew to the roof beam. "There she sits with the black man talking to her and a little yellow bird sucking between her fingers. Come down, Goody Nurse! Come down!" It was so dark overhead that seventy devils might have been perching on the beam without being seen. Still, Winthrop almost thought he saw them himself, the witch, the Devil, the yellow bird, and all. He looked away, at Goody Nurse's face. A single tear trickled down her withered cheek.

"See!" Mercy Lewis shouted. "See where the black man speaks in her ear!"

"The black man!" the girls all moaned. "The black man! Oh! He speaks in her ear!" The judges all fixed their gazes on Goody Nurse. She rolled her eyes upward, and shortly the girls did too, clear up into their poor young heads, so that only the whites were showing. Out of their chairs and onto the floor they tumbled, jerking their limbs and screaming.

"What does this black man say to you?" Judge Stoughton roared at the old woman. "Who is he?" The girls fell silent.

"I know nothing of it. There is no black man. How can I be sitting on the beam? You see that I am here before you."

"Impudence," Judge Hathorne muttered.

"You are bewitching these girls," Judge Stoughton said. "Can you deny it?"

"I do deny it. I am as clear as the child unborn. I am a Christian woman, Your Honors. I have been a good churchgoing woman my whole life long."

"How do you account, then, for the sufferings of these girls?"

"I cannot account for it. It may be that the Devil afflicts them in my shape."

This was an interesting point of law. What had Bernard said about it? The judges put their heads together to consider whether the Devil could assume the shape of an innocent person.

"No," Judge Hathorne said. "He cannot. The Lord God would never permit it." Certainly He would never punish an innocent person so, by allowing her to be suspected of witchcraft.

Everyone knew that the Bay Colony's recent difficulties—Red Indians and godless Frenchmen ravaging the northern settlements and shipping, the men who governed our colony embroiled in English politics and helpless against the French and Indian assaults—had at their root some fault in the people's Christian worship, a prayer too languid and a faith too dim, perhaps, or more likely a frontal attack by the Devil himself, aided by witches. The news that the colony's troubles were caused by a coven meeting in a pasture in Salem Village was greeted in Boston almost with relief. But the all-powerful God would have to permit such a thing to happen, explicitly, for reasons of His own. The alternative interpretation, that the men of Boston had misgoverned through their own lack of competence, was unthinkable.

And here sat Goody Nurse, the Devil's own weapon, a spearhead aimed at the very heart of Christ's Kingdom on Earth. An innocent woman? "Unthinkable," Winthrop repeated to himself.

Judge Nathaniel Saltonstall, whose education was less well grounded in Puritan theological principles than that of the other judges, frowned and shook his head. "Gentlemen, it seems to me—"

"She bites me! She bites me!" The Putnam girl pushed up her sleeve and held out her little white arm, marked with cruel red toothmarks. "Oh, Goody Nurse, don't bite me so! I tell you, I never will sign the Devil's book!" She fell in a fit. They all fell in fits. The judges' argument was forgotten.

WHEN THE JURY had finished its deliberations over the fate of Rebecca Nurse, they returned a verdict of not guilty. The old woman began to pray and give thanks to God, and the Nurse family embraced one another. Winthrop was startled by the verdict. The case had seemed plain to him, as it had to all the judges except for the bothersome Judge Saltonstall. But Winthrop supposed the Salem jurymen knew best. By the grace of God he would at least be able to return to Boston now and put this case behind him. The acquittal of Goody Nurse might very well mean the end of the witch business.

After a silence long enough to take a breath in, the girls began screaming and howling. Half of them fell to the floor, and the other half staggered toward the defendant, moaning, "Goody Nurse, Goody Nurse," and holding their hands out in front of themselves. Before they could reach her, they were struck flat down to the courthouse floor as if by an invisible hand. A horrible spectacle. Judge Winthrop was all over gooseflesh.

Judge Stoughton beat his gavel. "Blindfold the defendant!" The bailiffs grasped Goody Nurse's hands and put a blindfold around her eyes.

"Now bring the girls to her."

One by one the afflicted children were led to Goody Nurse. A bailiff held her hand out to touch them. When they were touched, the malevolent energy that had entered them through the witch's eyes flowed back into her hand again and the girls were healed.

Judge Stoughton said, "I would not impose upon the jury, but I wonder whether you gentlemen have sufficiently considered this case."

"We believed so, Your Honor," the foreman said.

"I wonder whether you have considered something Goody Nurse let slip. You will recall that she greeted the confessing witches as people who had been among her group. I found that telling."

The jurymen glanced nervously at one another.

"I charge you now to retire and reconsider your verdict," Judge Stoughton said.

———

WHEN THEY CAME back, it was with a verdict of guilty. Judge Stoughton lost no time in pronouncing Rebecca Nurse's sentence, as clearly prescribed in Bernard's *Guide to Grand-Jury Men*. "You shall be hanged by the neck until dead, and may God have mercy on your soul."

The bailiffs led her away, a crushed woman. The Massachusetts Bay Colony was saved from her evil designs, Winthrop supposed, and now the courts must deal with the other witches. He took out a handkerchief and mopped his brow. The day was very warm for June.

As the crowd began to file out of the courtroom, little Ann Putnam jumped up and began to shout, "Judge Stoughton! Judge Stoughton! I must speak!"

"Yes? What is it?"

"In my fit last night my seven little Putnam cousins, the dead ones, appeared to me in winding sheets, with napkins over their faces." The people stopped leaving. The whole room fell completely silent. Every soul in the place, even the Nurse relatives, riveted his attention upon the girl. "They said a witch had murdered them. They cried out for vengeance. They said I must come to you and tell you."

"Vengeance against whom?" Judge Stoughton said. The crowd held its breath. Winthrop awaited the girl's words with mild interest, but not with the fascination of most of the spectators, since he knew no one in Salem.

"Mistress Winthrop," Ann Putnam said. "Judge Waitstill Winthrop's wife. Ah! She afflicts me!"

KNIFE FIGHT

BY JOEL GOLDMAN

Every day is a knife fight. That's what I tell my lawyer first time I meet her.

"Travis," she say to me, "what am I supposed to do with that?"

"Shit, girl, you my lawyer. You figure it out."

We in a room at the jail where prisoners meet wit they lawyers, a guard watchin' through a window make sure I don't climb inside her pants and escape. Hard floor, hard chairs, hard everything.

Her name Elisabeth Rosenthal, Public Defender. She don't look like much. Hit me 'bout at my shoulders. Black hair cut short and tight. Wearin' black pants, black shirt, hangin' loose. If the girl got a shape, she hidin' it.

"You a lesbian?"

She cross her arms. "Yeah."

"Jew?"

"Two for two."

"So I got a Jew dyke for a lawyer. This shit is fucked up, man."

"Yeah, well, don't feel bad. Looks like I've got a black client who hates Jews and gays. I guess we're both fucked."

I look at her, girl smilin', maybe playin' wit me. "You sayin' you hate blacks?"

She shake her head. "I'm saying that we are what we are. I don't have a problem with it, but if you do, get over it. Johnnie Cochran is dead." She shove a paper across the table. "Take a look at this."

Court paper say I killed this dude Diego Hernández. Call it capital murder and say they wanna give me the needle. I read my name. Travis Runnels. I like the way it look, big heavy black letters.

"Way it is," I say.

"For now. We'll see what the jury says."

"What about a deal?"

She shake her head, not askin' how come I want a deal if I'm innocent. "No way," she say. "The DA is running for re-election."

I seen his ads on TV. Kevin Watts. He say vote for me 'cause I lock the niggas up. And the man a brother.

"What if I'm convicted?"

"You appeal. If you get the death penalty, the appeals can last ten to twelve years. Even if you lose, at least you win for a while."

"Can I win an appeal?"

"Depends on what happens at trial. If the judge screws up or I screw up, you might get a new trial."

"Whuju mean, if you screw up?"

"The Constitution guarantees you the right to effective assistance of counsel. I don't have to be perfect or the best. I can make mistakes, but I have to be just good enough that you get a fair trial."

"What's your track record?"

She take a deep breath, look at me hard. "I lose most of the time."

"How come?"

"Most of my clients are guilty."

"I'm innocent."

"Of course you are."

She don't smile or nuthin'. Girl's a fuckin' puzzle.

"Ain't you afraid you get me off, I go out and do it again? If I done it in the first place."

"I have nightmares about that," she say, sittin' across from me, lookin' at my file. She put the papers down. "On the other hand, if you go to prison, you might kill someone inside just because he looks at you the wrong way. Or you might get shanked in the shower because you're not in love with someone who's in love with you. There's a lot that can happen in your life I can't do a damn thing about, but this case isn't one of them."

She say all the right shit, but that don't mean she can get it done. "You jus a PD. What chance I got wit you?"

"Your only chance. The State has a witness that will testify you threatened to kill Diego Hernández before he was found carved up like a Christmas goose. The cops found a knife and Diego's blood in your car when they picked you up at your mother's house. Plus, you've already done time for armed robbery and manslaughter that was pled down from murder two."

I lean back in my chair, lift the front legs off the floor, rock back and forth like that shit don't mean nuthin'. "I hear all that. You got a job to do. You jus wanna know how hard it gonna be."

She puts her hands on the table, gets in my face, her eyes on fire. "That's right, Travis. I want to know how hard it's going to be to save your life."

I put my chair down. Stand so she lookin' up at me. "Like I tole you. Every day is a knife fight."

———

I MEET WITH Elisabeth the night before the trial. She give me a hundred-dollar suit to wear so I don't look like I'm guilty wearin' prison clothes.

Then she say the first thing gonna happen tomorrow is the lawyers pick the jury. She say she gonna tell the jury she only want people who can be fair, but she tell me she only wants jurors who don't trust cops and will feel sorry for a brother that was abused when he was a kid and never caught a break. Most of all, she say, she want jurors who don't like the death penalty.

"So you gonna lie to the jury."

She wearin' honey-colored glasses halfway down her nose, make her face soft. She take 'em off. Her eyes are dark gray and she got bags under 'em color of wet newspaper.

"It's not a lie," she say. "It's how I define fair."

I put my hands up. "You gotta lie, I can respect that."

She don't argue, jus act like she don't hear me.

"The jury wants to know what happened," she say. "If I can create reasonable doubt in their minds about the DA's version, you've got a chance."

"How you gonna do that?"

"You say you were at your mother's when Diego was killed. She backs you up. It's a lousy alibi, because everyone knows a mother will lie to save her child. But if the jury likes your mother, they might buy it."

I think about what she say.

"My momma a good woman even if she like her wine too much. Can't nobody not like her."

"Well then, I'll have to talk with her and make certain she hasn't been liking her wine too much when she testifies."

———

ELISABETH LEAN OVER to me after the judge swear in the jury, so close I can smell her. Soap. No perfume. She say the jury okay, but she say it the way I say, *Good evenin', Officer, nice to see you.* Seven women, five men. Four black, six white. Two Mexican. I look at them. They look away.

Kevin Watts, the DA, make his openin' statement to the jury. Brother talks whiter than Jay Leno. Wears a suit cost ten times the one I'm wearin'. Calls me a drug dealer. Says I cut Diego on account he don't pay me for some crack I sell him. Says I didn't jus cut him. Says I tortured him, cut out his eyes, and cut off his dick. That's why he say I deserve the needle. Makes me a bad motherfucker if I done it, that's for damn sure. I ain't sayin' I did or I didn't, but man don't pay, man gets cut. Way it is.

Elisabeth, she tell the jury the DA got no proof I done nuthin'. She say everythin' circumstantial and I got an alibi. My momma gonna testify I was watchin' TV at her house when Diego got hisself murdered. She don't talk as long as Watts, and she don't get worked up like he did neither. I was on the jury, I ain't believin' her. Girl sure as hell not perfect or the best.

The judge a white guy, no chin and no hair, tell the jury what the lawyers say ain't evidence. Then why he let them tell the jury anythin'? Don't make no sense.

The courtroom's cold. I rub my hands, keep 'em warm. Elisabeth whisper at me to stop, say it make me look nervous. The judge say he keep it cold so nobody fall asleep. The jury laughs like it'd be funny they fall asleep tryin' to decide if I get the needle. He tells them bring a sweater. I'm shiverin' in my suit. I look at the jury. They see me shake. Elisabeth puts her hand on my arm. I'm still cold, but I quit shiverin'. That's all that happens the first day. I go back to my cell, but I don't sleep.

———

NEXT DAY, ELISABETH make me stand when the jury and the judge come in the courtroom. Them jurors tuggin' on their sweaters makin' sure the judge notice, all of them smilin' and laughin' like they havin' a party.

Elisabeth say we stand out of respect whenever the judge and the jury come or go. I ain't got no fuckin' respect for people what gonna decide if I live or die and all they care about is what they wearin'. Ain't none of them fuckin' know who I am or what I'm about. They got the power and Elisabeth she got to play their game, but that don't mean I got to respect they shit.

Fred Barton be the detective on the case. He a fat fuck, his collar squeezin' his head till it swole up like a thumb somebody done hit wit a hammer. Him and the DA got they shit together playin' patty cake wit the questions. Barton he all about how Diego all cut up, the DA showin' the jury pictures of the holes in Diego's head where his eyes used to be and another close-up of the man's dick lyin' on the floor all bloody. Elisabeth she object like it her dick the jury lookin' at, but the judge tell her overruled and take a seat.

I watch the jury. Couple them white guys gettin' red, the women swallowin' hard like they gonna puke. I already seen the pictures. They bad, but I seen worse.

Barton go on sayin' how Diego was under investigation for sellin' drugs, mostly crack, and that I was the one what was sellin' the shit to Diego. Elisabeth, she take a piece out of Barton, walkin' around the courtroom like she own it, askin' him questions.

"Detective Barton, did you find any drugs on Mr. Hernández's body?"

"Yes, ma'am, we did. Several rocks of crack cocaine."

"Whose label was on them?"

Barton, he look at her like she crazy. "Street drugs don't have labels on them," he say.

"Well then," Elisabeth say, "was anybody's name on those drugs?"

"No."

"How about a receipt? Did you find a receipt or a canceled check or a credit card record showing who paid for those drugs?"

"No. That's not the way these things work."

"Of course they don't, Detective. Drug dealers don't operate like Wal-Mart. Everyone knows that. So you must have found some other physical evidence that proved my client sold those drugs or any drugs to Mr. Hernández."

Barton took a deep breath, looked over at the DA. "No, ma'am. We didn't."

"What? No photographs? No wiretaps? No fingerprints?"

"No."

"But you testified that the defendant sold drugs to Mr. Hernández and that my client murdered him when Mr. Hernández didn't pay for the drugs, isn't that right?"

"That was my testimony."

"And you told the jury that you relied on a paid informant who was part of Mr. Hernández's drug ring who told you that story about my client?"

Another deep breath. Motherfucker keep suckin' air he gonna blow up like a goddamn birthday balloon. "That's correct."

"And that paid informant, who previously did time in prison for assault with a deadly weapon and who the district attorney gave a get-out-of-jail-free card in return for his testimony, is the only source of evidence you have that Travis Runnels sold drugs to Mr. Hernández. Isn't that correct?"

"Yes, ma'am."

"And that paid informant is also the only witness who told you that my client threatened to kill Mr. Hernández. True?"

"True," Barton say, lettin' the air out like he an old grandpa can't breathe.

"And if that paid informant hadn't made such a sweet deal with the district attorney, he'd be on trial for selling drugs. True?"

"I don't know. I don't make those decisions."

"No, you don't, Detective. You just ignored his crimes and arrested my client instead. Nothing further."

Elisabeth sit back down. "How'd you like that knife fight?" she say out of the corner of her mouth.

"That's what I'm talkin' about," I say, sittin' high and feelin' fine. My girl kills.

Luis Pillco testify next. Pillco be the rat, a skinny dude got greased-back hair, no meat on him, jumpy like he lookin' to get fixed up. The DA take him through his paces. I don't look at him. Elisabeth, she eye Luis like he her next meal, squirmin' around in her chair, ready to jump his ass soon as Watts let go.

"Mr. Pillco, can you identify the man you heard threaten to kill Diego Hernández?" Watts ask Luis.

"That's him."

"Let the record show that the witness is pointing at the defendant, Travis Runnels," Watts say. "Had you met the defendant at some point prior to when he made that threat?"

"Yeah. Him and Diego and me, we was all in prison together. He was dealin' back then too, inside the joint."

Elisabeth shoot out of her chair so fast I thought she gonna land in the judge's lap. She come down in front of the bench, the judge coverin' his microphone wit his hand while the lawyers whispered, veins in Elisabeth's neck poppin' out her skin, Watts all silky. Elisabeth walk back to our table, her chin up, her hard eyes givin' me a beat-down.

"Objection overruled," the judge say.

"What do you mean, Mr. Pillco," Watts say to the rat, "that the defendant was dealing?"

"He was the man to see you needed to get fixed up. Pills mostly."

"Did the defendant tell you why he was in prison?"

"Yeah. Some dude stiffed him, so Travis say he cut him. Dude died. Travis made a real point of tellin' that story. Said man don't pay, man get cut. Way it is."

I feel the jurors' eyes on me, drillin' holes in my back. Elisabeth, she go stiff, makin' notes on her legal pad, keep from lookin' at me. There's a seal on the wall behind the judge's chair, a picture of an eagle, wings spread and arrows in its claws. I jus stare at that big bird, wonder what it be like to swoop down from the sky and rip a rat to shreds.

"That's it for today," the judge say. "We'll reconvene tomorrow morning at nine."

———

ELISABETH COME SEE me before court start. We in a witness room. A couple of chairs. No windows. Smell like old flop. She don't sit, so I don't sit.

"Travis," she say, "have you seen anyone in the courtroom you recognize, not counting your old prison buddy Luis Pillco?"

"I ain't seen nobody."

"What about your father?"

"Shit, I never met him. Wouldn't know if he was there or not."

"Sisters or brothers?"

"Sister live in St. Louis. My brother got hisself killed ten years ago."

"Friends?"

I shake my head. Don't have to tell her I ain't got any, none what would stand by me unless they was gettin' well doin' it.

"Your mother is a witness, so the judge won't let her in the courtroom until she testifies. Which means that I'm the only one in there who gives a rat's ass what happens to you. Luis Pillco kicked us in the nuts yesterday, and there wasn't a damn thing

I could do about it because you didn't tell me that you'd been in prison with him. Now the jury knows you were connected to Diego Hernández, that you are a drug dealer and you cut people who don't pay you. If you want this to be a knife fight, you can't take the knife out of my hand and let the DA stick one in your back at the same time. If there's anything else I need to know, this would be the time to tell me."

"What Luis say in court stay between me and Luis. We work it out another time."

"That's it?"

"That's it." Then it hit me. "How come you didn't know what Luis gonna say? You tole me the DA has to give you a list of witnesses and that you gonna talk to all of 'em."

Girl goes all red on me. "I've got a lot of cases. Wouldn't have mattered anyway. The judge was going to let him testify."

She leave me there waitin' for the sheriff's deputy to take me into the courtroom, wonderin' how close to jus good enough she gonna be.

————

Brenda Rudner in charge of the police crime lab. She say the cops found a knife hidden under the seat in my car. Say it had the kind of blade used to cut Diego. Say she trace the knife to the manufacturer, who tell her they sold it to a sporting-goods store in my neighborhood but the store got no record who they sold it to. Then she show pictures of bloodstains they found in my car and hold up charts showing the blood come from Diego.

Elisabeth take her time gettin' out of her chair, shufflin' her papers like she lookin' for somethin' 'cept I can tell it all for show, 'cause her eyes on me and not them papers.

"Ms. Rudner," she say, "whose fingerprints did you find on the knife that was recovered from my client's car?"

"We were unable to identify any prints."

"Are you telling the jury you found fingerprints on the knife but you couldn't tell whose they were?"

Rudner clear her throat like she know her foot in it. "Not exactly."

"Unfortunately, we need exactly. You see, the State wants to kill my client. So exactly would be very helpful. Did you exactly find any fingerprints on the knife?"

"No, we didn't."

"No smudges, swirls, partials, or latents?"

"No. Nothing."

"How do you explain that?"

"Someone wiped off any fingerprints that were there."

"Who?"

"I don't know."

"Did you find any blood, tissue, or DNA material on that knife?"

"No."

"Do you have any proof that my client ever touched that knife?"

"No."

"Did you examine the clothing my client was wearing when he was arrested?"

"Yes."

"Did you find any blood, tissue, or DNA belonging to the decedent?"

"No."

"What about the rest of his clothes. Did you examine them?"

"Yes. We didn't find anything that linked his clothing to this crime."

"Did you find any blood, tissue, or DNA belonging to my client on the decedent?"

"No."

"Given the bloody nature of this crime, do you find that unusual?"

"Not if the decedent didn't struggle."

"Are you telling the jury that the decedent did not struggle? That he offered no resistance while someone was stabbing and mutilating him?"

She crossed her arms, puttin' up her own fight. "It's reasonable to assume he struggled, at least at first."

"And even if the decedent didn't struggle, the killer had to have made contact with the decedent's skin when he gouged out the decedent's eyes and amputated the decedent's penis. True?"

"That's likely."

"And yet you found no physical evidence that Travis Runnels had any contact with the decedent's body. Isn't that also true?"

"It is."

"You inspected my client's car?"

Rudner lean back in the witness stand, glad to be talkin' about somethin' else. "I did."

"Inside and out?"

"Well, I didn't take it for a drive, if that's what you mean, Counselor."

"How about the door locks? Did you try them?"

Rudner squinted her eyes. She thumbed through her file. "No, I didn't. There was no need. The car was unlocked."

"Precisely. When the police found the car it was unlocked." Elisabeth give her a paper. "I'm handing you what has been admitted into evidence as People's Exhibit Six. This is a copy of Detective Barton's report. I direct your attention to the third page of the report. Please read the portion I have highlighted."

"Okay. *Investigating officer asked Mr. Runnels for permission to search his car. Mr. Runnels consented to the search. Investigating officer asked Mr. Runnels for the keys. Mr. Runnels advised that the car was unlocked because the locks were broken. Investigating officer proceeded with search and confirmed that locks did not work.* What's your point, Counselor?"

"Well, for starters, my client cooperated fully with the investigation, which seems a bit unusual if he knew that the murder weapon and the decedent's blood were in his car. But the real point is, the killer could have planted the knife and the decedent's bloodstains in the car because it was always unlocked. Isn't that true?"

"I don't know."

"But that scenario is entirely consistent with the physical evidence, true?"

"Yes, but—"

"Thank you. You answered my question. And it's also correct that there is nothing in the physical evidence that makes your scenario more likely than my scenario. True?"

"You're asking me to speculate. I won't do that."

"I agree. You shouldn't do that when a man's life is at stake."

The coroner, Dr. Kirk Semple, testify next. He tell the jury how he figured out whoever cut Diego was right-handed, how Diego standin' up when he got cut the first time and how the one what did it was taller than Diego. I'm right-handed, taller than Diego, and I ain't stupid. Dude hurtin' me.

Elisabeth don't get out of her chair. "How tall is Luis Pillco?" she ask Dr. Semple.

The doctor's chin dropped. "I have no idea," he say.

"Fair enough. Is Luis Pillco right-handed or left-handed?"

"No one provided me with that information. I couldn't tell you."

"So neither the police nor the district attorney provided you with the information you would need to rule out Mr. Pillco as a suspect, even though he was a known criminal associate of the decedent and had served time in prison for assault with a deadly weapon. True?"

"True," he say.

I look at the jury. They lookin' at Dr. Semple, shakin' they heads. Makes me hard.

———

FOURTH DAY. MY suit already wearin' thin. Before court start, I ask Elisabeth, she think Luis killed Diego.

"I've got no idea."

"Don't you know if he right-handed and taller than Diego?"

"Couldn't tell you. I wasn't paying attention. I'm betting the jury wasn't either. If he isn't, Watts has to bring him back so the jurors can see with their own eyes. If Watts doesn't bring him back, you can bet he's right-handed and taller. Hopefully, that's the way it will break and I'll have something else to talk about in my closing argument."

Watts bring Luis back to testify he left-handed and shorter than Diego. My stomach get cold and my dick get limp. Then Watts say the People rests. The judge look at Elisabeth.

"Ms. Rosenthal," he say.

Elisabeth stand, squarin' her shoulders, lookin' taller.

"The defense calls Shaila Dewan."

Elisabeth walk to the back of the courtroom, open the door, and my momma come in wearin' her Easter dress even though it October. She a big woman, her hips swayin'. She slow down when she get to where I'm sittin'. She reach out, takes my hand, squeezin' it tight. Her eyes are red and wet and she smells like wine.

Momma get on the stand and tell her story. Elisabeth thank her. Watts stare at Momma till she can't look at him.

"You love your son?" he ask her.

"Course I do."

"Enough to lie to save his life?"

"I ain't lyin'. He was with me."

"That's not what I asked you," Watts say. "Would you lie to save your son's life?"

"He's my son."

"Do you know what will happen to your son if the jury finds him guilty of capital murder?"

"I know."

"He'll be sentenced to death and executed. Do you want that to happen to your son?"

Momma, she hold her head up. "No mother wants that."

"Any mother would try to prevent that, don't you think, even if she had to lie?"

"Any mother what loved her baby."

"Because it's a mother's job to take care of her child."

"That's right," Momma say.

"Raise him right. To know the difference between right and wrong."

"I done my best. Travis he never had no father. I took him to church, but one of them priests done him wrong. After that, he wouldn't go back. That's when he started gettin' in trouble. It wasn't his fault."

"But the incident with the priest happened years ago and you never told the church, the police, the district attorney, or anyone else about it until after your son was arrested for murder, did you?"

"I didn't want to embarrass him."

Watts look through some papers on his table. Must be what lawyers do when they want the jury to know they gettin' ready for somethin' important. Elisabeth done the same thing. Watchin' him do it makes me have to pee.

"Your son is thirty-five. How old are you?"

Momma get her back up. "I'm fifty-one."

"How old was Travis when he moved out of your house?"

"He come and go a lot."

"I'm sure he does. How old was he when he was pretty much living on his own?"

Momma roll her eyes, countin' in her head. "Seventeen."

Watts nod. "You still cook for him when he comes over?"

"I do. He likes my meatloaf."

"How about his laundry? Is he like my kids, always bringing their dirty clothes with them when they come home?"

The jurors laugh. They all got kids. "I'm his momma. He ain't too old for me to do his wash."

Elisabeth studyin' her legal pad, not writin' a word. I start prayin', but I don't think God gonna listen.

"And you did his wash the day of the murder, didn't you, ma'am?" Watts ask, all smile and teeth. Momma don't answer. "You're not going to lie about a simple thing like doing the wash, are you, ma'am?"

"I done his wash," Momma say, her hand goin' to her throat to catch the words before they got out, the wine slowin' her down till it too late.

I grip the edge of the table. Elisabeth slide her hand over and ease mine back in my lap.

Watts walk over to the witness stand, puttin' his hands on the rail between him and Momma. He a big man. Momma can't see past him. She lean over, look at me. Her eyes wide, flutterin'.

"He asked you to wash his clothes that day, didn't he?"

Momma's head down. She don't answer till the judge tell her she has to say somethin'. Then her voice so quiet the judge tell her to speak up.

"Yes," she say. "He did."

"Why did he ask you to wash his clothes?"

She wipe her eyes, keep her head down. "They was a mess."

"A mess," Watts say. "What did he have on his clothes that made them such a mess?" Momma look at me again. "You don't need to look at your son. He can't tell you what to say. Not now.

Not in front of the judge and the jury. Now there's only one thing you can do. Tell us the truth."

Momma turn toward the jury, then back at me, then she stare down at the floor. "His clothes was all bloody."

"But you couldn't get the blood out, could you?" Momma shake her head. "So you went to Travis's apartment and got him clean clothes, the clothes he was wearing when the police arrested him at your house. On the way back, you probably threw his bloody clothes in a Dumpster. Am I right?"

Momma cryin' now, snot runnin' out her nose. "He's all I got. He's my baby."

Goddamn Momma and her wine.

———

It take two hours for the jury to find me guilty of capital murder. Only reason it take so long, the bailiff tole me, was on account of the jury wantin' to stay long enough so the county had to pay for they lunch.

Elisabeth come see me two days later wearin' a blood-red dress showin' a shape I didn't know she had. First time I seen any color in her or on her wasn't black or gray. Girl had a glow. We was back in the room at the jail where prisoners and lawyers talk. Asked me how they treatin' me.

"Better than you did," I say.

She shrug her shoulders. "I don't blame you for being angry, but it was a tough case. I did the best I could."

"Bullshit. You did what you said you had to do. Jus good enough to get my ass convicted."

She cross her arms, leanin' against the wall. "If I recall, Travis, you were the one who didn't tell me that you'd bragged to Luis Pillco how you'd cut someone who hadn't paid you."

"And you the one who say she got too many cases to go talk to Luis even though the DA tole you he their whole case."

She nodded, walked over to the table in the middle of the room. "I should have talked to Luis, but it wouldn't have mattered. The judge would have let him testify anyway."

"That's what you tole me, but one thing I learned on the street, it don't matter what you say so much as how you say it. You actin' so surprised and mad 'bout what Luis say make me look worse than Luis done. Make it look like I didn't tell you."

"I was surprised because you didn't tell me," she say. She sit down at the table, runnin' her fingers over the initials prisoners done carved on it.

"Ain't what Luis say."

She stop runnin' her fingers. "You're locked up. Luis is on the street. You couldn't know that."

"But you ain't denyin' it. One of my boys gone see Luis. He say you talked to him, knew what he was gonna say."

"Then you can't be angry with me for not talking to him," she say, smilin' like she beggin' me to smack her.

"Then all that shit about was Luis taller than Diego and was he right-handed, that was all an act. Shit! You knew he wasn't 'cause you talked to him. That boy was my only out. The jury mighta decided he the one cut Diego, but you made sure that the DA brung him back so the jury see I the only one what coulda done it."

"I took a chance," she say. "It didn't work."

"That the way it is?"

"That's the way it is."

I let that sit. Pull my chair around close to her; let her smell the jail on me. She start to get up. I grab her arm, see sweat poppin' above her lip. I talk low to her.

"My momma come see me yesterday. She say you come over to her house the night before she testified."

"That's right. I had to get her ready for her testimony."

"That why you brought her those bottles of wine?"

Elisabeth's eyes get wide lookin' at her arm turnin' red where I'm squeezin' her. Then she look at the door where the guard s'posed to be watchin' us, 'cept I facin' her and got my back to the door. No way he can see what I'm doin' and she know the guard ain't allowed to listen to what we sayin'.

She cough like somethin' stuck in her throat. "I thought we were going to win. I told her to save it until after the trial for a celebration."

I put my face right next to hers. "Now, I tole you my momma like her wine too much. You knew she'd have them bottles empty 'fore she ever open her mouth in that courtroom."

She yank on her arm. I let her go, keep her from screamin'. Now she sit back in her chair, squintin' at me like she tryin' to figure out how smart a nigga I am.

"Why would I want your mother to be drunk when she testified?"

I get out my chair, shove it against the table. "Damn bitch! I ain't no dumb ass! You made sure that jury found me guilty."

She get up and move for the door. I cut her off, back her up again.

"If you think it's my fault, you can appeal on the grounds of ineffective assistance of counsel, just like I told you before."

I ball my fist, cock my arm, but I don't let fly. "I asked you what chance I had and you say you my only chance, 'cept you don't tell me you gonna steal it from me. I scare you enough you do all that?"

Her face start quiverin', her eyes all wet, then hard. "Yes, Travis. You scared me that much. The DA had a good case on paper, but it had holes. They had no physical evidence to tie you to the murder, and Luis's criminal record and the deal the DA gave him made him a vulnerable witness."

"You coulda let him take the fall instead of me."

"I could have, except he was innocent and he wasn't my client. You were guilty. I couldn't take the chance that you'd get off."

"Why you do me like that? You ain't supposed to judge me. You supposed to be my lawyer."

She turn away from me. I put my hand on her shoulder, spin her back around. She slap my hand away.

"A few years ago, I won a case for someone just like you, and a month later he slaughtered the guy who testified against him, along with his wife and kids. That's when I said no more nightmares. I stopped caring about who I represented. You'll die in prison and I won't lose any sleep."

"I'll get a new lawyer. Tell him what you tole me."

She let out a sigh. "Of course you will. I'll be called to testify and I'll lie and the judge and jury will believe me, not you."

The door open and two deputies come in, the DA followin' right behind them. Elisabeth she look at me, her mouth open wide enough for my whole fist, but I don't swing at her.

"Your client authorized us to tape your conversation," the DA say.

"Like I tole you," I say to Elisabeth, "every day is a knife fight."

DEATH, CHEATED

BY JAMES GRIPPANDO

The doctor told me I have two years to live," she said. "Three, tops."

My mouth fell open, but words came slowly. "Damn, Jessie. I'm so sorry."

It wasn't the kind of news you expected to hear from a woman who had only recently celebrated her thirtieth birthday.

It had been six years since I'd last laid eyes on Jessie Merrill. The split had been awkward. Five months after dumping me, Jessie had called for lunch with the hope of giving it another try. By then I was well on my way toward falling hopelessly in love with Cindy Paige, now Mrs. Jack Swyteck—something I never called her unless I wanted to be introduced at cocktail parties as Mr. Cindy Paige. Cindy was more beautiful today than she was then, and I had to admit the same was true of Jessie. That, of course, was no reason to become her lawyer. But it was no reason to turn her away, either. This had nothing to do with the fact that her long auburn hair had once splayed across my pillow. She'd come to me as an old friend in a genuine crisis—and at the moment, she seemed to be on the verge of tears.

I rifled through my desk drawer in search of a tissue. She dug one from her purse.

"It's so hard for me to talk about this," she said.

"I understand."

"I was so damn unprepared for that kind of news."

"Who wouldn't be?"

"I take care of myself. I always have."

"It shows." It wasn't intended as a come-on, just a statement of fact that underscored what a waste this was.

"My first thought was *You're crazy, Doc. This can't be.*"

"Of course."

"I mean, I've never faced anything that I couldn't beat. Then suddenly I'm in the office of some doctor who's basically telling me, 'That's it, game over.' No one bothered to tell me the game had even started."

I could hear the anger in her voice. "I'd be mad, too."

"I was furious. And scared. Especially when he told me what I had."

I didn't ask. I figured she'd tell me, if she wanted me to know.

"He said I had ALS—amyotrophic lateral sclerosis."

"I'm not familiar with that one."

"You probably know it as Lou Gehrig's disease."

"Oh." It was a more ominous-sounding "oh" than intended. She immediately picked up on it.

"So, you know what a horrible illness it is."

"Just from what I heard happened to Lou Gehrig."

"Imagine how it feels to hear that it's going to happen to you. Your mind stays healthy, but your nervous system slowly dies, causing you to lose control of your own body. Eventually your throat muscles fail, you can't swallow anymore, and you either suffocate or choke to death on your own tongue."

She was looking straight at me, and I was the one to blink.

"It's always fatal," she added. "Usually in two to five years."

I wasn't sure what to say. The silence was getting uncomfortable. "I don't know how I can help, but if there's anything I can do, just name it."

"There is."

"Please don't be afraid to ask."

"I'm being sued."

"For what?"

"A million and a half dollars."

I did a double take. "That's a lot of money."

"It's all the money I have in the world."

"Funny," I said. "There was a time when you and I would have thought that *was* all the money in the world."

Her smile was more sad than wistful. "Things change."

"They sure do."

A silence fell between us, an unscripted moment to reminisce.

"Anyway, here's my problem. My *legal* problem. I tried to be responsible about my illness. The first thing I did was get my finances in order. Treatment's expensive, and I wanted to do something extravagant for myself in the time I had left. Maybe a trip to Europe, whatever. I didn't have a lot of money, but I did have a three-million-dollar life insurance policy."

"Why so much?"

"When the stock market tanked a couple years ago, a financial planner talked me into believing that whole-life insurance was a good retirement vehicle. Maybe it would have been worth something by the time I reached sixty-five. But at my age, the cash surrender value is practically zilch. Obviously the death benefit wouldn't kick in until I was dead, which didn't do *me* any good. I wanted a pot of money while I was alive and well enough to enjoy myself."

I nodded, seeing where this was headed. "You did a viatical settlement?"

"You've heard of them?"

"I had a friend with AIDS who did one before he died."

"That's how they got popular, back in the eighties. But the concept works with any terminal disease."

"Is it a done deal?"

"Yes. It sounded like a win-win situation. I sell my three-million-dollar policy to a group of investors for a million and a half dollars. I get a big check right now, when I can use it. They get the three-million-dollar death benefit when I die. They'd basically double their money in two or three years."

"It's a little ghoulish, but I can see the good in it."

"Absolutely. Everybody was satisfied." The sorrow seemed to drain from her expression as she looked at me and said, "Until my symptoms started to disappear."

"Disappear?"

"Yeah. I started getting better."

"But there's no cure for ALS."

"The doctor ran more tests."

I saw a glimmer in her eye. My heart beat faster. "And?"

"They finally figured out I had lead poisoning. It can mimic the symptoms of ALS, but it wasn't nearly enough to kill me."

"You don't have Lou Gehrig's disease?" I said, hopeful.

"No."

"You're not going to die?"

"I'm completely recovered."

A sense of joy washed over me, though I did feel a little manipulated. "Thank God. But why didn't you tell me from the get-go?"

She smiled wryly, then turned serious. "I thought you should know how I felt, even if it was just for a few minutes. This sense of being on the fast track to such an awful death."

"It worked."

"Good. Because I have quite a battle on my hands, legally speaking."

"You want to sue the quack who got the diagnosis wrong?"

"Like I said, at the moment I'm the one being sued over this."

"The viatical investors?" I said.

"You got it. They thought they were coming into three million in at most five years. Turns out they may have to wait another forty or fifty years for their investment to 'mature,' so to speak. They want their million and a half bucks back."

"Them's the breaks."

She smiled. "So you'll take the case?"

I was suddenly thinking about Cindy. Wives and old girl-friends didn't always mix. "I'll need to think about that," I said.

"Don't think too long," she said. "I fired my old lawyer yesterday."

"When does the trial start?"

"Two days ago. Tomorrow's the final day."

"You fired your lawyer in the middle of trial?"

It seemed almost corny, but I could have sworn that she'd batted her eyes. "All's well that ends well, right, Jack? Are you on board or not?"

———

THE TRIAL WAS in Courtroom 9 of the Miami-Dade court-house, and for the life of me, I couldn't understand why Jessie had been unhappy with her first lawyer. The case was shaping up as a slam-bang winner, the judge had been spitting venom at opposing counsel the entire trial, and the client was a gorgeous redhead who'd once ripped my heart right out of my chest and stomped that sucker flat.

Well, two out of three wasn't bad.

"All rise!"

The lunch break was over, and the lawyers and litigants rose as Judge Antonio García approached the bench. The judge glanced in our direction, as if he couldn't help gathering another eyeful of my client. No surprise there. Jessie wasn't stunningly beautiful, but she was damn close. She carried herself with a confidence that bespoke intelligence, tempered by intermittent moments of apparent vulnerability that made her simply irresistible to the knuckle-dragging, testosterone-toting half of the population. Judge García was as susceptible as the next guy. Beneath that flowing black robe was, after all, a mere mortal—a man. That aside, Jessie was a victim in this case, and it was impossible not to feel sorry for her.

"Good afternoon," said the judge.

"Good afternoon," the lawyers replied, though the judge's nose was buried in paperwork. Rather than immediately call in the jury, it was Judge García's custom to mount the bench and then take a few minutes to read his mail or finish the crossword puzzle—his way of announcing to all who entered his courtroom that he alone had that rare and special power to silence attorneys and make them sit and wait. Judicial power plays of all sorts seemed to be on the rise in Miami courtrooms, ever since hometown hero Marilyn Melian gave up her day job to star on *The People's Court*. Not every South Florida judge wanted to trace her steps to television stardom, but at least one wannabe in criminal court had taken to encouraging plea bargains by asking, "Deal or no deal?"

I glanced to my left and noticed my client's hand shaking. It stopped the moment she caught me looking. Typical Jessie, never wanting anyone to know she was nervous.

"We're almost home," I whispered.

She gave me a tight smile. I knew that smile—before I was married. I fought the impulse to let my mind go there.

The crack of the gavel stirred me from my thoughts. The jury had returned. Judge García had finished perusing his mail, the sports section, or whatever else had caught his attention. Court was back in session.

"Mr. Swyteck, any questions for Dr. Herna?"

I glanced toward the witness stand. Dr. Herna was the physician who'd reviewed Jessie's medical history on behalf of the viatical investors and confirmed the original diagnosis, giving them the green light to invest. He and the investors' lawyer had spent the entire morning trying to convince the jury that, because Jessie didn't actually have ALS, the viatical settlement should be invalidated on the basis of a "mutual mistake." It was my job to prove it was *their* mistake, nothing mutual about it, too bad, so sad.

I could hardly wait.

"Yes, Your Honor," I said, as I approached the witness with a thin, confident smile. "I promise this won't take long."

The courtroom was silent. It was the pivotal moment in the trial, my cross-examination of the plaintiff's star witness. The jury looked on attentively—whites, blacks, Hispanics, a cross-section of Miami. Anyone who wondered if an ethnically diverse community could possibly work together should serve on a jury. The case of *Viatical Solutions, Inc. v. Jessie Merrill* was like dozens of other trials under way in Miami at that very moment—no media, no protestors, no circus ringmaster. It was reassuring to know that the administration of justice in Florida wasn't always the joke people saw on television.

Reassuring for me, anyway. Staring out from the witness stand, Dr. Felix Herna looked anything but calm. My opposing counsel seemed to sense the doctor's anxiety. Parker Aimes was a savvy-enough plaintiffs' attorney to sprint to his feet and do something about it.

"Judge, could we have a five-minute break, please?"

"We just got back from lunch," he said, snarling.

"I know but—"

"But nothing," the judge said, peering out over the top of his wire-rimmed reading glasses. "Counselor, I just checked my horoscope, and it says there's loads of leisure time in my near future. So, Mr. Swyteck, if you please."

With the judge talking astrology, I was beginning to re-think my restored faith in the justice system. "Thank you, Your Honor."

All eyes of the jurors followed as I approached the witness. I planted myself firmly, using height and body language to convey a trial lawyer's greatest tool: control.

"Dr. Herna, you'll agree with me that ALS is a serious disease, won't you?"

He shifted nervously, as if distrustful of even the most innocuous question. "Of course."

"It attacks the nervous system, breaks down the tissues, kills the motor neurons?"

"That's correct."

"Victims eventually lose the ability to control their legs?"

"Yes."

"Their hands and arms as well?"

"Yes."

"Their abdominal muscles?"

"That's correct, yes. It destroys the neurons that control the body's voluntary muscles. Muscles controlled by conscious thought."

"Speech becomes unclear? Eating and swallowing become difficult?"

"Yes."

"Breathing may become impossible?"

"It does affect the tongue and pharyngeal muscles. Eventually, all victims must choose between prolonging their life on a ventilator or asphyxiation."

"Suffocation," I said. "Not a very pleasant way to die."

"Death is rarely pleasant, Mr. Swyteck."

"Unless you're a viatical investor."

A juror nodded with agreement.

"Objection."

"Uh," said the judge, "sustained."

I moved on, knowing I'd tweaked the opposition. "Is it fair to say that once ALS starts, there's no way to stop it?"

"Miracles may happen, but the basic assumption in the medical community is that the disease is fatal, its progression relentless. Fifty percent of people die within two years. Eighty percent within five."

"Sounds like an ideal scenario for a viatical settlement," I said.

"Objection."

"I'll rephrase it. True or false, Doctor: The basic assumption of viatical investors is that the patient will die soon."

He looked at me as if the question were ridiculous. "Of course that's true. That's how they make their money."

"You'd agree, then, that a proper diagnosis is a key component of the investment decision?"

"True again."

"That's why the investors hired you, isn't it? They relied on *you* to confirm that Ms. Merrill had ALS."

"They hired me to review her doctor's diagnosis."

"How many times did you physically examine her?"

"None."

"How many times did you meet with her?"

"None."

"How many times did you speak with her?"

"None," he said, his tone defensive. "You're making this sound worse than it really was. The reviewing physician in a viatical settlement rarely if ever examines the patient. It was my job to review Ms. Merrill's medical history as presented to me by her treating physician. I then made a determination as to whether the diagnosis was based on sound medical judgment."

"So you were fully aware that Dr. Marsh's diagnosis was 'clinically possible ALS.'"

"Yes."

"*Possible* ALS," I repeated, making sure the judge and jury caught it. "Which means that it could possibly be something else."

"Her symptoms, though minor, were entirely consistent with the early stages of the disease."

"But the very diagnosis—possible ALS—made it clear that it could be something other than ALS. And you knew that."

The doctor was wringing his hands. "You have to understand that there's no magic bullet, no single test to determine whether a patient has ALS. The diagnosis is in many ways a process of elimination. A series of tests are run over a period of months to rule out other possible illnesses. In the early stages, a seemingly healthy woman like Jessie Merrill could have ALS and have no idea that anything's seriously wrong with her body, apart from the fact that maybe her foot falls asleep, or she fumbles with her car keys, or is having difficulty swallowing."

"You're not suggesting that your investors plunked down a million and a half dollars based solely on the fact that Ms. Merrill was dropping her car keys."

"No."

"In fact, your investors rejected the investment proposal at first, didn't they?"

"An investment based on a diagnosis of clinically possible ALS was deemed too risky."

"They decided to invest only *after* you spoke with Dr. Marsh, correct?"

"I did speak with him."

I gestured toward the jury, as if inviting them into the conversation. "Would you share with the jury Dr. Marsh's exact words, please?"

Even the judge looked up, his interest sufficiently piqued. Dr. Herna shifted his weight again, obviously reluctant.

"Let me say at the outset that Dr. Marsh is one of the most respected neurologists in Florida. I knew that his diagnosis of clinically possible ALS was based upon strict adherence to the diagnostic criteria established by the World Federation of Neurology. But I also knew that he was an experienced physician who had seen more cases of ALS than just about any other doctor in Miami. So I asked him to put the strict criteria aside. I asked him to talk to me straight but off the record: Did he think Jessie Merrill had ALS?"

"I'll ask the question again: What did Dr. Marsh tell you?"

Herna looked at his lawyer, then at me, and said, "He told me that if he were a betting man, he'd bet on ALS."

"As it turns out, Ms. Merrill didn't have ALS, did she?"

"Obviously not. Dr. Marsh was dead wrong."

"Excuse me, Doctor. He wasn't wrong. Dr. Marsh's diagnosis was clinically *possible* ALS. You knew that he was still monitoring the patient, still conducting tests."

"I also know what he told me. He told me to bet on ALS."

"Only after you pushed him to speculate prematurely."

"As a colleague with the utmost respect for the man, I asked for his honest opinion."

"You urged him to *guess*. You pushed for an answer because Ms. Merrill was a tempting investment opportunity."

"That's not true."

"You were afraid that if you waited for a conclusive diagnosis, she'd be snatched up by another group of viatical investors."

"All I know is that Dr. Marsh said he'd bet on ALS. That was good enough for me."

I moved closer, tightening the figurative grip. "It wasn't Ms. Merrill who made the wrong diagnosis, was it?"

"No."

"As far as she knew, a horrible death was just two or three years away."

"I don't know what she was thinking."

"Yes, you do," I said sharply. "When you reviewed her medical file and coughed up a million and a half dollars to buy her life insurance policy, you became her second opinion. You convinced her that she was going to die."

He fell stone silent, as if suddenly he realized the grief he'd caused her—as if finally he understood my animosity.

I continued: "Ms. Merrill never told you she had a confirmed case of ALS, did she?"

"No."

"She never guaranteed you that she'd die in two years."

"No."

"All she did was give you her medical records."

"That's all I saw."

"And you made a professional judgment as to whether she was going to live or die."

"I did."

"And you bet on death."

"In a manner of speaking."

"You bet on ALS."

"Yes."

"And you lost."

He didn't answer. I couldn't let go.

"Doctor, you and your investors rolled the dice and lost. Isn't that what really happened here?"

He hesitated, then answered: "It didn't turn out the way we thought it would."

"Great reason to file a lawsuit."

"Objection."

"Sustained."

I didn't push it, but a little sarcasm had telegraphed to the jury the question I most wanted answered: *Don't you think this woman has been through enough without you suing her, jerk?*

"Are you finished, Mr. Swyteck?" asked Judge García.

"Yes. I think that wraps things up."

I turned away from the witness and headed back to my chair. I could see the gratitude in Jessie's eyes, but far more palpable was the dagger in my back that was Dr. Herna's angry glare.

Jessie leaned closer and whispered, "Nice work."

"Yeah," I said, fixing on the word she'd chosen. "I was entirely too *nice*."

———

JESSIE AND I were seated on the courthouse steps, casting cookie crumbs to pigeons as we awaited notification that the jury had reached a verdict.

"What do you think they'll do?" she asked.

I paused. The tiers of granite outside the Miami-Dade courthouse were the judicial equivalent of the Oracle of Delphi, where lawyers were called upon daily to hazard a wild-ass guess about a process that was ultimately unpredictable. I would have liked to tell her there was nothing to worry about, that in twenty minutes we'd be cruising toward Miami Beach, the top down on my beloved Mustang convertible, the CD player totally cranked with an obnoxiously loud version of the old hit song from the rock band Queen "We Are the Champions."

But my career had brought too many surprises to be that un-equivocal.

"I have a good feeling," I said. "But with a jury, you never know."

I savored the last bit of cream from the better half of an Oreo, then tossed the rest of the cookie to the steps below. A chorus of gray wings fluttered as hungry pigeons scurried after the treat. In seconds it was in a hundred pieces. The victors flew off into the warm, crystal-blue skies that marked February in Miami.

Jessie said, "Either way, I guess this is it."

"We might have an appeal if we lose."

"I was speaking more on a personal level." She laid her hand on my forearm and said, "You did a really great thing for me, step-ping in and taking my case in midstream. But in a few minutes it will all be over. And then I guess I'll never see you again."

"That's actually a good thing. In my experience, reuniting with an old client usually means they've been sued or indicted all over again."

"I've had my fill of that, thank you."

"I know you have."

I glanced toward the hot dog vendor on the crowded sidewalk along Flagler Street, then back at Jessie. She hadn't shifted her gaze away from me, and her hand was still resting on my fore-arm. A little too touchy-feely today. I rose and buried my hands in my pants pockets.

"Jack, there's something I want to tell you."

The conversation seemed to be drifting beyond the attorney-client relationship, and I didn't want to go there. I was her law-yer, nothing more, never mind the past.

"Before you say anything," I said, "there's something I should tell you."

"Really?" she said.

I sat on the step beside her. "I noticed that Dr. Marsh was back in the courtroom today. He's obviously concerned."

My abrupt return to law talk seemed to confuse her.

"Concerned about me, you mean?" she said.

"I'd say his exact concern is whether you plan to sue him. We haven't talked much about this, but you probably do have a case against him."

"Sue him? For what?"

"Malpractice, of course. He eventually got your diagnosis right, but not until you went through severe emotional distress. He should have targeted lead poisoning as the cause of your neurological problems much earlier than he did. Especially after you told him about the renovations to your condo. The dust that comes with sanding off old lead-based paint in houses built before 1978 is a pretty common source of lead poisoning."

"But he's the top expert in Miami."

"He's still capable of being wrong. He is human, after all."

She looked off to the middle distance. "That's the perfect word for him. He was *so* human. He took such special care of me."

"How do you mean?"

"Some doctors are ice cold, no bedside manner at all. Dr. Marsh was very sympathetic, very compassionate. It's not that common for someone under the age of forty to get ALS, and he took a genuine interest in me."

"In what way?"

"Not in the way you're thinking," she said, giving me a playful kick in the shin.

"I'm not thinking anything," I said, lying.

"I'll give you a perfect example. One of the most important tests I had was the EMG. That's the one where they hook you up to the electrodes to see if there's any nerve damage."

"I know. I saw the report."

"Yeah, but *all* you saw was the report. The actual test can be pretty scary, especially when you're worried that you might have something as awful as Lou Gehrig's disease. Most neurologists have a technician do the test. But Dr. Marsh knew how freaked out I was about this. I didn't want some technician to conduct the test, and then I'd have to wait another week for the doctor to interpret the results, and then wait another two weeks for a follow-up appointment where the results would finally be explained to me. So he ran the test himself, immediately. There aren't a lot of doctors who would do that for their patients in this world of mismanaged care."

"You're right about that."

"I could give you a dozen other examples. He's a great doctor and a real gentleman. I don't need to sue Dr. Marsh. The investors can have my three million dollars in life insurance when I die. As far as I'm concerned, a million and a half dollars is plenty for me."

I couldn't disagree. It was one more pleasant reminder that she was no longer the self-centered twenty-something-year-old of another decade. And neither was I.

"You're making the right decision," I said.

"I've made a few good ones in my lifetime," she said, her smile fading. "And a few bad ones too."

I was at a loss for the right response, and preferred to let it go. But she followed up.

"Have you ever wondered what would have happened if we hadn't broken up?"

"No."

"Liar."

"Let's not talk about that," I said.

"Why not? Isn't that just a teensy-weensy part of the reason you jumped into my case?"

"No."

"Liar."

"Stop calling me a liar," I said.

"Stop lying."

"What do you want me to say?"

She moved closer, invading my space again.

"Just answer one question for me," she said. "I want you to be completely honest. And if you are, I'll totally drop this, okay?"

"All right. One."

"If I had hired you from the beginning of this case—if you and I had been lawyer and client for six months instead of just a couple days—do you think something would have happened between us?"

"No."

"Why not?"

"That's two questions," I said.

"Why do you think nothing would have happened?"

"Because I'm married."

She flashed a thin smile, nodding knowingly. "Interesting answer."

"What's so interesting about it? That's the answer."

"Yes, but you could have said something a little different, like: 'Because I love my wife.' Instead, you said, 'Because I'm married.'"

"It comes down to the same thing."

"No. One comes from the heart. The other is just a matter of playing by the rules."

I didn't answer. Jessie had always been a smart girl, but that was perhaps the most perceptive thing I'd ever heard her say.

The digital pager vibrated on my belt. I checked it eagerly, then looked at Jessie and said, "Jury's back."

She didn't move, still waiting for me to respond in some way to her words. I just gathered myself up and said, "Can't keep the judge and jury waiting."

Without more, she rose and followed me up the courthouse steps.

———

In minutes we were back in Courtroom 9, and I could feel the butterflies swirling in my belly. This wasn't the most legally complicated case I'd ever handled, but I wanted to win it for Jessie. It had nothing to do with the fact that my client was a woman who'd once rejected me and that this was my chance to prove what a great lawyer I was. Jessie deserved to win. Period. It was that simple.

Right. Was anything ever that simple?

My client and I stood impassively at our place behind the mahogany table for the defense. Plaintiff's counsel stood alone on the other side of the courtroom, at the table closest to the jury box. His client, a corporation, hadn't bothered to send a representative for the rendering of the verdict. Perhaps they'd expected the worst, a prospect that seemed to have stimulated some public interest. A reporter from the local paper was seated in the first row, and behind her in the public gallery were other folks I didn't recognize. One face, however, was entirely familiar: Dr. Joseph Marsh, Jessie's neurologist, was standing in the rear of the courtroom.

A paddle fan wobbled overhead as the decision makers returned to the jury box in single file. Each of them looked straight ahead, sharing not a glance with either the plaintiff or the defendant. Professional jury consultants could have argued for days as to the significance of their body language—whether it was good or bad if they made eye contact with the plaintiff, the defendant, the lawyers, the judge, or no one at all. To me, it was all pop psychology, unreliable even when the foreman winked at your client and mouthed the words, *It's in the bag, baby.*

"Has the jury reached a verdict?" asked the judge.

"We have," announced the forewoman. The all-important slip of paper went from the jury box, to the bailiff, and finally to the judge. He inspected it for less than half a second, showing no reaction. "Please announce the verdict."

I felt my client's manicured fingernails digging into my biceps.

"In the case of *Viatical Solutions, Inc. v. Jessie Merrill*, we the jury find in favor of the defendant."

I suddenly found myself locked in what felt like a full-body embrace, Jessie trembling in my arms. Had I not been there to hold her, she would have fallen to the floor. A tear trickled down her cheek as she looked me in the eye and whispered, "Thank you."

"You're so welcome."

I released her, but she held me a moment longer—a little too long and too publicly, perhaps, to suit a married man. Then again, plenty of overjoyed clients had hugged me in the past, even big burly men who were homophobic to the core. Like them, Jessie had simply gotten carried away with the moment.

Right?

"Your Honor, we have a motion," said the lawyer for Viatical Solutions, Inc., as he approached the lectern. He seemed on the verge of an explosion, which was understandable. One and a half million dollars had just slipped through his fingers. Six months ago he'd written an arrogant letter to Jessie telling her that her viatical settlement wasn't worth the paper it was written on. Now Jessie was cool, and he was the fool.

God, I loved winning.

"What's your motion?" the judge asked.

Parker Aimes cleared his throat. "We ask that the court enter judgment for the plaintiff notwithstanding the verdict. The evidence does not support—"

"Save it," said the judge.

"Excuse me?"

"You heard me, Mr. Aimes." With that, Judge García unleashed a veritable tongue-lashing. He truly seemed taken with Jessie. At least a half-dozen times in the span of two minutes he derided the suit against her as "frivolous and mean-spirited." He not only denied the plaintiff's post-trial motion but he so completely clobbered them that I was beginning to wish I had invited Cindy downtown to watch.

On second thought, it was just as well that she'd missed that big hug Jessie had given me in her excitement over the verdict.

The judge leaned forward and used the friendly tone he reserved only for non-lawyers. "Ladies and gentlemen of the jury, thank you for your service. We are adjourned."

With a bang of the judge's gavel, it was all over.

Jessie was a millionaire.

"Time to celebrate," she said.

"You go right ahead. You've earned it."

"You're coming too, buster. Drinks are on me."

I checked my watch. "All right. It's early for me, but maybe a beer."

"One beer? Wimp."

"Lush."

"*Lawyer.*"

"Now you're hitting way below the belt."

We shared a smile, then headed for the exit. The courtroom had already cleared, but a small crowd was gathering at the elevator. Most had emerged from another courtroom, but I recognized a few spectators from Jessie's trial.

Among them was Dr. Marsh.

The elevator doors opened, but I tugged at Jessie's elbow. "Let's wait for the next one," I told her.

"There's room," said Jessie.

A dozen people packed into the crowded car. In all the jostling for position, a janitor and his bucket came between me and Jessie. The doors closed, and as if it were an immutable precept of universal elevator etiquette, all conversation ceased. The lighted numbers overhead marked our silent descent. The doors opened two floors down. Three passengers got out, four more got in. I kept my eyes forward but noticed that, in the shuffle, Dr. Marsh had wended his way from the back of the car to a spot directly beside Jessie.

The elevator stopped again. Another exchange of passengers, two exiting, two more getting in. I kept my place in front, near the control panel. As the doors closed, Jessie moved all the way to the far corner. Dr. Marsh managed to find an opening right beside her.

Was he actually pursuing her?

It was too crowded for me to turn around completely, but I could see Jessie and her former physician in the convex mirror in the opposite corner of the elevator. Discreetly, I kept an eye on both of them. Marsh had blown the diagnosis of ALS, but he was a smart guy. Surely he'd anticipated that Jessie would speak to her lawyer about suing him for malpractice. If it was his intention to corner Jessie in the elevator and breathe a few threatening words into her ear, I would be all over him.

No more stops. The elevator was on the express route to the lobby. I glanced at the lighted numbers above the door, then back at the mirror.

My heart nearly stopped; I couldn't believe my eyes.

It had lasted only a split second, but what I'd seen was unmistakable. Obviously, Jessie and the doctor hadn't noticed the mirror, hadn't realized that I was watching them even though they were standing behind me.

They'd locked fingers, as if holding hands, then released.

For one chilling moment, I couldn't breathe.

The elevator doors opened. I held the Door Open button to

allow the others to exit. Dr. Marsh passed without a word, without so much as looking at me. Jessie emerged last. I took her by the arm and pulled her into an alcove near the bank of pay telephones.

"What the hell did you just do in there?"

She shook free of my grip. "Nothing."

"I was watching in the mirror. I saw you and Marsh hold hands."

"Are you crazy?"

"Apparently. Crazy to have trusted you."

She shook her head, scoffing. "You're a real piece of work, you know that, Swyteck? That's what I couldn't stand when we were dating, you and your stupid jealousy."

"This has nothing to do with jealousy. You just held hands with the doctor who supposedly started this whole problem by misdiagnosing you with ALS. You owe me a damn good explanation, lady."

"We don't owe you anything."

It struck me cold, the way she'd said *we*. I was suddenly thinking of our conversation on the courthouse steps just minutes earlier, where Jessie had heaped such praise on the kind and considerate doctor.

"Now I see why Dr. Marsh performed the diagnostic tests himself," I said. "It had nothing to do with his compassion. You never had any symptoms of ALS. You never even had lead poisoning. The tests were fakes, weren't they?"

She just glared and said, "It's like I told you: we don't owe you anything."

"What do you expect me to do? Ignore what I just saw?"

"Yes. Like my first lawyer. The one I fired before I hired you. He just keeps his mouth shut. And you will, too. If you're smart."

"Is that some kind of threat?"

"Do yourself a favor, okay? Forget you ever knew me. Move on with your life."

Those were the exact words she'd used to dump me years earlier.

She started away, then stopped, as if unable to resist one more shot.

"I feel sorry for you, Swyteck. I feel sorry for anyone who goes through life just playing by the rules."

As she turned and disappeared into the crowded lobby, I felt a gaping pit in the bottom of my stomach. Ten years a trial lawyer. I'd represented thieves, swindlers, even cold-blooded murderers. I'd never claimed to be the world's smartest man, but never before had I even come close to letting this happen. The realization was sickening.

Jessie had cheated death.

Her investors.

And me.

MY BROTHER'S KEEPER

BY DANIEL J. HALE

The Pacific stretched to the horizon, smooth as velvet. Hints of jasmine wafted in the cool morning air. We glided through the meandering streets of the hushed enclave under a cloudless sky. Our shoes were whispers on the manicured pavement.

People call La Jolla paradise. For the past three years, it had been purgatory. My daily runs with this group of middle-aged megalomaniacs was the only thing that had kept me from sliding off the cliffs into hell.

We slowed to a walk as we passed the house in the crook of the Camino de la Costa. The other guys headed out to the brink of Sun Gold Point to cool down, stretch, and obsess over the market value of their portfolios. I jogged down the street toward my front gate and the long-legged blonde standing there in the black pantsuit.

The young woman turned toward me as I drew near. I stifled a gasp. I thought for a moment I was seeing a ghost.

"Hi, Uncle Robert." The voice was hauntingly familiar as well, but this was no apparition.

"Shawnie?" I hadn't seen her in over a decade, not since she was a gawky adolescent. I was shocked by how much she now resembled her mother. Like Mary Shawn in her younger years, Shawnie was a flawless beauty. I took a final step toward her. "What are you doing here?"

"You're unlisted." She let out a long breath smelling of cigarettes. Her chin began to quiver. "The number was in Daddy's cell phone, but it burned up in the fire."

Another fire? My stomach tightened into a knot. "Is Jimmy okay?"

Her eyes—her mother's big blue eyes—grew wide. "I didn't have your address, but I knew your house was on the ocean. I remembered what the place looked like from when Mama and Daddy brought me out here to see you and Aunt Elizabeth after Riley was born. I tried to find you last night, but it was too dark to tell which house was which, so I stayed in this moldy old motel on the beach and tried to get some sleep, but I couldn't sleep at all. It took half an hour to find your house this morning. Thank God you're here!" Tears trickled down her cheeks.

"Shawnie." I put my hands on her shoulders. "Tell me what happened."

"Mama's dead. Daddy's in jail."

———

SHAWNIE LOOKED OUT the window as the crowded jetliner climbed over the Pacific. The plane banked right and headed east over land. She looked at me and let out a long sigh. "I need a drink." *Just like her mother.*

Four Bloody Marys later, as if things at home were perfectly normal, she said, "I hate being packed in this plane like I'm a sardine." She pouted. "I thought you owned your own jet."

"I sold it."

"Couldn't we have flown in first class?" She looked out the window again. "Coach sucks."

I leaned back in my seat. "This is how I travel now."

I switched on the headlights as twilight faded to night. The rented Ford sedan's outside temperature indicator read 97. Condensation formed on the passenger-side window where Shawnie had pointed the air-conditioner vent away from herself, toward the glass. The heat and humidity alone would have been enough to keep me away from this part of the world. I had other reasons for vowing never to come back. But here I was, driving across the pine-infested river flats dressed in the suit I'd worn to Elizabeth and Riley's funeral . . . three years ago to the day.

The paper mill's sulfur reek began seeping through the vents.

"Wake up, Shawnie. We're almost there."

She checked her face in the mirror. I didn't understand why she bothered. She didn't wear makeup, didn't need it.

We drove through town, passing the Wal-Mart and the crumbling red-brick storefronts and the corrugated-metal structures. It could have been any one of a thousand other small Southern towns. I wished it were.

I wheeled the black sedan into a parking space outside a seventies-era concrete building with vertical-slit windows. "You stay here. I'll leave the engine running so you can keep the air conditioner on."

"You're gonna get him out of there, aren't you?" Shawnie's voice was so much like her mother's; if I'd had my eyes closed, I could have easily imagined it was Mary Shawn sitting in the car with me. "I mean, you have to get him out of there."

"I can't, Shawnie. Not tonight, anyway."

"I thought you were supposed to be one of the most high-powered lawyers in the country."

The taunt in her voice set me on edge the same way her mother's had. I wanted to snap at her, to tell her how ungrateful she was, but I'd learned my lesson long ago. I kept my cool.

"Sweetheart"—I smiled—"Jimmy's my brother. I want him out of there, too, but I'm no Houdini."

She shot me a puzzled look. "Who's Houdini?"

I just shook my head. "I haven't practiced law in three years, and I was never a criminal attorney." I switched off the Ford's headlights. "I know a good defense lawyer in Little Rock. I called him from the San Diego Airport while you were outside the terminal building sneaking that last cigarette. He'll be here day after tomorrow. I'll do what I can for Jimmy until then." I grabbed my suit coat and left the engine running. "Lock the doors after I get out."

The concrete was gritty under the hard leather soles of the shoes I hadn't worn since the graveside service. The distance from the car to the building was thirty yards at most, but it was so muggy I wanted to take off my jacket halfway down the sidewalk.

A middle-aged woman with frizzy hair looked up from behind the counter when I walked in the door. "Robert Hicks!" She bared her bad teeth. "You haven't changed a bit since the day we graduated."

If we'd gone to high school together, she couldn't have been more than forty-three. She looked like she was in her mid-fifties. I had no memory of her. I smiled and slipped into the drawl of my childhood. "Well, aren't you a sight for sore eyes!"

"Oh, I'm a godawful mess. Have been ever since Kenny Earl stole my savings and left me with the grandbabies and run off to Houston. I had to get me a second job at the E-Z Mart just to make ends meet."

I had no idea who Kenny Earl was. "Kenny Earl ain't worth spit."

"I swear, Robert, you're even better-looking now than you were senior year. Every girl in our class had a big ol' . . ." Her expression turned serious. "I'm sure sorry about your wife and son. That was just plain horrible news."

"That's very kind of you to say."

"What's it been now? Three years?"

I nodded.

"I'm sorry about your brother too."

"Speaking of Jimmy . . ." I loosened my tie, undid the top button, and leaned over the counter. "I know it's awful late, but could you get me in to see him?" I winked. "Please?"

Her yellow smile gave me my answer.

———

A POTBELLIED DEPUTY who said we'd played on the same Little League team showed me into a windowless room. Four tan plastic chairs circled a scratched Formica table. The overhead fluorescents emitted an annoying buzz. A large no-smoking sign dominated the far wall. The place smelled like an ashtray.

The deputy brought Jimmy into the room. He'd lost too much weight. His skin was ashen, his eyes sunken and hollow. He looked mostly dead. The life had started draining out of him the day he married Mary Shawn.

I had thought that once he was free of her, his situation would improve. I was wrong. Things had gone from bad to worse. It wasn't supposed to have turned out this way.

The deputy left the room. My brother sat across from me. He placed his hands on the marred surface of the table.

"Hi, Jimmy." The stale cigarette smell stuck in my throat. I coughed. "Shawnie tells me you're not talking to anyone."

He looked down as if he were inspecting the gnawed ends of his fingernails.

"I know what the sheriff says you did. I know he's wrong."

Jimmy just kept looking down.

"You didn't kill Mary Shawn any more than you killed her father."

He looked up.

"I'm not going to let you go to prison for something you didn't do. Not again." Water welled in my eyes. "You're the only family I have left. I can't lose you."

His sunken gaze locked on mine.

"Help me, Jimmy." I touched his bone-cold hands. "Tell me what happened."

He pulled away and looked down at the table again.

Ten minutes later, he began to speak.

———

I SQUINTED INTO the morning sun as I drove down the pine tree–lined country road. When I came to the clearing where I'd built the house for my brother, I pulled into the driveway alongside a red Mustang convertible. Its windows and top were up.

The melted remnants of a Mercedes-Benz sedan stood ten yards ahead, in what had once been the partially detached garage. Mary Shawn had commandeered the car from Jimmy after his last DWI conviction six months ago. She'd wanted the Benz ever since Jimmy bought it. Mary Shawn always got what she wanted.

I parked the rental car and stepped out into the hot sun. The convertible's engine was running. I looked inside. The driver's seatback was fully reclined. A half-empty bottle of Grey Goose vodka lay on the floorboard. As I looked around for some sign of the car's owner, a cloud of bluish smoke wafted over the hood.

I walked around to the other side of the convertible to find Shawnie sitting on the ground smoking a cigarette. Even in the heat and humidity, she still wore the black pants and jacket she'd had on when she showed up at my house yesterday morning. She looked up at me through her sunglasses. The lenses weren't dark;

I could plainly see that her eyes were bloodshot. I wondered if it was from the crying or the lack of sleep or the vodka. Her being so much like her mother, I'd put my money on the Grey Goose.

Even now, after a night of hard drinking, Shawnie was stunningly beautiful. Her thick, sleek hair glowed golden in the sun. Women would have killed for her high cheekbones, pouting lips, flawless skin. She was the epitome of classic beauty. Shawnie took it all for granted. *Just like her mother.* My wife had been jealous of Mary Shawn's looks. Throughout the years of our marriage, Elizabeth always wondered if something had happened between Mary Shawn and me. Nothing had, of course, but I was never able to explain why Elizabeth's suspicions were unfounded. I couldn't tell her. I'd given Jimmy my word.

I took Shawnie by the wrist and pulled her to her feet. "Where'd you go last night?"

"I couldn't handle it anymore." She took a drag from the cigarette in a theatrical sort of gesture, the kind of motion Mary Shawn had made when she smoked. Shawnie exhaled and said, "I had to get away."

"You left the rental car running in the parking lot. Couldn't you have at least left the keys at the front desk? Someone might have stolen it."

She shrugged.

I took a deep breath and let it out. "Where'd you sleep?"

"Here. In my car." She dropped the cigarette on the concrete and crushed it with one of her black stilettos. "The sheriff put that yellow tape stuff across the door of Daddy's apartment. I didn't have anywhere else to go."

"I got you a room at the Marriott on the interstate." I reached into my pocket, pulled out the keycard, and handed it to her. "You're in four-one-one. Like the number you call for information. You can remember that, right?"

She rolled her eyes at me. Either the lenses weren't as dark as she thought they were or she just didn't care if I saw. "Where's Daddy?"

"Still in jail."

Shawnie frowned. "What'd he tell you?"

"Not a word."

Perspiration beaded on my forehead. I looked over my shoulder. The shade of a large pine was only a few yards away. Beyond that, twin two-story chimneys stood watch over the rubble that had once been my brother's house. When I offered to build the place for him after I'd won my first big verdict, Jimmy said he wanted something made of brick, something simple that wouldn't require a lot of maintenance. I still had the blueprints of the house he wanted . . . and of the house that was actually built. Mary Shawn had insisted that the place be a two-story wooden structure with a tall staircase, a wraparound porch, and lots of gingerbread. She got what she wanted. Mary Shawn always got what she wanted.

I faced Shawnie. "I'm going to have a look around, try to figure out what to do until the attorney from Little Rock gets here."

She squatted and rummaged through the Louis Vuitton purse on the ground. She pulled out a lighter and a cigarette, then stood again. With the spiky heels she wore, it was an amazing feat of balance. She may have had a lot to drink last night, but she was apparently sober now.

"Go to the hotel and get some sleep." I turned to walk away.

She grabbed my arm and said, "I was hoping Daddy'd be out of jail by now . . ."

"And?"

She lit the cigarette. "The man at the bank won't let me draw on Daddy's trust. Mama had me on her account, but I used all that money to buy my ticket out to California. There's nothing left, Uncle Robert. I'm broke."

I wondered why we had to do this in the hot sun when there

was shade only a few steps away. I pulled my wallet from the pocket of my jeans and fished out three one-hundred-dollar bills. "Will this do for now?"

She motioned toward the rubble with her cigarette. "All my clothes burned up in the house."

I added two more hundreds and passed her the cash.

Shawnie didn't say thank you. She stood there biting her lower lip.

I was sweltering. "If you need more, speak up."

"The funeral home wants everything paid for up front."

"Which funeral home?"

She took a drag from her cigarette and blew out the smoke. "There's only the one."

"I'll take care of it." I wiped the sweat from my forehead. "Anything else?"

"My car payment's due."

"Where?"

"At the bank."

"I'll take care of it. I'll take care of everything. Just go to the hotel and get some sleep. I'll come get you for dinner later."

Cigarette hanging from her mouth, Shawnie picked up her purse, stepped into the convertible, and drove away.

There was so little left of the house, it took a few moments for me to get my bearings. I stepped over the crime scene tape, walked through what used to be the front door, and worked my way through the charred wood and broken glass to the base of the staircase.

When Jimmy had finally started talking in the jail last night, everything he told me was clear, coherent, chronological. I couldn't remember the last time I'd seen my brother sober. I wondered when he'd last been more than a few hours without a drink. Years ago, I imagined. Probably not since before he got out of prison.

Jimmy told me that Mary Shawn had called him from the house—it showed on the caller ID—threatening to tell Shawnie the truth about her father if Jimmy didn't come over right away. He'd put away several shots of Macallan by then, but it didn't matter. He didn't have a license, and he didn't have a car. He got one of his neighbors to drive him to the house and drop him off at the end of the driveway. He found the front door ajar. Mary Shawn was at the base of the staircase. Dead. Broken neck, as best he could tell. He figured she'd fallen down the stairs.

After Shawnie had started college, Jimmy finally got up the nerve to leave Mary Shawn. He moved into an apartment; Mary Shawn stayed in the house. When Shawnie graduated, Jimmy filed for divorce. Mary Shawn asked for the house, but it wasn't his to give. The deed was in my name. Mary Shawn's attorney told her as much. She was undeterred. She said she'd die in that house.

Mary Shawn got what she wanted.

Jimmy said that when he pulled his cell phone off his belt to call the sheriff, everything went black. He figured he'd passed out. When he came to, the place was on fire. He barely escaped. He knew people would think he'd done it again, that he'd killed someone in a fight, then burned down the house to try to cover his tracks. So he ran. The sheriff—the same sheriff he'd turned himself in to twenty-four years ago—picked him up on the road out of town.

My brother might have done a stupid thing by running, but the reasoning behind it was valid. It would be almost impossible to find anyone in the county who'd believe him to be innocent.

Twenty-four years ago, a justice of the peace pronounced Jimmy man and wife with Mary Shawn. Jimmy kissed his bride, walked across the street, and turned himself in to the sheriff for killing Mary Shawn's father and burning down his house with him in it. He said it was an accident, that he'd gotten into a fight with the old man because Mary Shawn's father had been roughing her up. Jimmy said he shoved the old man, and he had hit his head and died. He said he'd burned down the old man's house to try to cover up what he did. It wasn't the truth, but Jimmy stuck to the story. Shawnie was born while Jimmy was serving his fourth month in the penitentiary.

After five years of prison and a nineteen-year drinking career peppered with three DWIs and several dropped domestic violence charges, Jimmy had already been convicted in the mind of just about every potential juror. A change of venue or some other legal maneuvering might help, but it wasn't a certainty. If they sent him back to prison now, he'd die.

Elizabeth and Riley were gone, and as hard as it was to admit to myself, there was no bringing them back. Jimmy was the only family I had left. He hadn't passed out that night. Someone tried to kill him, and now he was being held for a crime he didn't commit. I had to save him while there was still time.

———

THE FIRST E-Z Mart was a bust. I drove to the one at the other end of town and walked inside. The woman with the bad hair from the county jail was behind the counter ringing up a carton of Camels and a bag of Funyuns for a sunburned man in paint-stained work boots. She didn't seem to notice me. I made my way to the back of the store and pulled a bottle of Perrier from the cooler. I waited there until the man in the work boots left and we had the place to ourselves. I hurried to the counter. The woman's nametag read *Patricia*. I still had no recollection of her from high school, but I doubted she'd go by such a formal name.

I approached the counter and looked her straight in the eye. "Hi, Patty."

She gave a yellow smile. "I didn't think you remembered my name last night."

"How could I forget?" I smiled back at her. "I take it this is your second job?"

She nodded. "It sure wears me out, but I have to do it. Got them grandbabies to feed and clothe."

"Listen"—I leaned over the counter—"I don't practice law anymore, but I'd like to help if I can. Would you like me to see what I can do about getting some of your money back from Kenny Earl?"

Mouth open, she nodded.

"Do you have e-mail access?"

"At the library." She spoke as if she were in shock. "I check my e-mails at the library."

I passed her what would have been my business card if I were still in business. "Send me an e-mail with every scrap of information you have on him. I'll see to it just as soon as I get back home."

"How long do you think that'll be?" She gave an embarrassed look. "I mean, how much longer are you going to be able to stay in town?"

"I'm not sure. I've got a criminal defense man coming down from Little Rock tomorrow. There's really nothing else I can do for Jimmy. My main concern now is Shawnie." A mud-encrusted Chevy pickup pulled into the parking lot. "She won't talk to me, but I know there's something going on. I'm worried about her."

"A lot of people are worried about her." Patty gave a smile. "Such a pretty thing—homecoming queen, just like her mama— but she's a drinker, just like her mama *and* her daddy. And she's well on her way to becoming a big ol' . . ."

I remained silent.

Patty waved her hands in the air. "Forget I said anything."

I stood upright.

"I really shouldn't say any more."

I nodded as if I understood.

She looked out the glass storefront. The man in the muddy pickup was still behind the wheel, talking on a cell phone. Patty's voice lowered to a near-hush. "I shouldn't be telling you this, but . . ."

It was hard not to smile. There's nothing like silence to get people to talk.

She leaned in over the counter. "The night Mary Shawn died, Shawnie was supposed to have been down in Dallas. She'd won a big shopping spree in some contest."

I nodded knowingly.

"But one of the deputies spotted her convertible at a cabin up in the hills north of here. Sheriff went up to give her the news about her mama. He found her alone, but there was no telling what she'd been doing up there before. Rumor is, she's been sneaking around with an older man, a doctor out of Hot Springs. Thing is, Sheriff didn't mention where he found Shawnie in his report. I think he kept it out of the record because it was an open-and-shut case . . . and the doctor's married . . . and he's the sheriff's cousin."

———

IT WAS DARK by the time I left the jail. I returned to the Marriott, put on a suit, and walked up one flight of stairs to the fourth floor. Light shone through room 411's peephole. I knocked. The peephole light remained steady until Shawnie opened the door. She wore an expensive-looking black dress. "Hi, Uncle Robert!"

"You should really see who's there before opening."

She just shrugged. A cigarette smell drifted out of the room.

"Were you smoking in there?"

Shawnie tilted her head to the side as if to say, *So what?*

"This is a nonsmoking hotel."

She shrugged again. "Can we go to dinner now? I'm starving."

The Red Lobster was a hundred yards from the hotel, but Shawnie insisted we take my rental car so she wouldn't scuff the soles of her new shoes. She tossed down an endless stream of vodka tonics before, during, and after dinner. She ordered the most expensive entree on the menu. She talked incessantly about the bargains she'd found while shopping. A few people in the restaurant stared at us as if they were amazed she could act so carefree with her mother rotting in the funeral home and her father rotting in jail. They also might have been wondering if I was the older married doctor out of Hot Springs.

We drove back to the Marriott, and I waited outside while Shawnie smoked what she said would be her last cigarette of the evening. I knew she'd have a few more in her room. She was a liar. *Just like her mother.* We rode the elevator to the fourth floor, and I walked her to her door. "Well, I guess this is good-bye."

"Don't you mean good night?"

"No. I mean good-bye."

Shawnie's flawless brow wrinkled. "I don't understand."

"I wanted to tell you at dinner, but I never got a chance. Jimmy started talking. He's going to plead guilty."

Shawnie stumbled back as if I'd just hit her.

"But he . . ."

"He what, Shawnie?"

"I didn't really believe he did it. I thought it was just an accident."

I shrugged. "The attorney from Little Rock's due here at nine tomorrow morning. I'm going to meet with him and Jimmy, help them nail down a plea-bargain strategy, then I'm taking the first flight back to California."

"But you can't leave yet."

"Of course I can."

Eyes wide, she shook her head. "You have to go to Mama's funeral."

"No, I don't."

She looked as if she could scarcely believe I would say anything but yes to her.

"I'm not going to bad-mouth Mary Shawn in front of you or anyone else, but everybody knows how I felt about her. I'm not a hypocrite."

"Well . . ."

"Well, what?"

"What about me? What am I going to do?"

"The sheriff's removing the cordon from Jimmy's apartment in the morning. I took care of the rent until the end of his lease. And I paid off your car. The bank's going to mail you the title." I reached into my coat pocket, pulled out a small wad of hundreds, and placed it in her hand. "There's five hundred there, and I had three thousand more transferred into your checking account. After that, you're on your own." I walked away and headed for the stairwell to return to my room on the third floor. "Good luck, Shawnie."

The words floated down the hallway after me. "I can't live on that."

I kept walking. "Then get a job."

"But you're rich! Mama said you could buy half the state."

I glanced over my shoulder. "I have no idea what Mary Shawn told you, but I'm not rich anymore."

"You made a gazillion dollars as a lawyer, and then you got that big payoff from . . ." Her words trailed off.

I stopped and faced her. "You mean the settlement from the trucking company? The settlement they paid me after that semi crossed the median and killed my wife and son? Is that the settlement you're talking about?"

She just nodded.

"You want some of that money?"

She nodded again.

It took effort, but I contained my anger. "I gave it away. I gave away almost everything. I kept enough to live on, but I can't afford to support anyone else." I turned and made my way into the stairwell. I stopped at the top of the stairs. The first flight down was long and steep.

Shawnie ran past me and stopped two steps below, blocking my path.

She turned to face me. "But . . ."

"But what?"

"What about the insurance money from the fire?"

"It was my house." I shrugged and looked past her, down at the landing far below. "Not that it matters. There's not going to be any insurance money. The policy doesn't pay in case of arson. Jimmy admitted to starting the fire. So that's that." I stepped to the left.

She moved in front of me again. "What about the trust you set up for Daddy? Can you sign it over to me?"

I shook my head. "The lawyers' fees will eat up most of it. The state will probably take the rest. If there's anything left, Jimmy'll need it to live on when he gets out. He's not young and able-bodied . . . like you." I stepped to my right.

She blocked my path once more. The skin around her lips went pale, then her cheeks turned bright red. "You can't just leave me here like this! I won't let you!"

"There's nothing you can do to stop me."

"Yes, there is!" She half-spat the words.

"Oh, really? How's that?"

"I want a million dollars, or I'll tell everybody the truth!"

"What truth?"

"Mama told me Jimmy's not really my daddy. She told me what you did to her the night he surrendered to the sheriff."

I just looked at her.

"You raped Mama, and you got her pregnant with me!"

I started to laugh. I laughed so hard, I could hardly control myself. I laughed so hard, it took a moment for me to realize that a stream of obscenities had begun flowing from Shawnie's pretty mouth.

The vile things she said about me I could let pass, but not the disparaging remark about Elizabeth. That's where I drew the line with her. It's where I'd drawn the line with Mary Shawn.

I looked down at Shawnie. As drunk as she was, it wouldn't take much to tip her off balance. Just one little push, and . . . But that wasn't going to get Jimmy out of jail. I had to stay focused on saving him. I lowered my voice. "I didn't rape your mother. I was never with her. I'm not your father."

"Yes, you are. Mama told me so."

"Mary Shawn was a liar." *Just like you.*

Shawnie's face grew so red, her blue eyes seemed to glow. Her hair looked like white flames.

I gave half a thought to telling her the truth about her mother and her grandfather, the truth about why Mary Shawn killed the old man, but I promised Jimmy I wouldn't. Ever. Some truths were too horrible to be told. Instead, I said, "Mary Shawn was pregnant when Jimmy turned himself in. My brother took the blame for what your mother did so you wouldn't be born in prison." I took a deep breath and let it out. "Once was too much. I'm not going to let him serve time for you again."

"Serve time for me?" She seemed to regain her composure. "What do you mean by that?"

"It's over, Shawnie." I pointed my finger at her sternum. "I know what you did."

She put her hands on her hips. She looked so nonchalant, it infuriated me. It would be so easy. Just one little jab, and . . .

I had to keep my cool. "You came home and found your mother dead. You stashed your car out of sight and you called Jimmy and pretended to be Mary Shawn and you got him to come over to the house. You were hiding when he walked in. You waited until he found Mary Shawn's body, then you sneaked up behind him and knocked him unconscious and set the house on fire."

A strange sort of calm came over her. "You can't prove any of this, Robert."

"If Jimmy had died in the fire, the money in his trust would have been yours."

Shawnie's expression showed nothing.

"I have just one question: Why were you so anxious for me to get my brother out of jail? Were you going to try to kill him again? Or were you just going to try to get your hands on some of the money you thought I had?" I let out a soft laugh. "Sorry. I guess I had three questions."

She shook her head and said, "This is ridiculous. I don't have to stand here and—"

"I had a chat with a certain doctor up in Hot Springs this afternoon. Guy about my age. Wealthy. Married." I smiled. "Horrible taste in mistresses."

The color drained from Shawnie's face.

"Seems your doctor friend broke off his relationship with you the night Mary Shawn died, the night you were supposed to have been in Dallas. He said you were very upset when you left the cabin. He was worried about you driving with all you'd had to drink. He followed you to make sure you made it home safe."

She stood there looking more like a wax figure than a human being.

"The doctor would be willing to testify that he saw you walk into the house ten minutes before that call Mary Shawn supposedly made to Jimmy."

Shawnie's blue eyes darted from side to side.

"You didn't really think you'd get away with it, did you?"

A siren blared nearby.

The police were probably just stopping a speeding motorist, but Shawnie must have thought they were coming to arrest her. She turned to run. When she did, she lost her balance. She began to fall. It was a long way to the landing below. I gave a fleeting thought to just letting it happen. But I couldn't. It wouldn't save Jimmy. I caught Shawnie by the arm, in the nick of time. *Not at all like her mother.*

——

THE PACIFIC STRETCHED to the horizon, smooth as velvet. Jimmy and I sat on my back deck with mugs of coffee and our laptop computers. He'd regained a few pounds over the past couple of months, and the La Jolla sun had brought back some of his color. He wasn't fully among the living yet, but at least he wasn't mostly dead anymore. He'd stopped drinking. He'd even started running with my group in the mornings. Everything was going to be okay. I just knew it.

My laptop dinged. I looked down to see an e-mail with *Thanks from Patty* in the subject line. I opened the note and read it. I didn't even mind the misspellings.

"Hey, Jimmy. Remember Patty Ingram?"

"Sure. Nice girl. Works in the sheriff's office. Kenny Earl Boyd took all her money and ran off to Houston with some stripper or something." He paused. "Why do you ask?"

"I just got a message from her." I smiled. "Kenny Earl returned all her money . . . with interest."

"How did you manage that?"

"I have my ways." I shut off my computer and said, "Good-deed-doing gives me an appetite. Wanna drive down to the Broken Yolk in PB and get some breakfast?"

Jimmy took a long drink of coffee, swallowed hard, then said, "Ever since you were a little kid, you never did give up. You always were a real bulldog. That tenacity made you a good lawyer. That and your willingness to do whatever it took."

"Thanks . . . I think." I stood. "I'm hungry. Let's go."

Jimmy didn't budge. "You know, your running buddies sure are a chatty bunch." He took another drink of coffee. "According to them, up until the day Shawnie came out here to get you, you hadn't missed a morning run in over three months. It was some kind of record, according to them."

I shrugged. "What's your point?"

"Well, you couldn't have flown commercial. It would have taken too long. You never would have made it back here by morning. Besides, with all the ID restrictions nowadays, your name would have ended up on the airline's passenger list. You're not that sloppy."

I was suddenly light-headed. I tightened my stomach muscles trying to keep the blood pumping to my brain.

"What'd you do? Charter a plane using an alias or something?" Jimmy took another sip of coffee. "Better yet, maybe you never sold your Gulfstream at all. I'll bet you transferred it to some entity you control. Heck, I'd even wager that you never gave away your money. A thousand bucks says you still have it all, every penny."

I just looked at him.

"And the shopping spree in Dallas that Shawnie won . . . She didn't really win it, did she? I wouldn't be a bit surprised if that entity you control sponsored the 'contest.' Stroke of genius, actually. Under normal circumstances, it would have been a surefire way to get Shawnie out of the house. You just didn't know about the doctor."

I eased myself onto the low stone wall that bordered the deck.

"You set it up so Mary Shawn would be home alone that evening. You snuck into town and went to the house. Mary Shawn was already drunk, of course—she was always drunk by sundown. You got her up to the second floor somehow. You pushed her down the stairs so it looked like an accident. You snuck out of the house, out of town, back to whatever airport you used. You flew back to La Jolla without anyone being the wiser. You joined your running buddies the next morning just like you'd never left town. That's your style, Robert. Clean and simple."

I took a deep breath, then let it out. "Jimmy, that's ridic—"

"Drunk woman home alone falls down a flight of stairs, breaks her neck, dies. It's the kind of tragic accident that happens every day. No one thinks anything about it."

I just shook my head.

"Shawnie coming back unexpected like that, her getting me over to the house and knocking me out and setting the place on fire, it really threw a wrench in the simplicity of your plan, didn't it?"

I let out a laugh. "You have one fertile imagination, Jimmy Hicks! Maybe you should use your new computer to write mystery novels." I stood and headed toward the kitchen. "Want some more coffee before we go to breakfast?"

"A man spends five years in prison, even an innocent man, he's bound to learn a lot about the criminal mind."

I stopped in the doorway and turned to face him.

"The thing is, some things are so obvious, a really smart criminal might not notice them."

My knees were suddenly weak.

"You know how I first started figuring it out?"

I leaned against the doorframe.

"You knew Mary Shawn was already dead when Shawnie reached the house."

I fought to stay standing.

"You never once mentioned the possibility that Shawnie might have killed Mary Shawn, even accidentally." Jimmy set down his coffee mug, leaned forward, and clasped his hands underneath his chin. "If she was going to try to kill me, why did you never for a moment think that she might have killed Mary Shawn, too?"

There was nothing I could do or say. It would have been pointless to try to deny it. I just looked at him.

"Your knowing Mary Shawn was already dead didn't really prove anything, of course. But it did get me to thinking. So I took my new computer and did a little poking around on the Internet. I found something real interesting. Mary Shawn died three years after Elizabeth and Riley got killed in that wreck. Three years to the day."

I drained the last of my coffee. It was cold and bitter.

"What'd Mary Shawn do?"

I looked out over the ocean and thought about the last morning Elizabeth, Riley, and I had had breakfast here on this deck. Water welled in my eyes. I could have said nothing. I probably should have said nothing. But Jimmy was the only family I had left.

I walked halfway to where my brother sat. I clasped my hands on top of my head. "A few months after you'd left Mary Shawn and moved into your apartment, she started calling me at the office asking for money. I kept saying no. While I was up in San Francisco working on a case, she called my cell phone. I'd had the number a long time, so I didn't think anything of her calling me on it—a lot of people I didn't want having the number had it. I expected her to ask for money again, but this time she threatened to blackmail me. She said she was going to call Elizabeth and tell her that I'd forced myself on her that night you turned yourself in to the sheriff. Mary Shawn said she was going to tell Elizabeth that Shawnie was my daughter, and that the time had come for me to make things right. It was all a lie, of course, but we both know that never stopped Mary Shawn." I lowered my arms to my sides. "Elizabeth and I had just changed our unlisted phone at the house, Elizabeth's cell, all our e-mail addresses, things like that. I just laughed and told Mary Shawn to go right ahead. I was going home that night, so I knew I'd be there before any letter would have time to reach her."

Jimmy half-stood, then he sat again. "But . . ."

"Mary Shawn called back a few minutes later. She told me she'd carried out her threat. I didn't believe her, but then she recited our new number. She said she'd only tell Elizabeth the truth if I wired a million dollars into her account."

"Oh God." Jimmy clamped his hands around the back of his neck.

"Mary Shawn had gotten the number somehow. I knew you weren't talking to her then. Best I can figure, Shawnie got the number off your cell phone and gave it to Mary Shawn."

Jimmy closed his eyes. "Oh Jesus. Robert, I had no—"

"A simple blood test would have proven Mary Shawn was lying, but that would take time, and then there was the issue of Shawnie's paternity. None of us wanted Shawnie to know who her real father was. I guess Mary Shawn was banking on that. She probably thought it was worth a million dollars to me to have her tell Elizabeth the truth and get it over quickly."

Jimmy sat there. His face twitched.

"I never told you this, but Elizabeth was always jealous of how pretty Mary Shawn was. She thought I pretended to hate Mary Shawn because I was secretly attracted to her. No matter what I said, Elizabeth was always suspicious that something had happened between Mary Shawn and me. Then Mary Shawn called saying those things and . . ."

Jimmy stood and walked toward me.

"I knew Elizabeth would be upset, so I hung up and called the house. There was no answer. I tried Elizabeth's cell, but it went straight to voice mail. I flew home. The police were there waiting for me."

"Oh Jesus, God, Robert." Jimmy was standing just in front of me. "Oh Jesus, God."

"If Mary Shawn hadn't called and told that horrible lie, Elizabeth wouldn't have taken Riley and left the house. They wouldn't have been driving on that road. If Mary Shawn hadn't called, Elizabeth and Riley would still be . . ." I buried my face in my hands. I cried so hard, I could barely get the words out. "Mary Shawn killed my wife and my little boy. I wasn't going to let her kill you, too. You're the only family I've got left."

Jimmy caught me when my legs gave out. He helped me over to the bench at the seaside edge of the deck. We sat there together looking out over the ocean. A lone wave washed in and out over the rocks below. Neither of us spoke for a long time.

I swallowed hard and wiped the tears from my cheeks. "I'll fly back tomorrow and turn myself in."

Jimmy gave me a hard look. "You never told Shawnie who her real father was, did you?"

I shook my head. "Some truths are too horrible to be told."

He turned his gaze back toward the ocean. "There at the end, Mary Shawn had been threatening to tell her. I know she would have eventually. It was just a matter of time."

I looked at my brother.

His eyes seemed to be fixed on a point far out at sea. "Seems to me, what you did, that's another one of those truths better left untold."

THE FLASHLIGHT GAME

BY DIANA HANSEN-YOUNG

D ad. Dad. Stop. I can't get involved. You know that," I said, twirling the flashlight. "I can't practice law, give you advice, write letters, file your lawsuits, or help you with your *pro se* schemes while I'm clerking for a federal appeals judge. I just can't."

"Think of this as a hypothetical," he said.

"Dad, we've had this conversation a hundred times."

"An anonymous hypothetical. I won't use any names."

I put my cell phone on speaker and listened to Dad while I played the flashlight game with Jaws. My cat spun around in a tight circle, a furry blur, chasing the beam faster and faster until he was so dizzy he staggered. I switched directions.

"It's pretty simple," Dad said, and I knew that it was a long, complicated story. Jaws loved long, complicated calls from Dad; they meant a really long flashlight game. "Someone like you with a mind like a steel trap will get this one immediately."

In reality, he was the one with a mind like a steel trap, an electronics engineer who studied math with Feynman at Cal Tech and had become an expert solving the problems created by his corporation's crappy telephone circuit boards, rushed too soon to market. He worked from home, mostly by e-mail and phone, because his boss recognized he was both invaluable and "a little rough around the edges," an epiphany that came after a dispute between Dad and an office co-worker over recycled paper towels. Now Dad sat at home every day, computer on, wearing only his Hawaiian surf shorts, waiting for bad news. This arrangement gave him time to make calls and write letters of complaint, for example, to Mega Office about a rude deliveryman, or to Verizon, who regularly turned off his service because he regularly paid at the last minute to punish them for turning off his service.

My dad, the dispute collector, was thrilled when I went to law school. He was ecstatic when I graduated summa cum laude. When I came home to Brooklyn to study for the bar exam, he installed a second office chair and meticulously copied practice questions onto flash cards. We studied together twelve hours a day, seven days a week. Unfortunately, because the answers were on the back of every flash card, Dad memorized every one. I took breaks only when some new circuit board broke. Once, I had four days off when Dad had to work on-site in Beijing. He came back with a picture of himself on a yak and a fresh list of complaints against the Chinese airline and Beijing hotel, neither of which answered his international certified letters.

After "we" passed the bar, his appetite for disputes became insatiable. Armed with his flash-card law degree, he followed up letters with *pro se* suits. His brokerage house was his first. They refused to let him use "F*** You" as his online password to view his 401(k) account. "First amendment," Dad said, and sued.

Dad was charming and courteous, even in his disputes. He became a regular in Civil Court, where the clerks knew him by name, loved him, and thought his teeny-tiny personality disorder was kinda cute. While I agreed with him that filing *pro se* lawsuits was a good way to get out of the house, I suggested other social activities, whereupon he started dating a sixty-year-old process server named Maria López who worked for the sheriff in the basement of Civil Court. I hadn't met her, so I kept my mouth shut, glad that he'd finally had a date, some twenty years after Mom died of breast cancer.

I heard Dad's papers rustle over the speaker phone. "Say someone has health insurance with prescription coverage filled by mail by Speedy Scripts. One day that person receives an e-mail telling him his warfarin pills are delayed."

"Coumadin, Dad. Warfarin is rat poison." I spun the flashlight at warp speed.

"Same thing," he said. "Anyway, this person wants to know why it's delayed, but this person can't find the prescription customer service number."

Jaws staggered to a halt and barfed.

"He has his dental card, so he is forced to call dental customer service, which of course has been outsourced to India."

The barf was mostly wheatgrass from the farmers' market, fairly easy to clean up. Dad abandoned the hypothetical while I got paper towels.

"Now, India has no idea why my prescription is delayed. I ask to speak to a supervisor. I get a Houston number. A Houston supervisor tells me they had to check the prescription with my doctor. What? What? Check what? Since when has warfarin been a controlled substance? He insisted the drug's name was Coumadin. I told him how wrong he was, and he hung up on me. I called my doctor. The receptionist cited FIRPA laws and refused to speak to me because she couldn't verify that I'm me. I demanded to speak to the doctor. He's on jury duty. I insisted she page him. Do you know what she said to me?"

"I can't begin to guess." I shot a little 409 on the barf and wiped it up.

"She told me that if I needed Coumadin, go buy some rat

poison at the hardware store and thin it out with a little orange juice. Why would she say something like that?"

"Were you shouting at her?"

"Never mind shouting, I want to file a class action against Speedy Scripts for callous disregard of my life by outsourcing critical medication customer service calls. I could die without my warfarin."

"Do you have any left?"

"Just a three-month supply. Do you think I would actually trust those people to send it on time?"

"Dad, then you weren't damaged."

"I can sue the doctor for being on jury duty. He has an obligation to do no harm."

"The Hippocratic Oath is not legally binding," I said. "You have enough Coumadin to kill all the rodents on the Q line." I turned on the flashlight beam. Jaws yowled with happiness.

"Are you driving the cat crazy again with that darn flashlight game?"

"No," I lied. "Dad, let it go. Send an e-mail to Lou Dobbs."

"Well, maybe," he said. "It is Sunday. But before I go to bed, I'll just run the Hippocratic Oath through LexisNexis."

LexisNexis. That had been a big fat Father's Day present mistake. "What am I going to do with you, Dad?"

"Lighten up, sweetheart. It's fun to be an attorney."

———

MONDAY AFTERNOON I was sitting in the judge's office. We'd finished going over oral arguments. The judge was telling me about a dispute she was having with a neighbor over a tree gone wild on the property line.

My cell phone vibrated. I peeked at the screen. Dad. The judge was my boss. Dad would have to wait.

"The roots destroyed their driveway. So okay, it had to come down. They said it was my tree so I should pay. I had the trunk surveyed," she said. "It was precisely half in their yard, half in mine. I said I would go fifty-fifty. They hired an ultrasound guy who did a calculation of root mass and found that there was six percent more on my side. So they claimed that the preponderance of the tree belonged to me, thus I should pay one hundred percent."

My cell phone vibrated again. *Unknown caller* flashed on the screen. Probably Dad turning off caller ID to see if I'd pick it up if I didn't know who it was.

"I said no and offered to pay 56 percent. They refused, sued me in small-claims court, and called *Judge Judy*. The show called me. A federal appeals judge on *Judge Judy*? I don't think so."

Vibrate. Text. *Call Benny Bail Bonds asap.* Oh crap. My stomach flip-flopped.

"Frankly," the judge said, "I don't know what to do next. Doesn't your dad have some experience with disputes?" She noticed my face. "What's wrong?"

"A call from Dad," I said, "then a call from Benny Bail Bonds in Brooklyn."

"Doesn't sound like good news." She leaned forward. "Take three days off. Straighten it out." She paused. "But before you go, can you just run Establishment of Tree Ownership through LexisNexis?"

———

IT WAS ELEVEN before my plane landed at JFK. Benny was waiting at the curb. He rolled his eyes when I slid the cat carrier into the backseat. Jaws farted.

"It always happens when he flies," I said. I rolled down the window. "Change in cabin air pressure." I buckled my seat belt.

"The police responded to an anonymous nine-one-one around noon," Benny, the *Law & Order* rerun junkie, said. "The caller, female, said she heard shots in an apartment in Carroll Gardens.

She thought the perp was still there." Benny shot through three red lights on Conduit and swerved onto Atlantic. "The officer who responded saw your father on the stoop with blood on his Hawaiian shorts and a gun in his hand. They brought him in."

"He called you?"

"No," he said. "Maria was driving by the Eighty-seventh and she saw him being taken in. He made her promise not to call you, so she called me, and I called you."

"Benny, watch it!"

Benny slowed to the speed limit and ran twenty red lights in a row before the twenty-first light turned green. "They don't synchronize the lights until midnight," he said. "Besides, there's no traffic."

———

BENNY, MY SECOND dad, ran a bail-bond business across from Civil Court in Brooklyn. His daughter Jessica and I had been best friends from second grade through NYU. We split up when I went to University of Chicago Law School and she went to Georgetown. Now she practices criminal law in New York. When I'm in town, we have drinks and swap horror stories about our dads.

Benny parked in the bus zone and insisted that he walk me to my dad's apartment. He checked each room. "All clear," he said. "See you in the morning."

I filled Jaws's litter box from a bag under the sink, then set him free from his carrier. He streaked for the clay while I filled up a water bowl and opened tuna from Dad's three-year supply of canned goods. I pressed the tuna dribbles into his food dish, found whole grain and mayo in the fridge, and made myself a sandwich.

I rummaged for coffee. It was likely to be a long night. For whatever reason, Dad had nothing but bags of Yerba Maté.

While I waited for the water to boil, I clicked on the local news and caught a grainy video of police marching Dad into the 87th Precinct. He looked like a Hawaiian ax murderer in handcuffs. "A sixty-five-year-old man is being held for questioning in the murder of Alfred Frattelli, thirty-six, a former deliveryman at Mega Office."

A Mega Office deliveryman? Cat crap! I vaguely remembered him telling me about some dispute with a Mega deliveryman. The kettle whistled. I had a bad feeling. Had Dad's disputes escalated to this? Nonsense. Dad was incapable of physical violence. "Frattelli leaves behind a wife." A picture of a happy couple flashed on the screen as the anchor signed off.

I needed to look in Dad's dispute files and read the Mega Office folder.

There were three drawers, labeled Current, Successful, and Un. Current was packed full of what looked like a hundred yellow folders, organized alphabetically. City Hall, Corning, China Airlines, David's Cleaners, Dixon's Coffee Shop . . . and there it was, after a three-inch-thick McDonald's file: Mega Office.

I sat down and flipped through a chronological series of letters. The first was to the Mega store manager, informing him that the deliveryman, one Alfred Fratelli, had cursed Dad after Dad refused to accept the ream of conventional paper Fratelli had carried up three flights of stairs (Dad had ordered recycled). Dad asked for an apology. Mega manager apologized. Dad didn't want an apology from Mega; he wanted Fratelli to apologize. Mega management wrote back that they would discipline Fratelli. Fratelli then wrote to Dad, a foul letter full of bad English and F words, which Dad copied and sent to Mega management. Two days later, Dad received another letter from Fratelli telling him he intended to cut off his nuts before he killed him. This time Dad sent a copy to the Mega CEO, asking for damages in the form of a contribution to the Humane Society spay and neuter program. The CEO replied that Fratelli had been fired and enclosed a copy of a check to the Humane Society for $10,000. Dad wrote a courteous letter of thanks. After that, there was nothing from Mega, but there were eight letters from Fratelli, describing what he intended to do to Dad. A graphic photo of a corpse was enclosed with the last letter. Then a copy of a police report Dad made, dated last week, and a background check on Fratelli that Benny ran for Dad on Friday. Fratelli had a long rap sheet, everything from simple assault to suspicion of murder. He also had a dozen domestic charges that were dropped by his common-law wife, Arlene Raposa. Dad had circled "Raposa" and put a question mark next to it.

Crap, double crap. I reached for my tuna sandwich. The plate was empty. Jaws energetically washed his paws.

The file burned in my hands. I am an officer of the court; nevertheless, family trumps ethics. The police would eventually get copies of the letters from Mega, anyway. I put the file in my purse on the floor next to my chair.

And then it occurred to me that investigators would be all over this place like Jaws on a sandwich. The prosecutor would offer all of Dad's dispute files as proof of his extreme combative nature, which they would claim had escalated to murder. But if all the files were gone . . .

I opened Dad's living-room closet, hauled out the water purification system, iodine tablets, and solar radios, and there it was, Dad's collapsible handcart. I took off my business-suit jacket and tried to load the files directly onto the handcart. They slid off. I found green (environmental, not the color) garbage bags, stuffed in the files, and tied the first load to the handcart. I rolled it out onto the landing. Fudge crap, if I bumped it down the stairs, someone was bound to wake up. I carefully lifted the cart and set it down on each descending step. Forty-four, including the stairs that led to the basement, where Dad had a storage locker. There the files would be safe.

But would they? A subpoena would include the locker. I dragged the handcart back up the stairs and out the door. I wheeled the first bag halfway down the block and hid it under a pile of a neighbor's garbage, which would be picked up at dawn. Four loads later, my DKNY blouse was soaked with sweat. My arms ached. I rolled the handcart back into the apartment and realized that the file cabinet stood empty. Anyone who searched the apartment would know that the files it held were missing. It had to go.

I wrapped each drawer, plus the frame, in blankets, loaded them onto the handcart, and hauled them out onto the street. The final load with the empty cabinet frame nearly did me in. Plus, it ripped my blouse. I could hardly make it up the stairs and back into the apartment. Water. Water. I needed water.

I was standing at the sink when I heard a key in the front door lock. What the hell? I grabbed a kitchen knife.

A short, compact woman with shiny black hair dressed in a pink jogging suit and carrying a matching pink bag tiptoed into the living room.

I came out of the kitchen with my knife. "Who the hell are you?"

"Maria López. Who the hell are you?"

"His daughter." I lowered my knife. "What the fudging crap are you doing here? And why do you have a key?"

She looked around the living room. "Where's the file cabinet?"

"What file cabinet?"

"The one that was here last night, the one full of disputes, including his dispute with Mega Office, whose deliveryman is *de nada*. I need that folder."

"The file cabinet's gone."

"What do you mean, gone?"

"Bye-bye. Aloha. *Adios*." I set the knife down on the side table next to the empty tuna sandwich plate. "I can't say any more."

It took her five seconds to get the picture. "Did you, ah, get a chance to take a look at the Mega file before it, ah, disappeared?"

I don't know why I lied. "No."

"Too bad," she said. "If your dad didn't do it, someone else did. There might be something in that file that would give us a clue who killed Fratelli." She looked at me.

I felt like I was in a Dashiell Hammett novel. "I wouldn't know about that."

"Change your clothes. I'll make us some Yerba Maté." God, she was bossy.

———

BY THE TIME I'd changed to jeans and a sweatshirt, Maria had set my cup of tea on the table next to the chair. The empty tuna sandwich plate and kitchen knife were gone.

"You didn't have to clean up," I said.

"*De nada*," she said. She lifted her cup of Maté. "My folks are from Peru. I drank this growing up."

Evidently Maria was close enough to Dad to keep her stash of Yerba Maté in Dad's kitchen. Dad, Dad, Dad. I sighed. "Dad's not guilty."

"Of course not," she said. She sipped. "He talks a lot about you and the cat. I thought you were clerking."

"Benny called me." I sipped. The tea was four times stronger than what I'd made. I tried not to gag. "I came on the first flight."

"Pay full fare for walk-up ticket?" I nodded. "Bastards," she said. "They always nail the walk-ups."

"One of Dad's complaints."

She leaned forward. "Don't you ever get tired of your dad's disputes? I do."

"Dad is what he is." Outside the window, I could see the sky getting lighter. Fatigue washed over me.

Maria stuck out her hand. Her grip was strong; her hands callused. "I'll be back in a couple of hours, drive you to the station. Get some sleep."

———

THE 87TH WAS a cinder-block building circa 1950. The green asbestos linoleum was cracked and gouged, waiting for a class-action lawsuit. It smelled like piss and French fries. Maria seemed to know the desk sergeant.

"Hey, Paco," she said. "What's the Fratelli situation?"

"We charged him. Murder two," he said. "Arraignment at eleven."

"This is the daughter," Maria said. "She needs to see him."

"Attorneys only," he said.

I flashed my New York Bar Association card. "I'm an attorney."

"I'll put the old man in a room," he said. He looked at my handbag. "You can't take that in there," he said. "Gimme."

Maria started to follow. He turned to her. "You can't come."

She flipped him the bird, then turned to me. "Tell him I need to be there."

"Actually, it's best if you don't," I said. "Whatever he says isn't privileged if you're there."

———

MY DAD, THE prisoner, had traded in his shorts for an orange jumpsuit. He looked depressed. I gave him a hug.

"I told Maria not to call you," he said. "She's getting on my nerves."

"It was Benny who called me," I said. "He's going to arrange bail."

"I don't want bail. I was falsely arrested. I didn't do it. They have no right to arrest an innocent man. I'm not going anywhere. I'm staying right here until they apologize and let me go."

"Dad, I want you out of here," I said.

"I'm making a statement on behalf of innocent prisoners everywhere."

It was pointless to argue. "Tell me what happened."

"Well, it's actually quite simple," he said. "It started when I ordered recycled paper from Mega Office."

I cut him off at the pass. "I read the file," I said. "Get to yesterday."

————

DAD HAD ACTUALLY been working on the phone trying to figure a work-around for his company's defective chip that had already been installed in a million cell phones. He was just saying good-bye when call waiting buzzed. He toggled to the incoming call.

It was a woman who said she was Mrs. Fratelli. She was crying. She said her life had been hell since her husband had started acting like a jackass. She told her husband she was leaving him unless he apologized to Dad. Her husband finally agreed. She'd fixed spaghetti Bolognese. Would Dad come to lunch and they could sit down, just the three of them, and talk it through? Make things right. Dad agreed and offered to bring an Italian Barolo. Come right over, she said, 314 Carroll Street, apartment A.

I was incredulous. "It didn't seem odd to you that someone whose husband sent you a picture of a corpse now wanted to sit down over spaghetti and apologize?"

"No. It was the right thing for him to do.

"I bought the Barolo and called a car service." When he got

there, a yellow sticky note on the buzzer box said *Out of Order. Come in.* The door was wedged open with grocery fliers. Dad went in, found apartment A, and knocked. The door opened. "The next thing I knew, I was laying on the floor with a gun in my hand, next to a dead man."

"How did you know he was dead?"

"The top of his head was gone," he said. "I ran out to get help. I was on the stoop when a police car rolled up. They pointed their guns and told me to drop the gun and get down on the ground. I didn't even know I'd carried the gun out. I did what they said. They handcuffed me, and here I am. Oh, and they charged me with second-degree murder."

I held up my hand before he could rattle off the flash-card definition of second-degree murder. "When the door opened, did you see anything?"

"No."

"When you ran out, was the yellow sticky note still on the buzzer box?"

"I don't remember."

"You have a mind like a steel trap. It's there somewhere, memorized."

He closed his eyes for thirty seconds. Opened them. "No," he said. "No yellow sticky note."

———

I TOLD DAD I'd see him at arraignment. I was walking down the hall when my cell phone rang. It was Jessica.

"Got your text message," she said. "You know Dixon's? Across from the courthouse, three doors down from my dad's office?" Dixon's. Wasn't that one of Dad's files? "Meet you there in fifteen."

"Let's get a bite to eat," Maria said as we walked back to her car. I shook my head. "I'm meeting Jessica," I said. "She's going to represent Dad at arraignment."

"I thought you were representing him."

"I work for a federal appeals judge," I said. "I can't represent clients, give advice, or practice law while I'm clerking. Nothing remotely related. I could lose my license."

"And we don't want that, do we?" She beep-beeped her key ring. "Well, between Jessica and me, we'll get him off."

I slid into the passenger seat. "Maria, I appreciate your affection for Dad, and your eagerness to vindicate him, but you can't be involved in these meetings or the prosecution can subpoena you and make you tell what was said."

Maria was silent all the way to the coffee shop.

"See you in a few minutes, at arraignment," I said. She did not answer. I closed the door. She drove away.

I downed three cups of coffee while waiting for Jessica. She rushed in, ordered more coffee. I briefed her while she drank. She looked at her watch.

"The arraignment is in two minutes." She waved frantically for more coffee.

"By the way," I said, "Dixon's seems like a nice enough little shop."

"One of your dad's favorites."

I pondered that while we rushed across the street to the courthouse. On the steps she stopped. "I need to see the Mega file," she said.

I reached into my bag.

The file was gone.

———

DAD ACTUALLY LOOKED cheerful when the bailiff led him in. Jessica had to explain three times to the judge that her client wanted remand. No bail. Dad flashed a V-for-Victory sign when they led him away.

Benny, in the front row, was the one who looked depressed. "First time I ever met anyone who refused bail," he said.

"It's a statement," I said.

"He's better off there while we sort this out," Jessica said. She turned to me. "Drinks at six? Blue Fin?"

"I heard the beers there are fifteen bucks a pop," Benny said. "Can I come?"

Jessica kissed him on the cheek. "No, Dad," she said. "I'll take you for pizza and beer at Sponzini's on Saturday night. Besides, we're going to talk about you."

———

JESSICA RUSHED OFF to a meeting. I hailed a taxi. "Prospect Heights," I said.

I thought about the missing file. I'd put it into my bag last night in the living room. Maria could have taken it while I was changing. But why? On the other hand, Paco at the 87th had had my purse while I was visiting Dad.

"Changed my mind," I said to the driver. "Eighty-seventh Precinct."

Paco was at the front desk, eating French fries.

I pounded the cracked marble top. "Did you take something out of my handbag?"

"What?"

"This morning. You take something out of my bag while you were holding it?"

"You accusing me of stealing?" He stood up. French fries sprinkled the floor.

"It was either you or Maria," I said.

"Vote for Maria," Paco said. "She's a real piece of work. Her whole family is."

I THOUGHT ABOUT what he'd said all the way back to the apartment. Jaws yowled for breakfast. I went into the kitchen and fried up a half-dozen free-range eggs. I scraped two into Jaws's dish and ate four. He turned up his nose and left the room.

"Eat that or die," I said. I looked around the kitchen. Something wasn't right. Something was different. I looked around again.

The shelf that held the Yerba Maté was empty. What the crap was going on?

I looked through the rest of the house. Everything seemed normal, except for the yellow sticky note on Dad's pillow, next to a key.

I can't take these disputes no more. Good-bye. Nice welcome-home present; Dad was going to love this—if he ever came home.

There was pounding on the door. "Police," someone shouted. "Open up."

I put the note in my pocket and opened the door. A uniformed officer stood beside some bozo in a wrinkled suit, who handed me something blue and folded with his right hand and flashed a badge with his left. "Search warrant," Wrinkled Suit said. "We're looking for a specific file that was in your father's possession. It's evidence in a homicide investigation."

"What file?"

Another officer came out of my old bedroom waving the Mega file. "In her suitcase." He handed it to Wrinkled Suit.

"What have we got here?" Wrinkled Suit said.

"No way," I said. "The suitcase is my property. This warrant doesn't cover my property."

"Tell it to the judge." Wrinkled Suit pointed to the door. "Come on."

"Am I under arrest?"

"Not yet."

"Then I'll pass."

"We'll be back," he said. He and his boys filed out of the apartment, leaving the door open.

"I can hardly wait," I shouted, and slammed the door shut. What the brimstone crap was going on?

Maria. It had to be Maria. For whatever reason, she'd taken the file last night and put it in the suitcase this morning when she came to collect her Yerba Maté. Why?

And then I thought of the yellow sticky notes, on the pillow and on the buzzer box. I had a bad feeling. Panic would be more like it. I had to get out of the apartment before they came back with a warrant and I found myself sitting in the cell next to Dad.

I was down one flight of stairs before it occurred to me that Wrinkled Suit may have left someone in front of the apartment to make sure I didn't leave. I went back inside. Jaws looked perplexed as I climbed out the kitchen window onto the fire escape.

"Eat your eggs," I said. I climbed down the ladder like I'd done a hundred times before, sneaking out to see a boyfriend Dad didn't like. I hot-footed it through the backyard, through to Sterling. I walked to Flatbush, ducked into RastaMan, bought a Jamaican patty, and ate it while I called Benny.

"Benny? Exactly what do you know about Maria López?"

"Bossy." He paused. "Come to think of it, I don't know much about her, except that your dad liked her."

"Can you run a background check on her?" I told him about the file, Wrinkled Suit, the sticky note.

There was a long silence. Then he whistled. "Come to the office."

I didn't know how smart or motivated Wrinkled Suit was. "Make it Dixon's."

———

I HOPPED A bus down Flatbush, got out at the Fulton Mall, and headed toward the court complex. I passed a Conway display of hoodies for $5. I bought a navy blue and a pair of baggy matching sweatpants. I paid, had the clerk cut the tags, and pulled them on over my own jeans and sweatshirt in the store.

Benny didn't comment on the hoodie. He had a big crap-eating grin on his face when he handed me two folded papers.

I looked at Maria's sheet. Bad credit, some unpaid credit cards. Married and divorced from Raymond López. Maiden name: Raposa.

"Raposa," I said out loud. I handed Fratelli's rap sheet to Benny and tapped the name of his common-law wife: Arlene Raposa.

"Bingo," Benny said. "I'll track down Maria's and Arlene's current addresses."

"Call me when you find them," I said.

"Better yet, I'll bring them to the Blue Fin," he said nonchalantly. "At six."

———

I TEXTED JESSICA and asked her to meet me at the Blue Fin at 5:30. She was late. We ordered apple martinis. I barely had time to fill her in before Benny arrived. The hostess led him right to our table. He immediately looked at the drink menu.

"Well, I'll be," he said. "They start at fifteen dollars." He ordered a thirty-dollar imported beer from Bavaria, brewed by monks, and then set out a photocopy of two DMV licenses. Maria Raposa. Arlene Raposa. "Maria never changed her name on her license." He tapped the papers. "Take a look at the address."

Both of them lived at 314 Carroll Street, apartment B, one door down from apartment A, where my dad had been bonked on his head.

The waitress set down Benny's beer. I tossed a hundred on the table. "We have to go," I told her.

"But he just got his beer," she said.

"We'll be back later."

———

WE FLAGGED DOWN a surly taxi driver who cursed when we said we needed to go to Brooklyn. But Benny had his butt in the backseat and he couldn't speed away. Traffic on the Manhattan Bridge was a nightmare. It took over an hour to get to the 87th.

Benny, Jessica, and I walked in. Paco was off duty, but talking story out in front with his buddies.

"Hey, Paco," I said. I waved the two DMV printouts at him. "Want a promotion?"

———

THE DEAL WAS, I wanted to be the one to knock on the door and confront Maria. I wanted to know why, so I could tell Dad.

"You think she's going to tell you why?" Paco said. "Ha."

Paco and his crew broke the crime scene seal on Fratelli's apartment A and hid inside. "Two minutes," he said, motioning down the hall, which smelled of burned empanadas.

I knocked on B. A younger, shorter version of Maria opened the door. "Yes?"

"Hello, Arlene," I said. "Maria here?"

"She's in the bathroom," Arlene said.

I pushed past her. Suitcases were open on the couch, half-full of Yerba Maté bags.

Maria came out of the bathroom in her towel, saw me, and bolted for the door.

"Why? Why?" I yelled, following her out into the hallway, where Paco stepped out of A and grabbed her arm.

"Hey, Maria," he said. "What say we put on some clothes?"

———

THE 87TH WAS hopping. Paco was the hero of the day, two collars for the Fratelli murder, plus springing the old guy.

Wrinkled Suit saw me and started yelling. "You have some explaining to do!" he said. "Plus there was a picture of a corpse in that file." He pulled out his handcuffs.

Jessica stepped in front of me. "Touch her and I'll sue your sorry ass for sexual assault."

———

PACO BROUGHT DAD out into the lobby. He was still in his orange jumpsuit.

"Dad," I said, "I'm getting you out of here."

"I'm not going," he said. "I'm innocent."

"Yes," I said. "We know."

He demanded the return of his Hawaiian shorts. They refused, citing them as evidence.

"Then I'll have to leave naked," he said. He started to unzip his jumpsuit.

"Keep the jumpsuit overnight," Paco said.

"You can change at home," I said.

"Home?" Benny snorted. "Oh no. We're all going to the Blue Fin."

"The Blue Fin, huh?" Paco's face lit up. "I heard their beers are fifteen bucks a pop."

"No, they start at fifteen bucks and go up," Benny, the world-wise sophisticate, said. "Two pages of them. You're going to flip a switch."

"I got Maria's paperwork to do," Paco said.

"We'll be there awhile," Benny said.

Just then, Dad saw Maria being led from the fingerprint room. She was wearing an orange jumpsuit.

Dad called to her: "Maria? Maria?"

She refused to look at him or answer before she disappeared through the doors that led to the holding cells.

———

We all sat around a table at the Blue Fin. Dad, Benny, and Paco were working a flight of exotic beer, Jessica and I were nursing apple martinis. The waitress popped by, and Benny ordered one each of their thirty-dollar appetizers.

"I'm not hungry," Dad said.

"You've got to eat something," I said. He shook his head. I turned to the waitress. "Bring him two orders of your seared ahi, stuffed with caviar." I turned to Jessica. "I'm paying," I said, thinking of my clerk's salary. I'd put it on Visa. Paco arrived, and Benny ordered.

Jessica saw my face. She also saw Benny order another flight, plus three bottles of assorted German imports. "Not a chance," she said. "I have an expense account."

"And an order of fries," Paco said.

"I may have to go across the street for those." The waitress looked out the window at McDonald's.

Dad looked at the golden arches, frowned, and started to open his mouth. I shook my head. "Speaking of disputes," I said, "what's with Dixon's?"

"I was helping Ed Dixon with his dispute against Visa."

"Oh," I said, wondering how I was going to tell Dad about all his files I'd tossed.

———

Waiting for our food, Paco spilled the beans, so to speak.

"Maria spilled her guts," he said. Fratelli was abusive. A jerk. A lowlife. Violent, probably a murderer, a dog who deserved to die. Fresh out of jail, he'd moved into the apartment down the hall from Maria and Arlene, whom he beat if she didn't spend the night with him and beat if she did.

The last straw was when she took a plate of empanadas to his apartment, as requested, empanadas she had accidentally scorched on account of she was looking up the address of a women's shelter in the Brooklyn yellow pages and forgot about them on the stove.

Maria knew about Dad's Mega dispute and cooked up a quick plan. Arlene called Dad and got him to come over. Maria posted the yellow sticky note on the buzzer box to make it easy for him to come straight to the apartment door. Arlene opened it while Maria popped him gently on the head with a rubber baton from the stash of weapons under Fratelli's bed, then left to phone in the tip from the corner booth.

"Why?" Dad said.

I tried to be gentle. "She was getting tired of your disputes," I said.

"Aw shucks," Dad said. "Aw shucks."

Paco downed a whole bottle in one breath. Wiped his mouth. Continued. "She came to your apartment looking for the Mega file to see if there was anything in there that could tie Fratelli to Arlene," Paco said. "She found you there and hung around, trying to get information. When you cut her out of the loop, she thought you knew she was involved, so she planted the Mega file in your suitcase and called in another tip, figuring it would keep you tied up for a few days while she and Arlene split."

"I didn't offer to put up bail," Benny said.

"They'll get a deal," Jessica said. "Domestic defenses are guaranteed acquittals these days."

"Especially when we ID that corpse picture that Fratelli had," Paco said.

The waitress brought food. I wrapped up one order of seared ahi, with caviar, in a napkin.

"I thought we were in love," Dad said. "Now I've lost my appetite." I wrapped his ahi in another napkin and put both bundles in my purse.

"You may have been in love, old man," Paco said. "But Maria's a piece of work, and in her case, family trumps love."

His words gave me an idea. I would invite Dad to visit me. Introduce him to the judge, a novice dispute collector. Then I'd treat them to dinner at an overpriced restaurant that had bad service, dishonest waiters, thieving coatroom attendants, slovenly kitchen help, and a menu known as Salmonella Special. I knew about it because my co-clerk's boyfriend took her there to propose and she became deathly ill after consuming the shrimp bisque.

It was a dispute made in heaven.

"Gotta go," I said. "I'm dead, and I gotta be on the first flight out. Oral arguments. Come on, Dad."

———

DAD NOTICED HIS missing file cabinet the minute he walked in the door. He opened his mouth. I held up my hand.

"Say nothing," I said. "This is a new beginning."

He was silent for a full thirty seconds. I could see him reviewing his files with his steel trap of a mind. Perfect memory. It was only a matter of days before he was back in the saddle.

"Kitty, kitty." I unwrapped the bundles of ahi and caviar and put them in Jaws's dish. Jaws came running. Dad saw him, and his whole face lit up. He rummaged in a desk drawer for a well-worn flashlight, switched it on, and started twirling the beam.

Jaws hesitated. Fish or flashlight?

He snatched a mouthful of caviar and then dove into the game, speeding in an incredibly fast circle. Dad, the flashlight king, really knew how to get him going. Jaws had been mine until I went away to law school, whereupon Dad had spent three years ruining him with the flashlight.

Jaws staggered. "I'm leaving Jaws with you," I said. "He'll keep you company."

Jaws barfed. Caviar. Tough to clean up with Dad's environmental crap cleaning products.

"You can't leave him here," Dad said, ignoring the barf. He changed directions. Jaws fell over. "You won't have anyone to play the flashlight game with."

I looked long and hard at Dad, the flash-card lawyer. "I'll always have someone to play the flashlight game with."

"Who's that?" Dad said.

"You, Dad. You."

And I went into the kitchen to get a roll of recycled paper towels.

MOM IS MY CO-COUNSEL

BY PAUL LEVINE

L adies and gentlemen, the state will prove that Dr. Philip Macklin intentionally drove his Mercedes sedan into the Santa Ynez canal. Why? To kill his wife and make a premeditated murder look like an accident."

Scott Gardner pasted on his solemn face and paused. Keeping quiet was the trial lawyer's most difficult task, but he wanted his words to sink in.

Premeditated murder.

"A homicide both heinous and cruel," he continued. "Dr. Macklin swims to safety as his wife gasps for air, black water engulfing her like a shroud of death."

A tad melodramatic, but Nancy Grace will love the sound bite, and the jurors will be moved by my passion.

Tomorrow.

Tonight, Scott Gardner, duly elected District Attorney of Santa Barbara County, spun his tale for the empty chairs of his conference room. A dry run.

"Earlier that fateful evening," he continued, "Dr. Philip Macklin, the man sitting right here . . ."

J'accuse! *Pointing his index finger like a rapier at the monster.*

". . . placed the drug Seconal in his wife's drink. You will hear evidence that alcohol and barbiturates were found in Mrs. Macklin's blood, and that both substances were present in a cocktail glass in the family living room. Not only that . . ."

Softly but gravely. Make them lean forward, thirsting for every word.

". . . Dr. Macklin's fingerprints were found on that glass, along with those of his wife. *He* mixed her drink, and when she passed out, *he* carried her to the car, a scrap of her blue satin blouse catching on the Spanish bayonet bush in the driveway. *He* drove at a high rate of speed down Santa Ynez Road, veered through a guardrail, over the embankment, and into the canal. Just as *he* had planned."

"You have a motive for all this?"

Scott wheeled around. "Jesus! Mom, I didn't hear you come in."

"Your father used to say I treaded softly as an angel."

"I think he was going deaf there at the end." She didn't laugh at his joke. She *never* laughed at his jokes. "Say, how'd you get past security?"

She smiled and gave a little shrug. "Aren't you going to get your hair trimmed before trial?"

Reflexively, Scott ran a hand through his shaggy mop. Next, he expected his mother to straighten his tie, tuck in his shirttail, and remind him to eat his veggies.

"No time, Mom. We pick a jury in the morning."

She sighed her disapproval. For a moment Scott stared at his mother, marveling at her elegance. A gold silk embroidered jacket with a matching skirt falling just below the knees. Armani or Gucci, he figured. Gray hair stylishly cut, glacial blue eyes, and a still-firm chin.

"So what's up, Mom? I'm a little busy."

"I'm here to help. It's not like you're in court every day. Not like your father. Now, there was a lawyer."

As opposed to me?

"And there was a man," she added wistfully.

Ditto, he thought.

"So, what's the motive, Scottie?" his mother said.

Scottie.

Jeez, how many times had he asked her not to call him that?

He turned to his imaginary jury. "And just why did Dr. Macklin kill his wife? Because he was deeply in debt, his psychology practice foundering. Because Mrs. Macklin planned to divorce him, and she was his cash cow."

"Cash cow? Dear God, what a vulgarity. Why not call her his *femme de miel*?"

"If I get any Parisians on the jury, I will."

His mother lowered herself into one of the conference chairs. She gracefully crossed her legs and reached into her handbag, some Italian number made of supple blond leather the color of hay and soft as butter. She tapped a cigarette out of a blue Gauloises Blondes box and said, "Sometimes, Scottie, I wonder if you're cut out for criminal law."

"The voters of Santa Barbara County think I am."

"Oh, come, dear. They didn't know they were voting for Scott Gardner, *Junior*."

That again. In any contest with his father, he would always come in second. Scott Gardner, Sr., had been DA for a dozen years before going back into private practice with his wife. Gardner & Gardner, LLP. For all those messy problems of the moneyed folk with big houses in the hills of Montecito and on the cliffs above the beach.

So, sure, Scott knew that a lot of voters mistakenly thought his old man was making a comeback, even though he'd been residing in a cemetery overlooking the Pacific for the past three years.

"God, how I miss your father," she said, lighting a cigarette in violation of state, county, and city laws.

"Me too, Mom."

"I should never have gotten remarried."

"After what you and Dad had, you were bound to be disappointed."

Scott once told his mother that her marriage was a lot like the Reagans'. Husband and wife adoring each other and basically ignoring their children.

She didn't deny the charge, saying simply that little tadpoles need to swim on their own, or something to that effect.

She tilted her head toward the ceiling and exhaled a puff of smoke. "So what's your proof this wasn't an accident?"

"Seventeen minutes. The car's clock stopped at ten eighteen p.m. Macklin called nine-one-one at ten thirty-five. What was he doing for seventeen minutes?"

"Maybe he was in shock."

"Paramedics say he was fine." Scott smiled, letting her know he'd covered that base, just like good old Dad would have done. "Say, have you eaten? Kristin's stopping by with cheeseburgers."

"Cheeseburgers?" Making the word sound like "herpes sores."

"And fries."

"Kristin never did learn to cook, did she?"

"Don't start, Mom."

"I'm amazed she's kept her figure. Must have been all that exotic dancing."

"Mom, she was a Laker Girl."

"So she was. A regular Isadora Duncan."

"If you want a burger, tell me now, and I'll catch Kristin at the In-N-Out."

"I'd rather eat glass." She tapped cigarette ash into an empty coffee cup. "What makes you think Macklin didn't dive into the water and pound on the car windows for seventeen minutes?"

"He never claimed he did. Not a word to the cops at the scene or in the hospital. What does that tell you?"

"His silence is inadmissible."

"I'm just saying, would an innocent man keep quiet?"

"Maybe. If he had to think things through."

"Why? To plan his lies for trial?"

"To tell a painful truth that would nonetheless prove his innocence."

"What are you talking about?"

"The holes in your case."

"Hey, Mom. It's one thing to play devil's advocate, but I've been over this a hundred times. There are no holes."

"Do you remember the night of the crash?"

"Hard to forget. The sheriff called me at home. I was at the scene in fifteen minutes."

His mother exhaled a perfect smoke ring. She'd learned the trick from his father. "Did the lovely Kristin go with you?"

He thought a second. "No. She wasn't home."

"Ten thirty at night. Where was she, donating blood at the Red Cross?"

"It was a Thursday. Girls' night out. Racquetball."

"Was she there when you got back?"

"Of course. I didn't get home until nearly dawn. Kristin was asleep."

"How was she in the morning?"

"I don't understand the question, Counselor."

"Yes, you do. I always told your father you were brighter than you appear."

"Gee, thanks, Mom."

"Was Kristin stiff or sore? Was she visibly injured in any way?"

"What's that got to do with—"

"The witness shall answer the question."

Fine, he'd play along. "I wouldn't call it an injury. She had a bruised cheekbone from getting hit with a racquetball."

"Easily covered, I suppose, by all that Estée Lauder foundation she trowels on."

The intercom rasped with a woman's voice. "Honey, can you buzz me in?"

"Only if you're bringing food." Scott hit a button and heard the lock double-click open.

"We haven't much time," his mother said. "Don't make me go through this when you already know the answer."

"Mom, I swear I don't even know the question."

"You're in denial, Scottie."

"Of what?"

"Let's say that Mrs. Macklin was supposed to be traveling that fateful evening. But a marine layer rolled in and the Lear couldn't get out of the municipal airport."

"Okay, she's fogged in."

His mother laughed, the sound of church bells pealing. "Oh my, yes. Was she ever fogged in. Anyway, she comes home and finds her husband in bed with a young woman. The woman was astride the miscreant in what I believe they call the 'cowgirl' position, and sure as shooting, her whoops and hollers would have been appropriate for a rodeo."

Scott heard the door to the anteroom open. "Honey," Kristin called out, "I'll be there in a sec, after I get some Cokes from the fridge."

"Take your time." He turned to his mother. "Your story doesn't make sense. If Mrs. Macklin catches her husband in flagrante delicto, no way she's going to sit down and have a drink with him."

"She doesn't."

"So what's with his fingerprints on the glass?"

"I assume she put Seconal in her whiskey, downed it, then dropped the glass. Her husband simply picked up the glass, perhaps to sniff it, or maybe he's a neat freak."

They could hear Kristin in the next room, the sound of ice cubes rattling out of a tray.

"You're saying she committed suicide," Scott said.

"Tried to. OD'ed into a semiconscious state."

"So what's she doing in the car with her husband?"

"What's down Santa Ynez Road? Three miles past the site of the accident."

He considered the question. "The Cottage Hospital."

"Exactly. If I were defending the case, I'd say Dr. Macklin felt enormous guilt over causing his wife's suicide attempt. He picked her up, carried her to his car, her blouse catching on that damn thorny bush. He's driving to the hospital at seventy miles an hour when he loses control around a curve and plunges into the canal."

"So why didn't he pull her out of the water?"

"Because he only had time to rescue one person, and no matter how heavy his guilt, he was in love with someone else. Stated another way, his wife was second on his triage list."

"Wrong. There was no one else in the car."

"You mean there was no one else there when the paramedics arrived. Dr. Macklin didn't call nine-one-one until his paramour—a lovely term, is it not? —left the scene. There's your seventeen minutes."

"So who'd he rescue? Who's this paramour?"

"How about a woman who hit her cheekbone on the dashboard when the car went into the water?"

He shook his head and his shoulders sagged. Of course, he knew. He just couldn't accept it. Not that or the knowledge of his own cowardice. He'd never challenged Kristin, and he'd never confronted his own unethical conduct. He wanted to punish Dr. Macklin. Not for homicide, because Macklin wasn't a killer. No, he wanted to punish Macklin for cuckolding him.

"So what do I do now?" he said.

"Scott, who are you talking to?" With a dancer's graceful gait, Kristin waltzed into the conference room in black yoga pants and a fluorescent orange sleeveless sports top. She carried a tray of food and drinks.

"Tell me!" he yelled.

"Tell you what?" Kristin asked. "What are you upset about?"

"Mom, what do I do?"

"Oh Christ." Kristin dropped the tray on the table, spilling a soda. "Not this again."

"Mom!"

He could still see Gayle Gardner Macklin, but her image was fading.

"Mom, don't leave me. Please!"

Trembling, Kristin said, "Scott, you know your mother drowned in that car."

"No! She's here now."

"Honey, you spoke at her funeral and bawled your eyes out."

Scott propped one hand on the conference table and struggled to his feet. He brushed past his wife without even seeing her.

"The judge should never have allowed you to handle the case," Kristin said. "I knew something weird would happen."

His legs felt rubbery as he staggered out, leaving behind his trial bag, the pleadings, the exhibits. His wife.

"Scott, where are you going?"

She dropped into a chair, sniffed the air. "Did you start smoking again?"

No answer. He was gone.

Kristin examined a coffee cup on the table. Inside, a half-smoked cigarette. She picked it up, the tip still glowing.

French. Just like her bitch mother-in-law used to smoke. A shudder went through her and she crushed the cigarette into the bottom of the cup. From the doorway, she heard a melodious voice.

"Kristin, dear. You look just darling in your workout gear."

She spun around in her chair.

Omigod.

"Last time we met, you were au naturel and grunting like a sow in heat."

Kristin steadied herself against the fear. Her words came in forced breaths. "What have you become? What do you want?"

"At long last, I am my true self. And all I want is justice."

Paralyzed, Kristin watched as Scott, wearing a woman's gray wig, his cheeks rouged and lips glossed, raised a handgun and pointed it at her chest.

QUALITY OF MERCY

BY LEIGH LUNDIN

*T*hank you, Your Honor. Yes, the prosecution is ready with an opening statement.

Ladies and gentlemen of the jury, good morning. We are here today to discuss, literally, a case of life and death: whether any individual has the right to take another's life. My job is to present the state's evidence, the state's view of this crime. Your job, based upon the evidence, is to render a decision about this crime, about this sad and unfortunate death.

Today, ladies and gentlemen, we come to this courtroom to try a defendant, to discuss and deliberate upon a death for which the accused freely admits responsibility.

My esteemed colleague at the adjoining table will tell you about extenuating circumstances, about euthanasia, about the right to die. Indeed, my opponent can rattle on for hours about it.

The state's position is: What about the right to life? If a society condones murder—and don't mistake that, with all its window dressing, this was murder—what kind of society would we live in?

Most of you, I'm sure, would rather be somewhere else. I certainly did not ask for this case. I didn't want it; no one wanted it. I *even like the defendant. I feel for the defendant. You may well like the defendant, too.*

I won't demonize the accused, I won't tell you the crime was diabolical, but—let us be clear—a homicide was committed, the law broken, a life taken, and we, my friends, live in a society of laws. As such, it is incumbent upon us to take note of the societal picture at large.

A crime of murder took place, and there is never, ever an excuse for taking the life of another.

That means, ladies and gentlemen, your only choice will be to render a verdict of . . . guilty.

———

HIS CERTAINTY SOLIDIFIED the day she forgot the children's names. It was strange, because she'd always accused *him* of being absentminded. Before, they'd always laughed self-consciously, but for a while now, she'd been forgetting little things. This time, forgetfulness seemed more than absentmindedness.

He convinced himself the first episode wasn't so bad, but less than two weeks later, he found her speaking to her mother, as if her mother were actually standing there, as if his wife were once again a little girl. It was startling; she was eighty-three, and her mother had been dead for twenty years. When, finally, his wife had come around, he comforted her and they'd cried together.

He felt frightened. For days, he debated whether to say anything more about it. Could he even be certain of connecting? But how could he not talk this out with her? After fifty years, sharing every thought had become an ingrained habit.

In the end, as with so many things, she was the one who brought the matter up.

"I'm changing, love. I'm afraid I'm slipping. In fact, I'm . . . afraid."

He sat silently, listening, as he had done so often. She was the one who could articulate, the one who could express thoughts he could never put into words.

"My forgetfulness, the mistakes . . . the other day I brushed my teeth with that dandruff shampoo out of the tube. And last month I burned myself. Sometimes I feel I'm losing my mind, that I'm disintegrating."

He smiled grimly at that, remembering once years ago when he'd blindly shampooed not Head & Shoulders but toothpaste into his scalp. Of course, he'd been thinking out a research problem, and everyone had smiled indulgently at yet another anecdote proving him the proverbial absentminded professor. They'd joked about it, said no one would be able to tell when he became senile. But this couldn't happen with her. "Come here," he whispered to her.

She was only seven or eight inches away, but she melded against him, crushing her silver hair against his cheek. The fresh scent of her, which he knew so well, filled his nostrils, and he felt the warm trickle of her tears upon his neck.

He had loved her for so long. It was more than fifty years since he had been the self-absorbed rake, the boy who couldn't keep it in his pants. Stern fathers locked up their daughters and hid away their wives, while mothers whispered about him, one or two with a burning gleam in the eye.

Then, he'd met *her*. Today, six decades later, he found it hard to remember a time without her smile, without her voice, without her cheek against his.

"I'm so scared," she wept, softly sobbing. "I don't want to lose what we have."

"We won't, we can't; we worked too hard to find it. We learned it, we earned it, remember? Besides, don't we have what those young TV psychologists call 'co-dependence'? Think of all the psychiatry we would have to endure to unlearn all this."

She nodded. Poor spoiled little rich girl and spoiled little poor boy; she'd learned about loving from him and he'd learned about living from her. They continued learning, every minute, every hour, every day.

He said, "It's only temporary, just a phase—like adolescence or menopause."

"No. No, we both know better. It has a name—only . . . only I forget what it is."

Glancing at her, he found her smiling. Her humor was one of her attractions.

"I seem to recall that our worst fear was we might be reduced to wearing Depends someday," he said.

"I'll be happy to trade." She nuzzled his neck; let her hand slip down his lanky frame.

He relaxed a little. Thank God she was again her old self. She wasn't impaired, mentally or otherwise, not really.

"Without Viagra, 'depend' is about all that happens these days. But I appreciate the thought."

She straightened. "Darling, let's see a doctor, a gerontologist. Let's hear what he has to say. This week, okay?"

————

"*SUNDOWNING*, IT'S CALLED," said the geriatrician, speaking as if she wasn't there. "Her experience of agitation late in the day is not uncommon. Keep her quiet during the day, reduce the stress at night. Sundowning may come from fatigue, or it may be related to shadows; we're not exactly sure. See that she naps in the afternoon. Cover the mirrors so she won't see a face she doesn't recognize."

"But my wife's prognosis?"

"Late in the early stages," said the doctor, making the onset sound like an oxymoron. "I'm terribly sorry, but you have to face the facts: from now on, I'm afraid you'll continue to observe further deterioration. I recommend you start looking for a good resident care program. I'll provide you with a list of suitable facilities. You'll want to start on this right away."

He *wanted* no such thing. Their greatest fear was separation, of being alone as the darkness descended.

———

"Let's take a trip," she said brightly. "New Hampshire, Vermont, and see the changing leaves. Let's see America, cruise across the Midwest perhaps, maybe Indiana, Iowa. It's autumn and the autumn of our lives; let's enjoy it."

And so from Maine they swept across New England into Pennsylvania, where for the second time she wandered off during the middle of the night. He sat terrified, staring at her picture on television, waiting for news. Any news.

Thank God, the police found her, wandering and confused, without a clue as to where she was. Unfamiliar, yet facelessly identical as fast-food restaurants and malls, motels confused her. With reluctance and tears, they turned homeward.

———

In her own house, she seemed to do better. She was almost her old—or rather younger self, he thought. As before, she cooked a little, listened to music, and dressed herself for church. One month passed, then two. Other than a minor episode instigated by the replacement of the old stained coffeemaker with a new model, she talked and acted as if her brain had mended.

He began to feel hopeful.

Then, one day, he noticed her favorite magazine opened to an article. About euthanasia. In the Netherlands. There, apparently, putting one's life in the hands of others was an acceptable practice. Even if—even if your relatives might be in a bit of a hurry to, well, to polish you off.

That same evening, the news broadcast a segment on Jack Kevorkian and his Alzheimer's patients.

He changed channels.

"Wait," she said. "Go back. No, not that channel. Not that one either. Oh no, it's over."

After breakfast he locked the house and strolled down to the library. He didn't understand why everyone seemed to think computers were too much for the elderly to handle. The Internet was a hell of a lot easier than using microfilm machines.

Before looking it up, he'd been under the impression Dr. Kevorkian's victims were terminal cancer patients. He was wrong. Dr. K's early subjects had been fearful of Alzheimer's. A number of articles suggested Kevorkian had been, to put it generously, precipitous.

He sat back and considered the gray irony, the bitter Catch-22 of old age: anybody frightened by the appalling effects of senility had too much mental clarity to be considered a candidate for euthanasia. On the other hand, if the afflicted were past understanding their own Alzheimer's symptoms, they didn't have the mental capacity to make sensible decisions and therefore weren't ethically rational enough to give their consent.

He signed off the computer and pondered the *should* and *should not*, the right and wrong of it all.

———

"Darling, I want you to do one little thing for me."

"Now, now, my dear, I don't know if I'm up to it." He winked a mock leer her way.

"If anyone could, you would, but that isn't what I meant."

"No, I suppose not. What do you want me to do for you?"

She hesitated. "If I worsen . . . I mean worsen a lot . . . I don't want you to let me go on like this. And I don't want you to agonize about it."

Tears stung his eyes.

"Poor dear," she said, "you're agonizing now, but listen, I have no one but you, no one else to rely upon. Always, I was afraid of losing you, that you'd go first, that I'd have to live out the rest of my life alone with only memories to comfort me. But this—no memories at all?"

He couldn't speak from the acrid torsion of his throat.

She dipped her fingers in the pooled tears from his eyes and drew them to her lips. "Don't cry, love. I know what I'm doing."

"None of us knows. Not you, not me."

"I know I don't want to succumb to Alzheimer's. We've read so much about it. Remember that Florida case? We watched those TV movies about it."

He knew she couldn't feel as controlled about it as she made it sound.

"Poor baby, I know," she continued. "What will you do without me? But think, love. What will you do *with* me if I'm incapacitated?"

He pushed the thought away. "But you're not, and you won't be. For better or worse . . ."

"This is decidedly worse, for we're talking about a cruel disease. We're talking about dignity. About quality. About life."

"False dignity! And what kind of quality?" He was angry. "It's you that made our marriage what it is. You kept us solvent following the Depression. Your letters kept me going during the war. You prayed for our sons in Vietnam and our grandchildren in Iraq. You worked so hard and had faith in me when I started the business. Do you think I could give up on you, even if I'd never loved you? I couldn't bear to let you stay in a nursing home."

"I'm not talking about a nursing home. I think you know that."

That was when he truly understood what she was getting at. He said, "How could you expect that of me? Me? I won't even kill a spider, and you ask me to destroy what I love most? Discard you like laundry?"

"No, my dear, not destroy it, save it. Other cultures have remarkable concepts about choosing when and where to end one's own life. I'm not so sure those ideas have any place for the young, but they have meaning for the old."

"I won't. This is madness. I can't."

She continued as if he hadn't spoken. "This is what I want you to do. I bought a little bottle. It's in the cupboard, next to the aspirin. When I can no longer . . . *function* . . . function normally . . . I want you to get the bottle out. You don't even have to give it to me. Just set it out, here on the bedstand. When I'm lucid, I'll know."

He shook, and cried, and argued, and in the end, she held him, petting him, cradling him as she'd done so often. By the time they'd exhausted themselves, if not the subject, he hadn't agreed, but he hadn't flatly refused.

———

SHE SEEMED RELIEVED, and for a while she was much, much better. It was he who suffered, feeling a dark gray mass hovering over them. Her clasping him close, her snuggling, her gentle teasing only temporarily dispelled the clouds.

Throwing the bottle away, or filling it with vitamins or perhaps sugar pills, crossed his mind. But she wasn't anyone's fool, not even now. She would know. Dejected, he sensed discarding the vial would only hurt her.

Then, with a flash of insight, he had the revelation. He suddenly understood the bottle was an ironic lifeline for her, an escape, a way out, a kind of hope. Even if he never set the bottle out, it seemed to comfort her to know it was there.

He watched as she grew more peaceful at night, almost content. She slept with her arms around him, spoon fashion, as they fell asleep. He prayed she couldn't feel the rivulets of tears sear his cheek, couldn't hear his heart break. He was sad and already lonely.

Numbness crept in around them both, stealing over them like the too-sweet redolence of day-old flowers.

———

THE ONSLAUGHT WAS sudden and fierce. By Wednesday, she began losing names and the occasional word from her vocabulary. Unexpectedly, she burst out crying in frustration. On Sunday, she wandered off after church. He found her minutes later, traipsing around the churchyard, the hem of her skirt clutched tightly in her hand, as if she were dancing, babbling to no one that Daddy let her hitch the horse. She prattled on like that the rest of the day.

During the afternoon, he cradled her, rocked her, walked her to the bathroom, and brushed her hair. He knew it wasn't her, not really, but he could no longer touch and talk to the woman he loved, the woman who'd defined who he was for all these years.

The edges of his life were turning brown, wilting like the fringes of autumn leaves.

He didn't dare trust her to cook. She confused salt with sugar, cinnamon with cumin. One evening she made a cream sauce recipe and measured in two cups of flour instead of two tablespoons. She fled weeping to their bedroom and refused to try again.

Shopping became a catastrophe. By the end of the month he'd stopped taking her along—it was too difficult tenderly managing her while trying to get the task done. But when he left her alone and returned home, he was terrified he would face some new crisis.

The crisis came in September, after a quick trip to fetch groceries. She didn't answer when he tapped the door with his toe. He could hear her inside, singing "After the Ball Is Over."

Setting down the bags, he let himself in. Smoke hung heavily in the air. He turned off the burner under the smoldering remains of a forgotten dish towel.

His darling sat spread-legged in the middle of the living-room floor, with a large pair of shears and her dress in tatters, remnants pinned to her antique rag doll.

"Hi, Papa." She looked up and smiled. "Papa?"

He suppressed a flash of exasperation.

She looked wonderingly around at the smoke. "Did Mama close the flue?"

"Come, sweetheart. Come along, before I go mad."

He helped her to her feet, held her, and noticed she'd wet herself.

That night he picked up the small bottle, stared at it for a long, long time. He wanted to weep, but no tears came. He wanted to sense pain, but he'd spent it all too recently. If he couldn't feel, he thought, he could go on, and he started to put the bottle back. But no, that was wrong: if he could feel, he could never do what he had to do.

He displayed the bottle prominently, near the coffeepot. Instead of going to bed, he put a worn disk on the record player and sat in the unlit living room. Finally, the tears began and washed over him, bathing him, mingling with his agony.

He entered the darkened bedroom, its gloom the same texture as the night in his soul. He watched her sleeping, childlike.

She stirred and, sensing him, opened her eyes to his pain.

Oh, how could he think of leaving the bottle out? First thing in the morning, he must put it away. Surely he could take care of her for the rest of his life. He could rise to the occasion; he *would* rise to it. Hadn't she dedicated *her* life to *him?* He could do this, yes, he certainly could. He was strong enough to bear this cross; it was a weight of no consequence. What had led him so close to despair? Vanity? Self-pity?

He lay down beside her, and she held him again, fragile as an autumn dandelion, held him softly until he passed into sleep.

On the kitchen counter, a small bottle, forgotten, stood sentinel beside the coffeepot.

———

THE NEXT MORNING glowed golden and bright. She had been up, but came back to bed to snuggle against him. These intimate mornings had long been his favorite, their raison d'être.

He rose, enjoying this time with her, and began shaving. Looking at himself in the mirror, he remembered. Oh Lord, he must be losing his mind. The bottle was sitting out by the coffeepot.

Flying suspenders and shaving cream, he scuttled out to the kitchen.

She stood there gazing out the kitchen window, reading his mind. "It's okay, love. It's okay. It's exactly what I wanted you to do."

"But I was wrong. We're both wrong. It's not the time. It never will be. We can't do this."

"But it is time, love. Oh, not today perhaps, or even tomorrow. But another day. Or night. A glorious day, and you'll hold me tight that night. I'll know when." She held out her arms to him, dispelling his mute plea.

The bottle disappeared, and he was relieved as, day by day, she became more cheerful. But every day he detected new signs of her sliding away.

One night she made a pot of tea, lit a candle, and drew him into bed. She stripped back his pajamas, kissed his body where the skin clung thinly to his ribs. She lay next to him, willing her flesh to be part of his. It wasn't making love, not in the sense of what it used to be; this transcended, it was better. And he knew through his tears that time was no longer with them.

———

AND SO, LADIES and gentlemen of the jury, this is the part of the hearing called the summation. You have heard a crime described. A crime of passion, yes, and, as my esteemed colleague suggests, a crime of compassion as well, but still a crime.

Certainly the most heinous crime man can commit is the taking of a life, deliberate murder, the only crime for which you can never compensate the victim.

Over the last few days, you've heard testimony about Alzheimer's disease, about impaired mental capacity and diminished responsibility. I'm sure pain and suffering ensued for both parties. The psychiatric expert introduced by the defense mentioned a kind of temporary insanity. You've heard the defense suggest the defendant may be senile, a pitiful victim of aged dementia. You've heard how it's kind to be cruel, and how our nation has become so gentle in delivering death.

All of this means nothing. It doesn't matter whether she cooperated with him or not. And it doesn't matter that you and I find great sympathy with the defendant, or have even grown to like her, as I know we all have.

What matters to society is that a premeditated homicide took place. You cannot simply poison your husband if he becomes inconvenient to you. Your husband or your wife today, your parents tomorrow, and then who's next? What if your children become inconvenient, or hyperactive, or incontinent?

That's why, ladies and gentlemen, that is exactly why you must find against the defendant, no matter how much you like her, or how sorry you feel for her. That's why, beyond any doubt whatsoever—you must reach into your own personal repository of justice, and find this defendant . . . guilty.

THE MOTHER

BY MICHELE MARTINEZ

A cross the length of the courtroom, Melanie Vargas met the young woman's eyes. *This is the hard part,* Melanie tried to say with her gaze, *but I know you can handle it.*

"What happened next?" she asked.

"I was reaching for my keys, but they were way down in my bag."

"Where were the men?"

"Behind me still, but getting closer. It was late enough that there wasn't no traffic on the street and it was real quiet. So I could hear their footsteps coming toward me." Her voice cracked. "They were running."

"Did you see their faces?"

The head defense lawyer leaped to his feet. "Objection."

Good sign, Melanie thought. *There was nothing objectionable about that question. He's trying to break my stride.*

"Rephrase it," the judge said, looking annoyed.

"What if anything did you see of the men's faces while you were trying to get your keys from your bag?" Melanie asked.

"I didn't see nothing. I was too scared to look up. I was just praying. Like, please, God, make them go away, and trying to get my keys out as fast as I could. My legs was shaking, and I couldn't hardly breathe."

"Then what happened?" Melanie asked gently.

On the witness stand, Gabriela Torres went visibly paler under a cloud of curly black hair. She was a tiny thing, five-two and slender, and looked about sixteen, although she was twenty-three. She was one of the best witnesses in an ugly case full of brutal people, untainted except for being a kingpin's moll, and the jury was eating her up. As Gabriela stared down at her hands, clenched before her on the podium, every juror's gaze was locked on her. She took a deep breath, and the entire jury breathed in with her and held, waiting for the horror show.

"They caught up with me," Gabriela said, shaking her head in misery.

"Did you see their faces then?" Melanie asked.

The defense lawyer moved to get up, but the judge, who was a fearsome old man and protective of this young woman, froze him in place with a glare.

"Yeah, I saw them when they were coming at me," Gabriela whispered. "I saw them good."

"Are either of the men who approached you that night here in the courtroom today?"

"Yes, both of 'em."

"Can you identify them for the jury?"

Now Melanie was the one holding her breath. Gabriela knew the attackers. Would she have the guts to ID them in open court? But she looked straight at the defense table and pointed, her hand steadier than Melanie's felt right then.

"That's them. Sitting there at that table. The two black guys. The big one who's missing his ear and wearing a blue shirt. And the other one with the fade haircut and the tattoo on his forehead. I won't never forget that tattoo. *Everybody Dies,* it said. *Everybody Dies.*"

"Let the record reflect that the witness has identified the defendant Edwin Smith, who is wearing a blue shirt and whose left ear is missing, and the defendant Rashad Baxter, who has a tattoo on his forehead that reads, *Everybody Dies*," Melanie said.

And she paused for a moment to turn the page of her trial notebook, letting the jury get a good long look at those two before Gabriela resumed her tale.

"Had you ever seen either defendant before the night in question, the night of March seventeenth of last year?"

"Yes. The second I saw their faces, I recognized 'em both. I knew them from the spot. They came in there a lot."

"How many times had you seen them before that night?"

"At least eight, ten times, maybe more."

"Together?"

"Yes, always together."

"And when you say you saw them at the spot, what are you referring to?"

"The pool hall on Myrtle Avenue I told you about. The one Orlando sold drugs out of."

"When you would see them at the pool hall, what would they be doing?"

"They'd come in to meet with Orlando. I'd be hanging with him, and when them two guys showed up, he'd say, 'Sit tight, baby, I got business,' and he'd take them in the back room, where they kept the product."

"So you believed the defendants to be narcotics customers of Mr. Jiménez?"

"Objection."

"Sustained."

"Directing your attention again to the night of March seventeenth, what happened as the defendants approached you?" Melanie asked.

"They both pulled out guns. I mean, scary-ass guns too, not

nothing little. The second I saw the guns, I started screaming real loud, thinking maybe Orlando would hear me and come out, but he didn't. Instead, the one with the tattoo, he hit me with his gun, hard, right across the face."

"Rashad Baxter hit you with his gun?"

"Yes."

"How did the blow affect you?"

"Well, I never been hit so hard before. When they say you see stars, it's true. It was like lights going off inside my head. Everything went white, and the next thing I know, I'm sitting on my a—on my butt on the sidewalk, bleeding like a stuck pig from this cut. I still got a little scar. But that's when the lady walked by, the old lady. My angel I call her now, but I didn't know her at the time."

"Did you subsequently learn her name?" Melanie asked.

The woman had just testified, right before Gabriela took the stand, and Melanie wanted the jury to make the connection.

"Yes. Her name is Carmen Marrero. She saw me there sitting on the ground, and I saw her, but *they* didn't see her. They were too busy messing me up."

"What did Mrs. Marrero do when she saw you sitting and bleeding on the ground?"

"Nothing. She was smart. She went right back in her house real quiet and they didn't notice. I'm just glad I was in such a daze. If I wasn't messed up, I would've called out to her, and then they would've seen her."

"What happened after Mrs. Marrero went back inside?"

"He, him—the one with the tattoo?"

"You're referring to the defendant Rashad Baxter?"

"Yeah. He pulled me up real rough and stuck the gun right up in my face. He say to me, 'Where Orlando at?' and tell me all sorts of things he was gonna do to me if I didn't take him to the apartment. See, because they had followed me, but they didn't know exactly which apartment was us."

"What threats did Rashad Baxter make to you?"

"The one I really remember is . . ." Gabriela paused. "Can I use bad language?" she asked, looking up at the judge.

"Tell the jury what Mr. Baxter said," the judge commanded.

"He told me if I didn't take them inside right away, he was gonna put the gun up my cunt and pull the trigger."

Some of the jurors gasped.

"So what did you do?" Melanie asked.

"I didn't do nothing. I started crying, and I almost fainted. They took my keys out of my bag and opened the outside door and shoved me in the hallway. As soon as I'm inside, I hear the handcuffs. I been arrested before, that time you asked me about when we started? So I know the sound of handcuffs. When I heard it, I thought, I'm dead meat for sure. The guy with the tattoo cuffed me behind my back, and the other guy, the one with the ear, he hit me and told me to shut up because now they in, they don't need me. If I want to stay alive one more minute, I better help out. Like that."

"What, if anything, did Mr. Smith ask you to do to help him?"

"He told me, say something while I'm unlocking the door, so Orlando wouldn't get suspicious. To tell him like, I was back or something."

"To say something when you walked in the door of your apartment?"

Gabriela's eyes filled with tears. "Yes."

"And did you?" Melanie asked.

The tears spilled over. "Yes! We went up to the door. They unlocked it and opened it a crack, and I said, 'Baby, I'm home.' Then Orlando, he come out of the bedroom and he saw me all bloody like that, and saw the two guys. He freaked out."

"Where were your children while this was happening?"

"Asleep."

"Were they in the apartment?"

"My God, they were in the next room! I'm praying the whole time, Please, God, *Díos mio*, don't let my babies wake up and walk into this shit. I'm thinking they were gonna kill my kids."

Gabriela was sobbing, but trying to control it. Melanie reached into her jacket pocket and pulled out a small package of Kleenex she'd been saving for a moment like this.

"Your Honor, may I approach the witness?"

"You may."

Melanie walked toward the witness stand as Gabriela cried. When she handed the girl the Kleenex, Gabriela looked at her with imploring gratitude.

"Thank you," she whispered.

The jury was riveted.

"Do you need a recess?" the judge asked, a touch of impatience in his voice.

Gabriela shook her head. "Sir, I'd rather just get it over with."

"You said your children were present in the apartment at this time," Melanie said, resuming her place at the lectern. "How many children do you have?"

"Orlando Junior, he's five. And Antonio is almost three now, but when this happened, he was just a little baby."

Gabriela was still sniffling, but seemed more composed.

"You said that when Mr. Jiménez saw you and the defendants, he freaked out. Can you describe what happened?"

"He ran back to the bedroom for his gun. See, he didn't have no gun or nothing when he came out, because he thought it was only me."

"Would he normally have carried a gun in that situation?"

"If someone came to the door, yeah, normally he would."

"To your knowledge, why would Mr. Jiménez bring a gun to answer the door?"

"Because he stashed in the house. I always told him not to. I was afraid of just exactly what happened. That was my nightmare. I tell him, You crazy stashing here where your kids live. But that was Orlando. He was hardheaded, and he ain't never listen to no woman about business."

"When you say Mr. Jiménez stashed in your house, what do you mean by that?"

Gabriela made eye contact with the jury. Melanie watched them react to her sad, pretty face. They might disapprove of her, but they couldn't help liking her and, more than liking, *believing* her.

"He kept drugs and money there," Gabriela replied.

"What type of drugs?" Melanie asked.

"Heroin, like he sold in the spot."

"How much?"

"A lot. He kept a lot. And money too."

"Where in the apartment did he keep the drugs and money?"

"He had a hide built in the closet in our bedroom."

"Can you explain to the jury what a hide is?"

"It's like a secret compartment. He built the wall out and made a space in there that you couldn't see by looking. It was big. You could fit like a hundred kilos in it, not that he moved that much product at one time."

"On the night of the seventeenth, to your knowledge, how much heroin was in the secret compartment in the closet?"

"Twenty keys, because Orlando had just got a shipment."

"That's twenty kilograms?"

"Yes."

"To your knowledge, did anybody other than yourself or Mr. Jiménez know about this twenty-kilogram shipment?"

"A lot of people knew. All the workers at the spot. And any-body who worked for the connect. Word got around."

"When you say connect, who do you mean?"

"The supplier of the drugs. He was a Colombian from Jackson Heights called Gordo. That means fat guy. All Gordo's people knew he'd just fronted Orlando twenty keys. That's why I always told Orlando he's crazy, that we gonna get hit someday. But he say he's gotta take care of his product. He's not gonna leave it with nobody else because everybody steals. He'd rather risk his life and keep his product close."

"But wasn't he risking your life too, and your children's?"

"I know." She gave a resigned little shrug.

"Directing your attention back to what was going on inside the apartment. What happened after Mr. Jiménez ran back to the bedroom to get his gun?"

"He slammed the door behind him, but it didn't have no lock on it and they busted it down right away. I got on my knees and crawled behind the couch, so I couldn't see nothing, but I could still hear. Everything was crashing around real loud, and glass was smashing. Orlando kept his gun in the drawer next to the bed, so he must have been trying to get to it. Then I heard a shot, and the next second, I heard him cry out. I knew he was hit."

"After you heard Mr. Jiménez cry out, what happened?"

"A lot of yelling. Orlando was still alive. They're telling him he better give up the product or they gonna bring me in the room and cut pieces off me until he do. He was telling them get the fu—get out, or he's gonna kill 'em. That was Orlando. Somebody step to him, he don't back down. But I heard 'em in there tearing everything apart, and eventually one said, 'Here it is. I found it.' They found the stuff. After that, I knew they'd kill us."

Gabriela stopped speaking and welled up again.

"Then what?" Melanie asked in a gentle tone.

On the witness stand, the young woman looked up at the ceiling and sighed, then swiped her knuckles across her eyes, wiping away tears.

"I heard shots. Three shots."

"Coming from the bedroom?"

"Yes. And I knew it was done. My babies' daddy was dead, and they gonna come for me and my kids next."

"What made you think they would come for you and your children?"

"Because they said so. When they was unlocking the door downstairs on the street, the one with the tattoo, he say to the other one, 'We gonna shoot her?' and the one with the ear say, 'Not yet.' So I'm down on the floor expecting to die. But then the miracle happened. My angel, *la Señora* Marrero, she had called the police, and I started hearing the sirens. Normally in my neighborhood, there's sirens all the time, but this was different. It was a lot, and you could tell it was right outside the building. The next thing, I heard the window going up in the bedroom. It squeaked a lot, so I knew what it was."

"What was the significance to you of the window going up?"

"We got a fire escape there, so I knew they was running. Running away like scared little girls. The next thing I know, the cops is busting in, and I'm screaming. I'm saying, 'Please, please, call an ambulance. They shot my man.' But it was too late. I went in the room. There was blood and brains all over the wall. Orlando's laying on the floor on the other side of the bed. The top of his head . . . it was just gone. He was dead."

And she put her hands up to her face and started to wail.

"No further questions," Melanie said.

And she walked to her chair at the prosecution's table and sat down, trying not to let the triumph show on her face.

———

MELANIE CHECKED HER watch. It was a little past four, the jury had been out for over two hours, and she was hoping for a verdict by five o'clock. Normally she didn't let herself get over-confident, but this case was more of a slam-dunk than any she'd ever seen. She had two incredibly sympathetic eyewitnesses— Gabriela Torres and the little old lady who'd seen her getting brutalized and called the police. She had the murder weapon, with Rashad Baxter's fingerprints and clear ballistics linking it to the bullets riddling the victim's head and upper torso. She had several cops, all African-American or Hispanic, solid and believable, who'd testified to the racially mixed jury that they'd surrounded the defendants coming down the fire escape carrying two duffel bags stuffed with heroin. Proof beyond a reasonable doubt was a tough standard, but what more could you want?

Melanie wasn't alone in expecting a quick verdict. The two defense attorneys, who might otherwise have gone back to their offices, were hanging around in the corridor, making cell-phone calls from inside the quaint old wood and marble phone booths that were scheduled to be ripped out in a coming renovation. The courtroom deputy had poked her head into the courtroom a couple of times to report that there was nothing to report yet—something she wouldn't have done if a long deliberation was expected. The DEA agent assigned to the case, who sat at the government's table with Melanie, had stepped out for a cup of coffee, but promised he'd be "back in fifteen, just in case."

So Melanie was alone in the deserted courtroom, expecting a verdict any minute, when the woman walked in. She looked to be in her late forties, heavy-set, with a close-cropped Afro dyed blond and big gold hoop earrings. She'd been in the gallery throughout the two-week trial. Based on eye contact and ges-tures, Melanie had decided early on that the woman was Rashad Baxter's mother. Now she was heading down the aisle straight to-ward Melanie, "irate family member" written all over her face.

Melanie stood up, the better to protect herself.

"Can I help you, ma'am?" she asked in a firm voice as the woman stopped in front of her, hands on hips.

"Why'd you stand up like that? You afraid I'm gonna hurt you?"

"You're Rashad Baxter's mother, right?"

"I'm Danita Baxter, yes. I guess you're afraid because you're trying to kill my son, so you know I got cause to be angry."

The prosecution was asking for the death penalty. That decision had been made by bureaucrats in Washington and the previous prosecutor on the case rather than by Melanie herself. But given that she'd be the one urging the jury to vote for death after they came back with a guilty verdict, it would be disingenuous to try to shift blame.

"I'm just doing my job, ma'am," she said. "I'm sure this is very difficult for you emotionally, but there's no point in making trouble. If you have something you want to say to me, tell it to your son's lawyer and let him convey it."

Melanie picked up her file and turned to leave.

"I'm his mother!" Danita Baxter cried. "He has kids! Doesn't none of that mean nothing to you?"

"What about Orlando Jiménez's kids? What about *his* mother? Rashad would've killed Gabriela and her children without a moment's hesitation if the cops hadn't shown up. You know that as well as I do. And you know this wasn't the first time your son killed somebody either."

"It ain't Rashad. It's the streets."

"Plenty of men grow up on the streets and don't become killers. Besides, he had *you*. It's not like nobody cared about him. I'm sure you were a good mother. He chose to become what he is."

The woman's eyes went wild with misery. "You don't know him! To this day he calls me every night to see how I'm doing, if I need anything. I got two of his babies living with me 'cause their mother got a drug problem, and they don't want for nothing. Not only that—he spends *time* with them. Those children are gonna suffer."

"Orlando Jiménez's children are already suffering."

"Two wrongs don't make a right," Danita whispered hoarsely. "And if you think Orlando ain't never killed no one, you're sadly mistaken. He killed women and children too. Ask anybody in Bushwick."

Melanie didn't need to ask. She knew those things to be true. Jiménez had been every bit as evil as the men who murdered him, and Gabriela Torres, Melanie's star witness, was his knowing consort. But so what? This case wasn't about them. If Melanie had been called on to prosecute Orlando or Gabriela, she would have done so to the full extent of the law. That didn't make her feel sorry for their killers.

Danita Baxter sat down heavily in the front row of the spectator benches and began to weep as if her son were already dead. She'd been in the courtroom and heard the testimony. She knew what the verdict would be as well as anybody else did.

"I'm very sorry for your loss," Melanie said, and turned for the door.

"Then why *do* this to him?" Danita cried out to Melanie's receding back.

Melanie was halfway down the hall before she realized that she had tears in her eyes. She took the elevator to the lobby and exited the building, blinking them back in the hot sunshine. At some point when she'd been working too hard to notice, spring had turned to summer. She'd found her first gray hair, and her daughter had shot up suddenly, seeming a lot older.

She found a seat on a bench in the plaza and watched the people walking by. Some nodded hello, others were strangers. Everybody went about their business, unconcerned with life's big questions. She didn't have time to think about those questions either. Some things were just too complicated to figure out, like where the truest morality resided in a situation like this one. Melanie put her head in her hands and practiced breathing in and out deeply to clear her mind, like she remembered from the one yoga class she'd been to, over a year ago now.

Her pager went off.

It was 4:53 when the jury filed in, and 5:10 when they filed back out, after having delivered the expected verdict of guilty on all counts. Normally, the fact that a jury had its collective eye on the clock would not have seemed remarkable to Melanie, or problematic, so she did her best to push those thoughts away. She looked around and didn't see Danita Baxter anywhere in the gallery.

The next day, Danita testified for her son during the penalty phase of the trial and said the expected things. How he'd been a loving little boy until he was five or six years old. How an absent father, a series of abusive father substitutes, and the streets had all conspired to turn him into someone else, but how he was still a good son and father.

When Danita finished her testimony, she stood up and walked calmly down the aisle, passing right by Melanie's table. Nothing passed between them, not a word or a glance, to suggest that they'd ever met before. They'd used up all their emotion the previous afternoon. For a split second, she even felt as if her encounter with Danita in the empty courtroom had never happened. But it was real, and it had happened. Why else, when the jury came back a day and a half later with a sentence of life without parole, did Melanie feel such relief?

RED DOG

BY ANITA PAGE

I t was cold as misery in the shed, but that wasn't why I was shivering. Mr. Davis lay dead on the floor and my mama was sharpening her ax. I had just turned fourteen that winter of 1910 and I was scared to think what would become of me.

When we heard Mr. Davis riding into the yard that night, we knew right away he was drunk. My mama used to say that when he was drunk you heard him before you saw him. She put on her shawl and went out to the barn. Even when he was sober, Mr. Davis would never put a blanket on the horse or give him hay.

While she was still at the barn he came busting into the house, yelling and swearing, where was his supper. His face was red and ugly, and he stank from drink. He threw off his coat and left it on the floor where it dropped.

When my mama came in from the barn, she told him he could stop yelling, she had his supper. While she was frying the meat, he started throwing things around the place. First the chairs, then the bread she had baked that morning. He threw two loaves right out the door and into the snow. Then he tried to pick up the frying pan from the stove and burned his hand. He started yelling that Mama had gone the length of her rope, that she was a dead woman.

I tried to stay out of his way like always, but that room was small and he took up the whole place.

He went banging into the other room, and my mama followed him. She'd hid her revolver in the patch basket that was hanging off the end of the bed. I knew she was scared he'd get his hands on it.

She'd bought the revolver to keep us safe after a man followed us from Foster's store into the woods. Mr. Foster had just paid my mama for her eggs, so we knew what the man meant to do. We ran like the devil up to the road, even though that was the longer way home. Later my mama was sorry she bought the revolver. She always had to change the hiding place so Mr. Davis wouldn't find it and shoot her.

Mama and Mr. Davis were yelling in the bedroom, and I went out of the kitchen onto the porch. I found those two loaves where he'd thrown them in the snow. I brought them in and got a knife and cleaned them off as best I could. I hadn't had my dinner with him tearing up the house. All this time I didn't pay too much mind to his carrying on because that's how it always was when he was drunk.

Then all of a sudden I heard a crash and he yelled, "Now I've got it and I'm going to kill you and put you in a box."

I dropped the bread and ran into the bedroom. Mr. Davis had torn that room up, knocked over the stand, pulled the quilt off the bed. He was calling my mama names and waving the revolver around. He could hardly stand up, he was so drunk. My mama had her back to the wall. She yelled to me, "Run up to the Ernhouts'."

I was too scared to do that. The Ernhouts were almost a mile up the road. If Mr. Davis shot my mama, he'd come after me, not to shoot me, but to do the things I knew he'd been thinking about for months, ever since I became a woman. I ran to her and hung on to her because I didn't know what else to do.

The truth was, I hated my mama, though not as much as I hated him. He told her to give him money, and she gave it. He beat her, dragged her around the house by her hair, and she stayed on, knowing that tomorrow would mean another beating. If I was a grown woman, I'd live like an animal in the woods before I'd stay with him. But that night I hung on to her. She was all there was between me and him.

He just looked at me and laughed and said, "Okay with me if I kill you both." He was coming toward us, still swinging the revolver around, when he stumbled forward and dropped it. Tripped on his own bootlace is what I think happened. Then there was a struggle for the gun. He was stronger, but he was drunk, and when the revolver went off he got it right in the throat. He fell to the floor with blood spurting from his neck.

Mama grabbed my arm and pulled me into the kitchen. We shut the door and leaned against it, listening to hear if he was dead or alive. Then we heard a thump and my mama said, "He's a red dog." That's the way old-time Catskill Mountain people say it when someone is killed.

He was on the floor when we went into the room. Mama got some rags and wiped down the gun and put it away. There was a place where the mattress came open, and that's where she put it. After she cleaned up some of the blood, the two of us wrapped Mr. Davis in the summer quilt. Then we dragged him out to the shed. My mama was a big woman, almost as big as Mr. Davis, but it was hard going, dragging him out of the house and all the way around back.

When I asked where we were going to bury him, my mama said, "Use your head, Lucy Ann. How can we bury him when the ground is froze up solid?" Then she sent me running to the house for the lantern.

I brought it back and watched her take the ax from the wall. Her hair had come undone and it tumbled down her back, black as night in the light from the lantern. As soon as she started to sharpen the ax with the whetstone, I knew what she was going to do. I'd seen her butcher hogs. She looked up and saw me shivering. She told me to go fire up the stove, get it as hot as I could, and then fill the bucket and start scrubbing the floor, get all the blood up from the floor.

That's how we spent the night, me scrubbing up the blood, my mama going back and forth from the shed to the house with the big tub she used for washing clothes. I wouldn't look to see what she was throwing into the stove, but you couldn't get away from the smell of it.

When dawn came up, our work was pretty much done. I don't think I've ever been so tired. My arms hurt like they were going to fall off and my knees felt like needles were sticking into them. All that was left of Mr. Davis were his bones. Some of the bones my mama pounded up fine and put in a box. She said she'd give those to the chickens. The rest she threw into the dirt cellar that was under the barn. The ground wasn't frozen there and my mama said that's where she'd bury them. But that was going to wait for another day because she was too tired to move.

Then we cleaned ourselves up as best we could and fell into the bed. When we got up, the sun was low in the sky. It's the only time in my life I ever slept from sunup to sundown instead of the other way around.

———

THE DAYS THAT followed were peaceful with him gone. But every time I heard a noise outside, I was afraid it was the sheriff come to ask about Mr. Davis. If people asked where he had gone, my mama and I were going to tell them he was over to Denville buying a cow. After a while, when he didn't come back, my mama would say that he'd gone off with another woman. That had happened before, that he had another woman, so it could have been true.

After about a week, Mr. Ernhout rode over to our place looking for Mr. Davis. He said Mr. Davis owed him money for the horse he'd gotten off him, that he was paying for a little each month. When I heard my mama tell Mr. Ernhout the story we had agreed upon, I didn't think he believed her. My mama was a truthful woman and a lie coming out of her mouth sounded like what it was. After he left I said to her, "Mama, I think he knows you were lying."

The next morning we were just finishing the milking when Karl Myerhoff found us in the barn. He was Mr. Davis's uncle. My heart jumped when I saw him in that dim light, thinking Mr. Davis had come back to life. There was a resemblance between the two, although Mr. Myerhoff was older and his clothes were clean and neat and he wasn't a drunk.

He followed us back to the house. My mama asked him to come in and sit down, but he wouldn't do that. He would never set foot in our place even when he came to see Mr. Davis. It was plain from the time my mama married his nephew that Mr. Myerhoff didn't have any use for her. He would speak his business on the front porch and then leave.

This time he asked my mama straight out where his nephew was. When she said he'd gone to Denville, he said, "You're telling me he walked twelve miles to Denville?"

I knew why he said that. He'd seen the horse in the barn.

My mama was just his size, so she could look him straight in the eye. She wrapped her shawl tight around her and said, "He told me he was going to Denville, and when I came back from carrying the eggs to Foster's, he was gone. Maybe someone came for him with a wagon. I don't know and I don't care how he got there. I'm just glad to have the peace and quiet."

That last part sounded like she was speaking the truth, so I was glad she said it. For the rest, I was afraid that Mr. Myerhoff knew she was lying.

When he left, my mama and I went inside and she started frying meat for our breakfast. I was surprised. I thought the meat was for our dinner. My mama said that if Mr. Myerhoff went straight to the sheriff, we might not be having dinner at our place. Then she said we'd better have our story straight.

I know the story, I said to her, the story about him going off with another woman.

Not that story, my mama said. If the sheriff and his men came and searched the place, she worried that they'd find the bones she'd buried in the barn cellar. If that happened, she was going to have to tell them that she'd shot Mr. Davis by accident.

"But, Mama . . . ," I said, and she stopped me from saying more.

"That's how we're going to tell it, Lucy Ann." She fixed me with her eyes, so I would know there was no arguing.

Then I started trembling and crying and couldn't get myself to stop.

"There's nothing to go on about," my mama said. "It was nobody's fault but his that the revolver went off. That's what I'll tell them, the sheriff and all, and they'll believe me because everyone around here knows what that man was like, the temper on him and the things he did to me."

Then why did we tell the story about him going off to Denville? I wanted to ask. And why did you chop him up and burn him? I didn't ask those questions, because I knew the answer. In her heart she was afraid that no one would care what he had done to her and no one would believe that he got shot by accident.

Later that day, when we came back from Foster's, the sheriff and his men were waiting.

"Are you Mrs. Margaret Davis?" the sheriff asked my mama. He was a sour-looking man with a pockmarked face.

She answered that she was and that this was her house and she would like to go inside. But they wouldn't let us in, only kept us out on the porch. I could see through the window that they'd turned the place upside down. Then two men came out of the barn. One of them had something in his hand. I knew before he got close enough for me to see that they'd found Mr. Davis's bones.

———

WE RODE INTO town with the sheriff, the cold wind whipping against us so it was hard to catch a breath. As soon as we got there, they took my mama away. For a long time I'd been thinking that as soon as I had my own money, I'd get as far from her as I could. But that day, when they took my mama down off the wagon, I cried like a baby. My mama had no family, and my father's people were out in Pennsylvania. They didn't want to know us after my mama married Mr. Davis. If the sheriff put my mama in jail, I had no home, no place to go to at all.

They put me up for a few days at Tyler's Hotel, with a woman called Miss Carter in charge of me. Then Mr. Myerhoff came to see me and said I was to go home with him. Before we rode out of town in his wagon, we stopped at Kaufman's Dry Goods. Mr. Myerhoff gave me five dollars and sent me inside to buy some things. I got a thick wool shawl and a blue skirt and some other things. I never before had so many new things at the same time.

Mr. Myerhoff had the feed-and-grain store in town. When I saw his big white house, clean and warm inside, with carpet on the floor, I thought he must be a rich man. His wife took me to a small room in back of the kitchen and said that's where I would sleep. I never before had a room all to myself.

I knew by Mrs. Myerhoff's face that if it was up to her, I wouldn't be there. She told me I would have to make myself useful in the house. I said I wasn't afraid to work. I was used to it.

Working for Mrs. Myerhoff was nowhere near as hard as what I had to do at home. And when she saw I knew how to do the washing and keep the place clean, she didn't seem to mind that I was there. In that house, I got to see how things could be when no one was drunk or swearing or breaking up the chairs. I made up my mind that someday I would live like that with my own family. If someone had said to me, Lucy Ann, you're going home with your mama today, I would have begged to stay on with the Myerhoffs. Every day I worried that I'd do something wrong and they'd send me away, so I tried to do just like they said.

In those months before the trial, Mr. Myerhoff would take me to see Mr. Sullivan, the district attorney. The two of them asked me questions, the same ones over and over. I figured that they were going to keep asking until they got the answers they wanted.

How did Mr. Davis come to get shot? It was an accident, I said. What had my mama done with Mr. Davis's body? I don't know, I said. That was partly true. I'd only seen her sharpen the ax and carry the tub back and forth from the shed to the stove.

Then they twisted the questions around, and it got harder for me to answer.

"Wasn't it true there was a lot of yelling and shouting?" Mr. Sullivan asked me. "Weren't you scared and confused? Can you say for certain that you didn't see your mama pull the trigger?" Then: "You saw Mr. Davis dead and you saw the ax and you saw your mama covered with blood. How do you suppose that blood got on her?"

When I didn't answer the way he wanted, Mr. Sullivan talked to me about the oath. He said when the trial came I was going to have to swear on a Bible that I would speak the truth. He said,

"Lucy Ann, if you see someone shoot and kill another person and lie about it, you can go to prison just the same as if you pulled the trigger yourself."

In the end I was afraid that if I didn't answer the way they wanted me to, Mr. Myerhoff would send me out of his house and Mr. Sullivan would make sure I went to prison.

One time, before the trial, I was taken to see my mama's lawyer. I answered his questions the way Mr. Sullivan had taught me. I could see Mama's lawyer wasn't pleased with me. I told myself that I hadn't put my mama in jail. From the time I was ten, I'd begged for us to run away. If she'd listened to me, Mr. Davis would never have got shot. And I told myself that when the trial started, the judge would hear about the beatings and the black eyes. Then he'd know that Mr. Davis got what he deserved.

———

IT WAS SPRING when the trial started. People were lined up on the grass outside the courthouse waiting to get in. Mr. Myerhoff and I didn't have to wait. We went right in and found our seats in the courtroom. That place looked to me like a church for rich people, with its marble walls and dark wooden benches and tall windows.

Every person stopped talking when my mama walked into the courtroom that first day. The sheriff was right beside her, like they were afraid she'd bolt and run. The people all stretched their necks to see her, some standing up until they were told to sit back down.

My mama walked with her head up, looking straight ahead. This was the first I'd seen her since the day we rode into town in the sheriff's wagon. Her hair was nice, combed back and twisted up neat in the back. She wore clothes I had never seen, a red shirtwaist trimmed in black and a black skirt. They wrote about it in the newspaper. That was one thing they got right. Later I found out that Mr. Hackett, her lawyer, helped get those clothes for her.

We had to stand up when the judge came in. Even in his black robe, you could tell he was a heavy man. He didn't have much hair on his head, but his eyebrows were the thickest I'd ever seen.

Mr. Sullivan and Mr. Hackett made their speeches, but I hardly heard a word they said. I knew any minute they were going to call me to put my hand on the Bible and swear to tell the truth. My mama and I never went to church much after she married Mr. Davis, but still I wondered what happened to people who swore on the Bible and then told a lie.

When the speeches were done, the other witnesses were made to leave the courtroom. Mr. Sullivan asked that I be allowed to stay since I would be the first to testify, and the judge agreed.

When I heard my name, I was trembling so hard I thought my legs wouldn't carry me to the front of the courtroom. My hand shook when I put it on the Bible. I looked to where my mama was sitting, then quick looked away.

Mr. Sullivan's questions were easy at first. Was my name Lucy Ann Simpson and was I Margaret Davis's daughter and was I acquainted with George Davis? I just had to say yes, sir, but even so the judge kept telling me to speak up.

Then Mr. Sullivan asked me about the shooting, about how I heard shouting from the other room and ran in and saw Mr. Davis waving the revolver around. He asked about Mr. Davis and my mama fighting for the revolver and about how I was so scared I couldn't be certain whether it went off by accident or on purpose.

That was true, I said. I kept my eyes on my lap because I was afraid to look up and see my mama's face.

"And when Mr. Davis lay dying on the floor, you saw the revolver in your mother's hands?"

"Yes, sir," I said. By this time truth and lies were so mixed up in my head, I hardly knew one from the other. But I do know I never said those things they put in the newspaper, that my mama's eyes were blazing like a cat's and that she pulled the trigger again and again. Ever since my mama's trial, I don't believe a word I read in the newspaper. If they say the sun is shining, I think to myself it must be raining.

Then Mr. Hackett, my mama's lawyer, asked me questions. He was a tall man with a thick mustache that he kept stroking like it was a furry animal.

"Do you like living in Mr. Myerhoff's house?" he asked. "Are you treated more kindly than you were by Mr. Davis? Do they buy you nice clothes? Would you choose to stay with the Myerhoffs as long as you could?" All I could answer was "Yes, sir."

When the judge finally told me I could step down, I was crying. As I went back to my seat, my mama and I looked at each other straight on for the first time. I expected to see pure hatred on her face, but it wasn't like that. Whatever she was feeling didn't show at all.

Other people put their hands on the Bible and swore to tell the truth. I suppose some of them did. One man talked about the blood in the cellar. With all my scrubbing that night, we didn't think about the blood dripping down between the floorboards. He talked for a long time, telling how he knew it was human blood and not from a pig or a cow. Another man went on about the bones that were under the barn, how he knew without any doubt that they were human bones.

I was glad when they called up Mr. Ed Buckley. He was a farmer who had known my mama since she was a girl. I didn't think he would say anything to harm her, but that wasn't how it turned out. He told how the sheriff asked him to come up to the jail and visit with my mama even though he didn't want to.

He told how he and Mama just sat talking about one thing and another.

"She talked to you about killing George Davis, did she?" Mr. Sullivan asked.

Mr. Buckley said, "Well, she said something about red-dogging George Davis and I told her I could hardly blame her, the way he treated her." Then Mr. Buckley looked straight at the sheriff and said that if he'd known the reason for his visit was to get evidence against my mama, he wouldn't have gone in there.

———

ON THE THIRD or fourth day, I don't remember for certain, Mr. Hackett called my mama up to testify. She was wearing a different dress that day, a black calico with white trim. I suppose he got that for her too, because I had never seen it before. When Mr. Hackett called her up, people got so noisy, commenting to each other, that the judge had to bang his gavel again and again.

Mr. Hackett asked my mama about the things Mr. Davis had done to her, the beatings and so forth, and how she was afraid for her life. This was where I had put my hope. I thought that if the judge heard what kind of man George Davis was, he'd say he deserved to die ten times over. But it didn't happen that way. Mr. Sullivan and the judge wouldn't let Mr. Hackett ask my mama those questions. Those questions weren't proper, they said.

Mr. Hackett argued with the judge, saying the questions were proper, that my mama feared for her life and that was why she tried to get the revolver away from Mr. Davis. But the judge had another idea. He said it didn't matter that my mama was afraid, because she didn't say she was trying to protect herself. She said the gun went off by accident. They went back and forth on this. At first I didn't understand what it all meant, but then I got the gist. The judge didn't care about the things Mr. Davis had done to my mama.

Then it was Mr. Sullivan's turn. When he asked my mama how she came to shoot Mr. Davis, she stuck to her story about how he waved the revolver around, threatening to shoot her, and when she tried to grab it, it went off. "He got shot purely by accident," she said.

Then Mr. Sullivan asked whether she had chopped off Mr. Davis's head.

The courtroom was so quiet then you could have heard a leaf fall to the ground. Everyone was waiting for my mama's answer.

She finally said, "I don't see what difference it makes, once a man is dead."

Mr. Sullivan asked his question two or three more times, and each time my mama gave him the same answer. By then there was laughing in the courtroom, not out-loud laughing, but snickering and the like.

Then Mr. Sullivan said, "I expect you know what a man's head is, Mrs. Davis."

My mama said, "I expect so."

"I will make my question very plain," Mr. Sullivan said. "Did you pick up an ax and chop Mr. Davis's head off?"

"Not when he was still living," my mama said.

"Am I to understand that you chopped off his head when he was no longer living?"

"That was when I did it," my mama said.

The judge had to bang his gavel then and tell the people that if the commotion didn't stop he was going to throw the bunch of them out of the courtroom.

After my mama stepped down, Mr. Hackett told the judge that he had a list of names, more than twenty, I think, of people who were ready to speak up for my mama. Two of them were justices of the peace my mama had gone to at different times, swearing an oath against Mr. Davis so they would put him in jail for beating her, but it never did work. The others were neighbors, people from town who'd seen her with her eyes blackened and clumps of her hair torn out.

But the judge wouldn't let Mr. Hackett call a single one of them up to speak. "Improper, improper," he said again and again. Listening to him, something changed in my heart. I stopped hating my mama. After all the beatings she had taken from Mr. Davis, here she was taking a beating from the judge, this time with his words.

———

THE NEXT DAY Mr. Sullivan and Mr. Hackett and the judge made long speeches. Then the jury went out to decide if my mama was guilty. I knew what they would decide before they even came back. I guess everyone else did too. There was no hope for my mama, not with the judge forbidding Mr. Hackett's questions.

———

MR. MYERHOFF TOOK me over to the jail in his wagon so I could spend time with my mama before they sent her to the prison up in Auburn. I was scared to see her, but I went anyway. When I walked in, the first thing she said was "Lucy Ann, you've gotten so fat I would hardly know you." Then I knew it would be all right, that she didn't hate me.

I cried and told her I was sorry I hadn't stuck to the story the way we planned. She said I wasn't to worry about it, that she knew what those people were like, how they twisted things around. Then she laughed and said she'd never had things so easy in all her years with Mr. Davis as she did in that jail. I suppose she was scared about going to prison, but she didn't let me see it.

Then I spoke up and told what had been on my mind for some

days. "I want to tell Mr. Sullivan the truth about that night," I said.

"And what would come of that?" My mama's eyes were blazing then. "Nothing you say is going to make them set me free." Then she made me swear to her that I would never say a word to Mr. Sullivan.

I had to make another promise too. When I said that if I got money of my own, I would take the train up to Auburn and visit her, she got all riled up. She didn't want me to see her in that place, she said.

I asked if it was so terrible there, but she wouldn't answer, just made me promise that I never would come. Then she said she would be happy to have my letters, and I promised to write to her every month.

The woman who was a keeper at the jail had showed her how to do fancy stitching, and my mama wanted to teach me. That was how we spent the rest of the morning, stitching on muslin, and talking just as if it was not the last time we would ever see each other.

———

I STAYED ON working for Mrs. Myerhoff until I was sixteen. Then I got work at the hotel, where I met Samuel McCoy, the man I married. I wrote to my mama every month, only missing one now and again. Sometimes she answered and sometimes she didn't, depending on if she was sick or if they punished her by not letting her write to me. She was a big, strong woman, but she became sickly soon after she got to Auburn.

The last letter I had from her was when my oldest boy was six. I guess she had been at Auburn for nine years. I hardly recognized her writing because her hand was so weak. She started by saying that she expected to die soon, but she wasn't afraid. She knew the next life would be better for her than this one.

She wanted me to know that two things in her life made her happy. The first was reading in my letters how well my family and I were doing. "The other thing I am glad about," she wrote, "is that I red-dogged George Davis, even if it was an accident. You and I both know that man deserved to die." Then she asked me to pray for her soul.

I remember looking out my back door with the letter in my hand, not knowing what to think. Here she was writing about that night just as if she'd forgotten the truth of it, that I was the one who had my hand on the revolver when it went off. I wondered if she was reminding me to stick to the story we had agreed on. But over the years I've come to see it differently. I think she found comfort in believing that she'd pulled the trigger, that she'd put the bullet in George Davis's throat.

A CLERK'S LIFE

BY BARBARA PARKER

Payday at Penniman, Wolfe & Mulloy. In the nanosecond they allow us for breaks I go to accounting to pick up my check. Rita sits at her desk, smiling up at me. Ever since we had lunch together at the Cuban diner last week, she gets this look on her face. She wants me to ask her out. Be nice to her. Something.

Rita says, "How's your mother?" She leans on crossed arms, making cleavage. The buttons strain on her shirt. She is not slender.

I pocket the envelope. "Still recuperating. Thanks for asking."

"So. Are you going back to school next month?"

"Probably not. Mom . . . you know."

"Yeah. That's too bad."

"Law school can wait. I don't mind. It's only a year."

Rita sighs. "Not many guys would be that decent." As I turn to leave, she says, "Warren? Are you busy tonight?"

"Tonight? Why?"

"The Latin Fest is at Bayfront Park. You're always working. You need to get out! Besides, it's free."

I can't think of an excuse to say no . . . except for one, sitting

263

in the apartment on Miami Beach. But it's Friday. What the hell. She's capable of putting her own dinner in the microwave. "Okay. I'll go with you."

Rita actually claps her hands together, a gesture that says more than it should. "Great. You want to meet downstairs at five thirty?"

"Well . . . let me call you. I have to finish something for Erika Mulloy. If it's not on her desk this afternoon, she'll slice out my heart with her fingernails." Erika's nails are legendary, the subject of jokes.

Rita giggles. Her supervisor glances over from her computer screen.

Ha-ha, funny man, but I've just insulted a name partner, the head of our commercial litigation division. Worse: I've blown off an entire five minutes. Erika Mulloy could cause me considerable pain, but I don't think she would fire me. Technically, I work for the managing partner, Louis Penniman. Erika snatched me to help out on a lawsuit involving shoddy construction of a luxury hotel on the Beach. I am her document-review slave, going through mountains of paper, searching for any scrap that bears on the issue at hand. Thrilling work.

On my way to the elevator I walk past the cubicles on the windowless side of the long, open corridor where the secretaries sit. Most of them are young and pretty. They don't look up. I am only Warren Kemble.

Rounding a corner, I hear jubilant laughter through the open door of Frank Delgado's office. I slow to a stop. Frank is a big rainmaker, head of our criminal department. He holds the firm record for most sexual harassment claims against him. He is telling someone about the PR expert he hired in the Talbot murder case, and how they got the client's parents on *Larry King Live*, and how Talbot was smart enough from day one not to open his mouth to the police. Just said, I'd like to talk to you, but on advice of my counsel, can't do it. Jesus Christ, if more of my clients would live by that rule—

A hand appears and pushes the door shut.

Yesterday Talbot was acquitted on charges of beating his girl-friend to death. He did it. We all knew he did it. The baseball bat was his, and he'd sworn to kill her if she left him. I saw the autopsy photos. Her nose was pushed sideways almost to her ear, and her jaw was knocked off her head. I went to the men's room and threw up.

Do I really want to work for these people? Except for Mr. Penniman, an attorney whose like you don't see anymore, the lawyers here are soulless phonies. I endure them. What choice do I have?

The elevator door slides open and I step inside. Jack Porter is already there, probably on his way back from court, as he's carry-ing his briefcase. Jack Porter is my age, a first-year associate, but he's got to be making a hundred K a year already. He works for Erika Mulloy. The small overhead lights gleam on his hair and the shoulders of his suit. I myself am wearing a blue shirt and khakis from the Gap.

The button for 14 is already lit, but I press it again and stand beside Porter, facing front. "I guess you heard about the Talbot case. Do you believe that verdict?"

Jack Porter's face is a fuzzy reflection in the polished wood. "What about it?"

"They bought his story. They thought he was innocent. Del-gado totally confused the issues, coached the client how to act, and made the victim out to be a whore. He put the blame on a killer who didn't exist."

"And your point?"

"My *point?* It's a perversion of justice. All Delgado cared about was polishing his reputation, not to mention paying for another vacation home."

I see Porter's reflected smile. "Justice. Okay. Try this on: without lawyers like Frank Delgado, the state would run the accused into the ground. The system needs Delgado to keep it honest. He did his job. Guilty, innocent—that's not your concern. Your job is to win. If you believe anything else, you need to go into social work, not law."

This is depressing. Porter is right, but it's still depressing. I step out of the elevator ahead of him. His office is in the same direction as mine, and he walks a few paces behind me. The corridor slices between the glass walls of the library. One of the secretaries is reaching for a book on the top shelf. Her skirt slides up her thighs, and her blond hair swings. What is it with these girls? They all have the same hairstyle, and they wear the same tight tops and short black skirts. She turns around. I lift my hand and smile, but she looks through me.

I hear a chuckle. "Hey, Kemble. If you're seen hunting hippos, you'll never get a shot at the gazelles." I hear Jack Porter's voice.

"What?"

"I heard you went out with that fat chick from accounting."

"We had lunch. And she isn't fat, she's—"

"Whatever. Look. In the hunting ground that is this firm, your prey want to get bagged, but only by a hunter who's on their level. If the beautiful young gazelles think you're not up for the long, hard chase, they'll never give you a chance."

I stare at him.

Porter shrugs. "Hey, man, that's how the game is played. Keep hanging with Fatty, you'll see."

My face burns. At the end of the corridor, we go in separate directions. I want to hate his guts, but I can't. He has a point, I guess. I find my way to the Pits. To the clerks' office with a view of another building. To my faux-walnut-veneer desk shoved into the far corner. Two of the other clerks share the space with me.

Denise and Mike. They glance up, registering my presence, but they don't speak. I sit down and log onto my computer.

Penniman, Wolfe & Mulloy employs 316 attorneys in five offices around the state, a branch office in New York, one in Mexico City, and another in London. Here in Miami there are ninety-six lawyers, seventy-two support personnel, and eleven law clerks. I, at twenty-nine, am the oldest of the clerks. I have completed two years at Ohio University Southern College of Law. I also have four years' experience working as a paralegal at a law firm in Dayton, Ohio. This means nothing. Denise is a senior at Georgetown; her father is on the D.C. Court of Appeals. Mike just graduated in the top 5 percent from Harvard. The other clerks are either from the Ivies or law-review editors at top state schools. The clients care about such things, thus enabling the firm to bill clerk time at $300 per hour. But Mike's salary is twice mine. He made sure to let me know about it. My colleagues are experts in theory, but they have never seen the inside of a courtroom; they are shockingly disorganized and ignorant about real life in a law firm. I offer suggestions where I can, but generally the reaction is, Fuck off.

My job, however, is secure. I was hired by Louis Penniman, the founding partner, who served with my father in Vietnam. After my mother's heart attack in February, I left school and flew down from Ohio to take care of her. She called Penniman to ask about an opening at the firm. My father saved his life, so you could say he owed us. I had expected to return to school for my final year, but now it's getting on toward August. My mother won't hear of hiring a nurse. The insurance has run out. This is not a happy situation, but what can I do?

At 5:23 I finish the report for Erika and log off.

———

"WHAT IS THE matter with you, Mr. Kemble?"

"Excuse me?"

"I told you to have this on my desk by five o'clock. Did I not say that?"

"I believe you said 'before I leave,' and I assumed—"

"You assumed? I said five o'clock. Five, not five thirty. Do you have shit in your ears?"

I wiggle the tip of my little finger in my ear. "It doesn't seem so."

She stares at me. I maintain my composure and smile at her. She lets out a breath and starts flipping through the pages. Her long red nails click against each other. They are like claws. Her mouth compresses. "This is not in the form I asked for. Only three citations from this jurisdiction? And where are the goddamn documents that support the factual stipulations? Did that not occur to you?"

"You're right. I'll make the revisions and include the fact stip support. How soon do you need it?"

She flips the folder closed and shoves it across her desk. "Monday. Have it back to me first thing Monday. Let's make that eight o'clock."

My weekend is screwed. Oh, wonderful.

When I don't reply, she says, "Did you hear me?"

"Yes, Erika. Monday. Eight o'clock."

"That's Ms. Mulloy. Do not call me by my first name. Clerks are not entitled to call me by my first name."

"I'm sorry."

"On time and error-free, Mr. Kemble. If you can't do that, you need to be in the mail room with Robert."

Robert is the mentally handicapped man who delivers the mail and cleans the break room. I smile reassuringly. "Don't worry. The report will be on your desk by eight o'clock Monday."

"Thank you. And shut the door when you leave." As the crack narrows, I hear her say, "What I have to put up with."

Turning, I see the little smirk on her secretary's face. She flips her long brown hair over her shoulder and goes back to her keyboard. Avoiding the gauntlet of cubicles in the corridor, I head for the stairwell. As I descend, the echo of footsteps comes from below me.

It's Jack Porter. He notices the folder clenched in my hands. "Hey, is that the report for Erika? I thought you turned it in already."

"She didn't like the format. I have to redo it."

He passes me. "Cunt. I'd put my foot in her ass and kick her down the stairs."

"What?" A laugh escapes, and I steady myself on the railing. "Don't say things like that, man. It might get back to her."

"Who's going to tell her? You?"

"Hell no."

"Then don't worry about it." He moves on up the stairs and disappears at the landing. The steel door on 15 clicks shut. Jesus. That guy. I laugh again. Like he read my mind.

Rather than return immediately to the Pits, I head for Louis Penniman's corner office on 16. He has a view of the city and the bay and Miami Beach. He invites me in, and we chat for a few minutes about the Talbot case. I feel that Penniman shares my opinion, but he is oblique. He won't openly criticize another partner.

The conversation turns to my father, the war, Vietnam, the sniper aiming at Lieutenant Penniman from the jungle, my father taking him out with a burst from his M-16.

I nod soberly. "A brave man."

"Gone too soon," Penniman says. "What about you, Warren? You fitting in here? Everything's good?"

"Yes, sir, absolutely. I'll be going back to law school in

January. If not, then next fall. I'm considering a transfer to the University of Miami."

"Wonderful. Good luck to you, Warren." Penniman puts a hand on my shoulder as we walk to his door. "You tell your mother I said hello."

I admire Penniman. He's in his sixties, but we have a bond. After I graduate, I think he would take me on. I can't say I like Miami, but one has to start somewhere.

Back in my office, I notice the time: 6:10 p.m. My cell phone is blinking. A message from Rita. "Shit." The others have cleared out already. Their computer screens are dark. I call Rita and tell her that Erika Mulloy had me in her office discussing a major litigation case. "It's big. Looks like I'll have to work on it all weekend. I really shouldn't even be going to the concert tonight."

Rita says she's already on her way home.

"What about the concert?"

She tells me to have a nice day.

"I'm really sorry," I say.

———

WITH MY SPIRITS lifted somewhat from my talk with Penniman, I stop by the market and pick up a bacon-wrapped filet mignon and a thirty-dollar bottle of wine.

After my father passed away, my mother decided to move to Miami Beach. She thought it would be glamorous. She bought a condo on Pine Tree Drive, a few miles north of the craziness of Lincoln Road and South Beach. The Pine Villa is from the 1940s, two stories, painted yellow with turquoise doors. A walkway goes from the street to the end of the building where my mother lives. Air conditioners hum in the windows. The yard is overgrown with tropical plants, and a couple of old pie pans with cat food sit under the bushes, a violation of condo regulations.

There is a small, discolored swimming pool in the back that nobody uses. The average age here is about seventy.

The sun has set, and the lights have come on. As usual, our next-door neighbor Mr. Perlstein is sitting in his lawn chair, knobby knees in Bermuda shorts, chin on his chest. Their door opens as I go by, and Mrs. Perlstein comes out. She is a short woman with frizzy gray hair.

"Warren, darling, wait a minute." She clumps down the steps. "How's Georgette? I haven't seen her in weeks."

"She's doing better, but her doctors want her to rest. Thanks for asking, Mrs. Perlstein."

Her husband snorts in his sleep and resettles himself. Mrs. Perlstein pulls me closer and says she knows how it is, taking care of an invalid. "Listen, darling, I'd love to come over sometime and keep your mother company. It might cheer us both up, you know?"

"Thanks, Mrs. P., but she's not really taking visitors yet. I'll tell her you asked about her." The truth is, my mother is prejudiced against persons not of her own religion. She says if she'd known there were so many of them in this building, she'd have bought somewhere else, but it's too late now.

At our door I shift the grocery bag and turn the key. "Ma? I'm home."

The sound of a TV game show drifts through her door. There is only one bedroom; I sleep on the sofa. I hang my suit coat on the back of a chair. When I knock and go into my mother's room, she's sitting in her lounger with her feet up. Her AC is on the arctic setting, but that's how she likes it, wearing a sweater and two pairs of socks. A contestant on *Wheel of Fortune* reaches over to turn the wheel. My mother says, "I thought you were going out tonight."

"Well, I decided to stay home with you instead. Are you hungry? I picked up a steak."

"You told me to eat, so I did. I had a frozen dinner. Where did you get the steak?"

"Epicure Market."

"Epicure!"

"It was on sale. I make sandwiches or cold cereal every night. Is an occasional steak too much to ask?" She starts to cry. Tears follow the lines in her cheeks. "What now? Come on, Ma, don't do that."

"We used to have money. We used to be something in this world. Look at me now. Your father is dead, God rest him, and I'm sick. I never expected my life to be this way."

"You'll get better." I pat her shoulder.

"Go eat your steak." She aims the remote at the TV, raising the volume.

In the kitchen I slice onions and garlic, and the steady thud of the knife on the cutting board soothes me. After dinner I take some chamomile tea to my mother, along with her pills.

She is contrite. "I love you, Warren. Your sister couldn't care less. You won't leave me, will you?"

"I'm not leaving, Ma."

"When you graduate, we'll get out of this stinking place and buy a gorgeous condo. You'll have a sports car like you always wanted. A Porsche!" She laughs like a girl. She asks about my day, and I make things up to please her. I sit on the end of the bed and tell her about Frank Delgado's case, and I tell her about Jack Porter, and she says Porter isn't half the lawyer I'm going to be, which I know isn't true, but I don't contradict her.

I stand up. "Listen, I need to go back to the office tonight. I'm working on a big project for Ms. Mulloy." It's a lie, but I need to get out of here for a while.

"Sure, honey. Don't work too late. I love you."

I pull the afghan up and smooth her hair. I don't like to kiss her. She has a smell, like old shoes in a musty closet. She's afraid to take baths, afraid she'll fall. I should hire someone to help her. I can't do it myself, can't see my mother's body like that. I hate myself for saying this, but sometimes I wish they hadn't revived her.

———

FRIDAY NIGHT. LINCOLN Road, barred to traffic, is jammed with bodies. The restaurants are full, and the shops and the coffee bars and nightclubs. Candles flicker on outdoor tables. There are languages I don't recognize. Gay men holding hands. Long-legged girls in hot pants. Purebred dogs on leashes. Street musicians with their guitar cases open for tips. A woman on roller skates bumps my shoulder as she veers around me. The heat of bodies presses in on me as I wait at Meridian for the light to change. A white limo floats by. South Beach smells of the ocean, of incense, of money and power.

I have been thinking about personal-injury law. My chances of getting into a top firm are, let's face it, pretty remote, but I can rent a space and build my own practice. I don't want rich clients. They're a pain in the ass. I'd rather work for normal people. They trust me, and I relate well to them. I could be making half a million dollars a year by the time I'm forty. I'd have a family. Jack Porter gave good advice about not settling for just any woman. But I haven't dated since I got here. I'm an ordinary guy, average build, short brown hair, brown eyes. On the surface, nothing special. Sad fact: women like a man with cash in his pocket and a nice car. They judge you on those terms. Tell a woman you're a lawyer, or even in law school, and her eyes light up.

The nightclubs are all glitter and noise, and inside them I see the beautiful girls leaning on the men. Some of them are prostitutes, no doubt. How much would a woman cost? It would have to depend on what you want from her. I could get cash on my mother's ATM card. She never checks the balance. Could I do that? No. I am, as Rita said, a decent guy.

My aimless stroll takes me to Ocean Drive and over to Washington Avenue, the crowds even more dense here. With no breeze the heat is stifling. I go into a bar to cool off, have a beer, and watch the people. When I come out, a light rain is falling. What time is it? Late. Up the street I notice a tall, well-built man with a blond woman hanging off his arm. The way he walks, a swagger, reminds me of someone. Is that Jack Porter? The girl laughs, her mouth wide open, her hair swinging across her bare shoulders. She's pretty. And she's drunk. Then I recognize her: she works at the firm. She was the girl in the library. Ashley, Courtney, Traci, I can't remember.

Trust Jack Porter to pick her up. If it is him. I'm not sure. They vanish among the crowd, then appear again walking toward Drexel, and I follow. The man has his arm around her. She stumbles, and her laughter echoes off the dark buildings. This area is almost deserted. It's late, and the clubs are closing. They turn the corner, and I catch up in time to see their shadows slide into the alley behind a row of closed stores.

The rain has turned to mist, shining on the pavement, dripping off the heavy foliage. I stand beneath an awning where the light can't reach me and listen. Voices murmur. The girl laughs again. There is nothing for a while, then she says, "Don't! Stop it!" Then I hear some grunting noises, a thud. More thuds. And then nothing. Nothing. My heart feels like a rope is around it, twisting, squeezing. Sweat runs down my back, my sides. I am frozen.

Footsteps move quickly away.

Stiffly, slowly, I force myself into the alley. The girl is lying on the cracked, filthy asphalt. Bare legs are sprawled, a shoe is off, and palms turn upward like pale flowers. Her hair is over her face. I wait for her to breathe, but her chest doesn't move. I lean closer and see the marks on her neck.

Stumbling, I catch myself, then run out the other end of the alley looking for him, but he's gone. I fumble open my cell phone to call for help, then slam it shut. They can trace my number, and they will ask me why I was in the alley. What would I say? I was following an associate from my law firm?

I find a pay phone and call 911, using a false name. And then I blend into the crowd and watch as the police cars and an ambulance scream past. I shield my eyes against the pulsing lights.

ON MONDAY EVERYONE is talking about her. Courtney Benson. That was her name. Courtney. The other girls at the firm are in shock, or crying, or blaming her for being careless. Her friends went home, she wanted to keep partying. Nobody at the club saw her leave with anyone. The police have no clues, no witnesses, nothing.

My insides are twisted. I can't think what to do. Should I accuse a man I have come to like and admire? A man I didn't see clearly? Who would believe me?

ERIKA MULLOY LOOKS at her watch. "It's nine fifteen, Mr. Kemble."

"Sorry. There was a line for the printer. I worked on the documents all weekend."

"I should give you a medal?" She uses the nail on her forefinger to flip through the report. "This earns a C-minus, but we're on the meter. It will have to do."

It's perfect. She knows it's perfect, she just wants to torture me for some irrational purpose that I can't comprehend. She points to a stack of banker's boxes by her door. "This came in response to our amended demand for discovery. I need the review completed by Wednesday. Flag the relevant sections. Color-coded, please."

"Wednesday. What time?"

"Nine o'clock. You have a problem with that?"

"No, ma'am."

She waves me out. "Chop-chop."

I want to hide in the storeroom and lean against the wall with the lights off. Instead, I get a cart and wheel the boxes down to 14, take a turn past the library, and then another turn until I get to Jack Porter's office. He has a view of the ocean. Law books are open on his desk. His cuffs are rolled up. He wears a Rolex, what else? His hands and arms show no marks of a struggle. He raises his eyes and looks at me, and a sudden chill makes my chest quiver.

He twirls his gold pen. "What can I do for you, Kemble?"

I reach for a plausible excuse to be here. "Erika. You're pretty tight with her. Could you give me some advice how to stop her from wanting to strangle me?" I chuckle to cover my bad choice of words.

Jack Porter glances past me to make sure no one is in the corridor. "I'll tell you what the bitch needs." His hand drops behind the desk and he pretends to grab his crotch. "A piece of this." He grins. "Hey, man, lighten up."

I back out of his office and flee with the boxes of documents. I veer into the men's room and lock myself in a stall. How could Jack Porter make jokes? Like he doesn't care that one of our own was murdered over the weekend. But why should he care? He probably didn't even know who she was. If he had killed her, it would show. Unless he's a sociopath. The hiring committee would have picked up on that, wouldn't they? Unless they're all sociopaths, a concept that does not seem totally irrational.

To calm my nerves I walk two laps of the entire law firm,

going up and down the circular stairs that connect the main lobby on 15 with the library on 14 and the partners' meeting room on 16. On the way to the Pits I stop by the break room for a soda. I drop my quarters in the machine. Robert is wiping down the coffee spills on the counter.

"Hey, Warren."

"What's up, Robert?" My hands shake getting the can open.

"Not much." He squints at me. "Are you okay?"

"Sure." I take a gulp of cola. "That Jack Porter. What an asshole."

"Who?"

"The new associate. Jack Porter. He was just hired. Harvard."

Robert nods. "Right. Why do you hate him?"

"I don't *hate* him, I just . . ." And I realize that there is *nothing* I can say about Jack Porter. In this law firm there is nothing unusual about him. "Harvard. La-de-da. I go to Ohio Southern College of Law. Ever hear of it? I'll be lucky to get a job with the Bumfuck, Arkansas, public defender's office making thirty grand a year."

"That's okay, Warren. You'll be a good lawyer, I know you will, because you care."

I toss the can in the trash and wheel the boxes of documents to my desk in the Pits.

Missing lunch, I work all day on Erika's fricking document review. It is mindless. It is excruciating. It is worth $300 per hour to somebody, and the clients, like sheep, believe it. I keep my head down and put yellow or orange or blue sticky flags on the pages.

Around six o'clock, Mike comes back from a meeting, and he and Denise start talking about Louis Penniman. I scoot over so I can see around my computer monitor.

"What did you say?"

Mike rocks back in his chair. "You didn't hear about it? Penniman's retiring."

"You're kidding."

"And guess who's going to be our new managing partner." Denise swings her immense tote bag over her shoulder and unfolds her sunglasses.

"Who?" we say in unison.

"Erika Mulloy."

"Oh fucking A." Mike drops his face into his hands. "Just shoot me now."

Denise frowns at him. "Erika is a strong and capable woman. Does that bother you?"

"No, Denise. It does not. What bothers me is, she wants to reduce payroll. That could mean you."

"No, Michael. You're wrong. She's looking to merge with another law firm. We have a bunch of empty offices on this floor. She won't cut back."

"We're top-heavy with partners. I think Erika will try to get rid of some of the less profitable divisions, like probate."

They argue pointlessly, and I return to my desk in the corner. I am breathless. I can't talk to Rita. She hates me now. I can't talk to Jack Porter. He would laugh at my petty problems. I push a stack of documents out of the way and leave the Pits. I take the elevator up to 16 and walk straight to Penniman's office.

He tells me it's not entirely true. He's not leaving, just switching to counsel status and a smaller office. "I'm sixty-five years old. I've had two heart bypasses, and I want to spend some time traveling with my wife and playing golf before I check out."

"Erika's going to fire me."

"Nonsense. There's too much work right now. But you go back to school in January, don't you? The minute you graduate, I want you to come see me, all right?"

I go back to the Pits and call Mom to let her know I'll be

working late. I work on the documents until early morning, until the words blur on the page and the muscles in my neck are on fire. She will have this report *before* Wednesday.

———

TUESDAY EVENING A shape appears through the security screen on the front door. The louvers rattle. "Hello-o-o?"

"I'll get it, Ma."

Mrs. Perlstein holds a casserole dish with a glass lid. She looks into the living room, trying to see around me. "I brought Georgette some chicken noodle soup. It's still warm."

"That's very thoughtful of you, Mrs. Perlstein. She's napping right now." I take the dish. "I'm sure she'll like it."

"Well. I'll come back some other time. Tell her I asked about her."

"I will. And Mrs. P.? Mom said to thank you for the cake you brought last week."

In her room my mother is working a crossword puzzle. Her glasses reflect the black-and-white squares. The TV is tuned to Animal Planet. Tigers of Nepal.

"Look. Mrs. Perlstein brought over some chicken soup."

"Jew food."

"Don't talk like that. Aren't you hungry?"

"You were late getting home. I ate leftovers."

I take the soup into the kitchen and pour it down the drain. I open the freezer and pull out a meatloaf-and-mashed-potatoes dinner. Seven minutes. The numbers on the microwave count backward.

The phone rings. It's my sister, Diane. "How's Ma? I've called five times in the last week. She never picks up."

I don't tell her the truth: that our mother doesn't want to talk to her. I say, "She sleeps a lot. But don't worry. She's fine."

"She's fine. Great. She's still pissed off that I didn't come down for her operation, but I *couldn't*. The kids, Steve, my fucking job—"

"I know, Diane. I know."

"This is ridiculous. Put her on, Warren. I want to talk to her *now*."

"Okay. Hang on." I walk down the hall to our mother's room and open the door. Cold air rushes out. I shout so Diane can hear me. "Ma, it's Diane on the phone."

She pencils in a word on her crossword puzzle. "I'm not here. I'm shopping at Neiman Marcus."

I go back to the kitchen. "Sorry, Diane. She's in one of her moods. She said to tell you she went shopping."

My sister sighs. "She's so stubborn. I thought this, you know, brush-with-death thing might have made her aware."

"Afraid not."

"What are your plans? I guess you're not going back to school next month."

"I can't. I have Mother to think about."

"Do I hear blame in your tone?"

"No, Diane. You've done all you can. I appreciate the check you sent, by the way. I don't mind being here. I didn't visit her much after I started law school, so I'm making up for it now."

This seems to cheer her up. What Diane doesn't want is for me to say she has to fly down to Miami, or pay for a nursing home, or cram her kids into one bedroom to make room for our mother in her house, God forbid. She wishes me well and signs off.

I look in on Mother. She's dozing again. I turn the TV down and leave her a note: *Ma, I'm at the office.*

———

It's NEARLY TWO o'clock in the morning when I type the last keystroke on the report. Eighty-six pages come off the printer. I bind them into a folder and put the folder into a big envelope with Erika's name on the front. I turn out the lights, go down-stairs, and wave at the security guard in the lobby.

I plan to drop the envelope on her doorstep. I've looked up her address, a house in Coral Gables near the University of Miami, whose law school I could not get into in a million years.

Banyan trees arch over the quiet streets and block the street-lights. There is no traffic at this hour. I am not sure which house is hers, exactly, so I park in the law school lot and walk. There are only a few other cars there, students working late in the library. As I get to the end of the lot, I see a black Porsche parked in the shadows under some trees. I notice the sticker for the parking garage in our building. It's Jack Porter's car. That's odd. He lives on the Beach.

I walk three blocks to Erika's street. Number 5206 is set back behind a low coral rock wall. A porch light is on. Crickets are chirping, and something rustles through the bushes. A small gray lizard darts across the sidewalk.

Her Mercedes is parked under the portico to my right. A light shines through a window at the other end of the house. I should drop the envelope on her porch and go, but I wonder whether she's working late or entertaining someone. Erika is divorced, but she's over fifty, and the idea of her in bed naked with a lover, pounding the headboard against the wall—I stifle a laugh and move silently forward across the yard. Her windows are closed against the summer heat. The curtains are drawn. I can't see past them.

The light goes out at the same moment I hear a crash.

Then nothing. No sound at all. What to do? Maybe she's hav-ing a heart attack, a stroke. I could save her. Not that she'd be grateful. Even so, I can't just leave her, can I?

Looking for a way in, I run around the house. I leap over a fallen palm frond and shove my way through a hedge. In the backyard, the light from the swimming pool paints the trees pale turquoise. I stop at the edge of the terrace. The sliding door is open. I can make out the kitchen, a dim light from a stainless-steel range hood, a hallway beyond.

An instant later a black silhouette appears in the doorway. He looks around and moves silently across the terrace toward the portico. He dodges around an umbrella table, rounds the corner, and disappears.

I shrink farther into the shadows, nearly trip when I collide with a tree. My breath claws at my throat. I can't go into her house. There aren't any pay phones here. I feel sick. The envelope has fallen to the terrace. I pick it up and run.

When I reach the law school parking lot, I notice that the Porsche is gone.

———

AT THE FIRM the next day, people gather in the break room, in the corridors, the library, talking about the murder of Erika Mulloy. She was strangled, no signs of a break-in. Detectives from the Miami Beach police have set up shop in two of the conference rooms. The phone lines buzz with inquiries from clients. Denise is crying. Mike and the other clerks jam into our office and discuss what will happen now. They are more interested in their jobs than in Erika Mulloy's demise. None of them is sorry she's gone, which I find appalling. Show some sympathy, or at least pretend to, so other people in the office don't see you for the assholes you are.

My thoughts keep going down the hall to Jack Porter's office. My legs twitch. I have to get up. I leave the Pits and walk around the corner, past his open door, glancing quickly inside. I turn and come back the other way. He is writing notes in a file, working as if nothing had happened. He wears a white shirt, and the sun through the window makes a blaze of light. It shines on his hair and dances on his gold pen. I am so tense my vision blurs. I lean against the wall outside his office.

My mind is a spinning compass needle. Jack Porter is guilty. No, he isn't. I have no evidence. I didn't see him. But I saw his car. Can you prove you saw his car? If I point them toward Jack Porter, why should they believe me? Jack will hire Frank Delgado, and he'll get away with it, just like Frank's other clients get away with it. Jack Porter will come for me next.

"Warren? Is that you out there?"

My mouth is dry. I can't speak. I slide over and look around the doorjamb.

Jack Porter puts down his pen. "What do you want?"

"Nothing. The police are here."

"And?"

"And nothing. They're talking to everyone . . . about Erika Mulloy. What happened to her."

"Okay. So?"

"Just thought I'd tell you."

"Fine. You told me." He keeps staring at me, through me. He *knows*. He knows that I saw him. He will come after me if I tell. We are *friends, goddamn it,* and I am afraid he will kill me. I will be his third victim. The law firm has hired a psycho, and there's no one I can tell.

"Warren? Shut the door, will you?"

———

THE POLICE WORK in three teams on the main floor. Lunch is ordered in, and only those with previous appointments are permitted to leave. They get to the clerks in the afternoon, and they call for me at 3:55 p.m.

A detective introduces himself as Sergeant Dennis Ryan and gives me his card, which has a gold shield on it. They ask the usual questions. I answer them. Name, address. "I live with my mother. Actually, it's her apartment. She's ill and I came down from Ohio to take care of her. I was in law school at the time. Mr. Penniman hired me to work here."

"And you knew Ms. Mulloy?"

"Of course. Everyone did."

"You were doing some work for her?"

"That's correct."

"We understand that Ms. Mulloy wasn't happy with your work, and she got on your case about it."

"Who told you that?"

"Is it true?"

"No. Not at all. She was demanding with everyone. I wasn't special."

"Are you nervous, Mr. Kemble? You're sweating."

"It's warm in here."

They ask me where I was last night.

"Home. I was home."

"Security guard says you were here until two a.m."

"Yes, working, then I went home. My mother can vouch for me."

"We might need to talk to her."

"Sure. No problem."

Ryan gestures toward my hands, which are loosely clasped on the table. "How'd you get the injury there, Mr. Kemble?"

I stare at my right hand. There is a red scrape across the knuckles. I hadn't noticed until now, but I remember. Last night at Erika Mulloy's house, moving back when I saw Porter come out, bumping into the tree—

The detectives are waiting. There is no choice. I have to tell them everything.

When I finish, they look at each other. Ryan's partner picks up a list, scans it. "Porter. I don't see that name."

"He's new. Jack Porter."

"Not here."

"Yes, he is. He's on Fourteen. He was just hired. He worked for Erika Mulloy."

"You want to show us?"

"He's going to deny everything. He's very convincing. If you don't arrest him, he'll come after me."

"Don't worry about that. Just show us where he is."

They follow me downstairs, past the library, around a turn past the Pits, then into another corridor, a row of closed doors. My legs are weak, and my lungs feel cold. "I saw his car. I'm sorry, I didn't write down the license tag. But it was him. What if he comes after me? Can you offer protection?"

"Which office is his, Mr. Kemble?"

I stop and point at Jack Porter's door. They knock. Porter doesn't say to come in. Ryan turns the knob. No one is inside. There's no computer on the desk, no phone, nothing.

I stare. "No, this isn't right. Where did he go?"

"Doesn't look like anybody was ever here."

"He's here. He has to be here." I push past them into the hall and open one door after another, a long row of offices. They are all empty. I am screaming, "Porter! Jack Porter! Where are you?"

THE TWO DETECTIVES and a uniformed officer escort me home, and Mrs. Perlstein stares as our parade passes by. I tell her everything is fine. Detective Ryan orders me to open the door. Technically he needs a warrant to enter, but I unlock it. I ask them to wait in the living room until I speak to my mother about this, but Ryan goes to her bedroom door and knocks. "Mrs. Kemble? It's the police. We need to talk to you, ma'am."

He rudely goes inside. A couple of seconds later I hear him cursing. He comes out with a handkerchief over his nose and mouth. He looks at me strangely as he speaks to his partner. "She's dead. She's *been* dead. Nothing left but a husk. Call it in. Get forensics over here."

"Ma!" I rush toward her door. "Let me in! I want to see her!"

"Sit down and shut up." They shove me onto the sofa. The uniformed cop speaks into the radio on his shoulder.

Ryan pulls a chair over. "What happened here, Warren?"

"I don't know. I don't understand this. She was fine this morning." I fold my arms across my body and rock back and forth, trying to figure it out, but I'm stuck in a nightmare. "I would like to call my sister."

"In a minute, soon as you tell me what you did last night."

I remember what Frank Delgado said: Don't open your mouth to the police. Tears burn their way down my cheeks, drip off my chin.

"Talk to me, Warren."

"I'm sorry. I can't. My mother just passed away. I can't talk to you now. I can't talk to you at all. I'm sorry, I would like to, I would, but on advice of counsel, I can't. I'm sorry."

TIME WILL TELL

BY TWIST PHELAN

L auren Winslow swept into my office a half hour after my
secretary left, twenty minutes before Security came on
duty downstairs. As slim as a fading hope, she wore a long
sapphire sheath that was sexy but modest at the same time. She
hung her wet umbrella on the coat tree next to the door and collapsed into her favorite chair, the one closest to my desk.

I turned over the spreadsheet I'd been reviewing and put on a
welcoming smile. "You're looking lovely this evening, Madame Prosecutor. What's the occasion?"

"Annual judges' dinner at the Downtown Club. If I'd known the
weather was going to be this bad, I would have rented a tux." She
brushed off the raindrops that spangled her hem, revealing a pair of
satin slingbacks with vicious heels. "They're roasting Galletti, so I
have to be there. Would you please just kill me now?"

Lauren going to an event for Glamour Boy Galletti? "An evening
of lawyers in white ties telling white lies—you'll be in your element,
Counselor."

She chuckled, a low sound of genuine mirth. She had deep-set
brown eyes, wavy chestnut hair, and a dusting of freckles so fine

I often wondered if I'd imagined them. "I think you'd hold your own, Tommy."

Lauren headed up the Complex Crimes Unit for the regional office of the Department of Justice. A dozen attorneys under Galletti were on a crusade against "sophisticated" criminals—corporate fraudsters, identity thieves, computer hackers, pay-for-play politicos, big-time polluters. "We're not interested in ordinary crooks," Lauren had told me when we first met. "We go after the smart people who've gone bad, the ones who screw over widows and orphans."

I held up an almost-empty tumbler of whiskey. "Care to get a head start on the festivities?"

She declined, as she always did during her impromptu visits. Instead, she stood up and walked to the window, all fine-boned elegance and height. What began as an afternoon shower had turned into leaden rain. It was an ugly day, exactly as forecast.

I wondered why Lauren was here. Usually she dropped by to regale me with some courtroom triumph—the defeat of a defendant's motion to suppress evidence, a unanimous guilty verdict, a plea that sent somebody away for twenty-five years. Her stories hinted at rules she had to bend, witnesses she had to bully into fatal admissions.

Tonight, though, she was different. There was something about her I hadn't seen before; she was wired, so electric she nearly set the air vibrating. I swallowed a mouthful of scotch, felt the warmth spread through my belly, and waited.

"Have I ever told you what brought me to Seattle?" she asked, gazing out at the city. Her skin was pale against the darkness on the other side of the glass.

"No." Although Lauren was familiar with my background, she had always been closemouthed about hers. I took another sip of my drink. In less than a week, I'd be downing mojitos instead of single malt.

She turned, and her dress pulled tight against her thigh. I glimpsed the outline of lace through the thin fabric and sucked in my breath. Lauren was the only woman I knew who wore a garter belt. Her legs were great, and outside the courtroom she preferred short skirts to pants. During our first meeting she had leaned across a table to hand a document to Nick, exposing a thin strip of smooth flesh at the top of her stocking. Nearly a minute had passed before I'd been able to focus on her questions again.

"It was four years ago," she said, turning away from the window to reclaim her chair. I could smell her perfume. She always wore the same scent—subtle but crisp, not too flowery. I imagined her touching the glass stopper to the hollow of her neck, dabbing it between her breasts . . .

I felt the heft of my new watch as I lifted the whiskey bottle from the desk drawer and replenished my tumbler. Audemars Piguet—the only brand Arnold Schwarzenegger wore. With its gold face and thirty-two diamonds rimming the bezel, the thing weighed almost a pound. The black rubber wristband made it popular among the yachties in Boca.

Lauren noticed my new hardware. "Check out the bling. I could hire another paralegal for what that cost."

More like two, I didn't say. Eighty thousand dollars, no discount for cash.

"What happened to the Rolex?" she asked. "Or was that a Patek Philippe in your briefcase?"

I put the bottle back into the drawer, next to the mini digital recorder. I touched the square red button and left the drawer open. "I still can't believe you snooped."

"Your driver shouldn't have left the backseat door open. And briefcases come with locks for a reason."

I was tempted to ask what part of *no unreasonable searches and seizures* she didn't understand. "Next you'll be telling me, if I carry cash, I deserve to have my pocket picked. You're lucky I didn't think you were a carjacker."

Lauren looked at me through her eyelashes. "What if you had, Tommy? Would you have shot me?"

"Jesus, how can you—"

"I never figured you for one of those big-watch guys," she interrupted. "Bonus from a grateful client?"

"If you're gonna keep asking questions, Madame Prosecutor, I want my lawyer." I said it automatically. *Not a big-watch guy.* I turned my wrist so the diamonds wouldn't show so much.

Lauren made a face. "Very funny, Tommy."

As hilarious as the Fourth Amendment, Lauren. Bad guys aren't the only ones who think the end justifies the means. I pulled at my drink. *Galletti knows it, too.*

Outside, headlights were yellow smears in the downpour, and a foghorn mooed. I knew I shouldn't spill the beans, but I couldn't resist.

"As a matter of fact, the watch is a going-away present to myself. Good-bye, perpetual rain; hello, eternal sunshine."

Lauren tilted her head. "You're moving? Where?"

I picked up the Prada sunglasses from my desk—another recent purchase—and put them on.

"Next week I'll be sitting on the private beach of one of the ritziest golf communities in Florida." Harbour View or Vista or something like that. Harbour with a *u* of course, and a gated entrance even more pretentious than the name.

Gated, alarmed, rent-a-copped. Drop-ins at the office were one thing, but I've never been keen on clients—or anyone else—showing up at my house. "And I won't be back," I added in my best *Ahnuld* imitation.

A small crease appeared between Lauren's brows. A big reaction, if you knew her. I took off the glasses, prepared to launch into my sun, beach, and golf riff. None of these things actually mattered to me, but the explanation had satisfied everyone else.

Few people ever surprised me like Lauren.

"So you're walking away before things are finished," she said.

"What do you mean? The practice is all wrapped up. Not that there was much to do. After what happened to Nick, things went into the crapper pretty fast."

When my partner got shot in our parking garage, the local news feasted on it for a week. There was a lot of speculation—fueled by an anonymous source—that it was a mob hit. That was enough to scare off old clients and keep away new ones. I regarded Lauren. And with my other reason to stay in Seattle leaving too . . .

"I'm not talking about your accounting firm," she said.

I looked at my watch, no longer giving a damn what she thought of it. "Aren't you supposed to be at Galletti's roast?"

Lauren tossed back her prodigal curls. Usually she wore her hair in a ponytail. I decided I preferred it loose around her face.

"I want to arrive late." Her tone turned coy. "Besides, don't you want to hear why I came to Seattle?"

It was impossible to stay annoyed with her. Besides, this could be our last evening together before I left. "Go ahead."

"Ever play Monopoly when you were a kid?"

You could get whiplash trying to follow her train of thought. "Sure."

"Did you know it's the only game where going to jail is an accepted risk?"

I put on an Uncle Sam scowl and pointed at her. *"Do not pass Go, do not collect two hundred dollars."*

Her eyes sparkled. "I used to really rub it in when my brother pulled that card. Sometimes I made him so mad, he'd kick me out of the game."

You're still pissing off the other players, Lauren. "All I cared about was collecting rent," I said.

"Spoken like a true accountant. So, Tommy, did Monopoly make us what we are today?"

I wasn't exactly sure what she was getting at, so I sipped my whiskey and stayed quiet. The rain increased its patter on the windows. It sounded impatient, like a dealer's fingers drumming on the felt.

Lauren broke the silence. "Private placement offerings put together by Merrill Bache—coal-mining deals. That's what brought me here."

She was talking about PPOs. If the investment banks won't touch you, they're a way to raise capital without jumping through too many government hoops. Lawyers and accountants vet you and your numbers, then brokers sell the deal to "accredited" investors, rich people who've been around the financial block a few times.

I always thought private placements were small-time. Give me a REIT any day. You pool investor funds to buy commercial rental properties or mortgages—that's serious money.

"I don't remember hearing anything about coal."

Since meeting Lauren, I'd made a point of keeping up with local financial and legal news. The deals must have gone down before I moved to Seattle.

"It was a pretty standard fraud. The geology was faked—there wasn't any coal. The investors got stuck with worthless holes in the ground."

I shrugged. "So a few of the privileged class spent the summer at their lawyers' offices instead of the beach."

"Not so privileged," Lauren said, her voice like ice. "The brokers sold units to anyone who walked in the door, even if they weren't accredited. Retirement savings, college funds, cushions against medical emergencies—they took in millions, tens of millions."

Although we'd never talked about it, I sensed that Lauren took investors' losses personally. I wondered if there was private history.

"The money was gone, of course." I tried to sound sympathetic.

"I followed the funds through three banks before the trail went cold. As usual, nothing was left stateside. Rich crooks don't need walking-around money."

"Promoter disappear, too?"

"As soon as the deal went south, he followed it."

I swirled the scotch in my glass. "So you were left with the professionals. I assume you picked the obvious target."

She nodded. "The brokers who peddled the deal. You know how I hate white-collar types who think the rules don't apply to them. When these guys tried to play games during discovery, it really ticked me off. I wasn't going to settle for a fine after that. I wanted them in prison."

"Any defense?"

"The usual." Her voice became singsong. "Each investor received documents describing the risks, the brokers had no way to know the attorneys hadn't done the due diligence or that the accountants had inflated the numbers, it wasn't their fault unqualified investors bought into the deal, blah blah blah blah."

"Did the jury buy any of it?"

"Not after it took the head broker a full five minutes to locate where the lawyers had buried the risk disclosures in the offering memorandum. The print was so small, he couldn't read it without borrowing the judge's glasses. Meanwhile, the projected returns were smack-dab in the middle of the first page, in typeface as big as the top line on an eye chart."

"I take it you won."

"Don't I always?"

That had been true for as long as I'd known her. Lauren was a real buccaneer. She tried cases other prosecutors would have passed on, and she was willing to do whatever it took to win, even if it meant sailing to the edge of legal boundaries, or beyond. *I get the message, Lauren.*

I took a long pull from my tumbler. "A criminal conviction makes a civil suit practically a slam-dunk. I bet some class-action attorney had a complaint on file the same day your jury came back." I could feel my neck getting red.

She plucked at a thread on her dress and looked bored. "Probably."

"What did the investors finally end up with? Ninety, ninety-five cents on the dollar?" I heard the edge in my voice, so I gulped some of my drink. I had to choke back a cough as the whiskey scorched my throat.

Lauren hitched up her dress so she could cross her legs. "A little more than a hundred, actually. The jury was generous with punitive damages."

I forced myself to look away from her slender ankles. "I bet you went after the attorneys and accountants, too." I set the tumbler down hard on my desk. Amber liquid sloshed over my hand.

"The law allows—"

"To hell with the law! The investors got back *more* than they put up. And they're no less greedy than the professionals you're so hot to put in prison. Most people wouldn't go near these deals if they didn't think they'd get a big tax write-off, plus beat the market. Why not be reasonable? Dial it back after things are more or less even again, go after *real* bad guys."

"I do! Lawyers and accountants are supposed to be the watchdogs who make sure offerings are legit. And the ones in these deals did more than look the other way. The promoter was smart, but not that smart. He couldn't have put the fraud together without professional help."

I made a calming motion with my hands, I was determined not to argue with her. Besides, it was an old debate. "Okay, okay, *these* lawyers and *these* accountants were dirtbags. You have my blessing to prosecute them."

She grimaced. "Easier said than done. I barely had enough evidence for a search warrant. By the time it was executed, they had shredded all the documents. I needed the promoter's testimony that the attorneys and accountants were in on the scam from the get-go."

I rubbed a thumb against the rubberized band of my watch. "Those guys can be hard to find once they're in the wind."

"The coal mines were in Kentucky, so I started there. I went to the town, talked to the guy's landlord, the people who leased him office equipment, even the waitresses at his favorite diner. Wasn't hard—I was raised in a place like that. Turns out the guy's Norwegian, grew up working on a family fishing boat. He immigrated to the States about ten years ago with plans to make it big."

"Let's hear it for the American dream!" I took a mouthful of scotch and let it sizzle on my tongue. I was feeling good again. "He must have played Monopoly when he was a kid."

Lauren glared at me. "I expected him to go back to Europe. But Immigration didn't have a record of him leaving."

"How about Canada?"

"They said he wasn't there either. So that left Seattle."

"Seattle? What made you think—"

"When we went through his office in Kentucky, we found a bunch of blank Seattle postcards and some country-western CDs in the back of a desk drawer. Apparently he missed them when he cleaned out the place."

"You thought he came here because of some *postcards?*"

"Don't give me a hard time, Tommy. It was all I had to go on. The databases—"

"I was wondering when you'd get to those." I heard that edge in my voice again. "Do you feds even bother with warrants anymore? Or do you just whisper the word *terrorist* and wait for the sysop to hand over the master password?"

Lauren's expression told me she wasn't in the mood for my privacy-rights rant. "Oh, we got the password all right, but the databases were a bust. There was nothing in the computers—no driver's license, no address, no credit cards."

I was impressed by Lauren's quarry. Despite disposable cell phones, false identities for sale on the Internet, and banks that were more interested in fees than references, it was harder than ever to live off the grid. "So what did you do?"

She flashed that luminous smile. "Drove around in the rain, hyped on caffeine. I went to bars, hotels, used-car lots—anywhere he might have gone or done business. *Nada*. It was as though he'd never been here."

Despite myself, I was getting interested. "Why not give up?"

"I almost did. I was running out of places to look. But I knew—I just *knew*—he was here. The local Norwegian community, the climate, the fishing, the postcards" —she ticked each one off on a finger— "made Seattle the most logical place for him to go to ground." She shook her head. "Thank goodness for clams."

"What do clams have to do with this?"

"I was eating lunch at this tiny joint downtown—"

"The one next to the bridge? You ever have the chowder?"

"Every Tuesday. White, with extra crackers." She ducked behind a grin. "And an Elysian Fields Pale Ale, no glass."

A noontime beer should be the least of your worries, Lauren. For half a second, I wondered if she would go to lunch with me. Maybe if I called it a bon voyage thing . . .

"Anyway, I was eating on the patio when the ferry came in from Bainbridge Island. That's when it hit me."

"A boat," I said.

"A boat," she repeated, clearly relishing the memory. "And I had five days to find it before I had to start working another case."

"The State of Washington must have a hundred thousand registered vessels. How did you think you were going to come up with the right one in time?"

"Make that three hundred thousand, plus transients." Lauren flicked invisible lint from her dress. "Still, it was no problem."

"Okay, I'll bite. How did you find the needle in a third of a million boats?"

"Did you know the DMV is in charge of maritime registrations?

It handles them just like cars. I sat in a back office and scrolled through the listings for vessels over thirty feet—the DMV guy said that would be the minimum size for someone to live on. I found it the second day." Her tone was only slightly smug.

"He couldn't have been stupid enough to put his name down as the owner."

Lauren looked offended. "Of course not. Besides, I didn't look at the owner registry. I figured title would be held by some offshore corporation. I went through the list of boat names instead."

"*Boat names?* Why would you do that?"

"Because men aren't sentimental, except when they are." She looked at my watch. "They can't hide the things that matter to them."

I tugged my cuff over the gold dial. "So did he go for a name from the old country? Or something dumb, like *Other People's Money* or *Sucker Bet?*"

"Wrong, and wrong. But I knew I'd found the right one as soon as I saw it." She grinned, and I half-expected to see canary feathers sticking out of her mouth. "The *Loretta Lynn.*"

"Isn't that a country-western singer?"

"You got it. Born and raised in Butcher Hollow, Kentucky."

"Why would this guy name his boat after her? He's Swedish."

"Norwegian." Lauren hugged herself happily. "Remember when I told you the coal mines were in Kentucky? Well, guess what town they're in."

"You've *got* to be kidding. I still don't see how the hell you made the connection with Loretta Lynn. I didn't think you were a country-western buff."

"I'm not. But the CDs he'd left in his office were all hers, except for—here's the good part—the soundtrack from *Coal Miner's Daughter,* the movie they made about her life."

The pride in her voice was beginning to grate. "So then what did you do?"

"The records said the *Loretta Lynn* was a converted trawler. The DMV guy said that meant it ran on diesel. I called around to the fuel docks until I found the one that knew the boat. The gas jockey ID'd an e-mail photo of my guy, and the Harbor Patrol took me out there. Two days later, I was waiting when he showed up with empty tanks and a grocery list."

"I suppose you called the media for the perp walk," I said into my glass. The tumbler was almost empty again, and I considered refilling it.

"Of course." She almost purred the words. "You know I love the look of a man in a monogrammed shirt and handcuffs."

"Yeah, those initials come in real handy when it's time to sort prison laundry."

The corner of her mouth twitched. "Always the clever one, Tommy."

Looking out the window, I could see the interior of my office reflected endlessly across the skyline, illuminated boxes filled with bland furniture, screen-savered computers, and generic wall art. As I scanned the warren of other buildings, I half-expected to see someone like me looking back. It made me uncomfortable, and I pulled my gaze back to Lauren.

"So why did you stay?" I fiddled with the thick clasp on my watch—opening it, snapping it shut, opening it again. The diamonds winked at me. "In Seattle, I mean."

Her reply was quiet, measured. "I met you, Tommy."

I stopped playing with my watch.

Lauren got up from her chair.

"Assuming that ridiculous sundial on your wrist is correct, I better get going," she said. "One of the secretaries let slip that part of tonight's program includes a small celebration in my honor."

The words jumped out before I could stop them. "A celebration?"

Her eyes drilled into mine. Anticipation shimmered off her.

"I'm leaving Seattle too."

I felt something flutter in my chest, forced my eyebrows up in feigned surprise.

"You're looking at the new DOJ liaison with the local SEC office." Lauren leaned forward and placed her hands flat on the desktop. Her fingers were long and tapered, the nails filed into perfect ovals. "In Boca Raton."

The change in her demeanor was subtle but unmistakable. *Damn.* Sooner or later, we always came to this point in the conversation.

"You may be clever, Tommy, but you're not clever enough." Her voice was as soft as cashmere, but underneath I could feel the chill of steel. "I'm going to get you. Three years left on the securities fraud SOL. And, of course, there's Nick. There's no statute of limitations on murder."

Even when I held the winning hand, she still made me feel like I was chasing the pot. Had I refilled my glass twice or three times? I passed a damp palm over my face.

"This isn't one of your coal deals." My tongue felt slightly too big for my mouth. "For starters, the REIT investors' lawsuit was tossed."

Lauren blew out a dismissive breath. "Plaintiff's lawyer jumped the gun. Doesn't affect the criminal prosecution."

"*Lack of evidence*—that's what the judge said when he granted my lawyer's motion to dismiss. If the plaintiffs didn't have enough proof to get past *more likely than not*, how are you going to make it all the way to *beyond a reasonable doubt?*"

The determination was plain on her face. "I'll find the evidence."

By any means necessary. I tapped my watch. "You know as well as I do, the more time that passes, the more memories fade, the more documents are lost, the more people decide to put all this behind them and move on. As for what happened to my partner" —I put on the sad expression I'd used for the reporters— "carjacking gone wrong. Real tragedy."

"Four thousand investors lost everything in your REIT, Tommy. *Four thousand.* Already there have been two suicides, plus God knows what other damage—divorce, derailed retirements, ruined careers—" Lauren paused, bit down on her lip.

But it wasn't my fault, I wanted to tell her. I'd been in hock up to my eyeballs to those deranged Russian bookies. They "let me" pay off my marker by washing their gambling profits through the REIT. I didn't know they were going to rip off the investors, too.

"And we both know Nick wasn't killed by any carjacker." Her voice had dropped to a whisper, and I had to lean forward to hear her. Our faces were so close, I could see the pulse beating at her temple and smell her perfume. *Definitely grapefruit. Maybe a little cypress?*

"He's dead because he decided to take the immunity offer and testify." She nearly spat the words. "Against *you.*"

Also not my fault. Since when did my partner the schmoozer ever bother to look into the mechanics of a deal? Nick's job was to bring in the business, not run it. When he stumbled onto the money laundering, I had no choice. Otherwise the Russians would have left me lying on that cold concrete floor.

Lauren pushed herself off the desk. "Run to Florida, run halfway around the world. It won't make a bit of difference. You'll never be able to put enough distance—or time—between us. More search warrants, new witnesses—I'll plant the damn evidence if I need to—I'll get the proof I need. Then it'll be like that hideous watch of yours was turned back to yesterday."

Her look of distaste stung. I dropped my eyes to the digital recorder in the drawer. I imagined I could hear its motor humming. *Everybody's on the run from something, Lauren. Or should be.*

"I'll see you in Florida, Tommy. Don't get too comfortable in your new place. Before you know it, you'll be moving to another gated community—the kind where Security carries pump shotguns instead of cell phones and the bars on the windows aren't just for show."

With a rustle of blue silk, she was gone.

I'll see you in Florida, Tommy.

The black October rain beat against the window. I checked my watch, drained the last of the scotch, and pushed back my chair. I picked up the recorder from the drawer, turned it off, and dropped it into my pocket.

The irony of where I was headed hit me in the hallway and kept me laughing all the way to the elevator. I punched the down button.

Galletti wouldn't have offered a talk-and-walk on the Russian thing if he suspected anything about Nick. Lauren must have been keeping her cards close. Made it sweet for me. Once her overeager—or dumb—boss put blanket immunity on the table, I had my Get Out Of Jail Free card. If I took his deal, I'd be untouchable for the murder.

As the elevator doors slid open on the parking garage, I thought back to that night. I hadn't expected Nick to struggle, let alone rip the watch from my wrist. The Rolex had fallen into a crack in the cement floor beside one of the support beams, wedged out of reach. I averted my eyes as I walked past the spot. What the hell had possessed me to engrave the damn thing?

My DNA, Nick's blood . . . The feds had already been over the scene. But Lauren was talking about a new search warrant. If she found the watch before I disappeared into witness protection, my deal with her boss would evaporate. I'd be facing the needle instead of twenty years.

The gray Buick was parked next to the exit ramp, its engine running, in one of the spaces with a good view of the main entrance. The air was thick with the stink of exhaust. I could hear tires swishing through the puddles at street level.

I slid into the backseat and rested my head against the plump leather. Galletti eagerly twisted around in the driver's seat. No doubt he'd seen Lauren leave. Jesus, the guy had it in for her so bad, he was going to be late to his own roast.

Our last meeting had not gone well. He'd moaned about my coming up empty-handed again. I'd dropped the bomb about my Florida move.

"We both know witness protection is gonna stick me in someplace like Oshfart, North Dakota," I'd told him when he finished squawking. "I want to see sun and beach and girls in bikinis one last time. Besides, isn't this all moot, like you lawyers say? If Lauren's moving to Florida, she's not your problem anymore, right?"

He hadn't been able to hide the ambition and spite in his hooded eyes. Galletti wasn't gunning for Lauren because she crossed the line. He wanted to take her down because every month she won more cases, more headlines, more fans. She wouldn't be the first prosecutor to parlay those into a glory ride. But it was a trip her boss wanted to take himself.

I let my eyelids close as his voice once again bore into my skull, more excruciating than the hangover I knew I'd have in the morning.

He asked me the question.

How many had it been this time? Two—no, three counts of prosecutorial misconduct, any one of which was enough to deliver Lauren's head—and career—to Galletti on a silver platter.

"Nothing." I shifted in the seat. The recorder jabbed me in the rib. "Didn't even get a chance to turn it on."

I got out of the car and went back to my office. I sat down at my desk, took the whiskey bottle out of the drawer, and poured slowly until my glass was full again. I thumbed the rewind button on the recorder and turned up the volume so I could hear her voice over the rain.

I'll see you in Florida, Tommy.

THE EVIL WE DO

BY JOHN WALTER PUTRE

T he light of the late afternoon was failing. Deep caverns of shadow had begun their conquest of the corners of the chamber. Already, the audience had lasted too long, and now its disposition was becoming increasingly testy. A muscle at the back of Maculano's neck had stiffened. The tightness was turning into pain.

"You forget yourself, Reverend Father," he heard himself being warned for yet another time.

"I apologize, Your Holiness," the priest repeated, again with a respectful inclination of his head. "I belabor these issues only out of the weight of my concern."

"Ahh, Vincenzo. I know you do. I know it." With fingers the color and texture of parchment, the Pontiff stroked the side of his short, stubbled beard. "Were you not among the few in these precincts I trust, I'd have ended our discourse long ago. My son, there are times I wonder if intelligence such as yours is a gift. I fear that, by the final standard of salvation, the child or the fisherman may well be better off. I say without hesitation both are happier."

Maculano lifted his head. "I've no doubt that Your Holiness is correct in both opinions."

The Pope reached toward a tasseled strip of burgundy fabric that dropped from the ceiling to hang within reach of his chair. A slight tug of his hand produced no sound within the room, but the appearance of two servants was all but instantaneous. He ordered candles for the chamber and, "Since the supper hour approaches, Father, perhaps some wine would be in order?"

"For myself, may I please decline, Holy Father? I have duties that yet require my attention. I must transcribe the mental notes I've kept of our discussion so that I will not misrepresent or fail to recall any of the guidance you've given me. If my responsibilities were otherwise, I would be honored beyond expression by your invitation."

The Pope offered a sad smile. "For your own peace of mind, Reverend Father, do not make so much of these difficulties you foresee. Heresy, spoken, is an offense against God. If written and disseminated, its danger—and so the sin—is far worse. When the construction of it is such as to bring ridicule and disrespect to the very institution of His Holy Church, the offense becomes inexcusable and impossible for even the most tolerant of His servants to overlook. A successful prosecution will not be nearly so difficult as you imagine."

"Yes, Holy Father." Maculano sighed. "With your invaluable assistance, I will continue my preparations. As always, Your Holiness, I'm in your debt."

"Go with God, Vincenzo. Be thorough, but make haste in your work." Urban made the Sign and gave the priest his benediction. "This is not an occasion on which the Church can be seen to be dilatory or timorous."

FRA VINCENZO MACULANO da Firenzuola by vow was a Dominican and, by training and profession, a military engineer. But like many who show talent and judgment in an initially chosen discipline, he had found himself drawn beyond the borders of his expertise toward challenges that placed less reliance on the application of prescribed formulae and more on situations in which insight and sensitivity became the paramount requirements. In Maculano's career, these attributes had carried him to the highest levels of ecclesiastical law. It was there that he'd spent his recent years acquiring his new learning and reputation.

He sat at his desk in the solitude of his private quarters, poised over a sheet of paper, transcribing his notes to his best recollection. Over the back of his neck, he wore a moist towel in the hope of ameliorating the ache that stubbornly refused to go away. At the age of fifty-nine, after an eager youth, he had acquired the habits of patience and scholarship, along with a proneness to the sundry infirmities that make themselves the gratuitous companions of seniority.

The remains of his supper of bread and cheese accompanied by a tankard of equal parts wine and water rested on a tray beside him. Beyond the window, the purple sky of the early spring was turning rapidly to a blanket of dark blue. The first, faint stars had begun to appear. The evening held the warmth of the coming season. Winter was easing its grasp on the city. At best, a mixed blessing. The plague was still the dreaded guest that lurked on the steps just beyond every threshold.

Behind the priest's back, a votary came like a specter into the room. Deliberately, he shuffled his feet, then shuffled them again a bit more loudly. Finally, he resorted to a muffled cough.

"I beg your pardon, Father," he said softly as the priest, with care, turned his head. "You have a visitor. Father Sinceri begs to speak with you."

"Sinceri!" Maculano drew a breath as he pushed himself up

from his chair. "Show him in, Umberto. Then bring us some wine and a pair of the silver cups."

The attendant bowed and left, returning almost immediately, leading a man who, by his gait and vapid grin, gave every appearance of being a portly, balding, and awkward fool.

"Carlo. Greetings. Come in. Come in," Maculano invited. "I offer you welcome to my small foreshadowing of Purgatory." He spoke aside. "Umberto, please, as I ordered."

The servant departed, taking with him the remains of Maculano's meal.

"Good evening, Father," Sinceri began. "Are you certain I do not disturb the studies of the Commissary General? If another time would be more convenient . . ." And with the measure and tone of those words, all the visitor's awkwardness and foolishness disappeared.

A highly reputed classical scholar in his own right, Lord Carlo Sinceri, like Maculano, had only his wit and practical experience to guide him in the intricacies of canon law. Even so, it had been Sinceri, in his role as Prosecutor for the Holy Office, who had taken the lead in formulating the questions that had been put to the accused during the day's session. And although the testimony had produced an unanticipated contradiction in the evidence, Sinceri's seemingly endless litany of boring interrogatories had had the effect of placing in order the chronology and details of the case in a manner more efficient and damning than any the commissary general could have devised.

"Not at all, my Lord Prosecutor," Maculano replied. "In truth, the moment of your arrival could not be more propitious. I've called for wine. Please. Use the chair with the padded stool. Put your feet up, if you like. We've both had a long and taxing day."

"Thank you for your consideration, Reverend Father." Sinceri let himself sink into the chair and, with some effort, lifted his legs onto the stool. "Mmm," he sighed as his muscles relaxed.

"The onset of blessed relief." He allowed himself a moment of contentment, then a moment more to give the mood the chance to dissipate. Then he wasted no more time.

"This trial is a hazardous business, Father, as you, above all, understand. Full of pitfalls and villainies at every turn. Too many masters, too many personalities. For every foreseeable outcome, the consequences are profound."

Maculano nodded.

"I'm informed you were successful in obtaining an audience with His Holiness this afternoon."

Resettling his feet, Sinceri left the statement to stand unamplified as Umberto arrived and poured the wine. The attendant began to return the decanter to Maculano, but Maculano directed that it remain beside his guest.

"I was able to do so," Maculano answered when the two were again alone. He added nothing except for a shake of his head.

"Well, we knew as much," Sinceri acknowledged. "We had no hope the inclinations of that master would change."

"Before we speak more, Father . . ." Maculano paused, deliberately giving weight to that which would follow. "Before we speak more of this, it is essential we are agreed between ourselves. You speak of masters. You are right to do so. It is said truly no man can serve two."

"Or three. A trinity of sorts." Holding up three fingers, Sinceri permitted himself a show of pleasure at the aptness of his analogy. "We've already named His Holiness. There remains Holy Mother, the Church, along with that more intangible master, the Truth."

"If the master that you and I serve is different . . ."

"For reasons of both duty and my personal respect for you, Father Commissary, I could not have come here this evening believing that were so."

"Nor, for the same reasons, could I have received you, Father."

Maculano held out his open palms in token of the confidence shared between them. "As for me, my first duty cannot be to any man, even though that man be the Bishop of Rome. As for the Truth? I'm a man bred to the application of science and equations. I do not pretend to know what 'the Truth' of either is."

"Nor do I," Sinceri agreed. "Nor how the birds are able to fly, nor which orb circles which. Like you, I have my hierarchy of loyalties. The one I place highest, next to God alone, is my duty to His Church."

"By 'Church,' you mean . . . ?"

"Oh, not the Church in the present." With a motion of his hand, Sinceri waved that concern aside. "The Church as it stands today will care for itself. Whatever the outcome of our undertaking, we may find relief in that. In the pond of the present, we'll make scarcely a ripple. No, Fra Vincenzo, not the present. It's more the Church of the future I fear for."

"If, in our findings, we ratify a determination that was someday proven wrong . . ."

"Then we—you and I—the Court of Inquiry, and the Pope himself—shall all become the burdens of the future Church's history. As you, yourself, have implied."

Maculano contemplated Sinceri's appraisal before offering his reply.

"It will be a delicate affair, Father Prosecutor. Do you have some thought as to how we might proceed?"

"How, but with all our honor, Father? We shall build a lie." Sinceri raised an eyebrow as he vainly searched Maculano's face for a reaction. "We delay. We deceive. Where the protocols of the trial do not allow for it, we bring forth the accused's defense, while all the time not appearing to do so. We extend the duration of the proceedings to provide the occasion. We ask our questions in such a way as to elicit his most exculpatory replies. In the end, we can only hope that he will make the best of the opportunity and that those who will render the final judgment will still have ears to hear."

"We are not without allies," Maculano observed.

Sinceri smiled thinly. "We may hope so, Father Commissary. But neither are we without adversaries."

———

A STEADY RAIN of the kind that farmers venerate had spattered the city's cobbles since before daylight. Maculano murmured a *Deo Gratia* for those among the workers of the fields who might forget to do so, despite the fact that it was he who was getting wet. He kept his cowl about his head and a thin blanket over that as he hurried along at a pace rapid enough to belie the grievances of his years.

Events surrounding the trial were cooking at a boil, with some unseen hand adding the wood and stoking the fire. Maculano had more than his own suspicions as to the identity of the cook who was urging on the temperature. He, along with Sinceri, had tried to bring about the opposite result. No matter. He might as well, he realized, have tried to work his will upon the tides.

Even through the beat of the rain, he heard the splashes of footsteps approaching from behind him, and then the strained rasping of someone out of breath.

"Reverend Father . . . good morning. May I be permitted . . . the privilege . . . of walking with you for a short distance?"

The robed figure now beside him was a much younger man. So much younger that, already, his normal rate of respiration was returning.

"We've not met before, Father Commissary. So I take upon myself a great presumption. I am Wilhelm, nephew to the late Adolf and cousin to Adam, Counts von Schwarzenberg. I believe you knew my uncle and have spoken often with my cousin."

"Yes. Most certainly. The Lord's blessing upon you, Wilhelm." Maculano could see the evidence now. The fairness of the Austrian's complexion gave the clue to the man's heritage in his face. "Your uncle was a wise and Godly man, and your cousin remains, as always, an ardent protector of the Faith. You may take honor in having such a family as an ornament to hold before you." Maculano kept up his stride not out of impoliteness as much as to avoid any more of a soaking than was necessary. "I see you've taken vows, Wilhelm."

"Not my final ones, Father. I'm yet a novice. Under the tutelage of another I think you know, Father Melchior Inchofer."

So the warning bells sounded.

"Yes, Father Inchofer. He and I, too, have had occasion to work together. He is, like so many of the Jesuit order, not only a pillar of the Faith but also a gifted master of logic and language."

"I'm pleased to hear you consider him so, Father Commissary."

"Tell me, Wilhelm, does Father Inchofer know that you've taken this opportunity to speak with me?"

"Why? Why do you ask, Father?" Wilhelm nearly stopped in mid-step, but recovered when he realized that Maculano's tread hadn't altered. "Have I done something wrong?"

"That depends, does it not? On the matter of intention. You've presented yourself as a novice, Wilhelm. That your training, as yet, remains incomplete doesn't give you license to portray yourself a fool."

"I . . . Father, I don't . . ."

"But I fear you do. And therein lies the problem, my son. You approach me being fully aware that your master and I are at work on what, in essence, is the same adjudication."

"Father, I didn't . . ."

"I caution you, Wilhelm." Maculano stopped, even as the rain collected and dripped from the fabric covering his head. "It's not my place to be your confessor. Nevertheless, I advise you out of our common knowledge of our Faith not to increase further your need to find the one whose place it is."

"Father!"

"You've sought unwarranted advantage, Wilhelm. I shall choose to believe you did so on your own initiative rather than at the bidding of your mentor. It was your hope that I'd be unaware that Father Inchofer—along with two other examiners—has been charged by His Holiness with the task of reading and criticizing the accused's *Dialogue,* and that each is to offer his independent evaluation of the volume's content."

"Father . . . my hope was no such thing."

"Oh? Was it not? Alternatively, then, did you suspect I could be flattered into relating my own conclusions and recommendations prior to the time and outside the proper circumstances for their revelation?"

"Fra Maculano, I've told you who I am and of my family."

"So how dare I suggest such things? Yes, Wilhelm. I'm sorry I have to. Because all that I said of your uncle and cousin was honestly spoken. It is, however, more than a personal matter between you and me. It is, instead, an issue of justice, a cause to which I'm sworn. The procedures we follow are intended to produce balance. If the elements are compromised, the result is imbalance, and through that imbalance, justice is compromised."

"Justice compromised or heresy protected? Which is it you mean to say, Father Maculano? Do not presume to lecture me on justice. I, myself, have studied the accused's *Dialogue* down to its most trivial detail. I have reviewed what there is of the heretic's defense. To call it a 'mockery' is to ridicule the word. His current playacting is nothing more than a pretense to gain him indulgence. Do you think it's lost that he wrote in Italian, so that any peasant can read and be deceived by his infamies? Or that he puts His Holiness's arguments in the mouth of an idiot, whom—should anyone miss the point—he names 'Simplicio.' Is this attribution, too, to be taken as unintentional?"

"*Quod erat demonstrandum.*" Maculano folded his hands, assuming a pose of modest satisfaction. "Go back to Father Inchofer, Wilhelm. Report to him what has taken place between us. The undisputed renown of his orthodoxy in defense against the errors to which these times are inclined has never deafened him to the requirements of protocol. He will realize, if nothing else, that he has a very great deal more in which to instruct you."

In the rain, Father Maculano turned and continued at his previous pace toward his destination.

———

"THE COMMISSARY GENERAL to see the Florentine prisoner."

"Yes. At once, Reverend Father," the guard responded.

The Vatican was a small and self-contained city. As the chief magistrate of the Holy Inquisition, Maculano was well recognized by the attendants who maintained the cells beneath the Dominican Convent at the Church of Santa Maria Sopra Minerva. At the sentry's entreaty, Maculano followed him through the maze of stone-lined corridors.

The quarters at which he arrived were not a confinement where the inmate lay in chains, but rather were among the more tolerable that, given its purpose, the jail had to offer. Behind the massive wooden door were two rooms that shared a high, barred window, a plank cot with a straw mattress, and even the additions of a desk, candle, and chair.

Its solitary resident rose from the side of the bed, rubbing his eyes as the lock snapped back and Maculano entered.

The Commissary General dismissed the guard and ordered that he close the door behind him as he left.

The prisoner's shoulders were stooped. His neck was bent. His age, Maculano knew, had already reached seventy years, but he looked more frail in his present surroundings than even the accumulation of the decades could account for.

"Holy Father." The figure bowed.

"Sit down, my son."

The prisoner kept to his feet. "Have you news?"

"Not of the kind I know you hope to hear," Maculano answered.

"Oh. What, then?" The old man sank slowly back onto the side of his bed.

"I've just finished lunch with the Lord Prosecutor." The priest reached inside the folds of his robe and produced half a roasted chicken. "Not the most appetizing or sanitary, I know."

Setting the gift of the fowl on the desk, the prisoner began to tear off a portion, then stopped himself and returned to kiss the priest's hand.

"Please. That's not needed," Maculano commanded. "The pittance is only because I know how far these conditions fall short of those to which you're accustomed."

"Bless you, Father."

"Enough." For a moment, Maculano felt compelled to look away. "Regarding your case, I regret that I cannot bring better news. I've met, as I said, with the Lord Prosecutor. For what it may be worth, we find ourselves in agreement as to the disposition of your interrogation. To begin, there will be a second interview, to be held this coming Saturday. I must tell you, the likelihood is that there will be at least another after that."

"So much? What else is to be said?"

"Unfortunately, a great deal. Clarifications regarding your testimony, particularly pertaining to the Imprimaturs under which your manuscript was published. The candor of your present assertion that you, yourself, reject the heresy considered in your treatise. As well as some prospective questions concerning the potential testimony of other witnesses."

"Other witnesses?"

"The Inquisition is not the only investigative arm the Holy See has at its disposal."

"I don't understand."

"It is not necessary you do. It is only necessary that every answer you give to our inquiries be scrupulously complete and honest in every respect."

"I have been so, Reverend Father."

"I believe you have tried to be. Allowing for the situation as it was, and as you have come to see it. Nevertheless, risks remain."

"If I've told the truth . . . ?"

"Men are imperfect. Their justice can be no better than they. Still, it is possible that, within the scope of human justice, you may be released—released, if only from bearing the strain of an appearance before the Court of Cardinals. In the context of a full and creditable confession of error, accompanied by your acceptance of the purging of all offensive passages from your publication, a simpler administrative or ecclesiastical solution might yet be found."

"The talk of penance?"

"Public, perhaps. Accompanied by an expression of total submission."

"I agree to the terms."

Maculano smiled sympathetically. "Alas, the option is not mine to offer. To no small extent, the cause of your difficulty has been your own imprudence. You've made some powerful people exceedingly angry."

"His Holiness." The prisoner shrank, as though that one thought had absorbed all his hope.

"Most significantly, yes," Maculano agreed. "At some point in your case, it is he who must decide if a formal prosecution is to go forward. Should he do so, all inquiry will cease and a charge of heresy will be entered against you. You would then be required to appear before the Court, where you will be given the opportunity to abjure the heresy and accept all assigned penalties and conditions." Maculano placed his hand on the man's shoulder. "The choices are that—or to be found by the Court to persist in heresy and thereby to incur excommunication and suffer all associated forfeitures."

"Would it mean torture?"

"Only if the Cardinals felt reason to doubt your abjuration. You will be advised of that liability in advance. If your renunciation is deemed sincere, you will yet likely be called upon to face some term of imprisonment and penance."

"A trial"—the prisoner's lips scarcely moved—"without the possibility of an acquittal."

"You will have ten judges," Maculano persisted. "The Lord Prosecutor and I have done our sums. We can find perhaps four who will regard you sympathetically. Three, or even two, is a more likely number."

"Cardinal Barberini, the Pope's nephew, will be one of my judges, will he not? Francesco was my pupil. He will not abandon me."

"Barberini, we believe, is in your favor. He resides even now with his uncle at Gandolfo. But were his influence sufficient to protect you, it follows you would not still be here. Sant' Onofrio, the Pope's brother, who summoned you to Rome to appear before the Inquisition, is also among your judges."

"Onofrio hates me," the prisoner grimly affirmed. "So . . . if His Holiness will not accept a lesser arrangement, and my cause goes before the Cardinals . . . even with my abjuration, it's your sense my imprisonment will continue."

"For some term, I fear, yes." Maculano stared down at the stones of the floor. "I believe that would be the worst case."

The old man pressed his face into his hands. "God forgive me, Reverend Father, for what I've done. I swear I meant no harm."

"God, my son, is all-forgiving. That is the one truth by which each of us may feel reassured."

For such solace as it may give you, Maculano thought. Were their situations reversed, the priest wondered if even he could have believed it.

——

"Two days ago, I wrote to Barberini," Maculano announced. "I'm trusting my fate he believes as we do. I pray my confidence isn't misplaced."

"The Cardinal has always been our best hope." Sinceri leaned back in his chair and folded his hands across the dome of his stomach. "He has a long-held affection for the accused. His voice is not one that His Holiness, even in his most rancorous mood, can brush aside with a simple ascription of enmity. Barberini is young. Amenable to new ideas, even if he remains unfree to hold them openly. What construction did you put on your note?"

"A delicate one, to put the best face on it. I could not, of course, address it to the Cardinal. Had His Holiness become aware of such a letter, as he almost surely would have, he would have regarded it as another conspiracy against him, thus discrediting us while bringing the Cardinal into disrepute by association. So, instead, I dispatched the correspondence to His Holiness directly, feeling confident that Urban would seek the counsel of a trusted nephew and that the document would thus find its seemingly inadvertent way to the Cardinal's attention by the hand of Urban himself."

"Were you to lose your office in Rome, you could always find outlet for your talents in the warrens of Byzantium," Sinceri reflected.

"I painted the matter darkly," Maculano replied, choosing to ignore Sinceri's observation. "I outlined each difficulty I could find in making the prosecution's case, as well as the catalogue of bureaucratic bungles that allowed the manuscript to reach publication in the first place. If your case against the accused succeeds, my Lord Prosecutor, you may thank me for illuminating your accomplishment. I did not, in actual fact, propose a bargain, but at several junctures left the suggestion that a half loaf of bread is better than none."

"Allowing the Cardinal to consider the invitation to a compromise, even if Urban, on his own, surely will not."

"Just so," Maculano acknowledged. "Though I feel safe in saying that Barberini has already foreseen that possibility. From the note, he will know, at least, that others have seen it too."

"When do they return from Gandolfo to Rome?"

"I chose not to ask, fearing the question might be taken for an encouragement of haste. I'm trusting that Francesco, who is not without the legendary Barberini sagacity, will intuit our curiosity concerning the date and inform us by such means as he finds appropriate. Meanwhile, I hope we can still hold to a temperate speed, allowing for a thorough exploration of the many nuances the prosecution involves."

"Oh, dear Reverend Father! Tell me how a man of God becomes so adept in the ways of the swindler." Sinceri muffled a laugh into a mostly covered smile. "How much time do you estimate?"

"With good fortune, enough to permit a third session. Tomorrow is the first of May. Let's say toward the middle of the month. I think that's as much as we can hope for."

Sinceri's expression became concerned. "I have not been to the prison, Father Commissary. I have not seen the condition of the accused. I have, however, heard stories."

"They're true," Maculano attested. "Which is why I plan, at the conclusion of today's interview, to place a petition before my

Lord Prosecutor. I shall cite the age of the accused and his health, as well as the openness and piety he exhibited in our first session and which he shall exhibit again today. I will suggest we are more likely to receive his cooperation and thus learn the truth of this matter if we show some modest compassion. I will propose that, instead of continuing his incarceration under the direct supervision of the Holy Office, it would be in the interest of all to return him to his previous state of house arrest at the Villa d'Medici."

"I fear, should I consent to the Commissary General's petition," Sinceri mused, "that I shall lose the high regard that I presently enjoy from His Holiness."

"Pray, do not let it concern you, Father Carlo. I'm sure you shall regain it when you achieve the conviction you seek."

"Yes. Thank you, Fra Maculano. I'm sure I shall." The prosecutor's grin became sardonic. "Even if only you and I will know the price we will pay for my success."

———

"What did you think?"

Sinceri cocked his head to one side in a manner that suggested he was trying to pick some harmonic or other from the ether. "I've rarely seen such joy in a man's face," he decided. "He'll sleep at the Medici villa tonight in such comfort as he's never known. Don't you find it ironic, Father, the way the world is fulfilled by its opposites? The accused's whole life, until this circumstance, has been spent in relative abundance. Tonight he'll find that luxury again. But he'll treasure it with a gratitude as never before."

"I was thinking of what he conveyed in his testimony."

"Yes. That too. Being deprived of his high regard has stripped away much of his arrogance. The intended result, assuredly, and yet, in a man of such greatness, I admit I find it disturbing. How he clings to the new learning, to the empiricism of his *Dialogue*! He thinks, if he just makes some amendments . . ." Sinceri stared out at the late afternoon. "He hasn't yet come to realize the work is dead. That it will be placed upon the Index no matter what changes he consents to."

"Sustaining that optimism was in our interest—and also in his," Maculano confessed. "Still, I don't see how the result you predict can be avoided."

A tentative knock fell on the door.

Maculano gave the instruction to enter.

"Excuse me, Reverend Fathers." The cleric bowed formally. "I am commissioned to deliver this to Father Maculano personally."

"Very well, then." Maculano accepted the envelope and sat again as the bearer left and closed the door. "It carries no indication of the sender," he announced for Sinceri's benefit.

"Which suggests an obvious possibility."

Maculano opened the parcel with a small blade he drew from his robe. "Barberini," he confirmed, looking up from the signature. His eyes returned to the page.

"He tells us that Urban remains displeased with my tentativeness. He reiterates that His Holiness believes he has been depicted scandalously and feels deeply betrayed."

"His Holiness has received the submissions of the *Dialogue*'s supplementary critics?"

"I'm coming to that. He has, almost a month ago. The Pope finds them persuasive. Inchofer's most of all. He believes that, once the Court has considered them, the outcome will be assured. Moreover, Barberini reports that some of the judges have also seen the documents or else have been made aware of their substance, and that the reactions of those judges have further bolstered His Holiness's confidence. Francesco says that he'll seek more definite knowledge, including a head tally, if he can obtain one."

"When will we know what he finds?"

"He plans to return to Rome the second week in June. Urban knows this and is at ease that the affair should come to its end at that time." Maculano looked up at Sinceri. "So a third appearance of the accused is permitted, and even some weeks beyond that. But with the Cardinals' arrival, events will move quickly. By the middle of June at the latest, all will be over."

For a moment, Sinceri held his silence; then, "I see a darker horizon in this, Reverend Father. I've the sense that all chance for a bargain has passed. That a formal hearing cannot be averted. Barberini has nothing to say regarding an alternative?"

"Nothing." The Commissary General rose stiffly from his chair and, on his way across the room, picked up a tray from a table. He looked for a final time at the envelope and its contents, then subjected both to the flame of a candle and consigned their burning remnants to the tray.

When he was satisfied with the conflagration, Maculano turned back to the Lord Prosecutor.

"At the Cardinal's order," Maculano explained. "He says that, as I value his friendship, so should I honor his confidences."

———

"You set a modest table, Fra Maculano. Modest, but delectable in every morsel." Francesco Cardinal Barberini patted his mouth with his napkin. "I've a fondness for basic cooking, the kind done by women in simple kitchens. It's one of the reasons I tolerate travel. Country inns serve the same variety of fare."

"I'm pleased you enjoyed it, Your Eminence." Maculano tilted his head to acknowledge the compliment.

"I cannot pretend to draw the Cardinal's distinctions." Sinceri laughed at himself. "I'm afraid I am, in every meaningful sense of the word, omnivorous."

"Truly?" Barberini glanced toward the prosecutor's nearly full plate. "From tonight, I would not have suspected it, Father."

Sinceri's eyes narrowed as the Cardinal's skepticism moved the focus to the reason for their meeting. His lips parted slightly. "Well, let us say that tonight there's a matter we all have on our minds. Your presence in Rome brings with it the prospect of a final curtain. Can it ever be said that the man condemned honestly enjoyed his last meal?"

"You make your point, Father Sinceri." Barberini paused to tip the edge of his glass toward his host. "A good wine, also, Father Maculano. But with regard to the man our Lord Prosecutor speaks of . . . So that our minds may be as one, let me review for you the case against the accused as I have been privy to hear it discussed. Its substance comes to three parts:

"First, the science. Whether the Ptolemaic or Copernican system is correct? The question is decided. The Ptolemaic is correct. The Copernican is heresy. Were I, myself, to weigh the matter, I might conclude that the question remains too contentious for final disposal, while, at the same time, giving the advantage to Ptolemy. But what I think is not an issue. The Church has settled the argument for me.

"Second, the instructions. Fifteen years ago, when seeking permission to write about the two systems, the accused was informed of the Church's determination regarding the Copernican heresy and told that he could neither hold nor teach the doctrine. So much is written and not in dispute. What is not written anywhere, as the testimony that you have taken has exposed, is whether the accused was also advised that he could not write about the alternative theory even in the context of a hypothesis to be refuted. Although others insist he was so told orally, the author claims to have no memory of such a prohibition. A convenience? I leave it to you. Which brings us to the context he has chosen for his writing, as the framing relates to his intent.

"Put simply, in the *Dialogue*, the Copernican advocate wins at every mark. Moreover—and greatly complicating the difficulty—the Copernican's Aristotelian opponent is shown to be a brainless incompetent, a buffoon—who uses precisely the same arguments that Urban himself used in discussions with the author all those years ago.

"My uncle, good Fathers, is a stubborn and arrogant man. Yet, it is only fair to say he has been grievously provoked."

"Well stated, Francesco," Sinceri acknowledged. "You draw up the case like a noose."

"As you have cause to know, I wish it were otherwise," Barberini replied. "Not because I feel the accused is innocent. I regret to say that, despite my affection for my former teacher, I cannot bring myself to find him so. But I also believe, as do you, that his conviction may well create for our Church a looming disaster. I know enough of dogma to be wary of it. Even the straightest road has an unexpected turn somewhere ahead. It may be so in the matter of Copernicus, from whom the accused has taken the substance of his text. If it is, the cause of the Church will not be served by its conviction and incarceration of the astronomer's most eloquent advocate."

"We thank you for advising us," Maculano said.

Barberini's expression remained grave. "I wish, too, I could leave having done no more than underscore the challenge before you.

"Tomorrow you have a fourth appointment scheduled for testimony by the accused. It will be his last opportunity. On Wednesday, the day after, at their regular meeting, the Court of Cardinals will fulfill its formal role. The prisoner will attend. His Holiness has rendered his decision."

"The affair has reached that point, then." Maculano exhaled. "We, both of us, owe a great debt to Your Eminence for your supreme efforts."

"Thank me for nothing, Fathers. The matter is out of your hands. And out of mine."

"The accused is charged; the Cardinals will sit to hear his abjuration and deliver sentence?" Sinceri had not been sure whether to frame the sentence as a statement or a question. The indecision had shown in his voice.

Baberini answered: "All I can tell you with certainty is that at least seven of the Cardinals will attend Wednesday's session. I can tell you also that I will not be among them, for the simple and absurdly self-contradictory reason that, in the absence of a compromise resolution, I cannot bring myself to hold for or against the accused. I can tell you that Borgia will probably not be there either. Of Zacchia, I remain unsure. Though whether either chooses to appear is of no consequence.

"As to the Court's proceedings, you each know the law better than I. The heretic, so adjudged by His Holiness, will appear in the white robe of submission and contrition and be provided the opportunity to enter a written statement, which he may also read, swearing his renunciation of the heresy and freely accepting any and all penalties the Court may prescribe."

"These penalties will include . . . ?" Maculano asked.

"What you will have guessed," the Cardinal affirmed. "Assuming the judges accept the abjuration, they will follow His Holiness's recommendations and condemn the offender to imprisonment within the Holy Office for a term to be sustained at the Court's pleasure, plus the performance of associated penances. The entirety of the *Dialogue* will be placed on the Index of forbidden books and prohibited from being read or further published. Should the heretic's statement or demeanor, in any way, prove unsatisfactory . . ."

"It couldn't be worse," Maculano muttered harshly. He hurled his cup across the room.

"I agree with you, Father," Barberini conceded. "It could not be worse."

———

"HE IS FREE."

Maculano and Sinceri sat over lunch at a prepared table in Maculano's apartments.

"How can it be?" Sinceri asked in astonishment.

"You're correct, Father. I exaggerate," Maculano conceded. "Barberini's work is with us still. The sentence remains unaltered, except that Urban has agreed that the venue of incarceration be changed from the cells of the Holy Office to the residence of the Tuscan Ambassador."

"Thanks be to God," Sinceri breathed.

"Thanks be, as much I think, to mortal pride." Maculano's lip curled. "Gloating in the completeness of his victory, Urban feels he can afford to be magnanimous. Even so, Ambassador Niccolini has attempted to press the matter further. He's asked His Holiness to pardon the prisoner because of his repentance and his continuing great works of charity, and to permit his return to Florence. So far Urban has refused, but Niccolini is prepared with a second proposal, under which the sentence would be limited to a period of five months to be served in the residence of the Archbishop of Siena. For his part, the Archbishop has already consented to the arrangement. Niccolini has hopes that since this variation involves no repudiation of the conviction itself, it may yet gain His Holiness's favor."

"I pray it will," Sinceri replied. "For the good it will do the man for what remains of his earthly life." The prosecutor looked across at his host. "Our greater cause, the one in which we began, however, remains undone beyond any pretense of resurrection."

"But a good fight, Carlo. Worth the effort."

"A needless fight, Fra Vincenzo." Sinceri's expression clouded. "The price we pay for a failure of faith."

"That's bitterness speaking. You pronounce too harsh a judgment, my friend."

"Do I?" Sinceri contemplated a slice of bread he held between his fingers. His voice was quiet. "I'll tell you what I know. Don't fear, because it's very little. Our Faith is what it claims to be, a thing to be believed. As long as we remember that, for those who choose to accept it, it remains an impregnable bulwark. But when we feel the need to prove our Faith by imposing on it human logic, we employ a man-made tool that carries with it the pathway to a thousand human errors. Worse, when we then try to use that flawed concoction to account for the endless subtleties of the natural world, we multiply the chances of error by another thousandfold."

Maculano reached across the table to offer his guest a selection of olives. "And still, we have this to be grateful for." He smiled. "Though posterity may not forgive us our failure, we may, at least, take comfort in the certainty it will never remember our names."

For a moment Sinceri considered the bowl and the words.

At last, the Lord Prosecutor's expression mellowed. A thin smile came to his lips. "Yes. You're right, Fra Vincenzo. If it's not a sin to regard life too seriously, it is nonetheless surely an impediment to its enjoyment."

He transferred an olive onto his plate, then placed a second beside it.

NIGHT COURT

BY S. J. ROZAN

I t had been a hell of a long time since they'd held night court
here.

For sure, Murph reflected as he entered the robing room,
that was a good sign. It meant things were under control, the
crazy times past. And good riddance. Those years had been
tough, gangs duking it out block by block here in town, meth
labs at the end of every country road, the entire county awash
in a chaos of drugs and guns. That rats' nest took some serious cleaning, some tough talk, and tougher action. But they'd
straightened it out. For a while now they'd been living in what
Rossi called a Golden Age, an Era of Order and Peace.

Of course, Rossi couldn't drink coffee without calling it the
Elixir of Life, so his characterizations were suspect. Still, no
one could deny things were better now. Nor could anyone deny
that he, Murph, had had a lot to do with it. He was in charge
here, and he'd made that clear as often and as forcefully as he'd
had to. He'd instituted new procedures and streamlined exist-
ing ones, not afraid to jettison some of the old ways and, when
necessary, the old personnel. He'd gotten objections and whining, sure. People had their little fiefdoms. They expected to be

able to go on indefinitely doing what worked for them, even if in the larger picture they and their systems were roadblocks, not . . . what was the opposite of a roadblock? Murph sighed. *You're getting old, kiddo,* he told himself, groping for the heavy velvet drapes. He pulled them tight, made sure they overlapped to keep light from leaking out, then flicked the switch.

Why was it, he grumbled as he looked around, that now that things were better, the county peaceful and prosperous, this courthouse was still a dump? You'd think the town fathers would take more pride. All the place needed was a little paint, a few yards of new carpet. God knew, enough of his annual income, and everyone else's, went straight into the town's coffers. They should be able to spare a few coins to polish the brass occasionally.

But taking pride, that was always a problem. Me, me, me, everything was self-interest these days. Not that looking out for you and yours was a bad thing. What depressed Murph was how many people couldn't see that certain things—like taking pride, like hard work, like loyalty—weren't only abstract virtues, they were part and parcel of self-interest. When everyone benefited, everyone benefited—why was that so hard to understand?

The case they were trying tonight, for example: that's what it was all about. Another greedy bastard thinking me, me, me.

Murph slid the hangers in the judges' closet, searching out the smallest robe. Even that one was too big, the way it always had been. He shrugged into it and examined himself in the standing mirror. He had to admit what was looking back was worse than it used to be. His skin was getting looser as he got older, and the chicken neck sticking out of the folds was genuinely comical.

If truth be told, these masses of black cloth, even when they fit, made everyone look like the Sorcerer's Apprentice. Of course, for night court they could have dispensed with them. And with the formal reading of the indictment, people standing when he walked in, all that. They could have gone with a level of informality unacceptable in these rooms in daylight. But Murph, who'd been the one to institute night court to begin with back in the crazy days, had understood the need for pomp and tradition. They put the weight of history and the stamp of legitimacy on the proceedings. It wasn't exactly Shock and Awe, but it worked. From the beginning, the night court juries' verdicts were accepted as legitimate and Murph's sentences carried out assiduously and immediately.

Murph sat at the robing-room table and read the paperwork Rossi had given him. Rossi's fondness for flowery phrases applied, thank God, only to speech. On paper he came through as precise and detailed, and Murph read what he'd provided with appreciation. Murph already knew the general outline of the case. Nothing got this far without his active involvement. Only he, after all, could assign a case to night court. But the indictment laid out the particulars, and the accompanying material included both sides' witness lists, their evidence, and an outline of their arguments. Rossi was a terrific clerk. Murph knew he dreamed of a judgeship, but he was relieved and grateful that Rossi understood it wasn't going to happen. Murph had given considerable thought to succession; he couldn't go on forever. Given the declining rate of night court cases lately, this might even be his last. He had no intention of resigning his position, but as to his presiding here, he wouldn't be surprised if it didn't occur again.

And, he thought with a crooked smile, *I've already lasted longer than a lot of people had predicted.* But eventually he'd be gone, and the man who stepped into his job would have to be a big thinker, like Murph, not a detail man. He'd have to command respect right from the start, to keep chaos from erupting again.

That, in fact, was the real reason they were holding night court tonight.

Oh, the case was real enough, worthy on its merits. But it could have been dealt with in other ways. It was the men who had come up in the rotation for the prosecution and defense that had made up Murph's mind to bring this case to trial.

For the prosecution, Cameron. A dedicated man, hardworking and loyal, but lacking in imagination. Actually, he had enough to see himself in Murph's job, Murph knew that. But not to truly understand what it would mean. It was on Jefferson, who'd be representing the defendant, that Murph's eye was trained.

And tonight's was a terrific case, perfect for what Murph needed. Leopold, the weasel in the defendant's chair, was guilty as sin, in Murph's personal, and highly informed, opinion. If Jefferson managed to convince the jury there was any doubt and they let Leopold go, Jefferson would come across as a golden-tongued genius. If not, this loss wouldn't stain his reputation. His willingness to take the case had already impressed people with his sense of fair play.

And as a bonus, both men were quick and efficient. That was vital. Night court, from the beginning, had been limited to three hours, strictly enforced. An hour for each side to present its case and rebut the other guy's, a half hour for jury deliberations, a half hour for Murph's bench rulings, the sentence, and general cocking around. They started at one a.m. and were out by four. Inviolable, and they all knew it. It worked, too. Cases were argued, verdicts rendered, and sentences passed and executed well within their time limit. Murph sometimes thought it was a pity the day guys couldn't be here to take lessons.

Speaking of which, it was one on the nose, and here was Rossi, opening the door.

Murph took his seat on the bench, after which the assembled

multitudes, who had been bidden by Rossi to stand, sat also. Not that they were all that multitudinous: night court didn't allow spectators. The only people here were directly connected with the case. The attorneys, the witnesses, Rossi, the guards, the jury. And the defendant. Murph watched Leopold squirm. The guy looked pale. Well, he ought to. He was in big trouble.

For the next two-plus hours, everyone played their roles with skill and seriousness. Cameron presented the prosecution's case: the defendant had systematically stolen from, defrauded, and betrayed his employer. Cameron's lack of imagination served him well. He avoided hyperbole, supporting every allegation with testimony and evidence. Murph approved of this approach. Leopold was such an arrogant, unrepentant schemer, he was almost larger than life already. If Cameron had tried dramatics, the jury might have begun to wonder if Leopold really could be that blatant, or that stupid.

In fact, that was Jefferson's defense strategy. In addition to calling Cameron's case largely hearsay and opinion, he tried to plant doubt in the minds of the jurors as to whether anyone with two brain cells to rub together would have stepped so far outside such clearly defined lines. The guy was a great talker, and Murph saw a frown on a juror every now and then.

But Jefferson lost. Deliberations were short, and Leopold was convicted. Because he was guilty. He was so effing guilty, Murph could have sentenced him two weeks ago when his duplicity and greed came to light, without going through the hassle of night court. But it had been worth it. Jefferson had wowed the jury, the witnesses, the guards. He'd lost because this case was unwinnable, but word would get out. He'd be treated with a new respect, and that had been Murph's real aim: to raise Jefferson's profile. So when Murph began to make it clear Jefferson was the heir apparent, opposition, if it existed at all, would be minimal.

Murph thanked the jury, banged the gavel, and passed his sentence. Leopold blanched and started shaking. Murph stifled an irritated sigh. The sentence couldn't have come as a surprise.

Guards clasped Leopold's arms and propelled him from the courtroom. His eyes were wild; if it hadn't been for the gag, he'd be howling for sure. Everyone else could be trusted to keep quiet, but after they'd had such trouble at the first night court, Murph had ordered that the defendants be silenced before sentence was read.

He checked his watch. Three thirty. Not bad at all. He dismissed the jury, thanked the attorneys with a particular nod to Jefferson, and waited for everyone to stand so he could leave the bench and return to the robing room. He shed the black robe, listening to the quiet sounds of the courtroom emptying. The rule was, when court was done, everyone out fast; but he was Murph, so, hanging the robe, he gave himself a moment to reflect on the trial, and all the past trials, his years presiding here in this institution he'd created. He felt a twinge of nostalgia at the thought that he might not be back, and a glow of satisfaction at the thought of his protégé, Jefferson. He left, quickly and silently.

He didn't check on the guards, who were responsible for carrying out the sentence. They knew their jobs. They'd wait with the prisoner in the alley until everyone was gone. By morning, when the real judges, the real juries—the people who legitimately occupied this courthouse—arrived, Leopold would have been found. This time where in the rotation? That's right—down by the creek. The headlines would scream about "execution-style" killings. The mayor and the county executive would make fiery statements decrying lawlessness. There'd be a flurry of activity, but it would fade. Lawlessness. Hardly. That's what had been wrong with this county in the crazy days, before Murph took over the meth labs, the girls, and the gambling. Now citizens could walk the streets without fear of stray bullets, and revenue flowed in an orderly stream. Every now and then a mutt like Leopold thought he saw his main chance, and order had to be reestablished.

In a way everyone would understand.

Night court.

Murph ambled down the dark street, pleased with the peace and quiet of this town.

HARD BLOWS

BY MORLEY SWINGLE

W"hich one is yours?"

The raspy voice was an unwelcome intrusion. Jack Hogan glanced at the man sitting next to him on the bleachers at Star Power Gymnastics. Jack suppressed his irritation. The guy had no way of knowing he had just interrupted the closing argument Jack was rehearsing in his thoughts for next Thursday's jury trial. His inquisitor was just one more father of a budding gymnast, trying to make conversation while waiting for his daughter's practice session to end.

"She's the one in the bright blue leotard," Jack said, pointing to Amber.

Jack refrained from posing the reciprocal question requesting the man to identify his own daughter. Jack did not want to participate in an extended conversation. He would barely be able to carve out sufficient minutes between now and next Thursday to adequately prepare for the Porterfield jury trial, a particularly tough rape case certain to boil down to a swearing match between the victim and her rapist. At a key point in his closing argument, Jack was going to recite a list of factors showing that the teenage girl should be believed when she said she did not consent to the sexual intercourse. He had come up with seven good reasons so far. He was hoping to add three more. Ten would pack a more biblical punch for the jury.

As a prosecutor with a heavy caseload, Jack was always in the throes of preparing for one trial or another. He had discovered long ago that if he chose a seat on the bleachers farthest from the gymnasium door, most of the other parents would stay away from him during his daughter's gymnastics lessons and he could silently practice his opening statements and closing arguments in relative privacy. By necessity, Jack was a master at using his time efficiently.

It had almost worked on this weekday evening. Most of the parents were clustered on the bleachers near the entrance to the cavernous room. Only Jack and the one talkative father sat on this side of the gymnastics academy. A former warehouse, its high ceilings and mat-covered, spacious floor made a serviceable gymnasium.

"She sure knows what she's doing on that balance beam," the man said. "She's impressive."

"Thanks," Jack said. He forced himself to refrain from bragging about Amber's gymnastics talent. She had always been one of the best gymnasts in her age group. She'd been doing perfect round-off cartwheels since she was four years old. She was fearless on the balance beam and the parallel bars. She was naturally graceful on the floor exercise. Jack was proud of her. He enjoyed watching her practice sessions, even if he did use the time to hone his courtroom oratory. He stole a look at the gymnastics instructor, Leesa Beecher, a former national champion. It didn't hurt that the teacher typically wore a tube top and tight gym shorts during the lessons. She had the best-looking ass he'd ever seen. That's what twenty years of gymnastics would do for you, he supposed. Since he was happily married, he always tried not to openly gawk. "Happily married" did not mean you did not look.

It meant that out of consideration for your wife you tried not to get caught looking.

Jack wondered if Wendy had gotten home yet. After seeing a few patients at the hospital, she had gone to St. Louis for a training seminar for speech pathologists. He looked forward to hearing about her trip. His wife had a knack for turning any episode of her life into an entertaining story. That was one of the things he loved most about her. Maybe the three of them could pick up some Chinese takeout when he and Amber got home from gymnastics.

"What do you do?" the man asked.

Once again, Jack hid his frustration. Apparently a conversation was going to be unavoidable. So much for the closing-argument rehearsal.

"I'm a prosecutor. Jack Hogan, county prosecuting attorney."

Jack held out his hand. Most likely the guy had heard of him. Jack was frequently in the news.

The man stared at the outstretched hand. For a moment Jack thought he might not shake, but the man eventually clasped his hand. Jack practically winced at the power in the grip.

"Prosecutor, huh?" the man said. "Sounds like an interesting job."

"It is," Jack said, examining his hand for broken bones and bruises. "I know it sounds corny, but there's a lot of job satisfaction in knowing you're helping make your community a safer place."

"I'll bet there is."

Jack watched Amber as she moved to the parallel bars and began dusting her hands amid a cloud of chalk. The lithe twelve-year-old girl moved with the grace of a seasoned athlete. It gave him tremendous pleasure and pride just to watch his only daughter walk across the mat. It would be interesting to see which sports she chose to play in high school. Unlike her father, she was good at them all. So far, gymnastics was her true love.

"Do you ever worry you might send an innocent man to jail?"

Jack glanced at the man, so determined to engage in chitchat. Alert gray eyes were staring at him a bit too directly. Did he detect a hint of insolence in the tone of voice? Jack was not sure. The man's face was strong-jawed and clean-shaven. The iron-gray hair was longish, hanging over the ears but not touching the shoulders. The man was slender, but his muscle-bound torso rippled with power. He wore a skin-tight black Grateful Dead T-shirt, stiff new blue jeans, and a red St. Louis Cardinals warm-up jacket. He had the look of an aging bodybuilder.

"A prosecutor has an ethical duty not to prosecute an innocent man," Jack said. "I teach my assistant prosecutors to dismiss a case if they develop a reasonable doubt about a defendant's guilt. Better to dismiss it than risk the chance that an innocent man might be convicted."

The man raised his eyebrows.

"Well, I sure didn't know prosecutors thought that way. I assumed you *all* just collected scalps and sought convictions at any cost."

"Real life isn't like it's portrayed on TV," Jack said. "In fact, most prosecutors take to heart the famous quote from Justice George Sutherland that the prosecutor should strike hard blows but fair ones. Our duty is not simply to convict but to achieve justice."

Jack had quoted the line so many times it came out of his mouth like a speech. He debated whether to elaborate by discussing the equally famous comment of Justice Robert Jackson that the prosecutor had more control over life, liberty, and reputation than any other person in America. By simply filing a charge, a prosecutor could destroy the reputation of any member of his community. If Jack mentioned the quote, though, it might sound like he was bragging about the importance of his job. On the other hand, if he took the time to fully explain his deep sense of responsibility to make sure he did the right thing in every case, his conversation with this man might last a very long time. The gymnastics lesson was only half over. A full hour still remained. He really did not want to spend the entire time talking with this guy. If he could somehow extricate himself from the conversation, he might still be able to hammer out a few more kinks in the Porterfield closing argument. The trial was going to be upon him before he knew it.

He glanced again at the man. The pale gray eyes were fixed on Jack's face. Didn't the guy know it was rude to stare?

"Do you ever worry that someone you sent to prison might get out and come after you?"

This guy was asking all the typical cocktail-party questions thrown at a prosecutor. Jack decided to give his standard answer. It happened to be the truth.

"I suppose that's a risk of my job. I've had a couple of threats over the years. But very few of the people I prosecute are truly evil. Most committed their crimes because of temporary weakness, greed, or lust, or because they were drugged out or mentally imbalanced at the time. Once they're caught and get their heads screwed on straight, they realize they did wrong and deserve some punishment. They don't hold it against the prosecutor."

"You ever prosecuted a truly evil man?"

"Oh, sure. I get a few sociopaths every year: the sexual predators, the murderers who stalk their victims. They usually get such long sentences you don't have to worry about them getting out."

They sat in silence for a full minute, watching the gymnasts. Jack was beginning to think he might be able to get back to his closing-argument rehearsal, but the next question drove away all thoughts of the impending Porterfield trial.

"You don't remember me, do you?"

Jack's attention ratcheted up to red alert. He turned and studied the man's face with renewed interest. He was supposed to know this guy? What was he, about fifty years old? Six feet tall? Maybe one hundred and seventy pounds? He was fit, with a torso that seemed almost too big for the rest of his slender frame. His hair was the boring gray color of a steel frying pan. His nose had clearly been broken once upon a time.

"Have we met?" Jack asked.

The man laughed. It was an unpleasant sound, loud and jarring. Jack glanced at the other parents on the far side of the room, but no one was paying any attention to them.

"Have we met! That's funny, Mr. Prosecutor. Look at me again. Closer. Surely you recognize me."

Although the man had laughed, he was not smiling. His gray eyes glittered with something, either excitement or rage. A faint scar ran from the left eyebrow up a jagged course across the man's forehead and disappeared into his hairline at the left temple. Nothing sparked a memory for Jack. For all he knew, this man was a complete stranger.

"I'm sorry, but as far as I can tell, I've never seen you before in my life," Jack said. "Keep in mind, I meet lots of people in my job—witnesses, defendants, cops, lawyers, judges, jurors. I'm just not remembering you."

The gray eyes were cold and shiny, glittering like a metal railing sheathed in winter ice.

"I sure remember *you*, Counselor. For fourteen years I've thought about you every single night. I'd lie in that prison bed, remembering the way spittle flew from your mouth during your closing argument, and especially that smug, self-satisfied look on your face when the judge read the jury's guilty verdict out loud. I'd recognize you anywhere, anytime, Jack Hogan."

Jack felt his heart pounding. Okay, the flight-or-fight adrenaline jolt had apparently kicked in. Well, he wasn't going to run away. He'd just have to deal with whatever this guy had in mind. He was glad there were witnesses.

"You really don't remember me, do you?"

The voice was rough and gravelly. Its tone was incredulous.

"No, I don't. But you have to remember, my office prosecutes twenty-five hundred cases a year, divided among six prosecutors. Maybe it's a good thing your prosecutor doesn't remember you. The really bad ones tend to stand out."

Jack offered a halfhearted smile.

The man laughed again, a mirthless, harsh sound.

"Surely you remember your *murder* cases."

Murder? Well, that significantly narrowed down the list of former defendants. Still, he did not recognize the man.

"I've had sixty-six homicide cases," Jack said. "Are you saying I prosecuted you for murder?"

"Look at me!" the man hissed. "You not only prosecuted me, you convicted me. You sent an innocent man to prison!"

Jack stared hard at the angry face. A glimmer of recognition tugged at his memory. Make the hair dark brown, but much thicker. Unbreak the nose. Take away the scar. Thin down the face and restore its lost youth. Yes, the man looked familiar, especially the eyes. But still, Jack could not place the guy.

"This is freaking unbelievable," the man said. "I've been looking forward to this moment for fourteen years and you don't even remember me! I have to tell you, it takes a bit of the fun out of it. It makes me hate you even more, seeing how little ruining my life meant to you."

"I didn't ruin your life," Jack said. "*You* made your choices. If I prosecuted you for murder, it's because you killed somebody. Don't blame me for doing my job."

"Doing your job? You just told me your job is to strike *fair* blows, to *only* convict the guilty. You sent me to prison for shooting a man in self-defense. You *knew* it was self-defense, but you filed the charge anyway. You railroaded me, mister. You were like an evangelical preacher exhorting the jury to ship me off to prison to *send a message* to other would-be killers. Send a message! You must have said it ten times. *Now* do you remember me?"

Jack flipped through his mental Rolodex of murder defendants, especially those who had raised the affirmative defense of self-defense. This wasn't Pete Flamingo. Nor was it Barry Seltzer. This guy was definitely not Tom Barkley.

"You know," Jack said, "I use that send-a-message closing argument a lot. You haven't really narrowed it down too much for me."

The man's eyes narrowed.

"I've got this vivid image of you, Hogan. You're telling the jury that the chain of justice is only as strong as its weakest link. You're claiming the chain is composed of witnesses who report the crime and have the courage to testify in court, policemen who investigate the case, prosecutors who present the evidence, jurors who use their common sense to reach the right result, and the judge who rules on evidentiary issues and imposes an appropriate sentence. You urged the jury to use its common sense to send me to prison. You begged the jurors not to be the *weak link* in the chain. *Now* tell me you don't remember who I am!"

Jack raised his hands apologetically.

"Sorry. I use that chain-of-justice analogy in most of my closing arguments. Actually, I stole it from Vincent Bugliosi, the prosecutor of Charles Manson. I picked it up from one of his books. I figured if it worked for him, it would work for me."

For the first time, Jack noticed the man's right hand resting inside the side pocket of his St. Louis Cardinals jacket. It occurred to Jack that the man might well have a gun in his hand. This was bad. Jack never carried a gun. He was unarmed. He owned a six-shot Smith & Wesson revolver, but he always kept it in a drawer in the nightstand next to his bed.

"What's your favorite movie, Hogan?"

"What?"

"Your favorite movie. I figure you for a chick-flick kind of guy. What is it, *Sleepless in Seattle*?"

Jack felt a twinge of optimism. Maybe if they talked movies, this encounter would end more pleasantly than he expected. Perhaps this convicted murderer just wanted to air his grievances and tongue-lash Jack with insults.

"*To Kill a Mockingbird,*" Jack answered. "Gregory Peck plays a lawyer who represents an accused rapist. I'd have to say it's my favorite."

"What a coincidence, Counselor. Gregory Peck stars in my favorite movie too. Maybe you've seen it—*Cape Fear*. I've watched it at least twenty times. It's about a guy who gets out of prison. The ex-con is played by Robert Mitchum. He stalks a lawyer who was a key witness against him in his rape trial. He blames him for landing him behind bars. It's an old black-and-white movie. The lawyer, Gregory Peck, is a condescending, arrogant type, sort of like you. He thinks he's a real big shot. I'll tell you, though, he gets plenty scared when the ex-con starts sniffing around his daughter."

Jack felt alarm bells ringing in his head as the man's gaze shifted to Amber. She was doing a handstand on the parallel bars. A boiling rage began churning Jack's gut.

"They did a remake of *Cape Fear* in 1991," the man continued. "Robert De Niro played the convict. Nick Nolte was the guy he was after. Nolte was De Niro's former lawyer, who'd screwed up De Niro's case. De Niro was a real badass, man, absolutely covered with tattoos. One said, *Vengeance is mine.* Seen those movies, Hogan?"

"No."

"You should've, Mr. Prosecutor, what with your job and all. As good as the movies are, though, the book was even better. That's usually the case, don't you think, the book is better than the movie?"

Jack did not respond. He was trying to decide what this man would do if he simply stood up and started walking away. Did he really have a gun in his pocket?

"Yeah," the man said, "the book was better. John D. MacDonald wrote it. It was called *The Executioners* when it came out in 1957. In the book the guy getting out of prison is seeking revenge against that key witness whose testimony put him in prison. He's coming after the witness and his family, not his own defense lawyer. You read the book?"

"No," Jack said.

"To me," the man continued, "both the movies and the book would be more realistic if the ex-con was after the prosecutor. What do you think, Hogan?"

Jack stared into the cold eyes. "In my experience, the defendants are usually madder at the judge and the cops than they are at the prosecutor. They seem to realize the prosecutor is just doing his job."

"Wishful thinking, Hogan. I don't care how mad a man might be at his lawyer or the judge, he's always gonna be madder at the prosecutor. The prosecutor's the one who filed the charge, who could've dismissed it at any time, who could've plea-bargained it to something that didn't involve prison time, who gave the impassioned closing argument urging the jury to send the guy to prison. No, the prosecutor's always going to be number one on my hit list."

"I told you, I was just doing my job."

"Yeah, I heard you say that. But sending an innocent man to prison, that wasn't *in* your job description, was it?"

Jack glanced again at the side pocket of the Cardinals jacket.

A gun barrel or a finger was poking against the fabric, pointing directly at Jack's side. To Jack, it looked more like a gun barrel than a finger. He groped for something to say.

"Which one's *your* daughter?"

It was the question he'd thought about asking at the very beginning of the encounter, the one he would have asked had he been interested in making polite conversation.

"My daughter? She's dead. Leukemia. Got it while I was in prison. I didn't even get to go to her funeral."

"I'm sorry."

"Yeah, you're sorry, Hogan. You're a sorry piece of shit."

"Look," Jack began.

"No, you look! Not only did my little girl die, but my wife divorced me while I was doing my time—the time *you* gave me. She remarried a factory foreman. They've got five kids now. Five kids! He must bang her every night. Now she won't even return my phone calls. Last time I talked to her, she said she'd get a restraining order if I ever tried to call her again."

"That's a shame," Jack said.

"Ain't it, though? Oh, I almost forgot to tell you, I got gangraped behind the wall by a bunch of Blood Stone Villains who thought I was a snitch. I was innocent of that charge too, by the way. I'm no snitch. Never have been. I keep my mouth shut. But it happened just the same. That's something else I blame you for, Hogan. In fact, it's hard to put in words just how much I hate your guts."

"What do you propose to do about it?"

The gray eyes shifted again to take in the beauty of young Amber Hogan.

"For starters, there's your daughter."

"If you touch her . . ."

"If I touch her, *what!* What are you gonna do, Hogan, lock me up? Call me nasty names? Ask a jury to *send a message* for what I do to her? It's gonna be worth it, Hogan. I mean, just look at her. She must be your pride and joy."

The unmistakable click of a revolver being cocked came from the depths of the Cardinals jacket.

"I've got a message for *you*, Mr. Prosecutor. I'm gonna kill your daughter, right here today. I lost mine. It's only fair that you lose yours. I brought a gun and a knife with me. Only question left is whether I'm gonna shoot her or carve her up with the blade. Truth is, I haven't decided yet."

Jack glanced again at the gun barrel pressed against the jacket. If he lunged at the guy, he was sure to be shot. If he were shot, could he still protect Amber? Would the man kill her anyway, with Jack already dead? He tried to decide what to do, how to stop this man. What would be best for Amber?

The convict smiled. Jack felt a chill shoot up his spine, cold dancing fingers of death.

"After I kill your daughter, if I get out of this gym alive, my next stop will be your home. I'm gonna kill your wife, Wendy. You two still live on Oak Street, don't you? That big house, the yellow brick job with the wrought-iron railing and the three-car garage? Of course you do, what am I saying? I was there this morning, watching your wife leave for work. She was wearing that nice conservative black pantsuit. I noticed she switched to a white coat once she got to the hospital."

"You followed my wife?"

"I've been out of prison for over a month now, Hogan. I've devoted myself to learning all I can about your family. Your daughter, for instance. She doesn't ride the bus, even though it comes right by your house. Her daddy drives her to school every morning. Same exact route. Same exact time. Like clockwork."

Jack glanced at the pocket containing the gun. The barrel was pointed right at Jack's chest.

"Once I kill your wife," the man continued, "I'm gonna see if

I can find four guys who could stomach the thought of raping the sanctimonious Jack Hogan, and you'll get a taste of everything I went through these past fourteen years because of you. Everything except the bankruptcy. You know, I went from being a successful businessman to being a broke ex-con because I spent all my money on lawyers to fight the bogus charge you brought against me. I had to sell my dry-cleaning business to pay off my legal bills when I went to prison."

"Bart Thompson."

"Bingo. You remembered. I'm flattered, what with those thousands of cases you've prosecuted. How could I expect you to remember a simple case where a business owner shot the irate husband of an employee and claimed it was self-defense? I'm old news, aren't I? Water under the bridge. A flyspeck of a case. Boy, you sure nailed me in cross-examination, didn't you? How many times did you ask me if I shot him in the back?"

"Three."

"Yeah, and I admitted it every time. I shot him in the back, damn right I did. The prick came to my office, accusing me of having an affair with his wife. He was yelling and screaming. He threatened to kill me. When he spun away from me toward my credenza, I thought he was going for a gun. I pulled my Beretta from my desk drawer and shot him. I was telling the *truth*. I honestly thought I was protecting myself. I didn't know he was unarmed. But did you care? No!"

"The jury didn't believe you."

"*You* were leading them around by the nose, Counselor. I have to tell you, enlarging that photo of the dead man's back with the entrance wound right between his shoulder blades, that was a good stroke. So was your stunt of making a poster of the medical examiner's diagram. You were relentless in the way you drove home the point I shot the guy in the back."

Jack said nothing.

"You were impressive in closing arguments too," Bart Thompson continued. "I can see you now, pointing at me, thundering, 'Send a message to the community, send a message to Bart Thompson, send a message to would-be killers out there—it is *never* justified self-defense to shoot a man in the back, to gun him down in cold blood.' That's what you said, Hogan, isn't it?"

"Sounds pretty close."

Jack now remembered that particular closing argument well. He had spent countless hours working on it, honing it to perfection. The location of the bullet wound had been the strongest piece of evidence against Bart Thompson. The killer had shot his victim right in the middle of the back. Jack remembered heaping scornful ridicule on the defendant during summation: "What was the victim doing? Running *away* or *backing* toward his shooter? Either way it was not self-defense. Shooting a man in the back is a cowardly and criminal act. Don't let Bart Thompson get away with murder!"

Bart Thompson's case had been Jack's tenth murder trial. Since he spent most of the trial focusing upon the witnesses and the jurors, it was understandable that he did not recognize the defendant many years later. Besides, Bart Thompson had aged. Man, had he aged. Prison would do that to you.

"You took everything from me," Thompson said. "All by refusing to believe me when I told the *truth* that I really thought that wild-ass cuckold was trying to kill me. Hell, I wasn't even sleeping with his wife."

"I was fair to you," Jack said. "You told your version to the jury. You had your chance to convince them. They found you guilty beyond a reasonable doubt."

"Hard blows, but fair ones, I get it." Thompson sneered. "Charge them all and let God sort them out. Is that how it works?"

"No. Not at all. The prosecutor can exercise discretion. I never want to prosecute an innocent man. I just didn't believe you."

"I guess that was my misfortune, wasn't it? The great Jack Hogan didn't believe me." Bart Thompson stared at Jack silently for several long seconds. Jack glanced across the room at the other parents. It was mind-boggling that not one of them had noticed the heated conversation. Where were the busybodies and gossips when you needed them?

"Well, I've made up my mind," Thompson said, his voice low, barely above a whisper. "Shooting's too quick. I'm gonna gut her with the knife. I won't be needing this."

Bart Thompson withdrew a large revolver from his pocket and placed it on the bleachers between them. It was already cocked. Thompson stood up and smiled wickedly at Jack.

"The knife is a switchblade, in case you're interested. I figure to open up her belly first."

Grinning, the convicted murderer instantly broke into a run, heading directly toward Amber, his right hand snaking back inside his jacket pocket. It was all happening so fast. With horror, Jack realized he had only seconds to save his daughter.

He grabbed the gun and rose quickly to his feet. Instinctively, he assumed the stance he had practiced so often at the firing range. He knew he had to shoot fast, before Thompson got any closer to the gymnasts and put the girls in the line of fire. He brought up the gun and trained it on Thompson.

The earsplitting explosion produced an instant ringing in Jack's ears. He fired just one shot. He was oblivious to everything but the sight of Bart Thompson running toward his daughter. The instant Jack fired the gun, Thompson staggered and pitched forward onto the mat, crumpling like a puppet whose strings had been cut.

Jack heard screaming, probably the voices of the gymnasts. He heard yelling, probably the adults. He heard oaths being shouted at Bart Thompson, probably coming out of his own mouth.

Carefully pointing the gun at Thompson, almost daring him to make another move, Jack advanced toward him slowly. Thompson lay facedown on the light gray mat, his right hand thrust into his jacket pocket. He was still breathing.

Pointing the gun at Thompson with his right hand, Jack used his left to pull Thompson's hand from his pocket. The hand was empty. Jack slipped his own hand into the pocket. No knife. Jack patted the other pockets, finding nothing.

"Roll me over, Hogan," Bart Thompson rasped. "I want to see your face."

Jack took a moment to glance around the gym. The girls huddled on the floor between the balance beam and the vaulting horse. Tears streaked frightened faces. Parents crouched on and around the bleachers on the other side of the room, all eyeing Jack warily. Leesa Beecher, the instructor, was frantically talking on a cell phone, undoubtedly answering the questions of a 911 operator.

Jack reached down, grabbed the shoulder of the Cardinals jacket, and rolled Bart Thompson over. A growing pool of red blood already a yard wide covered the mat underneath the body.

Bart Thompson was smiling. It was the first time his grin had seemed genuine all evening.

"You recognize the gun, Counselor?"

Jack glanced at the gun in his hand, puzzled. It was a Smith & Wesson revolver, just like his own. Wait a minute. Surely it wasn't.

"Yeah, it's yours," Thompson said. "I stole it this morning. Don't worry, I didn't mess up your house. No fingerprints, no DNA, no signs of forced entry. No one will be able to tell I was ever there."

The gray eyes were flashing with triumph.

"That's right, Mr. Prosecutor. You just shot an unarmed man with your own gun in front of more than thirty witnesses, including your own daughter. And you shot him in the back as he was running away from you. In the *back*, Jack!"

The eyes began to grow dull, life ebbing away, but the dying man was still smiling.

"Good luck in court, Counselor. You're going to need it."

CUSTOM SETS

BY JOSEPH WALLACE

Martin County Courthouse, Shoals, Indiana. February

It was like a dance, Zhenya thought.

A strange, slow dance, full of rites and rituals she was just beginning to understand. Women and men in white shirts and dark suits, sitting behind long tables, reading from books, shuffling papers, popping up to talk, talk, talk to the grim-faced man sitting behind a desk up above the rest, and to the twelve silent, staring people trapped behind wooden railings on the side.

A performance where everyone else knew what would come next, as if the actors and the audience were all sharing a language, a vernacular that escaped only her.

A performance with a life at stake. Two lives.

Zhenya knew where she was, of course. She wasn't stupid. She'd traveled for two days, taking bus after bus, to a town, a state, a region she'd never even heard of before she found it on a map. To be here, in this big, pale stone building that looked like something built back home half a century ago to house a hundred families. She'd come all this way, to this uncomfortable wooden pew, just to watch the dance.

She'd watched a hundred similar performances on television before she'd come. There was a whole channel that showed nothing but them. But that was different—there were always words running across the screen, always people to explain what was going on, what all the endless talking meant.

But here she was on her own. Every once in a while, two of the men would step up to the big desk, to the judge. Then it would be his turn to drone on and on, sometimes speaking quietly, other times loudly enough for everyone to hear. She'd worked hard to learn English at school and since she'd been on her own, but his accent and the speed of his words made it hard for Zhenya to understand him.

So instead she just watched his face. It was round, pouchy, with flesh that sagged beneath the cheekbones and chin. But the judge's eyes were bright, and she could tell that he was following everything that was being said, even if she wasn't able to.

Good.

He had a strange nose. It started straight, but then bent sideways, as if it had been broken once and fixed badly. Perhaps he'd been a fighter. Or perhaps his father had hit him.

Zhenya reached up and touched the bump on the bridge of her own nose. She knew about broken noses. And about how hard you had to be hit for yours to break.

Most were strangers to her, of course, the people in this courtroom. All but one: the broad-shouldered man with the dark, wiry hair who sat at the table four rows in front of Zhenya, his back to her, facing the judge and the jury.

This man Zhenya knew too well, even though she'd never seen him before.

Yngblood. That's what he'd called himself. And now he must have felt the force of Zhenya's gaze, because he shifted in his chair, reached up to scratch his neck, and then finally twisted his head around to look at the small crowd in the pews. But before his eyes found her, his lawyer, a man in a suit that seemed too large for him, touched his arm and brought his attention back to the judge.

Zhenya's heart pounded.

Something must have happened, some decision made, because suddenly there were people moving around, a young woman carrying a big piece of cardboard to the front of the courtroom. The people in the jury box all leaned forward.

Speaking loudly, one of the lawyers lifted up a sheet of paper that covered the piece of cardboard, revealing the image, blown up to poster size, of a tall, slender girl with an oval face, luminous dark eyes, and black hair that fell thick to her shoulders.

The girl was wearing very short shorts and a bikini top. She was leaning forward and smiling at the camera.

She was, perhaps, thirteen.

People stirred and made noises. The judge barked at them. Yngblood stared down at his lap, the back of his neck turning pink.

Now one of the lawyers was talking about the girl in the picture. Zhenya heard words like "graceful" and "childlike" and "innocent." All around the courtroom, people were nodding their heads.

Zhenya laughed, a sharp, sudden sound that made people stare at her. Biting her lip to keep the laughter inside, she shook her head in apology, then reached up and ran her hand through her short blond hair.

Childlike. Innocent.

He had no idea what he was talking about, this lawyer.

Arkhangelsk, Russia

In 1989, just a year before Zhenya was born, treasure hunters found a great trove on the banks of the Dvina River in Arkhangelsk. People said it had been buried nearly a thousand years earlier.

Most of the objects were silver coins. They had been brought from all over Europe, at a time when Arkhangelsk was a great port city. People traveled there to live, to seek their fortunes, or just to stop briefly on their passage through the great northern continent. Even the Vikings had come, once.

But now it was just a gray city, with faceless apartment blocks left over from the Communists, and garbage on the streets, and no place for a girl to escape to, unless she wanted to throw herself in the river.

Zhenya rarely even left her room. She was not permitted to, except to attend school, to study math and science and English. At school she was known as a quiet, pretty girl, with fair skin and long legs and big dark eyes and an expressionless face that never revealed anything about her soul.

Not that she believed in souls. All she believed in was surviving till the next day, and doing what her father and his brother, Mikhail, told her to do. She'd learned long ago that she had no choice but to listen and obey.

When they told her to stay away from strangers, to stay silent among acquaintances, she did. And so, at ages ten, twelve, Zhenya had no friends, no one she could trust, no one to talk to. She didn't know anybody.

But thousands of people around the world knew her.

United States District Court, Philadelphia. April

This was the one who'd called himself BMOC.

He was a high-school teacher, it turned out, and girls' soccer and softball coach, though of course he'd lost those jobs months ago.

From what she could see from the back of the crowded courtroom, he didn't look much like an athlete. Soft and white, like the kind of bread you'd find on the grocery shelves here in America. If you pushed a finger into him, she thought, the dent you'd make would stay there.

Maybe he'd played sports as a child, in school, before he got so soft, and that was what made him an expert. Or maybe they couldn't pay much, the school, and he'd been the best they could get.

And maybe he'd taken the work so he could be close to the girls.

Zhenya had been sitting there all afternoon, waiting. Now it was time. One of the lawyers, a young man in a dark suit that reminded her of a knife blade, let his nasal, piercing voice get louder. Then, as happened every time, he pulled out the pictures. One, of Zhenya in a short sundress, lying back, bare legs spread, panties showing, was poster-sized, for all to see. But the others were smaller, private, for the eyes of the lawyers and the jury alone.

Protecting the audience from the shock. Still, the people around Zhenya shifted and murmured, a low, uncomfortable sound.

Innocents.

One by one, the members of the jury looked at the pictures, then raised their heads to stare at BMOC.

The girls' coach put his head in his hands and began to cry.

———

THEY BEAT HER, of course, her father and Mikhail.

But they were careful about it. They'd punch her in the stomach, and then photograph her in lingerie that hid the marks. Or avoid showing her arms if they were bruised. But when they slipped, when they hit her in the face, they covered up the bruises with makeup. One kind when the marks were purple, another for when they had faded to yellow.

But they knew they couldn't go too far. And that, Zhenya knew, was the only thing that kept her alive.

Mikhail, he was the one who lost control. She could see it in his eyes, the way the whites would shine all around the black irises, the way his pupils would become as small as pinheads, the way his thick cheeks would flush and his mouth would hang open as he drew his fist back for the next blow.

He would have killed her, Mikhail, if her father hadn't been there to stop him. To pull him off, to shout at him and send him away to calm down.

Her father was more careful, because he understood that they'd have nothing if she died. That she was the reason they could buy a Lada, drink more expensive vodka, go out to restaurants while she hunted up a couple of eggs or a hunk of bread in the apartment.

But even so, her father never pretended that he felt anything else toward her, and he always let her know how easily he could withdraw his protection.

"You try to run off," he said to her, "and I will find you. I know everyone, and you know no one."

She said nothing.

"I will leave you alone with him. And then we will float your body down the river with the logs."

He brought his face close to hers. "Do you believe me?"

Of course she did. So she behaved herself, and waited.

And began to dream of an alternative future.

United States Courthouse, Fort Worth. May

These ones were mean. You could tell it by looking at them, even from a distance. They sent out waves of anger as they sat side by side in the echoing room, with their thick arms and red faces and stains under their arms. Looking at each other all the time, shaking their heads, as if they couldn't believe the way they were being treated.

Brothers, like enough to be twins.

Interceptor and ScrewU. They'd always seemed to be the first to comment when a new set of photos went up, and what they always said was coarse, lewd, cruel.

Zhenya noticed that no one came to the courtroom to support them. No wives, no parents, no friends sitting in the first row to offer words of comfort and encouraging looks. Just the two of them, with their smirks and their sweat, and an audience of curious strangers.

And Zhenya, of course, sitting in the back with her hands clasped together so tightly that her knuckles were white.

———

IT HAD BEGUN when she was ten.

Her father had come into her room carrying two big bags. One was full of new clothes. At first Zhenya had been thrilled—she couldn't remember the last time he'd bought her something—but as she dug eagerly through the bag, she could feel the smile freeze on her face.

"What are these?" she'd asked, pulling out something that looked like it was made from strings. "They are for me?"

"Put them on," he had said. "Those ones."

At first, she hadn't even been able to tell which end went where, but eventually she'd figured it out. While she dressed, he rummaged around in the second bag and came out with a camera.

Even then Zhenya hadn't been stupid. She'd understood.

In her new clothes, she'd looked down at her skinny body, then up at her father. At the camera's single eye.

"Who will see me?" she'd asked.

"Get on the bed" was all the answer he'd given her.

CUSTOM SETS

Pima County Justice Court, Tucson, Arizona. September

It was fall, but the sun was blazing in the sky, and the breeze that rattled the shaggy palm trees did little to cool the baking air. Zhenya and some of the others sought out scraps of shade and waited to be allowed to go back into the courtroom.

"Why are you here?"

Zhenya froze for a moment. She felt like she couldn't breathe. Her legs tensed, and without hesitation her eyes sought out the nearest corner, the closest spot where she could run, get lost in the crowd, disappear from view.

Then she regained control of herself and turned to look at the woman who'd asked the question.

They were standing beneath the courthouse's green dome, which reminded Zhenya of the mosques back in Arkhangelsk. Inside, the judge, a woman with a face like a hawk's, had gotten angry over something and everyone had been shooed outside so the lawyers could argue. Now they all stood here on the sun-baked plaza, sweating.

"Excuse me?" Zhenya asked.

The woman was old, at least fifty, with a too-tight tanned face and hair that had been bleached blond. But her expression was friendly. "I come to watch the show," she said. "It's something different every week. Better than television or the movies."

Zhenya waited for a moment. Then, nodding, she said, "Yes, better than the movies."

The woman grinned and held out her hand. "I'm Bonnie, by the way. Bonnie Wright."

"Jane," Zhenya said, shaking the hand. It was hard and dry. "My name is Jane."

"Pleased to meet you, Jane. Where're you from?"

"New York."

Bonnie's eyes widened a little, but she didn't ask for any more details. "So, what do you think of this guy?" she said. "What's his name again?"

Zhenya nearly made a mistake. "Warlock," she almost said. "He calls himself Warlock." But then she realized that this hadn't been mentioned in the courtroom, that no one knew what he called himself when he wrote those horrible messages, when he described what he would do to her and what she would look like by the time he was done. No one knew, except her.

"I'm not sure," she said finally. "I don't remember his real name."

That was a mistake too, which caused Bonnie to give her a curious look. Even after all this time, it was hard for Zhenya to guess exactly what English words to use. You could get yourself in trouble so easily and barely be able to figure out why.

But it also protected her, this hesitation, this difficulty in putting sentences together. No one here, no one in America, was ever suspicious of her—they always gave her the benefit of the doubt. She could have used a vile word, and she had learned quite a few, and people would still have thought she didn't mean it.

"This man," she said. "Do you believe he is guilty?"

Bonnie shrugged and frowned. "I don't know," she said. "He *seems* like a nice guy. Not at all what I expected."

Someone called out from the front door of the courthouse, and they turned to go back inside. "And you," Bonnie asked. "What do you think?"

Zhenya just shook her head. She didn't yet have the words for what she thought.

———

THEY CAME TO America when she was fourteen, Zhenya and her father and Mikhail. Leaving Arkhangelsk, leaving Russia, behind without a backward glance. Taking the train to Moscow, endless hours jammed between the two big, sweaty men in a crowded train car that smelled of old food and cigarettes, before boarding the enormous airplane for New York.

She could have escaped at any time, she knew that. Cried out, screamed, called attention to herself. In Pskov station, both her father and Mikhail fell asleep on the bench, and for ten minutes, perhaps more, Zhenya could have just walked away.

But she had nowhere to go. The streets of Russia were full of fourteen-year-olds who had run away. They did not have happy lives, or long ones. Zhenya was more afraid to leave than she was to stay.

Also, she was too busy revising her plan. She hadn't expected them to leave home so soon.

Thousands of men they had never met paid for the Aeroflot flight, at $24.95 U.S. a month, thirty euros, who knew how many yen or pounds. Men who waited each week to see Zhenya in teddies and short shorts and bikinis with the tops off, her hands covering her breasts.

Never quite showing them as much as they wanted, but always enough to leave them dreaming of more.

Unless they paid extra for custom sets. Then their dreams did come true.

———

"WHY DO THEY do this?" Bonnie Wright asked as they took their seats in the cool, dim courtroom.

"Look at those pictures, I mean," she went on, bringing her shoulders up. "Those men. How can they—think about children that way?"

Zhenya let her eyes blur. She knew. Of course she did. She knew exactly what it was that appealed to some men, a lot of men, when they looked at pictures of her. And not just her—because she had learned there were countless other girls out there, going through what she had.

"It's disgusting," Bonnie said.

No, Zhenya thought. *Much worse than that.*

———

THEY MOVED TO Rego Park, Queens, a part of New York City that was already full of Russians. The stores had signs in Cyrillic, and the rhythm of the language she overheard on the street made it seem to Zhenya that they'd never left home. She knew her father had chosen this place because they would be completely invisible here. No one ever knocked on the door.

Two days after they arrived, he bought a new computer, a big new television set, and a new camera, much fancier than the one he'd had in Russia. Twice a week now, since she no longer went to school, he would photograph her dancing, holding stuffed animals, lying on her bed in a bathing suit, in lingerie. Wearing clothes sent by the men who were staring at her in their own homes, mere hours after her father took the pictures.

And the custom sets too got more frequent, more daring. Sometimes now she had to stand there, in front of her father, naked. But it was all the same to him. From behind the camera, he looked at her with eyes as black and expressionless as a crow's.

At first the money poured in. Zhenya, allowed outside only rarely and under close supervision, spent the hours reading *Novoe Russkoe slovo* and sometimes copies of the American newspapers left behind by Mikhail.

And she watched the television, soon finding the channel that showed only court cases. After that, she watched it whenever she could, closely, even obsessively.

In this way she learned about America and, saying words and sentences aloud in the empty apartment, practiced speaking English the way the Americans did.

She searched every inch of the four rooms when the men

were out, discovering all the places her father had chosen to hide things he didn't want anyone to find. And for the first time, her heart pounding, sweat beading on her forehead, she went to his fancy new computer and saw herself the way others saw her.

In the weeks that followed, she went back many times and taught herself much more. How her father uploaded the photos of her. How he ran the site. How he could go anywhere he wanted online and no one could ever see him.

And again, based on what she had learned in this new country, she dreamed of what she might do. Still, shaking with fear at the mere thought, she doubted that she would ever be brave enough to go ahead with it.

Until one day when Mikhail decided she was being too fresh with him and punched her in the stomach. As she lay there on the floor, he stood over her and looked down and told her something she hadn't known.

"You're getting too old," he said. "Soon you will be worthless to us."

Zhenya was seventeen.

"But before that happens, we will make you someone else's problem," he said.

She could guess what *that* meant. So the next time they went out, her father and Mikhail, to drink vodka with all the other expatriate Russians, Zhenya finally, after seven years, began to act.

———

WARLOCK SAT IN a chair to the right of the judge's desk. He was tall, with curly blond hair and a well-trimmed beard. Blue eyes and a face that looked like it had done a lot of smiling. Long arms that rested on his knees in front of him, slender wrists and delicate hands emerging from the sleeves of a dark suit.

He showed none of the desperation that gripped Yngblood in

Indiana or the girls' coach in Philadelphia, or any of the barely restrained rage of the brothers in Texas. Warlock looked like someone who had been brought here by mistake, who knew everything was just a misunderstanding, who expected to walk away and go back to his real life.

Explaining in a strong, convincing voice how mistakes had been made, how he had no idea, how in a million years he would never. As Bonnie Wright had said, he looked and sounded like a nice man. An innocent man.

Zhenya knew the truth. But would the rest, the twelve silent ones in the jury box, see it too?

———

THEY TALKED ABOUT her.

All the time.

Her father had christened her the Divine Dvina, and the members of her forum called themselves her Dvotees. They acted like friends who shared a secret, who understood each other more deeply than anyone else in their lives understood them. For them, the forum was a refuge, a hiding place, *home*.

Dvina's Dvotees. Dozens of them talking there some days, but five more than all the rest. The five who felt most strongly: Yngblood, BMOC, Interceptor, ScrewU, and, most of all, Warlock.

They talked about her eyes. Her smile. Her legs. Her breasts.

Her breasts, which, she discovered, had grown less appealing to them.

"Oh, the time is coming," BMOC lamented. "She's almost graduated to grannyhood already."

Grannyhood.

"Yeah, isn't it sad when they grow up?" asked Interceptor. "At least we'll always have the old sets, from when she was still cute."

"I hate fuckin' puberty," ScrewU said.

Zhenya looked down at her body. At the flaring bruises from Mikhail's most recent blow, the close-bitten fingernails, the fine hairs on her arms—which some Dvotees didn't like—the swell of her belly, her solid legs, her wide, high-arched feet.

When was the last time she'd studied herself so closely? She couldn't remember. Maybe never. Because it wasn't her body, it was theirs. And now they didn't seem to want it anymore.

"I'm letting my subscription lapse when it runs out," someone said.

"Me too," said someone else. "If I wanted to look at a teenager in a halter top, I'd just go down to the mall."

"Or the beach," BMOC said.

"Oh, shut the fuck up with all your whining."

That was Warlock.

"In a bad mood?" someone asked.

"He's always in a bad mood."

A pause. Then Warlock again: "I know some things you don't know."

"???" asked BMOC.

A longer pause. Then Warlock said, "Let's take this to chat."

Their screen names all disappeared from the forum screen. With a few quick strokes, Zhenya followed them into the private chatroom. Her father had set it up just as she would have: no one could see her there, but she could see them.

"So what's your secret?" BMOC asked.

"I'm going to meet her," Warlock said.

"WHAT?!"

"Spend as long with her as I want."

"Sure you are."

"Believe me or don't believe me, I don't give a fuck."

A long silence. Finally BMOC said, "How?"

"$$$$$."

And the Warlock went on to explain what he was going to do

with Dvina once he had her. Do to her. The description took up half the computer screen, but Zhenya made it only through the first six lines before she lost control and found herself crouched over the bathroom toilet, emptying her insides into the still, stained water.

———

FIRST THE PROSECUTOR stood and began to talk. She was beautiful, dark-skinned and black-haired, with high cheekbones and a mouth that turned down at the corners. Her voice was low, but somehow it still carried across the room.

"I have a question for you," she said to the jury. "Do you want this man out in the street, free, in the same room, on the same street, in the same *world*, as your daughters?"

Then it was Warlock's lawyer's turn. As short and lumpy as his client was tall and handsome, he jabbed the air with his right index finger as he talked. He told the audience and the jury about all the good works his client had done. And he talked about doubt. He said there was just too much doubt for the jury to convict. Proof was needed—and where was the proof?

"Don't let your emotions put an innocent man in jail," he said.

While Warlock stared down at the table in front of him, the picture of wounded innocence.

"Make the right choice," his lawyer said.

The audience seemed to be holding its breath. Watching from the back, Zhenya felt herself grow cold. They were going to believe him, those twelve people in the jury box. She could tell. They were going to believe all those pretty words, and Warlock was going to go free.

All around, Zhenya heard people exhaling. Beside her, Bonnie Wright turned her palms upward.

"I don't know what to think," she said.

———

"AND AFTER THAT," Warlock wrote, "I'll share her with you."

"Get real," Yngblood said.

"No, I'm serious—unless, of course, you think she's too old."

"I'd still do her," said Interceptor.

"When is all this happening?" asked BMOC.

"Very soon."

Zhenya sat looking at the words on the screen. *Very soon.*

"What if she doesn't want to?" BMOC asked.

"Oh, she will," said Yngblood. "She'll do whatever her father says."

Zhenya wondered if she'd waited too long.

Bending over the computer, she hit the Reply button, typed in, "Hi, guys!" and pressed Send.

A moment later she saw her message pop up, under the screen name The Real Dvina.

Turmoil in the chatroom.

"Do you want me to tell you what I'm wearing right now?"

Torn jeans and a stained sweatshirt, her usual clothes when she wasn't being photographed. Her mouth had a sour taste, and she knew she still smelled of vomit.

"Fuck you," said ScrewU. "You're just some guy who hacked his way into here to dick with us. I'd like to put my fist through your face."

"Oh, it's me," The Real Dvina typed. "And I can prove it."

"How?"

"I have a new custom set, my best ever."

"Fuck you," said ScrewU again.

"Only people who ask nicely," The Real Dvina wrote, "will get it."

She logged off and went into her room to change. Then she went into her father's bedroom and retrieved his fancy new camera. She'd long since figured out how to work the timer, and now she took twenty-seven photographs of herself, doing things she had never done before.

Including some things she imagined Warlock would like.

When she went back to the computer, all five of the men had asked nicely.

In their fashion.

———

GUILTY, SAID THE jury in Shoals, Indiana.

And the one in Philadelphia.

And the one in Fort Worth.

The verdicts were no surprise, according to the audiences in each courtroom. "Cut-and-dried cases" was an odd phrase Zhenya heard more than once. "We don't have much tolerance in this country for child porn," one woman said.

But Zhenya already knew that. She'd learned it from the television.

In each case, the evidence was found right there on the men's computers. Sometimes the police, the FBI, had found pictures of more than just Zhenya. Worse pictures, with other girls in them.

Hearing his verdict, Yngblood sat as still as if he'd turned to stone. The coach, BMOC, collapsed, weeping, and had to be carried from the courtroom. Interceptor and ScrewU cursed the judge and jury, shouted and spat and ended up writhing on the floor, beefy policemen with red faces sitting on them, clicking on the handcuffs.

Zhenya was there for each of the decisions, just as she'd borne witness to nearly all the testimony. She took little pleasure, though, because always in the back of her mind was the one case that had not yet been decided. The most important one.

Warlock's trial was different from the rest. He had the best lawyers, the most money, and (it seemed to Zhenya) the most burning desire to stay free. His trial was delayed once, again, still another time. And then, when it finally started, his lawyers fought hard, brought in witnesses of their own, battled the prosecutors fiercely at every turn. By contrast, Warlock himself was always quiet, respectful, convincing.

When all the testimony was finished, when the lawyers had made their final speeches, the jury left the room and stayed out for a whole day, and another.

As the time passed, Zhenya became more and more certain that Warlock would go free. And then he would come after her, to punish her for destroying his life.

If that happened, if he managed to find her, Zhenya knew what she would have to do.

———

HER FATHER SLAPPED her across the face. Her feet left the ground, and for a moment she felt as if she were flying. But then gravity caught her again, and she fell to the floor. The wood was cool against her bruised cheek, and the taste of her blood was in her mouth.

They'd come home too soon, he and Mikhail.

"What have you done?" he asked her in Russian.

She didn't reply.

"You are not allowed to talk to those men."

She was silent.

"Get up," he said. But when she did, he knocked her down again, a blow to the stomach that made her think she would never breathe again.

"You think you can take our business? Make money for yourself, not us?"

She didn't reply.

"Get up."

She got onto her hands and knees, and this time it was Mikhail who stepped forward and kicked her, his heavy boot thudding against her ribs. Again she almost flew, but this time when she landed, she rolled and twisted and got back to her feet faster than they expected. Making low, gasping sounds in her throat, she ran, but not for the front door. For her bedroom.

The two men followed. There was no lock on her door.

They found her lying on her bed, curled into a ball, hugging her pillow. "No," Mikhail said, laughing. "No time for sleep."

He reached down, grabbed her shoulder, and rolled her over. That was when she came up with the knife, the one she'd taken from the kitchen drawer weeks ago. Her arm swung around in a fast arc, and with open eyes she watched the four-inch blade enter Mikhail's throat just below his stubbly jaw.

There followed a moment of complete silence. Mikhail's eyes went wide as he stared at her. Then, choking and gasping, drowning, he fell backward onto the floor, leaving the knife clenched in her hand. His blood sprayed upward, a red fountain that drenched her and the bed alike.

Zhenya had been dreaming of this for years. She'd waited so long only because she needed to grow strong enough to carry it out. Never realizing that when the time came, her anger would give her all the strength she needed.

She came off the bed, and this time she flew, really flew. Landing on her father's back as he tried to run, hearing him cry out in terror, ripping upward with her right hand, feeling the blade slice through his flesh until it reached something harder, and then cutting through that too.

They went down together. Zhenya rolled clear and watched as he twisted and writhed and fought the air, watched until his crow eyes turned dull and he lay still.

Then she went and took a long, hot shower. When she was

done, she inspected herself in the bathroom mirror. It wasn't as bad as she feared. Nothing seemed broken, and most of the blood hadn't been hers.

As she always had, she covered up her bruises with the makeup her father had bought for that purpose. Then she went to the secret drawer where, not believing in banks, he'd kept his money. *Her* money, really. A lot of it, enough to travel wherever she wanted to go in this big, empty country, if she so chose. And no one would ever find her. No one even knew she was here.

But she wasn't ready, not quite yet. Her father and Mikhail had come home before she had finished her preparations.

First she went back to the computer and sent her last custom set on its way.

Then she picked up the telephone and made a call to Washington, D.C. Whatever happened next—and she had hopes—she'd learn about it from the news media, which in this country never stopped talking.

Finally, as she had dreamed of for so long, she packed her clothes and left the apartment for the last time.

———

"WE FIND THE defendant guilty," the foreman of the jury said several times.

Warlock sat down hard on his chair at the defense table, looking as if he'd been hit in the head with a hammer. Beside him, his lawyer frowned and shrugged and started gathering his papers. The judge thanked the jury.

"Wow," said Bonnie Wright. "I just wasn't sure."

"Will he go to jail?" Zhenya asked.

Bonnie gave her a curious look. "Honey, weren't you listening? He's going away for two hundred years."

Zhenya gasped.

"It's the law here in Arizona," Bonnie said. "A mandatory sentence of twenty years per count for possession of child pornography, with no chance of parole. They found him guilty of ten counts. Do the math." She looked over at Warlock, who was slowly getting to his feet. "That man will die in jail."

As they watched, a pair of officers walked Warlock up the center aisle toward the door. His composure shattered at last, he seemed stunned, almost blind with shock and fear. As he passed, he suddenly lifted his head and looked directly at Zhenya. His gaze sharpened, and a muscle jumped in his cheek.

He knows me, Zhenya thought.

At the same moment Warlock started shouting. "It's her!" he said. "That's her—the one who set me up! The one who sent me those pictures. It's her—I swear—"

But for the first time Zhenya understood something others didn't. The officers merely glanced at each other and grinned. One of them wrenched Warlock's arm, so hard that his words changed into strange, guttural cries. Before he could get control of himself again, he was out the door, the sound of his garbled shouts still echoing in the quiet room.

Zhenya forced herself to look at Bonnie, afraid her new friend would see through her. Would she recognize in the face, in the body, of this short-haired, blond, well-dressed young woman the dull-eyed, half-naked girl of the photos?

But all Bonnie did was shake her head and laugh. "What was *that* about?"

Zhenya gave a cautious shrug.

"Well, good riddance to bad rubbish, I guess," Bonnie said.

Who knew what that meant? But it sounded like a final judgment she could live with.

———

SHE AWOKE DISORIENTED and frightened. Then she remembered and, stretching, leaned her forehead against the cool glass of the bus window.

The landscape outside was dry, sere. Where was she? Utah? Nevada?

It didn't matter, since she didn't yet know where she was heading. But one thing she did know: when she got there, when she chose to step off the bus, her life would begin at last.

BANG

BY ANGELA ZEMAN

ana, I'm sorry." Sophie Black's whispered words sounded unnaturally loud in the glass box of a room. The nurse had disconnected the noisy machines, useless now, and the silence pressed heavily. Sophie shuddered at hearing a sigh from the man hovering at her back—like a vulture impatient for the last pump of his next dinner's heart. Turning her head, she hissed, "Back off!" He retreated, but didn't leave the room.

She slipped her square, unlovely tan hand under the thin blanket to grasp what was now a claw with yellowed nails. Her most-loved friend's hand.

Parchment-thin eyelids opened. Eyes that could once, with only a glance, daunt a powerful opponent. The wasted remains of the woman on the bed moved her lips: "Stop."

Sophie understood. Dana knew how sorry she was. She shouldn't waste time over it again. Time was against them both.

Sophie edged closer. "You're nearly dead." Cruel words, but Sophie knew her friend's intolerance of lies. Dana never found kindness in deception. She clenched her teeth, refusing the grief that promised to consume her, although tears flowed silently down her cheeks.

"Tell me what to do. What do I do?"

Dana's face twisted as she tried and failed to speak. Sophie rubbed a sliver of ice across Dana's crusted lips.

The only color left in the ghostly face was the black of her irises, now dull as raisins. Gone the lush swag of rich burgundy hair. Gone the arches of expressive brows. Few lashes clung to the staring eyes, eyes that still revealed a brilliant mind. The oxygen feed draped across Dana's pillow, ignored. A vinyl bag of colorless liquid hung useless from the metal rack, its tube disconnected from her arm. Her veins had collapsed.

"Nuclear plant," she finally managed. "Tell them." She stopped to draw a breath. "Nuclear plant. Fremont."

Sophie recoiled. "Wait. Tell them? You mean—I'm to stay out of it? No! I can't let you die like this and do nothing." She gripped the hand a little harder, wanting Dana to feel her determination, but not wanting to hurt her.

"No. You'll die too."

"I don't care!"

"I care. Tell them. Nuclear plant."

"NO!"

Sophie blinked in shocked realization. Dana was dead.

"That's it." The voice, coming from behind her, was loud. His impatient tone angered her. She clung tighter to her friend's hand. Such extreme suffering had seemed too strange, too unreal, until this moment. Never to be with her or talk with her again. Sophie couldn't imagine it.

Since the official had picked her up at JFK from her Panama flight yesterday, she'd seen nothing on his face but a smirk that seemed permanent. Only his unshaven cheeks and pungent rumpled clothes verified the sleepless hours he claimed to have put in on this case. *Case*, thought Sophie. She rose stiffly, pulled herself away from the bedside.

He gestured with a thumb. "Down the hall. Room fourteen-twelve. Thought we'd save you that long, nasty trek to our offices. Bereaved as you are." He held the door open for her.

Bereaved. What a silly-sounding word for a raw, unfillable hole in a person's life.

She swept by him, stunned and expressionless, long past reacting to the trefoil radiation warning sign on the door. Her shearling coat flapped open to accommodate her long-legged strides. Dana's coat, borrowed. Sophie would be cold, if she could feel, more used to desert heat than this New York December. Unlike Dana, Sophie ignored makeup and haircuts, and considered clothes as merely protection from unfriendly elements.

As she walked, she swiped a sleeve across her wet face. Her pointed chin lifted; her blue eyes, pale against her deep tan, glazed with the intensity of her thoughts. She snatched up her long, ragged, sun-bleached hair and snapped a rubber band around it to keep it out of her eyes—a habit that, Dana could've warned the official, signaled that Sophie would tolerate no distraction. Dana had often mailed her sunscreen and the latest in outdoor gear, accompanied by scoldings to take better care of herself. Dana had often . . . Sophie snapped her mind back to the present.

When they entered the room, he gestured toward a metal folding chair. The only chair in the closet-sized room. She kicked the chair aside. A button at the end of a wire lay on an otherwise barren metal desk. The wire snaked beneath the desk and vanished. She decided not to kick the desk, although the impulse was strong. Sophie's eyes flicked a disinterested glance toward a woman already in the room.

Sophie took a step into her tormentor's personal space, just an inch too short in her thick work boots to look at him eye to eye. "Tell me what you've been doing to find her murderer."

He was a big man, tall, approaching forty, dark-haired, and thick with muscle. He leaned toward the tiny receiver and spoke: "Tape seventeen, Dana Fallon Case Number N-one-one-four-one—UNY. I'm Edward Eisner, temporary appointee New York State Assistant Director of the Office of Homeland Security. Also in this room is U.S. Attorney Georgina Moore, federal prosecutor for the Southern District of New York. The time is five thirty-six a.m., Tuesday, December twelfth, two thousand six. Two minutes ago, Ms. Fallon expired."

The U.S. Attorney was a medium-height, forty-something matronly black woman with hair trimmed tight against her head and an almost military posture. She wore a red suit of soft woven wool, swathed in a matching fringed shawl, but if she felt warm, her face didn't show it. She held out a hand. "Georgina Moore, Dr. Black. Sorry for your loss." Sophie looked at her as if surprised she could talk.

"What's on those sixteen previous tapes, Director?" she asked, turning back to Eisner.

Ms. Moore withdrew her untouched hand.

Eisner resumed speaking for the recorder: "We're in University Hospital, room fourteen-twelve, questioning Dr. Sophie Black, alleged friend of the victim. Dr. Black has a PhD in forensic pathology, cultural archaeology, and"—he consulted a small notebook—"anthropological science." He turned to Sophie. "Lot of degrees. What do you know about radiation poisoning?"

"Now that I've witnessed it firsthand?" she asked bitterly. "Too much."

"She say anything in there we didn't hear?"

"You hovered over me, what could you miss? And I'm not an alleged friend."

"Lesbian?" This from Ms. Moore.

Sophie glowered at her contemptuously. "No. Has nobody ever watched your back without sex involved?"

"Watched your back . . . ," mused Eisner. "Interesting way to define friendship."

Ms. Moore said, "We've been retracing Ms. Fallon's last days, trying to pinpoint the time and location of her—exposure to the radioactive isotope. We can't get beyond a dinner meeting she attended three weeks ago in D.C. So we think, tentatively, that was the day she was poisoned. Two Mortensen University professors attended that dinner, plus another academic gentleman and the university president." She paused. "You two received your doctorates in anthropology together at Mortensen, didn't you?"

Sophie, without looking at Ms. Moore, moved her head, a barely interested assent.

Ms. Moore continued: "We have the CVs of the four gentlemen and a stack of references. Hard to see any of them being in a position to steal radioactive material."

Sophie looked up at this. After a pause, she said, "Yeah, it is."

Ms. Moore added, "We're informed by the Health Protection Agency that this form of isotope required high-grade technical skills and a sophisticated scientific process to produce. The autopsy might reveal its geographic origin, but that takes time."

Eisner said, "So we're tracing others known to be around her earlier that day, and each person's movements backward—"

"Following the radioactivity, I get it," said Sophie. She sighed, her anger draining into despair.

Interest flickered in Eisner's eyes. "Sure. That's what you do, right? Look at bones and pottery, then figure out who they were and all that. Except centuries ago. Talk about a cold trail." His tone was admiring.

At her surprised look, he said, "Until your friend got sick, I was Homicide. NYPD."

"Promotion or demotion?"

His glum smirk returned. "Anybody in mind for your friend's death?"

"What do you mean? You heard her. Fremont, the Long Island nuclear plant. That's what you do, isn't it, Mr. Eisner?"

"What?"

"Monitor antiterrorist security?"

They looked at each other in silence.

Anger riveted her again. "You must think terrorists caused Dana's death, or you wouldn't be here! Dana's career was one investigative crusade after another, and her latest targeted nuclear plant security. Speeches, op-ed columns . . . CNN! About how our nuclear plants sit virtually unguarded, ripe for terrorists. She demanded prosecution of the federal appointees running them. Fremont topped her list. Wouldn't they, wouldn't Fremont especially, want to shut her up? Their guilt is ridiculously obvious!"

" 'Ridiculous' being the key word," Eisner said. "Why point fingers at themselves? Besides, we checked Fremont. Nothing missing. All records confirmed."

"Records can be falsified!"

Ms. Moore asked, "Are you familiar with Ms. Fallon's will?"

Sophie snapped her head in Ms. Moore's direction and stared. "What?"

Eisner said, "You inherit everything."

"Oh." Sophie made a dismissive noise. "Our wills. She's like that, organized and . . ."

"You get the apartment."

"Which you tore apart," Sophie snapped. "She would've been furious."

Eisner shrugged. "Time's tight. Agents also searched her D.C. townhouse. They might've been a little rough. Sorry."

Ms. Moore said, "You live out of a duffel bag on subsidy money.

I'm supposed to believe you forgot you're heir to millions? She was a highly successful woman, and from a wealthy family."

"That never mattered. She knew I hate the responsibility of owning things, so she shared."

"From what we discovered, she practically mothered you," said Ms. Moore.

Sophie almost smiled. "She always said I wasn't housebroken." She thought for a minute. "You investigated me?"

Eisner and Moore gave no reply.

She exhaled. "Her family dumped her. Dana's work required a spotlight, she always said they were allergic to publicity. I never had family. We made our own family." She shot a glance at Eisner. "So, yeah, we watched each other's back. She was the only person in this world who cared about me. What's money, compared to having her?"

Ms. Moore's eyelids lowered to slits. "Well, Congress failed to pass their budget for next year, producing a crisis in science financing, throwing thousands of scientists out of a job. What about you?"

Sophie slowly pulled the chair upright and straddled it. "I've never needed government grants."

Ms. Moore's eyebrows lifted. "Until now. According to our information, Mortensen dismissed you. What did you do wrong?"

Sophie said nothing.

"They were covering your expenses exclusively. Why was that?"

"Publicity. They're—were—eager to claim credit for my group's project. When we reveal our conclusions, they'll be front and center for global media attention. Publicity attracts donations, enhances their reputation, which attracts the more elite students—sort of an endless wheel of profit producing." Sophie looked away. "I'm exploring European sources."

Ms. Moore said softly, "But I hear your project is unpopular. Won't that hurt your chances to find new funds?"

Eisner glanced at Ms. Moore. "Why? What's she doing?"

"Genome mapping. She and her group are trying to solve one of the great mysteries of civilization: the specific origin of the first *Homo sapiens*. They're tracking migrations using DNA. Studying how and when the different ethnic groups formed through gradual mutations. I hear it's working well, especially via pockets of indigenous groups."

Eisner squinted. "What?"

Sophie nodded. "True—in Alaska, the Amazon, anywhere we can find them. People who've lived a long time in especially close-knit isolation make it easier for us to track adaptations through several generations. But many are so unsophisticated, it's hard to get them to understand why we want samples of their blood . . . they get upset. They're barely aware of a world outside of their own boundaries, let alone how DNA works." Sophie exhaled helplessly. "We give them medicine in trade for their help, but . . ."

Ms. Moore continued: "Her findings threaten some tribes' religious beliefs. For others, their assumed origins give them claims to income and land ownership. The results of her work could change boundaries, religion, history, income. Lots of anger."

Eisner almost laughed. "She's messing with money and religion?"

Ms. Moore added softly, "And race."

Sophie raised her hands in frustration. "It's overreaction. We're talking fifty thousand years ago. Only scientists will care. Maybe medical research . . . but what has that got to do with Dana's murder?"

"How much grant money?" asked Eisner.

"Massive lab fees. Archaeological digs. Travel. Salaries." Sophie shook her head.

"Ms. Fallon's millions would certainly bridge your funding gap," said Ms. Moore. "And if your project succeeds, you'll change global history! You'll earn prizes. Fame. All the money you could ever want will fall in your lap."

Sophie frowned. "Not just me. The whole group. And we're building on the work of many others . . ." She fell silent for a long moment. "I don't understand." She looked at Eisner, blue eyes dull with pain. "Your presence means somebody thinks it's terrorism. You think I'm a terrorist? Or do you think I killed Dana for her money? Which is it?"

Eisner considered her. "There could be a connection. You travel through some of the world's nastiest spots, Dr. Black. You cross borders, trek straight through warfare, you were even airlifted across Afghanistan—by Afghan guerrilla fighters."

She looked taken aback. "How did you learn that?"

He shrugged. "As the only beneficiary of your friend's demise, plan on staying in town."

She bolted to her feet. "You're accusing me?"

Eisner began straightening up the room. "You'll hear from us."

Color rose in her face. "You can't force me to stay here! I'm supposed to meet Dr. Guzman in the morning!"

"Who?" asked Eisner, pausing.

Ms. Moore murmured, "Nobel Prize–winner Xavier Guzman. The first to decipher a complete genome map."

"Exactly. We're flying together to Nicaragua tomorrow." Sophie wrung her hands in agitation. "This trip took months . . . No! I'm going!"

"Ah," said Eisner. "Then lucky your best friend died according to your schedule."

She recoiled as if he'd struck her.

"You go nowhere until Dana Fallon's murderer is found," said Ms. Moore crisply.

Sophie swayed, but said nothing more.

"End of session. Time, six twelve a.m." Eisner plucked the tiny receiver off the desk, began winding the cord into loops. He dropped it and a small box into a briefcase. "I don't think you understand, Ms. Black. I can do whatever I think necessary. New times, new—everything."

Eisner left the room. Ms. Moore followed, shoulders bowed as if carrying a heavy load. She paused and held out a business card. "If you think of anything, find me. A bad way to die."

The door swung shut and she was alone. Alone as she hadn't been since she first met Dana Fallon, her new roommate, freshman year at Michigan.

It was as if she were five again, when her mother coolly informed her that her daddy had died during the night. She'd added, "Just as well. I planned to divorce him anyway." Then a blank yawning chasm of years: unnoticed, unwanted, untouched, leaving her with a shaky notion that possibly she didn't really exist. When her mother died twelve years after her father, Sophie's life didn't change, it merely continued. Until her first day freshman year at college.

Dana Fallon had dragged the silent, self-effacing Sophie into what was to be their first shared dorm room and drilled for information, a deadly interviewer even then. She pulled out of Sophie the barren details of her existence. Dana then explained to Sophie that she, on the other hand, had a massive family, enormously wealthy—which had disowned her, appalled by Dana's future plans. "We're both orphans," she concluded.

Sophie's stricken sympathy caused Dana to laugh and grab her in a fierce hug. "Silly thing! We'll just be orphans together!" Sophie had blinked awake under Dana's fierce grip. She became, mysteriously, no longer a burden to herself. Both were anthropology majors, but on widely diverse tracks. Sophie craved to understand the development of past civilizations, but Dana was determined to shape the development of future civilizations, using her flair for public media.

Dana captured Sophie with her noise, toughness, hilarity, and confidence. And touch. Dana literally dragged Sophie to class, to parties, on double-dates, to meet influential people. The relief of having her existence confirmed by someone outside herself was almost painful. They entered and left Michigan, Columbia, and then Mortensen University together, always at the top of their class. Separate but inseparable. Or, as Dana always said, "moon and sun." Never a doubt that Dana was the burning, brilliant sun.

Eisner's words echoed in Sophie's mind: "Lucky your best friend died according to your schedule."

Sophie walked to the elevator, thinking of nothing else.

———

AT FIVE P.M. the same day, the lowering dusk had already made Sophie's car invisible where she'd backed it beneath a canopy of drooping pine tree branches far out east on Long Island. She'd rented something generic and dull green, deciding against Dana's flashy Jag. Despite Dana's coat, the cold had worked its way into Sophie's bones. Once in a while, she touched her hair or her face, absently irritated by the cloying stickiness of makeup and hairspray. But the Fremont nuclear power plant held all her attention.

After this morning's events, she'd split into two distinct parts—a physical body unable to feel and a mind unable to gather a thousand shards of thoughts into a plan. Shock, she supposed. Didn't care. She passed the afternoon huddled close to the roaring fireplace in Dana's luxurious apartment, studying Dana's research, mentally replaying Eisner's comment: "Lucky your best friend died according to your schedule."

A plan would come. Whenever she entered a site—a possible

future dig, an unremarkable spot to other eyes—each time she knew that beneath her feet waited clues to direct her next steps. Her best tool was patience. Today Fremont was her site.

As minutes passed, Sophie sat motionless in the shadows.

Every fifteen minutes Sophie started the car to rewarm the engine. She feared no heat scanners, which Dana had recommended to the nuclear plant in several speeches. No dogs, either, according to Dana's research.

Snow was coming. Soon and heavy, she judged by the crackling dryness of the air and rapidly failing light.

Beyond the grove of pines, thirty feet of cleared ground fronted a ten-foot-high chain-link fence topped with rolls of barbed wire. An incongruously ungated gap in the fence allowed employees to drive inside and park, then disappear to work among a cluster of pale yellow buildings. On the left side of the entrance a guard sat, booted feet propped on a small desk, cozy in a glassed-in booth, which was obviously sealed to retain heat—she doubted he would hear her if she screamed. He was absorbed in a magazine. Sophie saw the long body of a semiautomatic rifle racked up on the wall behind his head. She recognized the type and wondered if he regularly cleaned it; it tended to jam from dust.

A massive windowless tower behind the office buildings dominated the compound.

The icy, pine-drenched air emphasized the silence.

Finally, the guard sat up and muttered into a portable radio. She couldn't hear what he said, but could guess. He'd been drinking from a massive thermos. He probably wanted a toilet break and a refill. He shrugged himself into his coat, tucked his magazine and thermos under one arm, locked the small door behind him, and strolled toward a side building. No replacement appeared.

Sophie glanced at her watch—six thirty—and moved. She estimated fifteen minutes. She ducked under the metal chain which laughably barred the entrance. Under her coat she wore a navy jumpsuit she'd found in Dana's closet. It closely approximated the uniform of plant workers she'd seen in Dana's photos. Sophie wondered what Dana had discovered while wearing it.

She slipped through the door of the largest building and walked into a veritable cocoon of heat. A hallway confronted her. She had to choose, left or right. She opened her coat to the heat and sauntered down the left-hand passage. Swinging from her neck was another token from Dana—a press pass issued by this plant, granted a year ago when Dana's investigations began and she'd still been welcome here. Sophie had thought it might bolster her disguise. Or bring luck.

Pushing her lipsticked lips into a smile, she cracked open each door she passed, glancing swiftly inside. The fourth door revealed a large room full of people sitting and moving around long tables, mostly eating, talking loudly. She considered entering—maybe she would overhear something helpful—when across the room a man sitting at a crowded table looked up, then stood, staring straight at her. An unexpectedly familiar face. He darted toward her. In a panic, she stumbled backward, blundering into two people trying to enter the room behind her. They exclaimed loudly in annoyance. Several people looked her way. Quickly she turned and ducked her head, pushing out between the two, muttering, "Sorry. Sorry."

In the hall, she broke into a trot, back to where she'd entered. Outside, she bolted. In the still cold air she could hear feet pounding after her. His feet? No time to turn and look. All she could hope for now was escape.

Her rental instantly started, and ignoring the circular exit road, she cut straight uphill and across the lumpy frozen ground, threading between tree trunks until she lurched up onto the access road to the highway. She cursed the inadequate engine, but blessed her habitual preference for four-wheel-drive vehicles.

The highway appeared empty of traffic, with two lanes on each side of a low cement divider that forced a right turn. The wrong way. She shot across the divider. At the car's first bounce, she wrenched the wheel left to ease the impact of her tire rims when they hit the concrete edge. She pulled into the inner, fast lane. No streetlamps on this back-country road. Only the information signs were illuminated, green islands of light.

Suddenly she became aware of a car behind her. She glanced into her rearview mirror. The darkness had swallowed all but a pair of headlights, maybe fifty yards behind and approaching fast. Why no other cars? Surely this place shouldn't be so deserted at—she glanced at her watch—seven o'clock. Long Island overflowed with communities, and she was even close to the beaches! Damn it. Beaches in December. Stupid, stupid, and obvious. Dana would've thought of it.

Wishing desperately for inspiration, she jammed the accelerator to the floor, but could get no more speed. The headlights behind her crept closer. She heard the power in the engine following. Something heavy and expensive. Fast.

She stared up into the rearview mirror at the headlights behind her. Maybe she'd panicked over nothing. The following car could be a coincidence. Maybe she'd come out onto the highway ahead of someone else, a stranger. She'd seen him for only a second. And he had no business here. The man she saw had fit in among the employees . . . No. She'd made a mistake. It was probably a mistake.

Another well-lit sign flashed by. The chassis of her car shook and its engine rattled like a tin box full of cans. Sophie had been stranded in every terrain, in every type of vehicle. She could tell by listening, this one would soon quit unless she slowed down. If her follower was a stranger . . . she took a deep breath and twitched her shoulders to loosen her neck muscles. Snowflakes began to show in her headlights. The storm had arrived.

Suddenly the other car passed her on her right, bursting out of the darkness and startling her. It pulled in ahead of her too swiftly for her to see the driver. A dark Mercedes sedan, she noted. Reflected lights flashed painfully from its high-gloss paint, obscuring its color and damaging her night vision. Then the Mercedes braked hard. The cars slammed together.

Sophie reflexively braked. "Bastard!" She twisted the wheel right, fishtailing in her haste to get to the outer lane.

She exhaled in relief as she saw only crumpled metal at the end of her hood. No real damage, but now she sat so rigidly her back no longer touched the seat.

The Mercedes also switched lanes and hovered close behind. Too close.

Okay. No stranger. No mistake.

The two cars sped down the lonely highway as if connected, only a few feet apart. Darkness was now complete except for the bright white sheet of falling snow illuminated by their headlights.

Sophie twisted the wheel again, skidding in her haste to get back to the left inside lane. Again the other car followed. Then Sophie, gauging the strengthening snowstorm, decided she wanted to get off the highway. She had no speed, but she had experience.

Sophie swerved right, lunging across the lanes. Captured by its own momentum, the heavier Mercedes shot straight on.

She tapped her brakes. In seconds, her car was bouncing easily on the sloped graveled shoulder. As she slowed, she pulled deeper into the grass verge, tucking close to the overshadowing pines. She stopped, shifted into Park. Snow surrounded her like a white wall. She killed her headlights.

Far ahead, she watched the Mercedes brake. Moving too fast to handle the thickening layer of fresh snow, the car skated diagonally across the road. When the tires grabbed the rough gravel, the car lifted and rolled gracefully, onto the passenger side, onto the roof, then onto the driver's side. The abused metal moaned as it ground against the gravel for the last few yards, then came to rest upright. Sophie screamed, her fists covering her mouth.

Something in the Mercedes made a hissing sound. Then a figure, a man, crawled out through the passenger-side window. Leaning on the battered car, he groped his way around it until he reached the pavement. He dropped to his knees. Sophie shifted into gear and let her car roll forward. She stared, trying to identify her attacker. About thirty feet away, she braked and flipped her lights back on. In the sudden glare, the man held up an arm to shade his eyes.

In that moment Sophie knew him for certain. Victor Rubinski, director of the Jones-Formen Foundation, the doorway institution that screened scientists like her to allow her access to grants. The man who'd persuaded Mortensen to fire her from her own project—after which she'd run to Dana, whining about her troubles. Dana, who always covered Sophie's back. And now here was Rubinski, at a nuclear plant. As if he belonged. Dana. He must've murdered Dana. And now he'd tried to run her down on a deserted highway. How had he known she would come here? Sophie's thoughts whirled in confusion.

He pulled himself upright and staggered toward her. He raised the arm not shielding his eyes and stretched his hand toward her, as if offering her something. A blinding flash burst from his hand. Simultaneously she heard a loud thunk and her headrest jolted. She punched her lights off again and dove sideways, below the dashboard.

Sophie listened, shivering, but heard only the faint tapping of snowflakes on her windshield. She wondered what to do. Then it came to her. She, Sophie, was meek, quiet, confident only in jungles and deserts. Dana was powerful, clever, combative, like a trumpet in war. She would be Dana.

Straightening in her seat, she stamped on her car's accelerator.

With a loud thump, as loud as the thumping of her own heart, she rammed him.

He flung out his arms as his body flipped backward. Then he was gone.

She braked, then twisted in her seat to look. In the red glow of her taillights, she saw him in a bundle on the ground. The bundle moved. She shuddered, and the image of Dana's last seconds of agony, her ravaged body, flooded her mind. She rammed her gearshift into reverse. This time she felt the hump of each set of wheels. She braked. Panting, she huddled over the steering wheel, head down. Dana would make sure he was dead, wouldn't she? A bolt of fear shot through her. Dana would look.

Seconds passed, minutes, marked by the ticking of her cooling engine. Finally, still unable to look up, she eased shakily out of her car, leaving the door open. The interior light beamed a snowy shaft across the white highway. The only sounds were the shush of snowflakes as they filtered through pine boughs and the thin rumble of her car's idling engine.

When she reached where she thought he'd be, she saw nothing. In a haze of shock, she circled the Mercedes. Looked underneath. Searched among the tree trunks in the woods. No body. An object lay at the edge of the highway, not yet covered by snow. She walked up to it. A gun: a .38 revolver.

"Rubinski!" she screamed, whirling where she stood. The falling snow muffled her voice. Again she looked at the handgun.

Using a pen from the pocket of Dana's coat, she did as she'd seen detectives do on television—slid the pen into the trigger guard to lift it untouched. Before reentering her car, she placed the gun and pen onto the floor of the backseat. Gasping to catch her breath, she slammed her door, put the car into gear, and drove.

It was nearly nine when she reached Manhattan. She slipped

Moore's card from her pocket. An address had been scribbled on the back. Soon she parked on a side street near Fifth Avenue, in the East Seventies. She entered the apartment building and asked for Ms. Moore. The doorman called upstairs, then nodded her toward the elevator. "Press forty," he said.

Ms. Moore stood waiting in her open doorway, wrapped in a padded silky housecoat.

Without a word, Sophie walked past her, then plopped herself uninvited in the middle of a sofa. They looked at each other for a long moment. Finally, Ms. Moore closed the door and sat in a chair opposite the couch. She asked, "Have you had dinner? Would you like some coffee? You look frozen."

Sophie didn't answer. Ms. Moore slipped her hand into her robe pocket, pulled out a pager, pushed buttons. She leaned back into the soft cushions and waited.

After a pause, Sophie asked, "If a person . . . did nothing wrong herself . . . but knew of a crime. And for personal reasons said nothing—"

Ms. Moore interrupted. "Maybe an accessory. Depends on circumstances. Coercion, if it can be proved, might exonerate—"

"I knowingly profited from . . . doing nothing."

"Still depends."

Two loud thuds were heard at the door.

Sophie, trembling, met her eyes. Ms. Moore admitted Eisner, who, one step inside the apartment, stopped short. He examined Sophie on the couch. "I was already on my way up." He peeled off his wet coat and draped it on a coatrack behind the door. He glared at Sophie. "You're getting Georgie's couch all wet."

Sophie looked at him, taken aback. "Oh. Sorry." She removed her wet coat, but rolled it into a big ball and kept it on her lap. She stared down at it.

Eisner collapsed into a chair. "Now you're getting yourself all wet. What the hell are you wearing?"

Sophie didn't move or speak. Looking at Ms. Moore, Eisner held up his hands as if to ask, *What?*

Ms. Moore sat again in her chair. "She says she might be an accessory to a crime."

Eisner looked at Sophie. "What crime?"

Ms. Moore, slightly exasperated, said, "We hadn't gotten there yet."

Eisner pulled out his notebook, now damp and tattered, then sat back. "Shouldn't you be home packing?"

Sophie's head jerked up. She stared at him wide-eyed. Finally: "Oh. Nicaragua." She looked away again. "That's over."

Eisner frowned, puzzled. "Okay." Then he leaned forward. "What crime, Dr. Black?"

"Theft."

"Theft of what?" asked Ms. Moore.

"Of artifacts. Stolen from . . . Dana called them my 'dog and pony shows.' I'd do one every few months, or when I found something special. The university would invite wealthy supporters, serve wine and cheese. Slides and a speech from me, as project leader. The interruptions to my work were annoying, but—that's why they funded me, after all, for publicity." She paled and looked away. "Dana wrote my speeches. She said I have poor communication skills."

Eisner rubbed his eyes. "She's right. Okay, believe it or not, I'm with you. Somebody stole artifacts you brought to D.C. for exhibitions to impress the moneymen."

Sophie looked relieved. "Yes. Months ago somebody complained that a statue had never returned from Mortensen. I mean, the only reason I'm allowed to borrow these things is because the countries trust me to bring them back. So . . . I looked into it. I tracked through the bills of lading. The statue had never even been listed for transport. When I examined earlier shipments, I discovered other items had vanished. I'm guessing, but

I'm sure the thief is selling to collectors. Some collectors can be ruthless."

"Were the missing artifacts valuable?" Eisner asked while making notes.

"You mean, like gold? Sometimes. But technically, all antiquities are irreplaceable, and thus priceless."

"And you figured out who the thief was."

Sophie exhaled. "Yes."

Eisner said, "With proof?"

"Is his blackmailing me proof?"

"In my book. What hold did he have over you?"

Sophie said weakly, "Obvious, isn't it? My work. When I confronted him, he laughed. He reminded me of his power over my funding. I'd never destroy my life's work just to stop him from making a little profit, he said. And—he was right. I was arrogant. I thought what I was doing was so important that the thefts didn't matter in comparison. So I did nothing. At my next dig, though, I couldn't continue. Those people trust me. And their antiquities, their histories, are important to them, as important as my work was to me. I realized I'd made a terrible mistake. I told him he had to stop. That's when he cut off my funding. Then he told me Interpol would be interested in my activities. He'd set me up to look like the thief."

"He can do this?"

"He's doing it. He stole only from remote areas with few resources. Documents are easy for a man in his position to manufacture. My reputation is good, but pitted against his?" She shook her head.

Ms. Moore said, "Ah. Then you confided in Dana. Who watches your back."

"I never intended for her to do anything. But she"—Sophie took a moment to swallow—"she refused to let me ruin myself. She said she would make him her private crusade. She would stop him, protect me, and I could continue my work. She's very . . . strong. And clever! So I agreed."

Ms. Moore considered her. "And then she was poisoned."

"God, yes."

Eisner said, "But this type of radiation only comes from—"

"Nuclear plants. Yeah, I read Dana's research. And right before she died, Dana named Fremont. I thought she was saying that somebody from there poisoned her. She told me to make sure you knew that. Still protecting me."

Ms. Moore frowned. "So her murder had nothing to do with your stolen antiquities?"

"I didn't—I still don't see how it could! But either way, I had to do something. So this afternoon I went to Fremont. And I saw him!"

Ms. Moore's eyes narrowed. "Who? The thief? At Fremont? Who is this person? Who killed Dana Fallon?"

Sophie clutched her head. "Me! My selfishness. I never thought about her being in danger, I thought only about myself! The only person in the world who loved me, and I killed her!"

Ms. Moore leaned across the table and grabbed her hands. "Cut the melodrama. You didn't kill her! Who is the thief?"

Sophie shook her head. "You wouldn't believe me. Besides, it makes no sense." She looked at Ms. Moore. "Because I just killed him. And he's not dead."

Ms. Moore threw up her hands, then stood and began to pace. "You killed him?"

Eisner demanded, "What happened?"

"I got inside Fremont. Dana was right, it's way too easy. And I saw him in the employees' cafeteria. He saw me too. I got out fast, but he chased me. In a big dark Mercedes sedan, I couldn't tell what color it was. So shiny it half-blinded me. He tried to ram me. I pulled off the road. He handled his car badly, all that snow. He crashed. He crawled out of his car, though, and—he damn near shot me in the head! I panicked. I ran him down."

Eisner goggled. "Deliberately?"

"Twice."

Ms. Moore stopped her pacing and stared. "Twice?" And after a pause: "Twice? What's his name?"

"Victor Rubinski, director of—"

Ms. Moore interrupted: "Director of the Jones-Formen Foundation. That gatekeeper institution for scientific grants." She whirled to face Eisner. "The fourth guy at Fallon's dinner."

Eisner flipped open his cell phone. "Where was this car crash?"

Sophie thought, then described the last green sign she'd passed before stopping. "I don't know much about Long Island, sorry."

He made two calls. Ms. Moore went into her kitchen. Sophie sat huddled miserably on the couch, sunk in thought. In fifteen minutes, Eisner's cell phone rang. Ms. Moore returned from the kitchen, the aroma of hot coffee following her. Eisner listened, then sighed. "Thanks." He glanced at Sophie. "Some crackups due to weather, but no Mercedes of any type. You're sure about the make?"

Sophie nodded.

He shook his head. "No car or body found, Georgie. But Rubinski does own a Mercedes S600 Metallic Capri Blue sedan. That's shiny dark blue, if you drop the sales pitch."

Ms. Moore frowned, then let out a sound, half laugh, half exasperation. "Well, she did say he wasn't dead. Give me a minute to dress."

Eisner eyed Sophie. Ms. Moore said, "Let her come. I'd like to hear what he says when he sees her."

In twenty minutes they were pushing the doorbell at an elegant Murray Hill townhouse owned by Victor Rubinski.

When a man opened his door, before he could speak, Sophie let out a muffled squeal. Eisner elbowed her. "Victor Rubinski?"

Rubinski paused to wrap his maroon bathrobe tighter and cinch the belt. He was a long-faced man with thinning brown hair, in his late fifties, lean except for a small paunch, a few inches shorter than Sophie. "Yes?"

"Eisner, Homeland Security. I'm sure you remember U.S. Attorney Moore. A few minutes of your time." Rubinski hesitated, but Eisner swept him aside with a heavy arm, and made room for the two women to enter. He stepped in and closed the door.

They stood in a long, darkly paneled hallway, crowded together. Rubinski made no move to invite them in any farther. "Ah. Hello, Sophie. Surprised to see you here. Hah, you've combed your hair. I am surprised!" His drawled words revealed a faint European accent. He looked up at Eisner with a pained smile. "And you're here because?"

"Your car, Mr. Rubinski."

"My car?"

"Where is it?"

Rubinski's eyebrows lifted. "I suppose . . . in the garage. Where I left it last Friday, after I drove home from Washington."

"Where's this garage?" asked Eisner.

"Oh, come now. Around the corner, on . . . on Thirty-sixth. What's the fuss?"

"We'd like to see it," said Eisner.

Rubinski made an exasperated noise. "Get a warrant. Isn't that the drill?"

Eisner sighed. "Don't need one, Rubinski. Nobody seems to remember that."

Rubinski darted forward, as if intending to shoulder through them to get to the front door.

As he rushed past Sophie, she sidestepped and blocked the

door. She blurted, "You can't just arrest him! He tortured Dana! Think what she suffered!" Ms. Moore touched her on the shoulder, but Sophie wrenched away.

Rubinski snarled, "Hah! This woman's a known criminal. To accuse me—"

Suddenly a gun appeared in Sophie's hand. She slammed Rubinski against the wall and dug the muzzle deep into the soft spot beneath his ear. He gaped, mouth opening and closing like a fish drowning in air, but made no sound.

She wiped tears from her cheek with her shoulder. With her thumb she drew back the hammer. "You monster! You think I'd let them tuck you away in some cell? Pay for what you did with jail time? No death penalty in New York."

Eisner and Moore, startled, separated, and moved deeper into the hallway.

Rubinski suddenly recovered his voice. "I told you she's a criminal! You, Homeland, grab her! Do something!" He tried to jerk away, but she had him pinned too well with her body.

Eisner didn't move, but gestured at the gun. "You good with that?"

Rubinski snapped, "Of course she is, you cretin."

Ms. Moore sighed. "Deserts and jungles, Ed. I believe him." She said softly to Sophie, "Do you think shooting him will hurt him enough? Could anything hurt him enough to pay for Dana's suffering?"

Sophie didn't answer, but glanced uncertainly at Ms. Moore.

Rubinski, in a burst of new energy, struggled hard, but Sophie stiffened her hold. She hesitated, then shoved the gun harder against his neck. "Where's your brother or cousin?" she suddenly demanded. "In the trunk of your Mercedes?"

Rubinski's mouth opened halfway and stayed there.

Sophie continued: "Where's the car? Not in any heated garage, not with a body in it."

Eisner said, "In it?"

"Has to be. Too cold to dig a hole. And this happened—what. Two hours ago? Now that I think of it, the guy I hit crawled out of the passenger side. I never saw a second person, but it was so dark. Took me a while to get up the nerve to check that he was—and I couldn't find him! Rubinski could've pulled the body into the car. I looked all around, but never inside the car. I never thought of a second person. Hard to total a Mercedes. I bet he drove it away, hid it in Long Island somewhere near a train station."

Eisner nodded. "I can buy that."

Rubinski snapped, "Why would I be at Fremont!"

"Fremont, Rubinski?" Eisner asked with interest. "Who mentioned Fremont?"

"What relative? And how did you guess?" Ms. Moore stared at Sophie.

"No guess. People are my subject." Sophie smiled bitterly. "I'm a trained observer of physiognomy. If I was fooled, the resemblance had to be close, probably a brother. A cousin, at most. Victor's standing here, so I must've killed his relative."

Eisner said, "We knew he had a brother, didn't know he worked at Fremont."

Rubinski said, "He didn't. Consultant. And only a half-brother. Hardly a real sibling." Then Rubinski grinned. "Fortuitous, don't you think? Dana Fallon got the public all roused, leading Fremont to hire poor Jerry to patch up some engineering carelessness." He added sullenly, "Greedy piece of shit, charged me a fortune for that bit of isotope. Then elbowed in on my . . . business." He gestured at Sophie. "Still. She murdered him! She confessed it right in front of you!"

Ms. Moore considered this. She eyed Sophie, who kept her attention steadily on Rubinski. "You flew in at JFK yesterday from Panama, right?"

Sophie frowned. "Yes."

"Not Dana's gun?"

"No."

"So, you, ah, found it . . . where?"

"In the road. It fell out of his half-brother's hand after he shot at me."

"Ed, arrest Rubinski. Attempted murder will do to start. We'll sort out the details and the, ah, *twice*, in the morning. Please, carefully, relieve Sophie of Mr. Rubinski's, or his brother's, weapon."

She smiled at Sophie. "We might manage to rescue a few fingerprints."

Sophie hesitated, a worried frown on her face as she replaced the hammer. "Check the bullets. When people load, those are the fingerprints they usually forget to wipe off."

Rubinski gasped.

Eisner said, amused, "I've, uh, heard that."

"Honey, trust Ed. Come with me. Let's get you warm."

Sophie took the pen from her pocket, inserted it into the trigger guard, and handed both revolver and pen to Eisner.

GOING UNDER

BY LINDA FAIRSTEIN

I had dreamed about getting the gold shield ever since I was a kid. My grandfather's detective badge—gleaming yellow metal framing cobalt-blue enamel—had attracted and intrigued me for as long as I could remember. I had obeyed my parents' demand that I finish college, but four days after graduation I joined the rookie class at the New York Police Department's academy, to become a cop.

Promotion from the uniformed ranks to the detective bureau can be a long and hard-fought battle. Some officers seem content to walk a beat for their entire careers, while others take daring risks and perform heroic acts to merit the shift to plainclothes investigations. You can't sit for any exams to get the job the way you can for administrative posts. And I had no one looking out for me down at Headquarters to push me along the way.

There was nothing I wouldn't do, I had vowed to myself the morning I came on the job, to earn that shield.

———

"ARE YOU OUT of your mind? You think I'm gonna volunteer to let some guy molest me when I'm not even conscious?" I looked across the table at Mike Chapman, who was chewing the last bite of his cheeseburger as the waitress slipped the check under his plate.

"Chief of detectives asked for you personally."

"He doesn't have a clue who I am, does he?" At the time, I had been working in uniform for two years, assigned to a patrol car on Manhattan's Upper West Side.

"Not really. But when I told him you'd been moaning all over the station house about your abscessed wisdom tooth, he smiled for the first time in half a year."

I pushed away from the table. A week of evening shifts, 4:00 p.m. to midnight, had exhausted me completely and drained me of my normal good humor. I had spent most of this tour handling a domestic dispute in a high-rise on Riverside Drive, trying to determine which of the two intoxicated combatants had wielded the first broomstick. The last thing I needed to find when I got back to the command on West 82nd Street was Chapman, who waited for me while I showered and changed into jeans and a sweater. We had walked to a bar on the corner of Amsterdam Avenue, where I nursed a drink while he made me the offer he knew I couldn't refuse.

"What's the deal, exactly?" I asked.

"Lieutenant Borelli says the chief has promised a promotion to whoever agrees to go undercover on this one. Two weeks from today, you could be a third-grade detective. You wouldn't pass up a shot at *that*, would you?"

Chapman worked in the detective squad at the same precinct. He knew I was hungry to get out of uniform and start doing real investigative work, but he also knew that my chances of doing that any time soon—barring some serendipitous arrest of a notorious serial killer—were slim or none.

"I've got principles, Mike. I just can't see myself saying yes to letting some pervert—"

"No problem, pal," he answered, paying our tab at the bar. "I respect you for that. Sandy Denman's been begging me for the case, anyway. She'll be thrilled you don't want to step up to the plate on this one."

"What time tomorrow does Borelli want to see me?" I hated Sandy Denman. She'd been on the job only half as long as I had, but Denman had grabbed the commissioner's attention by talking two jumpers in a suicide pact down off the Brooklyn Bridge. One week before that, she had interrupted a robbery in progress at the back door of City Hall, an hour before the mayor's scheduled press conference on the latest figures confirming reduced crime rates in the Big Apple. I'd be damned if I would let Sandy get the shield before I did. "And exactly what do I have to let this dentist do to me, anyway?"

———

THREE DAYS LATER, on Tuesday morning, I sat in the reception area of the office of Melvin Trichner, DDS, filling out his patient information form using my real name, Samantha Atwell. When I completed the paperwork, I was ushered into one of the rooms at the end of a long corridor and invited to sit back in his reclining chair and relax.

"This is an awfully thick book, young lady," Trichner said, grinning at me through his bonded, bleached teeth, as he lifted Poe's *Tales of Mystery and Imagination* from my lap and placed it on the counter behind him. "Do you like the macabre?"

Somehow, I had thought the heavy tome would hold my short denim skirt in place throughout the examination, but I didn't protest when Trichner removed it and leaned in to inspect my mouth. "I love thrillers," I answered, before he spread my jaws, hooked his little round mirror on my tender gum, and peered at the lower left quadrant, which had been throbbing madly all week.

My hands gripped the arms of the chair as he poked around at the impacted tooth, and I tried to distract myself by staring at the garish assortment of neon-colored flowers and tropical birds which decorated his Hawaiian-style shirt.

"Yes, that baby has got to come out," Trichner announced, rolling away from me on his four-wheeled stool. "How's Thursday morning?" He picked up my chart and studied it to make sure I had answered all the questions about current medications and physical history.

"I'm terrified about the pain," I murmured to him in my whiniest voice.

"I'll give you some pills to hold you over these couple of days."

"Not that pain. I mean, I'm worried about how much it will hurt when you pull my tooth."

Back came a flash of the phony smile, as he clasped his hands on top of mine and rubbed them together several times. "I'm absolutely painless. Some Valium before the Novocain," Trichner offered, "and you'll have nothing but pleasant dreams. Have you got a friend who can take you home afterward? You'll be a bit woozy for a few hours."

"Yeah," I said. "My boyfriend can do that."

"Great. You just dream about him while I put you under. I promise, it'll be an erotic experience."

———

"BINGO. THAT'S JUST the language he used to describe what would happen to each of the other victims. This is a 'go.'" Chapman was pumped as he drove me back to the station house from the dental office on Central Park West and 81st Street.

While Borelli and his men plotted the technical procedures for the video surveillance that would monitor our encounter, I sat in the squad room reading the case reports on the first three complaints.

Victim number one was a student at Barnard College when she had visited Trichner eighteen months earlier. She had awakened from the anesthesia in his office after an extraction, certain that he had been kissing and caressing her. She went straight back to her dorm and told her roommate, who brought the young woman downtown to make a police report. Like most professionals, Trichner benefited from people's perception that they are unlikely to be criminals. Instead of arresting the dentist, Detective Conrad Sully had asked him if he could think of any reason for his patient's bizarre recollection.

"Of course I can," Trichner said, calmly handing the veteran investigator a brochure that described the sedative he had used. "If you read this, you'll see it cautions that the drug is hallucinogenic. What that means is that sexual fantasies are a frequent side effect when we use it."

Sully took the pamphlet back to his office, called the student to tell her that she had imagined the entire experience, and closed the case out by writing the word "Unfounded" at the end of his report.

When the second witness showed up in the same squad room eight months later, the lieutenant referred her complaint to his expert, Detective Sully. This time he didn't even have to leave his desk. The nineteen-year-old hairdresser, who reported that she woke up with her clothing in disarray and a faint memory of being fondled and kissed, read the literature herself before Sully replaced it in his case folder. She left the precinct believing that she had falsely accused poor Dr. Trichner because of her drug-induced intoxication. Sully's brain was sometimes thicker than his brogue.

Mike Chapman was working with Sully when the third victim walked into the station house the week before last. She was an ingénue who had played in a few television soaps and had been referred to Trichner by her brother when she needed a root canal.

"This gotta be some kind of wonder drug," Chapman remarked. "No other dentist in town has this problem, but all Melvin's patients are dreaming that he's slobbering over 'em."

The circumstances were unique, and no one in the department had ever investigated a matter like this before. Lieutenant Borelli wanted to explore a way to get evidence against Trichner that couldn't be attacked in a courtroom as the product of a witness's imagination. He took his idea to the chief of detectives for approval.

"Borelli asked the chief if he could send in an undercover policewoman and apply for a court order to conceal a video camera in Trichner's office, both to protect the patient and to secure the evidence," Mike said.

"That's legal?" I asked.

"You'll make history, kid," Chapman said. "First time it's ever been done. The chief had to call the district attorney's office to draft the order. They analogized it to a wiretap. The prosecutor told the judge that an audio bugging device like they use in taps wouldn't do any good in a situation like this. This bum doesn't need to utter a word to these women. You could send a dozen undercover cops in, but they'll be sedated too. Without a camera, we don't have any way to prove what's going on inside. We don't even know what crime he's committing."

"What makes you think he'll hit on *me?*"

Chapman gave me the once-over. "You're his type, Atwell. Long and lean, dark hair, mid-twenties. And a little bit flaky. I'm betting he'll want to touch, Sam."

"What'll you charge him with? I mean, what does he do, exactly?"

"That's the mystery, Sam. Nobody remembers, nobody knows."

———

I GOT TO the precinct at six a.m. on Thursday. It was a steaming hot summer day, so my tank top and tube skirt looked appropriate to the season and didn't leave much to the imagination. The tech guys from the department had broken into Trichner's office the night before—a court-authorized burglary—and hidden their camera behind the louvered air-conditioning duct, which was perched conveniently above the dental chair. A video monitor was set up in the basement of the building and wired through to the recording device, so Borelli could supervise the operation from underground. In the bottom of my shoulder bag, a Kel transmitter had been secreted, so that the backup team could hear all the conversation between Trichner and me, and I could summon them at any moment if I was aware of trouble.

Mike was to accompany me to the office and pose as my boyfriend. The minute Borelli observed any improper conduct while I was sedated, he would beep Chapman so he could race down the hallway, open the door to the examining room, and interrupt Trichner in the act. I had signed on for a little bit of sexual abuse—caressing and kissing at worst—but not for anything more invasive than that.

The Muzak was piping in a soulless orchestral rendition of Diana Ross's "Touch Me in the Morning" when the receptionist waved me into the rear of the office to begin the procedure. Mike was singing the lyrics as he watched me walk away. A routine teeth-cleaning appointment makes me tremble under the best of circumstances. My anxiety about the procedure seemed palpable as I entered the narrow corridor to surrender myself to Trichner's wandering hands.

Melvin, as he told me to call him, closed the door of the small room after he entered and flipped on the light switch, unknowingly starting up the camera as he gave it the juice. He chattered with me about my personal life as he scooted around on his stool, setting his tools in place for the extraction. Then he lifted my shirt and put the stethoscope against my chest, announcing to me that I had a good, strong heartbeat.

"Think loving thoughts," Trichner told me, stroking my arm as he wrapped the tourniquet in place before he gave me the injection. "You look nervous—they'll calm you down."

The last things I remember before going under were the sound of the Boston Pops segueing into a syrupy version of "Feelings," the sight of a flock of shocking-pink flamingos on Trichner's shirt, and the warm whoosh of the sedative as he pumped it into my slender arm.

———

I WAS LOST in a thick fog. Somewhere off in the distance, I could hear the scraping noise of the door pulling open along its metal tracking, the sound of a familiar voice, the scuffling of several feet, and the words "You're under arrest, Doc."

The fog thickened and my head rolled from side to side. Someone lowered the headrest on the dental chair and leaned me backward. My eyes flickered open to a display of the pink flamingos, swaying now against a turquoise landscape that was moving with them in undulating waves. The lids closed again, as I continued fighting the nausea.

The noise was gone, and this time there was only a woman in a nurse's uniform, holding my shoulder back against the chair. When I tried to move, she explained that I needed to rest in that position, to increase the supply of oxygen flowing to my brain. I was awake, and conscious only of the intense pain in my jaw.

Lieutenant Borelli insisted that Chapman drive me to Roosevelt Hospital, in order for a physician to draw blood so that we could be certain of what drugs Trichner had administered to me. On the way over there, I asked what had happened while I was under.

"Melvin went right to work extracting your tooth. The moment he finished, he pushed the tray which was holding all the dental equipment out of the way. Then he actually lifted you out of the chair and propped you up against his body, holding you in place by wrapping his legs around you."

"But didn't I do—?"

"Do anything? You were in the twilight zone, pal. You were as limp as a rag doll."

"Do I want to know the rest?"

"He lifted the back of your shirt and unhooked your bra. Then he started to caress you, moving his hands around in front, to touch your breasts."

"Didn't I feel that? Didn't I try to stop him?"

"Are you kidding? It's like necrophilia, Sam, only your body was still warm. No wonder these women can't remember anything. None of them even realized he pulled them out of the chair."

"How could he take the chance that I wouldn't come to in the middle of all this and just start screaming at him?" I asked.

"Not a chance. By standing you up, he makes sure the oxygen doesn't flow to your brain fast enough. You're not gonna regain consciousness until he settles you back in the proper position. You'd never know what happened, as all these complaints prove."

"How long did you let it go on?"

"The guys beeped me as soon as he started to fondle you. Sexual abuse in the first degree. We had our felony—didn't need another thing. When I pulled open the door, he had his hands on your rear end, squeezing it and rubbing himself against you. That's where I stopped him."

"Did he say anything when you burst in?"

"Yeah," Mike answered. "Trichner told me he was just trying to resuscitate you. That you had gone into respiratory distress and he was trying to help you breathe. Cool as a cucumber."

"What if the judge believes him?"

"Like the DA said when I called to tell her how it all went down, squeezing the buttocks is *not* a recognized means of resuscitation in the medical community. Let him test it out in the Riker's Island infirmary, Sami. I'll be taking Melvin downtown to his arraignment from here," Chapman told me as he left me in the ER. "Call you later."

The lieutenant had one of the guys drive me home, where I spent the rest of the afternoon napping off the anesthesia, nursing my sore mouth, and calming my fatigued nerves after a sleepless night. I was too drained to bother with a can of soup. When the pain hadn't let up by dinnertime, I spent some time in front of the bathroom mirror, surveying the damage of the excavation.

Mike called me at eight o'clock. "Meet me in an hour at the Palm."

"Let's do it another night. I really don't feel like—"

"Don't be such a wimp, Sami. Bring an ice pack for your jaw and get over there."

The cab let me off in front of the restaurant on Second Avenue. It was a New York classic, with lobsters so big you wouldn't want to meet them in a dark alley and enough beef to give a cardiologist nightmares. I walked inside to meet Chapman, who was sitting at the bar with Sully and the team of detectives who had worked the case.

"I'm buying," Mike said. "The judge just set bail for Trichner at fifty thousand dollars. He told the defense attorney that if the videotape showed that his client's hands were anywhere south of Ms. Atwell's mouth during this dental appointment, he didn't want to hear any argument on the merits of the People's case."

"Why did you have to pick *this* place?" I asked, massaging my swollen cheek as I tried to ignore the incredible smell of the grilled sirloins, fried onion rings, and hash browns the waiters kept bringing out of the kitchen to the surrounding tables. "The last thing I want to think about right now is a thick steak."

Mike bit his lip as he realized my problem. "Sorry, I wasn't thinking. We just didn't want any more courthouse quiche. I had a real craving for red meat. C'mon, have a drink."

"I can't do that either. I'm on painkillers, remember?"

"Give her a Shirley Temple, straight up," Chapman told the bartender.

The throbbing in my jaw was still intense.

"What are you still so crabby about, Sami?" he asked me, as the maître d' told us our table was ready and we carried our drinks over to sit down for the meal.

"You're not gonna believe what that creep did, Mike. He pulled the wrong tooth." An hour ago, when I had examined myself at home, I had discovered that the tooth that had been giving me all the trouble was still there, surrounded by the inflamed gum. In front of it was a gaping hole, where a perfectly healthy molar had been when I awakened this morning.

"The poor fool was in such a hurry to get his arms around you that his fingers must have slipped a bit, Sami. You thought undercover work would be easy? C'mon, we've got something to take your mind off your discomfort, right, guys?"

In front of my seat was a serving platter with a domed lid over it, like they use in restaurants to keep the food warm when it's being served.

Sully reached across me and lifted the handle. More welcome than the choicest filet, there sat a blue-and-gold shield, with my name engraved below the most beautiful word in the English language: *Detective.*

"Cheers, Sami. Borelli says you'll get the real one next Friday, at the promotion ceremonies. And Trichner, he'll get a new degree too. DDS—Dentist Desires Sex. I think they call it a conviction where I come from. You put that pervert out of business for us. Welcome to the squad."

I popped a couple of Tylenols with my drink and sat back in the chair, repeatedly stroking the smooth surface of the shiny badge with my fingers and feeling no pain.

ABOUT THE AUTHORS

Phyllis Cohen is a native New Yorker and a resident of Manhattan. After retiring from a thirty-five-year career in the New York City public schools, she undertook a mini (micro?) second career as a freelance writer, writing nonfiction at first and then moving on to fiction. About her fiction, she writes: "The short stories I have written are of many genres—crime, science fiction, relationships—but there is a common element throughout them of character and human interest." She is married to Herbert Cohen, a semiretired electronics engineer and a member of MWA, whose published work includes several mystery stories and a science-fiction novel.

Jo Dereske is originally from western Michigan, but has lived in Washington State since 1978. She is the author of seventeen books, including the Miss Zukas mystery series set in Washington and the Ruby Crane mystery series set in Michigan. She currently lives in the foothills of Mount Baker.

Charlie Drees admits that when it comes to his literary preferences, he's a mystery-genre snob. "Chances are, if someone doesn't die, I won't read it." "By Hook or by Crook" is his first story accepted for publication. (Everyone remembers the first time, right?) A licensed psychotherapist with over twenty years' experience, he lives with his wife in Manhattan, Kansas—the Little Apple.

Eileen Dunbaugh currently makes her living in the publishing industry, where over the years she has worked at a variety of jobs. She is a dedicated mystery reader who decided it was time to try her hand at writing the type of fiction she loves.

Linda Fairstein, one of America's foremost legal experts on crimes of sexual assault and domestic violence, led the Sex Crimes Unit of the District Attorney's Office in Manhattan for twenty-five years. A Fellow at the American College of Trial Lawyers, she is a graduate of Vassar College and the University of Virginia School of Law. Her ten best-selling crime novels have been translated into more than a dozen languages. The eleventh book in her series, *Lethal Legacy*, was published in February 2009. Her nonfiction book, *Sexual Violence*, was a *New York Times* Notable Book of the Year. She lives with her husband in Manhattan and on Martha's Vineyard. For more information, visit her Web site at www.lindafairstein.com.

Kate Gallison lives in Lambertville, New Jersey, with her musician husband and their cat. She has three private-eye novels and five traditional mysteries to her credit. The *New York Times* called her writing "excitement of an off-beat variety"; *Booklist*, "superb black comedy"; *Kirkus Reviews*, "Well-bred work." Her Mother Lavinia Grey stories were the talk of the Episcopal Church. Under the name of Irene Fleming, she writes a series about a woman producing silent movies in the early days of the industry. She is descended from a convicted Salem witch.

Joel Goldman is the author of the Lou Mason series of legal thrillers, which have been nominated for the Edgar and Shamus awards. *Shakedown*, the first book in his new series featuring FBI agent Jack Davis, was published in 2008. Joel lives in Kansas City. Learn more about him and his books at www.joelgoldman .com.

James Grippando is the national best-selling author of sixteen novels, including *Born to Run*, the eighth installment in the acclaimed series featuring Miami lawyer Jack Swyteck. "Death, Cheated," is the never-before-published short story that transformed Jack Swyteck from a stand-alone hero in *The Pardon* (1994) to a recurring character in *Beyond Suspicion* (2002). James is also the author of "Operation Northwoods," another Swyteck short story, and *Leapholes*, a novel for young adults that was a finalist for the prestigious Benjamin Franklin Award. James's books are enjoyed worldwide in twenty-six languages. He lives in South Florida, where he was a trial lawyer.

Agatha Award–winning author **Daniel J. Hale** is a past executive vice president of Mystery Writers of America. Hale holds an MBA from Cornell University and a JD from Arkansas's Bowen School of Law. He teaches creative writing at Southern Methodist University, his alma mater. Learn more at www .danieljhale.com.

Diana Hansen-Young was born in Bellingham, Washington, in 1947, into a community of depressed Mormon Swedish farmers. In 1966 she moved to Hawaii, ran for the State Constitutional Convention in 1968, and won a seat by ninety-three votes. She went on to run for the Hawaii State House of Representatives and won. After losing a congressional race, she started painting scenes with Hawaiian women. For the next twenty-five years, she turned her paintings into a business of postcards, clothing, books, and children's videos. In 1996, she developed severe arthritis in her right arm and hand and could no longer hold a paintbrush. For years she had also been writing plays, novels, and short stories, and tossing them in boxes. Now she dusted them off, closed the business, and traveled to New York, where she earned an MFA in musical theater writing from New York University. Her Off-Broadway musical, *Mimi Le Duck*, starring Eartha Kitt, premiered in New York City in 2006. A member of Mystery Writers of America, she now writes full-time.

Edward D. Hoch (1930–2008) was a past president of Mystery Writers of America and winner of its Edgar Award for best short story. In 2001 he received MWA's Grand Master Award. He was a guest of honor at Bouchercon, twice winner of its Anthony Award, and recipient of its Lifetime Achievement Award. The Private Eye Writers of America honored him with its Life Achievement Award as well. Author of more than 975 published stories, until his death he had appeared in every issue of *Ellery Queen's Mystery Magazine* for the past thirty-five years.

Paul Levine is the author of four legal thrillers featuring Steve Solomon and Victoria Lord, squabbling Miami trial lawyers. *Solomon vs. Lord* was nominated for the Macavity Award as best mystery novel of 2005 and also for the Thurber Prize for American Humor. *The Deep Blue Alibi* was nominated for an Edgar Award in 2006, and *Kill All the Lawyers* was a finalist for the 2007 Thriller Award. His most recent book is *Illegal,* a thriller set in the world of human trafficking. The winner of the John D. MacDonald Award, Levine also wrote the Jake Lassiter novels and *9 Scorpions,* a thriller set at the U.S. Supreme Court. Levine was co-creator and co-executive producer of the CBS television series *First Monday,* starring Joe Mantegna and James Garner.

He also wrote twenty-one episodes of the military drama *JAG*. More information at www.paul-levine.com.

Leigh Lundin, a Florida resident, has lived and worked in both the United States and Europe, and only recently turned to writing. Leigh was honored with the Ellery Queen Readers' Choice Award in April 2007, the first time it has been won by a first-time author.

Michele Martinez is the author of the critically acclaimed thriller series featuring Manhattan federal prosecutor Melanie Vargas. Her books—including *Most Wanted, The Finishing School, Cover-Up,* and *Notorious*—have won awards, been named to numerous "best" lists, and been published in many languages. Her short fiction has been published in several anthologies. A graduate of Harvard College and Stanford Law School, Michele spent eight years as a federal prosecutor in New York City, specializing in narcotics and gang cases. She lives in New Hampshire with her husband and two children.

Anita Page's short stories have appeared or are forthcoming in *Murder New York Style* and in the journals *Word Riot, Mouth Full of Bullets, Mysterical-e, Ball State University Forum, Jewish Horizons,* and *Heresies*. While working as a freelance journalist in upstate New York, she learned about the events that would later inspire the story "Red Dog." Anita Page and her husband live in the mid Hudson Valley, where she taught and now writes full-time. She recently completed her first novel, a dark-edged traditional mystery set in the Catskill Mountains.

Barbara Parker used to practice law, but she gave it up to create fictional attorneys who make more money, have more fun, and never lose their cases. Best known for her "Suspicion" series of legal thrillers set in Miami (the first was nominated for an Edgar Award), she has penned nonseries novels as well. Her latest project, *The Dark of Day*, published in 2008, features a high-profile murder among the rich and decadent on South Beach. Before becoming a *New York Times* best-selling author, Barbara earned an MFA in creative writing from Florida International University (Miami). She has previously published one story, for the anthology *Miami Noir*. Doing "A Clerk's Life" reminded her why she left the profession: it is far easier to write about lawyers than to be one. She lives in South Florida, a few blocks from the ocean.

A Stanford graduate and former plaintiff's trial lawyer, **Twist Phelan** writes critically acclaimed short stories, suspense novels set in the business world, and the legal-themed Pinnacle Peak mystery series. Find out more about Twist and her work at www .twistphelan.com.

John Walter Putre is a former academic, teacher, and administrator who began writing full-time in 1984. His two mystery novels, *A Small and Incidental Murder* and *Death among the Angels*, were published in 1990 and 1991 respectively. "The Evil We Do" is Putre's first venture into the short-story genre. He lives with his wife and feline companion on Virginia's Eastern Shore, where he is currently at work polishing the final draft of a suspense novel, tentatively titled *Treason*, set in North Africa and Spain during the Second World War.

S. J. Rozan, a native New Yorker, is the author of eleven novels. She has won the Edgar, Nero, Macavity, Shamus, and Anthony awards for Best Novel and the Edgar Award for Best Short Story. She is a former Mystery Writers of America national board member, a current Sisters in Crime national board member, and president of the Private Eye Writers of America. In 2003 she was an invited speaker at the annual meeting of the World Economic Forum in Davos, Switzerland. In 2005 she was guest of honor at the Left Coast Crime convention.

Morley Swingle is the prosecuting attorney for Cape Girardeau County, Missouri. He has prosecuted 71 homicide cases and more than 120 jury trials, some featured on the *Oprah Winfrey Show*, *Dateline*, and *Forensic Files*. His historical mystery/thrillers include *The Gold of Cape Girardeau* (winner of the 2005 Book Award from the Missouri Humanities Council and praised as "absorbing courtroom drama" by Elmore Leonard) and *Bootheel Man* (a finalist for the 2008 William Rockhill Nelson Award for fiction). His true crime/humor, *Scoundrels to the Hoosegow: Perry Mason Moments and Entertaining Cases from the Files of a Prosecuting Attorney*, hailed as "engrossing" and "highly recommended" by Vincent Bugliosi, is described as a combination of *Law & Order* and *Seinfeld*.

Joseph Wallace grew up in Brooklyn, New York, where—despite his best efforts—he somehow managed to stay away from court-rooms. During more than twenty years as a nonfiction writer, he's traveled the world, gaining invaluable material for crime sto-ries, while frequently ending up in places no sane tourist would want to visit. His first story appeared in 2006's *Baltimore Noir*, edited by Laura Lippman, and since then he's placed stories in *Hardboiled Brooklyn*, *Bronx Noir*, and *Ellery Queen's Mystery Magazine*. He's thrilled to be included in *The Prosecution Rests*.

Angela Zeman is the author of *The Witch and the Borscht Pearl*, a novel using characters from a series published in *Alfred Hitch-cock's Mystery Magazine*. Her work receives high praise from *Pub-lishers Weekly* and other venues. Her story "Green Heat," first published in *A Hot and Sultry Night for Crime*, edited by Jeffery

Deaver, was selected by Otto Penzler and Nelson DeMille for *The Best American Mystery Stories: 2004*. Her stories often appear in anthologies; for instance: Nancy Pickard's *Mom, Apple Pie, and Murder*; Stuart Kaminsky's *Show Business Is Murder*; a Spanish-language homage to Raymond Carver; and Mystery Writers of America's 2008 anthology *On the Raven's Wing*, published in honor of Edgar Allan Poe's 200th birthday. She also contributes to nonfiction publications, such as the award-winning *The Fine Art of Murder*. More information can be found at www.AngelaZeman.com and under "FaeryHillProductions" on MySpace and CrimeSpace. She contributes to www.Criminal Brief.com, the short-story weblog.

ABOUT MYSTERY WRITERS OF AMERICA

Mystery Writers of America, the premier organization for established and aspiring mystery writers, is dedicated to promoting higher regard for crime writing, and recognition and respect for those who write within the genre.

COPYRIGHTS